THE SINS OF AN HEIR

MK LORBER

Three
Pom
Press

The Sins of an Heir
By MK Lorber

Published by Three Pom Press

ISBN e-book: 978-1-7359717-4-2
ISBN Paperback: 978-1-7359717-5-9

Cover Design by Bianca Bordianu at Moonpress/moonpress.co

To the squares who don't fit—

Forget changing your shape. Instead, sharpen your edges.

CONTENTS

CHAPTER ONE

Borderlands of Midpointe, The Militia Territory
Present day...

There were two kinds of people in the realm — those who arrived late and those who arrived fifteen minutes early.

Then there were the gods with their sense of humor, favoring relationships between the two.

Midafternoon sun highlighted the fresh coat of wax on Maia's bedroom floors. Four gleaming posts framed a simple cream-colored quilt on her bed. It would be hours before she could crawl beneath its familiar embrace.

She sighed.

Maia was a champion of schedules. Her friends, sweet and carefree, wouldn't recognize a timepiece if it whacked them in the eye.

They often teased her about her punctuality. She often put them in an affectionate headlock for their tardiness.

"If you're on time, you're late," was her father's favorite adage.

Arrive before everyone else. Work hard. Leave last. Hurry to the next duty. Repeat.

It had served her well as she rose through the ranks of Morvak's militia. First as the only female soldier to complete training. Now as a lieutenant and an assistant trainer to her commander, Gavyn.

The only deference she received was this small space she used for her private quarters. While Xavier, the territory's leader, thumbed his nose at tradition and allowed her to join the ranks, he drew the line at her sharing bunks with the men.

At first, the separation bothered her. It took years to earn the fighters' trust and acceptance. While the additional barrier made her task more difficult, it didn't take long to appreciate the privacy.

Besides, her room connected to the barracks, so she was never far from her comrades.

"Bollocks." She fumbled the bindings on her leather cuff. A graduation gift from Xavier to match the mark on her neck, she never left her room without the pair. "Come on. Come on. I don't have time for this."

Maia was never late. And today, when her entire territory traveled to the Castle to witness Gavyn's fight in the arena, was not the moment to start.

But a first-year fighter had approached her after morning training, inquiring about a particular take-down he couldn't master. Then a group of third-year students asked her to observe their sparring. She coached from behind the ring ropes, yelling pointers, stopping the match to fix stances, or demonstrating a new counterstrike.

Her stomach grumbled. She'd missed the nooning meal, too.

As she scooted forward on her stool, she glanced at her reflection in the vanity's looking glass, muttering. Her hair was still damp from her hasty dip in the stream. She tossed her second cuff back in its box and fashioned a lopsided plait.

Knock. Knock. Knock.

What now? Who was still here?

"Just a moment," she called out as she pinned the tail of her braid.

Most left the compound with Xavier and Gavyn, traveling the half-day trek to the Castle as a contingent. Only the kitchen staff and a few fighters on patrol remained. Perhaps they found something. Or someone.

There was evidence of a person lurking around the compound. Whoever it was knew their way around, eluding capture. When they caught him…

Maia ground her teeth.

She stood, snatched her other cuff, and padded across her room. Maia opened the door with one hand and struggled to tie the bindings with the other. Gah. She looked down at the offending bit of cord.

Her first mistake.

A large body slammed into her.

They fell to the ground, twisting in the air. Her attacker took the brunt of the fall, but the impact still forced a gasp.

Maia's world spun. One minute she glimpsed a burlap sack obscuring his features. The next, her shoulder blades dug into the wooden floor, and rough fabric abraded her cheek.

She wedged a forearm against his neck and swung at his face. The sloppy hook failed to land.

His chest pressed against her, trapping one arm between them. He secured the other above her head.

She bucked against his weight. If she could create some space between them, she could wedge a knee and make him sorry he ever dared to tangle with her.

"You coward. Take off that mask and fight me." Panic loosened her tongue. She shouldn't goad him, yet she couldn't stop herself. "Or does shame keep your beak and feathers covered? You yellow-livered chicken."

Breathe. Think. Think. Think.

He was male based on size and feel. Bigger than a trainee but a stone leaner than Gavyn. A muscular build filled out a faded black tunic and all too common fighting leathers.

If she could just—

Maia shifted her weight and rounded her shoulders.

Ahh. If she could just free a hand, she could poke him through the slit he cut in the hood for his eyes.

Too late, she felt more than saw him grab her wrist, pinning it with the other above her head.

"Stay still." His voice was garbled, an unnatural tone as if he wished to disguise it. "I'm not here to harm you."

She couldn't place its owner. Another deep breath failed to calm her riotous thoughts.

"You won't get away with this," she said, the words small and shrill. Her chest heaved. "You... you won't get away with this."

He pushed his face against her collarbone, and his chest expanded.

Did he just sniff her? Why this—

Too irate to be afraid, too stubborn to submit, she arched her back and twisted.

"Stay still," he repeated as he pulled a length of rope from the back of his waistband. He cinched it tight around both wrists. Fibers scraped against her skin, burning as she fought his hold. "I said—"

Maia locked her legs against his lower back and waited. When he finished the task, she jerked her head forward.

He dodged the blow at the last second. Her forehead narrowly missed smashing his nose.

"You better clear off," she said and tugged against the bindings. "I will track you through the mountains if I must."

He stilled as if considering her threat. With slow, deliberate movements, he squeezed her hands, earning a yelp. Her attacker sank back on his heals and cocked his head to the side, assessing.

If she could wrap her ankles higher on his torso, maybe she could pull him back down. Maia repositioned her feet.

That was her second mistake.

He took advantage of the shift in pressure and stood, breaking her lock.

Another length of rope materialized from his waistband. He grabbed her upper arm and drug her across the room to the foot of her bed like an exasperated parent who lost their sanity and hauled their children out of a shop.

Her legs thrashed under her. Years of training vanished when she needed them the most.

She swore. Her bare feet smacked against the polished wooden floor, unable to find purchase to slow his progress.

He spun her around and cradled her body. His chest to her back. With him wedged against her, he eliminated another opportunity for a head butt.

Maia watched, her body paralyzed, as he tied her wrists around the leg of the footboard. The bed was five paces from her vanity. Another ten from her door. The lone window faced the stream, but its rush of water would drown her cries for help.

The familiar scent of pine hit her nostrils.

Everyone and their neighbor in the Militia territory used the simple soap. The apothecary in the market sold it in bricks.

This was real.

This wasn't a dream. She couldn't wish it so.

This must be the bastard lurking around.

Maia stared at a spot on the wall above the window. Her heart thudded against her ribs. Her breaths came in shallow spurts. Otherwise, she might've noted the hint of another fragrance teasing her nostrils.

"I look forward to the chase."

Maia ignored his taunt and resisted the urge to test the rope tethering her to the bed. She sneered but kept silent as he slipped out of her chambers without a backward glance.

Footsteps echoed down the barrack's center aisle.

She loosed a breath when they faded. Sweat — borne of frantic rage and a sliver of embarrassment at her predicament — beaded along her temple.

After she figured out how to free herself, Maia would start the hunt. He could hide. He could run. She would follow him to the edge of the peninsula to return this favor.

Maia wasn't looking forward to recounting tonight's events with Xavier and Gavyn.

She closed her eyes. *Gavyn.* Her stomach dropped. She would miss his fight.

Some soldier she was.

She lost awareness of her surroundings. Failed to subdue an attacker in her own chambers. And wouldn't stand with her friends and adoptive family against the Castle.

At least her father wasn't here to witness her shame.

He'd always said, *"If there is one thing worse than arriving late, it is not showing up at all."*

CHAPTER TWO

The Militia Compound
One Week Later…

Maia wanted to strangle the man standing across from her. But she was at her wedding.

And he was the groom.

"It's time," Xavier, her leader-turned-officiant, announced to the small crowd.

"Enjoying the view?" Erik smirked.

She ignored the taunt and forced herself to take a step closer.

The sun hung on the horizon, illuminating the waxy greens of the late summer foliage adorning the skirts of Morvak Mountain. Old oaks stood sentry at the edge of the gushing river and framed the sultry pinks and vibrant oranges. Romantic for someone with a tender heart and the right partner.

Not that Erik was that partner. Nor did he care about the landscape.

The spectators — she refused to think of them as guests — took their seats.

She tilted her head back and mouthed, "I've seen better."

Lies. For many, his looks alone fulfilled a fantasy. At one time she'd thought him handsome, too.

With close-cropped hair the color of a mink's pelt and honey-flecked eyes, there were few in the territories who would disagree.

His cheekbones were as sharp as his tongue, his jawline as hard as his obstinate head. They shared the same olive skin that darkened three shades with the first long days of spring. While her complexion came from the clan of huntsmen living on the western edge of the mountain range, his stemmed from noble lineage.

"Relax, Kitten. I don't want to be here either. But we need to sell our infatuation, so at least pretend you don't want to stab me." Erik snagged her hand and kissed her knuckles. "Remember, we are madly in love."

Ignore him. Just... ignore him...

Maia focused on the arch of flowers anchoring the altar. She didn't dare glance at Xavier, the man responsible for this mess. One glimpse of her face, he would call the whole thing off.

Instead, she studied the red blooms. They were woven between braided twigs and green fronds. Pretty and useless, but she appreciated the gesture.

Someone sneezed from the front row.

"We are gathered here today to witness..."

A trio of singers stood to her left, their muted voices a pleasant backdrop for Xavier's opening remarks.

She closed her eyes, allowing the traditional hymn to wash over her. She'd imagined this day for years. She never thought...

Maia swallowed against a burning sensation then opened her eyes. Weird. She hadn't eaten anything today.

A simple black tunic stretched across Erik's wide shoulders, his broad chest. The top two buttons were open, revealing a copper chain and a small pendant. A recent addition, one she dismissed.

Her gaze lingered on his ears, their pointed ends evidence of the heritage his magic had disguised for many months.

Erik was Faeblood. A Lord sent to spy on her family. The male who tied her up and left her in her chambers while Gavyn fought in the Castle arena.

His father, a High Lord, had questioned the roots of the militia's loyalty. So he'd sent his son, his heir, to join the ranks and report his findings.

More fox than wolf. More cunning than brute. Erik moved like a predator. Quickly and quietly. Deadly. And the look he gave her now...

Maia hunted too often in the densely-packed woods surrounding her home not to recognize when she was prey. Albeit angry prey. One who carried a grudge, not to mention a weapon.

As Xavier concluded the customary introduction, the singers wrapped up their final verse. A moment of silence lapsed, broken by muted sniffles from the back.

"The stars favor us tonight." Xavier gestured to the first twinkle at the edges of the realm. "The gods bless this union."

Maia shifted. Her skirts grazed the forest floor.

Instead of a traditional white gown, she wore an illegal dagger strapped to her thigh and a snarl on her face. A borrowed dress concealed the blade. She forced herself to relax her lips.

The weapon was old — a gift from her father on her fourteenth birthday, a month before his sudden death. A decade had passed since that dreadful day, but it was as sharp now as when he kept it on his person. Nary a rust spot to be found.

The snarl was new — six months of shy smiles transformed into threatening scowls overnight upon learning Erik's true identity.

She smoothed out the invisible wrinkles of her loaned sundress, a rose-colored linen she reluctantly donned for the ceremony.

The swooping neckline gathered on the swell of her chest. With grim satisfaction, she caught Erik's gaze straying there more than once. While the color of the fabric complimented her deep tan, she detested the saccharine pink. It was too late to change.

Besides, no one cared what she wore anyway.

She had something old and something new and something borrowed. Now she needed something blue.

The call of a bullfrog carried on the light breeze, blending with the harmony of innumerable crickets. Fireflies danced at her ankles, their bright bellies floating up from the tall grasses like candles hovering mid-flight.

A wee lass bounded up to them and cupped the air. She bumped into Erik's leg, drawing a chuckle from Xavier.

Erik broke away from the ceremony and captured a few fireflies, releasing the bunch in front of her. When she failed to catch the nearest, he guided her tiny hands with his. Together, they wrangled the last one before it floated away.

A harried woman shuffled to the altar, an apologetic smile on her face. Erik patted the girl on the head and nudged her forward. Xavier cleared his throat and resumed the next round of blessings.

The reprieve was over.

Maia fidgeted with her collar, wishing for a small bouquet to occupy her hands. Tonight, they would travel to the Castle. Her gut clenched. Perhaps she ought to forgo supper, lest she lose it at his feet.

Not that he didn't deserve it.

She didn't know who earned her ire more — Erik for his treachery or Xavier for failing to disclose it sooner. Or herself, for falling for his looks, his pretty lies.

"You look ravishing," Erik said with a savage grin. He cupped her elbow, crowding her space. "That dress is divine. My gratitude to whomever picked it out."

Too stunned by the compliment, Maia missed the subtle implication she required another to choose her clothes. She may have preferred the simplicity of her militia uniform, but she *could* dress herself for the occasion.

"Don't grow accustomed to it." She wrenched her arm free. "My time at the Castle will be brief. I shall return to my usual attire soon enough."

The sooner the better.

In an ironic twist, Xavier was sending her undercover in the Castle as Erik's wife. Simple. Get in. Wear some frilly dresses. Send home evidence of the Faeblood's strategies. Get out.

"You mistake my admiration." Erik raised an eyebrow. "I assume every bride wishes to hear she is beautiful on her wedding day. While I enjoy this new look, I prefer you in leathers. Too bad I won't have the pleasure of peeling off this fluff."

"We may disagree on many things, but in this you are correct," Maia hissed. "Your traitorous hands aren't welcome anywhere near my body."

"For now." He inclined his head as if accepting a challenge.

Was it possible to want to stab and kiss someone at the same time? The prick.

Arrogant men surrounded Maia, an occupational hazard. Every spring, she put a new crop of soldiers in their place. While seasoned fighters treated her with respect, there were always a few overgrown lads who needed to be cut down several notches when they first arrived at the compound. She loved her duties, even the vexing parts.

Xavier cleared his throat and held out his hand. "The cords."

When did the singing stop? Were they at the final blessing already?

Erik dug into his back pocket, producing three thin, tightly-braided sections of rope.

Right. Cords — a mark of commitment in this life and the next. Maia glanced down the makeshift aisle.

Flower petals in various shades of red twirled at her feet, dividing the crowd in two. Faces pink with excitement, or several pints of mead, stared back at her. The newest militia fighters stood in the back. Villagers, who made the trek to the compound, comprised the middle.

Her family, with a range from serious to outright hostile expressions, stood in front.

Those in Xavier's inner circle knew of his plan. If they failed to school their expressions, everyone in the territory would know too.

Erik lifted her wrist to his mouth and nipped the sensitive skin, the touch feather-light.

He shouldn't have such pretty lips. She swallowed the urge to rip her hand away. *Get it together, Maia. He is the enemy.*

Too bad her fascination hadn't diminished the second she'd learned of Erik's mission. Months of writhing against him in the grappling pit — all under the pretense of working on his ground escapes — had primed her body to respond any time he was within twenty paces.

"Careful, my Lord." She fluttered her lashes. Under her breath, she added, "I will cut you while you sleep."

"Erik," Xavier growled under his breath. "Clasp her hands."

The strap of the dagger's sheath twisted on her thigh, sliding in the fine sheen of sweat coating her skin. Her palm itched for its weight. It wouldn't be the first time Erik tasted the tip of her blade.

Too bad it posed an unnecessary risk. His father might have sent minions to witness this spectacle. Drawing the illegal weapon was not worth the punishment it would bring to her family.

"Small wounds," she leaned in and whispered as Erik entwined their fingers. "I will splay your skin open where no one will notice. Every time your tunic rubs against the raw flesh, you will think of me."

"I look forward to it." He dipped his head and kissed the soft spot in front of her ear. "Anytime you need to play, let me know."

"You're demented." She leaned back. The heat from his body added to her flush. "Absolutely insane."

"Maybe I just want to see you smile."

Xavier ignored their banter and wound the royal blue cord, the longest of the bunch, around their hands. Frayed ends dangled between them along with the last threads of hope that this was all a dreadful nightmare.

"We are here today to share the union of Erik Siodina and Maia Braenough. They will join those who crossed the Veil of Matrimony, binding their souls in this life and the next."

Maia swallowed.

The wedding bond was irrevocable. The oath written in the stars.

Both in the territories and at Court, divorce was not an option. Couples could live separate lives. Birth offspring out of wedlock with another. But never speak the vows again.

She'd spent a restless night rallying her conviction.

Maia would do anything for her family, including binding herself to Erik and sacrificing her chance of happiness — what her mother and father had shared — if it meant gaining advantage in Xavier's undeclared war on the Castle.

Humans, save for servants and Red Guard, weren't allowed at Court. Xavier saw an opportunity to place a spy in the enemy's den and took it.

But an hour before the ceremony, Erik had pulled her aside, insisting she drink an elixir. He claimed it was a potion that nullified the marital oaths, scrubbing them from the constellations.

Despite his amorous attention, a benefit for those in attendance, he was here under duress too.

Maia gulped the elixir down without hesitation. She'd survived the putrid drink. At least it hadn't been poison.

"With the stars as my witness do you, Erik Siodina, take Maia Braenough as your bonded wife?" Xavier wrapped the ends of the green cord around their joined hands. "In sickness and in health? In this world and across the Veil?"

"I do." Erik took another half step forward.

"With the stars as my witness do you, Maia Braenough, take Erik Siodina as your bonded husband? In sickness and in health? In this world and across the Veil?"

"Aye—" Her voice croaked.

Erik ran the tip of his nose across her cheek.

What the hell was he doing? Xavier wedged an arm between them, looping the final green cord as she said more firmly, "I do."

"As the ancient gods foretold, a bonded pair is mightier than the combined strength of the individuals. Do you, Erik Siodina, pledge to hold your marriage to Maia Braenough above all other oaths? In times of uncertainty and in prosperity? In this life and beyond the Veil?"

"I do." Erik pulled back, regarding her through heavy lids.

She couldn't decipher his look.

"And do you, Maia Braenough, pledge to hold your marriage to Erik Siodina above all other oaths? In times of uncertainty and in prosperity?" Xavier positioned the final gold cord. "In this life and beyond the Veil?"

Her tongue stuck to the roof of her mouth, so she nodded.

"You must say the words." Xavier clasped their hands.

She hesitated, then said, "Aye."

"The final cord — a gift from the goddess Alemonia —

drapes over the wedded pair, bestowing fertility on the couple. It signifies Maia Braenough's acceptance into Erik's line. We shall henceforth know any children born of their union as *of Siodina*."

Erik frowned.

She wasn't thrilled about this part either. At least she didn't need to worry about unintended pregnancy. Not only would they never consummate their union, but couples wishing for children required a fertility tea for conception.

Something scratched the back of her hand. She blinked once. Twice. Then three times in quick succession.

She was married.

She had a husband.

Dear gods, she was Erik's wife.

"May I present..." Xavier said, the words far, far away. She recognized her name. His. "You may kiss..."

It was customary to seal the vows with a kiss. She hadn't given it much consideration last night. Or yesterday. Or every morning since Xavier had declared his intention to send her undercover.

The corners of Erik's mouth tipped up. Not a smile, nor a smirk. It was a tiny show of emotion that softened his features. One he reserved for their sessions in the training barn.

Maia would've missed it if she hadn't been studying him so closely.

Xavier unwound the cords.

Time stilled. Blood pulsed between her ears. The cheers and hollers from the crowd faded. Even the crickets stopped chirping.

Erik cupped the sides of her jaw, his thumb trailing across her cheeks. Two pools of molten chocolate held her in place. Up close, the honey flecks peppering his eyes kept the hue from becoming dull. His mouth parted and his tongue darted out, running along that obnoxiously full lower lip.

Remember, we are madly in love.

Her arms slid around the back of his neck. She ran her fingers through his short hair. A prickly velvet. Much like his personality.

She understood her body's reaction. What it meant. And what it didn't. Like an old friend, she welcomed the rush. Instead of meeting Erik's lips halfway, she pushed on her tiptoes, smashing her mouth against his.

Pressure at the base of her head kept her in place. She recognized the moment he took control.

Erik angled his mouth, tugging her lip between his teeth. Her lips parted. His tongue swept inside. A spicy scent clung to him, a heady mixture of crisp and sweet. The kiss was ravenous.

She gripped the front of his tunic. To steady herself. Not to pull him closer.

Somewhere in the distance, a moan melded with the applause. Before she could determine its owner, his arms wrapped around her, and the ground fell away from the tips of her slippers.

He deepened the kiss as she clung to his shoulders.

This was better than her dreams — the ones she refused to acknowledge in the light of morning. More vivid than all the restless nights put together. And she suffered plenty.

He was the first to break away. Something she would dwell on later.

"So beautiful." His mouth grazed her jawline. Kiss. "So enchanting." Kiss. "A sleek Kitten. Soft fur hiding sharp claws."

He licked her throat.

The throb between her legs matched the thump of her heart against her ribs. A sharp, piercing pain interrupted the steady beat. It had the same effect as a bucket of water dumped on her head.

He bit her.

"You bit me." She wrenched out of his hold and took a step

back, rubbing the tender spot. Tiny splotches of blood coated her fingertips. "You bit me. Why you—"

Erik Siodina was many things. A scoundrel. A liar. A cad. But none of the names left her mouth.

"You... you..."

"I couldn't help myself."

If he'd looked contrite or lost in the moment, she would have forgiven him. Instead, the corners of his lips settled into arrogant smugness. For the witnesses or her? She didn't care.

"Besides, it is customary amongst Faeblood to mark your bride." He ran his tongue over his canines. "The wound will heal."

Another mark. Unlike the cords, one she couldn't take off. Maia ground her teeth.

Her body moved on its own. It dropped into her fighting stance, muscles aligning with ease. Her arm cocked back and formed a fist.

The punch connected with Erik's jaw. A satisfying thud jerked his head to the side.

His chest heaved. Erik wiped his mouth with the back of his wrist, and a streak of blood coated his skin.

Hearty chuckles from the crowd drowned out quieter, dignified gasps.

Pride and delight warred with the pain coursing through her hand. Aye, that hurt. But it was worth it. So worth the bruise her knuckles would sport tomorrow.

It may be a day late, but it looked like she would wear something blue after all.

CHAPTER THREE

Erik, the sole heir to the most sadistic Lord sitting at the High Table, was a married Faeblood.

News of the ceremony would reach his father by nightfall, carried on the tongues of the Castle spies he recognized in the audience.

And what a way to start their union.

There was likely some symbolism in Maia's punch, but instead of dwelling on it, he threw an exaggerated wink over his shoulder.

"Foreplay," he said to the spectators as if including them in the jest.

Predictable laughter followed, the fighters easy to entertain.

He rubbed his jaw and forced another grin for his enchanting wife.

His wife. Whoever crafted the centuries-old vows was either a fool or a genius.

Fool. Marriage was a miserable state of affairs, as confirmed by his parents' loveless union. Or genius. Vows written in the stars were necessary. Why else would two individuals live together, grow to hate each other, and stay mated for all eternity?

"I require a word with my bride," Erik said to Xavier.

The pain in Maia's hand would dwindle soon, but the swelling and bruising would last for days. No reason for her to suffer.

"Be quick." Xavier crossed his arms and flicked his chin toward the stream.

"I'll return her in half an hour."

"Ten minutes."

"Twenty. And not a moment less."

"Not a moment more." Xavier didn't wait for Erik's acknowledgement. He pivoted on his heel and joined the crowd as they weaved through the forest and headed to the courtyard. Dismissed.

"I have nothing to say to you." Maia took a step back.

"Not here." Erik closed the distance between them and leaned down. "We must speak but not here."

Alone with his bride, the nighttime sounds faded to a hum. It wasn't difficult to imagine his father's reaction to the wedding.

Erik not only broke his engagement to Lady Stella, a match made while he slept in a cradle, but he went and married a human. While he didn't care whether magic ran through Maia's veins, his father would.

The Ladies at Court would, too.

Upon learning of Erik's treachery, Xavier had enacted *Lex Talionis*. An eye for an eye. In his case, a life for a life. Erik owed Ember, a Faeblood healer hiding in the Militia territory, for saving his sorry hide; and he owed Xavier for not seeking retribution for Erik's infiltration into the militia's ranks.

But Erik was pissed.

His begrudging respect for Xavier evaporated the moment the leader demanded Maia return with him to the Castle. She was many things — a scrappy soldier, a feisty friend, a sensuous siren — and unfortunately, loyal to a fault. Like all men in power, Xavier played on that weakness, sacrificing her in his conflict with Erik's father.

"Stop fidgeting." Erik captured her wrist, adding more pressure when she attempted to pull out of his grasp.

Dear gods, she was breathtaking.

Maia's beauty had clocked him like an overzealous boxer all those months ago when he'd first set eyes on her, sparring in the ring with a recruit twice her size. She'd put the arrogant upstart in his place. Right then he'd known — with her body slick with perspiration, her chest heaving from exertion — that she was trouble.

Her features were delicate, emphasized by a pert mouth and upturned nose. But nothing about Maia was fragile. And while the vigorous militia training created a sleek frame, it failed to erode her soft curves.

She was famous in the training barn for her grappling — hard to trap, harder to pin. A slick escape artist on the ground. He rubbed his jaw. Her right hook wasn't lacking either.

He didn't lie when he said he preferred her in fighting leathers.

She boasted the most glorious backside — a fact that he and every other unattached fighter at the compound noticed.

Erik wanted to throttle the lot but he resisted. His father sent him to the compound to spy, not brawl like a rutting bull with every male who got within five paces of her.

Maia was conventionally beautiful, with long, dark brown hair the color of the rich loam his most fickle plants favored. More than once, he imagined wrapping his fist around the thick mass, pinning her underneath him.

She wore it tied back from her face most days.

But every so often, like tonight, she left it unbound, cascading over her shoulders, a thick curtain down her back. He stifled the urge to bury his nose in the silky tendrils, to squeeze her tight. To whisper, *"Everything will work out."*

Unlike the scheming Ladies at court, Maia didn't need his help. Just once, though, he wished to come to her rescue.

Maybe it was the reason he concocted the fake elixir. He couldn't stand the look on her face when Xavier announced his plans to send her undercover as his wife. Erik didn't believe in the vows, but it was clear she did.

"Come," was all he said as he tugged her along.

Neither of them spoke as they ventured deeper into the woods.

Gods, he wished he could leave her here, tucked away under Xavier's protection. Safe. Sound.

Maia would struggle to fit in at Court.

For one, she was human. Her rounded ears gave her away. Pointed tips were a useless trait passed down to pure offspring, lost the moment human blood entered the line.

Two, she carried herself in the image of a proud warrior, a stark contrast to the simpering Faeblood in the Castle.

The nobles were a product of their parents' inflated sense of entitlement. They acted like a pack of hyenas, posturing for leadership at the expense of genuine friendship. If a kind soul grew amongst the rot, the inhospitable environment would smother them before their official presentation.

While Erik successfully avoided his sire's notice most days — doing just enough to fulfill his duties to the nobles, navigating the scheming mothers at Court (aye, his engagement didn't prevent their attempts at ensnaring him for a son-in-law) — Maia would be a beacon for his father's gaze.

She would wear a target on her back. All for becoming Erik's wife.

The Ladies at Court would shun her at best. Plot her demise at worst. And his proud, human-hating father would lock her in the dungeons to control Erik's every move. He did it twice before. He would do it again.

They followed the stream until they reached a sharp bend. Erik halted. The water coursed around them, crashing into large boulders and sending plumes of spray into the air. Perfect. The roar would cover their words.

Maia tugged at their clasped hands. "Erik, what—"

"Shh." He lay a finger on his lips and held tight. In her ear he whispered, "This is not a conversation I want overheard. Stop pulling your hand away."

Warmth flooded his fingertips. The syrupy sweet taste of a cast coated his throat. Magic followed from his fingers to hers, easing the puffiness around her knuckles.

"Aye," he said as her eyes widened. "I'm a healer."

He admired the two small puncture wounds on her neck. The bleeding stopped mere seconds after his bite. No reason to erase them now.

"But your injuries in the arena… why didn't you mend them? Why did you need Ember to heal you?" *Why did you risk her discovery?* She didn't need to add.

Maia tugged her hand free. This time, he let it go.

"A tale for another day," he lied. Maia didn't want to hear his story, not really. Erik held up a finger, cutting off her next question. "Listen closely. Life at Court is treacherous. The minute you ask too many questions or feel sorry for someone or show a morsel of decency… the nobles will use it against you."

"That's barbaric."

"Not everything is fragrant red roses and consensual face punches." He ran his hands through his short hair. "Xavier sheltered this entire territory. You're soft. All of you."

"I'd rather be soft and honorable than a wretch without a compass." She balled her fists at her side.

"You're ignorant of the world." He paced between two

smaller saplings. "Not everyone has the luxury of doing what's right. There's no shame in survival."

"I'd rather be an outcast than live without bearing."

She wasn't getting it. Tender-hearted Xavier and his teachings. He created an entire brotherhood of saps. Strong fighters. Loyal to the end. But saps all the same.

Morals were a liability in the Castle. Erik did what was necessary. Nothing more. Nothing less. He was only one person. Not enough to make a difference anyway.

"An outcast?" He took a menacing step forward. "You'll be dead."

She stumbled back.

"Ah, you are finally seeing the picture." He closed the distance between them. Erik wanted to trace her ear's rounded edge with his tongue. Instead, he snarled, "Watch your mouth at Court. Xavier may grant you leeway to speak your mind, but the Faeblood nobles will not afford you the same indulgence."

He counted her breaths.

Her chest moved with three deep inhales before she finally said, "I liked you better when you didn't speak."

"I can find other ways to occupy my tongue."

"Kiss me again and you'll find my blade in your belly. This time, Ember isn't here to save you."

"A wager, then." An excuse to take her mind off tonight. "You'll beg to kiss me before the Grimoire Games."

Plenty of time to win the bet.

In three months, the Castle would host the annual event. The Games served as a chance for the territories to compete against one another. An opportunity for the Faeblood to lord over their human populace. And for one lucky winner, or winning team, a coveted invitation to join the ranks of the Red Guard, the nobles' personal soldiers.

The natural boundaries of the mountain divided Morvak's populace. Humans belonged to one of seven territories, working the land or family trade. Their annual tithe supported the Castle and its magical ruling class. Citizens scrapped out an existence while Faeblood Lords and Ladies basked in comfort. The leeches.

But the Red Guard were an anomaly. A chance for humans to live in the Castle. To earn a handsome wage and pass on the position to their heirs, lifting their line out of poverty. Unlike servants.

"Since there is no way in all the realms I will willingly kiss you again," she said, wiping her hands on her skirts, "I accept."

He couldn't see under her dress, but Erik *knew* her. No way she would attend their wedding without a dagger strapped to her thigh. Risky. Reckless. Maybe it made him a cad, but it did something for him.

"And what do I get when I win?" Maia asked. "When you beg me to kiss you?"

There it was. That fire, the one that dimmed after he'd tied her up in her chambers. A hasty, foolish plan to keep her safe. And he'd been right to do it. Earned an assassin's blade in the gullet likely meant for her.

Another truth she wasn't ready to hear.

"A favor." He let the words settle. "You could do worse than earn my marker. I expect the same in return."

Her nostrils flared.

"As much as I want to play with you, time draws to a close. Go. Say your goodbyes to your family. Don't drink any mead. We leave for the Castle tonight. I want to slip into the fortress while the nobles sleep off their revelry." And because he could, Erik added, "As much as I love imagining what's under that dress, we will set a quick pace. Change back into your leathers."

He leaned over, emphasizing the last demand. The copper pendant nestled under his tunic swung free. Erik never wore the tarnished chain in the training barn, worried it would snap during sparring.

By the Court's standards, the necklace was worthless. But to him, the simple charm with its worn inscription was priceless.

"So soon?" Her voice was soft as if she only just realized his intentions. Perhaps Xavier never explained Erik's haste to return home.

"I plan to tuck you in my bed before the sun burns the last drops of dew off the mountain air."

In my bed, his words echoed. While this arrangement made his life more difficult, a selfish part of him didn't mind her there.

He'd craved her for months.

Still, he was Faeblood. She human. They were enemies. Their lives could never blend. If he were smart, Erik would demand Xavier find another way for him to repay his debt because she was a complication.

With her sharing his chambers, he was bound to do something idiotic — like kiss her first. And how the hell was he going to avoid mating her?

While no doubt an enjoyable distraction, he didn't want to confuse the stars. The herbal elixir they drank before the ceremony was nothing more than a swig of apple cider and crushed Crimson Gillyflowers.

He'd lied.

Sure, it was low. Even for him. But Maia needed the illusion. Erik didn't question why he wanted to protect that for her.

There was no spell to break a spoken oath. At least, none that he knew. Erik would scour the Castle archives until he found an antidote, preferably before Maia discovered that he fed her a potion of pretty lies. He would be there regardless, searching for clues to his mother's disappearance.

His fingertips absentmindedly brushed the charm.

Life was simple for people like Maia.

They couldn't see beyond their nose, sorting everyone into

two distinct sides — good or evil. She was a naive dreamer and belonged on the virtuous half. His father on the other.

Then there was Erik, who didn't know where he fit. Nor did he allow himself to care. Not anymore.

"Unless you want to kiss me, move out."

~

MIKEL PALMED THE ROCK IN ONE HAND, THE SHARP CREVICE IN the other.

He shifted his weight to the side. Jagged stone pierced the thin soles of his boots. He embraced the pain, the heightened sensation aiding his balance.

It wasn't as if he couldn't afford a new pair.

As Xavier's scout leader, he received a generous salary. Added to the coin from his weekly fight purse, he could commission new shoes every day for the rest of his life. But thicker, protective leather meant less feeling. Less feeling meant less nimbleness.

His comfort was a worthy concession.

He chucked the rock, hitting the Castle's foundation. It was an effort not to throw it at the nearest Red Guard's head but knocking him out would sound an alarm. Tempting, but unwise.

The rock collided with a patch of loose pebbles, sending several cascading down the steep trail.

As intended, the two sentries whirled in unison. One smacked the other on his shoulder and pointed in the opposite direction of Mikel's hiding spot.

"Did you hear that?" the taller guard asked in a hushed tone. "What do you think—"

"Shh. Quiet." The shorter, squatter guard ran his hands down his trousers. "No idea. But I'm not going over there."

"You must. 'Tis your job."

"Says who?" The second idiot shoved a finger in guard number one's chest.

"I'm older," the first one hedged. "I outrank you based on age."

"You can't even qualify with a bow." Guard two straightened. "What makes you think you outrank me when you can't hit the broad side of Lady Newhiel's arse with an arrow? You go. I'll stand watch."

"I'm not going alone."

Come on, you fools. Take the bait. Mikel resisted the urge to drum his fingers on his leathers. *Take the bait.*

"Fine. Let's go together." The short one elbowed his companion and gestured to the door hidden in the shadows. "It's not as if anyone uses this tunnel. In another hour, the dandies will be too drunk to stumble down to an old servants' entrance."

"Thank the gods. Our shift is almost up. I have a tankard of ale and a warm bed calling my name. I'll be glad when the commander rotates us back to the great hall."

The tall guard took a hesitant step forward. Then another.

"This post is the worst. Why the hell does Lord Siodina want an ancient, unused passage guarded?"

"Shh. Don't say his name. He might hear you."

"Nonsense." The taller guard chuckled. "You listen to the maids too much."

"Still..."

"He's mortal like the rest." Guard number one kicked an exposed root. "A bit o' magic running through his blood doesn't prolong his life or enhance his hearing any more than yours or mine. Soon he'll die like the others. A new Lord will take his place, and we will still be here, jumping at their every whim."

"Better than scrounging a life in the territories." The second filed behind his friend. "Poor bastards."

Red Guard. Mikel shook his head. Idiots, but how could they be anything else?

He stood, careful not to make a sound as he crossed to the tunnel.

A battered wooden door greeted him. He held his breath and tested the old handle. It twisted with ease. Huh. Someone kept the locks and hinges oiled.

Mikel slipped inside. He shut the door behind him and leaned against the wall. Dampness from the dark tunnel clung to his skin. The cool stone wall seared his tunic as he slid down into a crouch.

He rubbed the thick scars on his wrist.

Even after three decades, the sensation never returned to the skin. He drew a shaky breath. The Castle smelled like any other mountainous stronghold — a combination of mildew and greed and subterfuge.

An overwhelming stench reeking of his past.

CHAPTER FOUR

A barrage of visitors to her private chambers had kept Maia occupied for the last hour.

Most wished her well, requesting regular gossip from the Castle. Her adopted brothers, the ones who wore cuffs and identical tattoos at the base of their necks, offered advice ranging from *keep your guard up* to *gut a few of those Faeblood suckers for me*.

She cupped her neck with both hands, letting her head hang.

Xavier's tattoo graced one side of her throat. A permanent declaration for when cuffs were impractical. Now, Erik's bite anchored the other. To the Court, they represented her past and her future, but Maia and her family knew where her heart lay.

"Leave your cuffs." Xavier leaned against the doorframe, his presence taking up most of the opening.

She welcomed the brittle edge of his voice.

Maia traced the supple leather bands, not quite ready to remove this part of her identity. It took her five years to earn them, a year longer than most recruits.

She would wear them again soon enough. Once she figured

out how to blend into high society. Two months was all she needed. Three at most.

Xavier entered, uninvited, and pulled out the stool tucked under the vanity.

"Make Erik give you some fancy baubles." He straddled the seat. His voice lowered an octave. "My cuffs draw too much attention."

Maia sank onto her mattress, not daring to look away. Whatever last words Xavier had for her, she needed to sit. She played with her left cuff, twirling it around and around. It was do that or vomit. Several deep breaths held the worst from climbing the back of her throat.

"Let it out." The corner of Xavier's lips curled in a feral smile.

He didn't mean her supper. How did you admit your fears to the man you'd looked up to your entire childhood?

Xavier became a hero the moment he'd sheltered a grieving widower and his scrawny daughter. She recalled little about her journey to the Militia territory, trailing her dazed but determined father. But she remembered Xavier's eyes. His kind smile.

As a child, she'd thought it amusing that he was younger than her father. But age had little to do with leadership. Xavier was larger than life.

"Can I?" Her voice croaked. "Am I free to admit that I'm scared? I've only ever been a soldier. What if I fail? What if I don't want to leave? I don't think I could refuse you."

They owed him so much. Her father spoke of debts. Of honor. He poured every ounce of himself into Xavier and this territory. The militia. She could live two lifetimes and never balance their ledger.

All these years later, she still sought Xavier's approval.

"Aye, you can." He dragged the stool closer, its legs scraping the wooden floor. "Tell me to find someone else. Tell me to kick rocks in the Underworld. Perhaps somebody should."

"Jade is your conscience." Maia nudged his boot, smiling softly. "I'm not suited for the role."

Jade, her close friend, was Xavier's childhood sweetheart. No. That wasn't quite right. They never became lovers, and Jade seemed to thrive on disregarding his authority and questioning the soundness of his orders.

"I can find someone else," he repeated.

Simple as that. And he would. But at what cost?

"No." Another small smile. "Erik and I wed. The Castle will not accept someone else."

"Listen, I know you spoke vows, but they don't mean anything. Those pure-blood fools might prattle on about lines and family names, but the rest of us don't. The stars don't care. It's all a bunch of nonsense and superstition."

But her mother and father cared. For a time, Maia had too.

She never told Xavier about the elixir. A simple oversight, one she should remedy. Perhaps it would assuage the lines between his brows.

"Xavier, we—"

"I need to know I'm sending you in there with a clear head." The words tumbled out in a near growl. He didn't give her time to respond before adding, "I have spies in the Red Guard, my allies have others among the servants. But I don't want to miss this opportunity. Send a letter every three days. If you miss one, I will assume the worst."

"Wait. Slow down." She sprang up and paced. "You don't use carrier fowl. I can't put my discoveries in parchment."

"Address them to Jade. Write whatever drivel the Castle would expect. Consider it proof of life."

He grabbed her wrist as she neared, stilling her.

"Take care to disguise your intent. I don't need details unless something is urgent. You can save those for your return."

She nodded. Easy. Get in. Quill to parchment every few days. Get out.

Maybe if she repeated it over and over, she would believe it.

In truth, Maia wasn't sure she could blend in with society enough to fool them into loosening their tongues. She was a soldier. Not a courtier. She never made time for the softer things. Dresses. Tea. Gossip. Her father never valued that sort of education for his daughter.

No matter. A good soldier adapted.

"I have two tasks while you are there." Xavier released her arm. "One, I need you to locate a book. A journal of sorts."

"What does it look like?"

"Small. Navy." Xavier hesitated. "Lord Siodina carried it on his person for years, never allowing another to touch it. Six moons ago, it disappeared."

Six moons ago. She blinked. Six moons ago, Erik joined the militia.

"Erik doesn't know where it is. What it is," Xavier said as if reading her mind. "Though he confirmed its existence."

"And this book," she hedged. "It's important?"

"My gut tells me it is." Xavier cupped the back of his neck. "My spies in the Castle can't locate it. Since its disappearance, strange things have been occurring in the territories. Too many to assume they aren't related."

"If your spies can't find it, why do you think I can?" She didn't ask about the occurrences. If Xavier wanted Maia to know, he would tell her.

"As a Lord's wife, you are allowed more movement. Plus the marriage oath opens doors. Figuratively and literally. Your blood is rumored to unlock passages that keep my spies out."

"Xavier, I can't—"

"You can," Xavier said in the same tone he used when addressing the entire militia. "Trust your instinct. If something feels rotten, leave."

She stifled the urge to straighten. "The other task?"

"I want you to enter the Grimoire Games."

To what end? Nobody in Xavier's territory ever bothered before. Why would they? And what if she won? Too many questions. None made sense.

"You'll need a physical outlet." He stood. "The politics will test your temper, and I can't have you maiming the Ladies. Think of the scandal."

"And if they discover my true intentions?" She didn't dare voice the rest.

"I will burn their comfortable lives to the ground. Send them to the gods as nothing more than ash and dust." He strode to the door. Over his shoulder he added, "Make no mistake, I will visit their worst nightmares if they dare harm a single hair on your head."

"You'd do that? For me? But your plans..."

"My plans be damned." He stalked back into the room. His big body loomed. "You are family. Those bastards spied on me for years. They know how far I'll go to protect you. Take care. Lean on Erik. He has enough morals left to keep you safe."

"I fear you overestimate his character," she said in an even tone though she wanted to hurl the words at him.

"Brilliant." Erik's voice curled over Xavier's shoulders. "It's not every day a Faeblood hears praise from an esteemed territory leader. Oh, am I interrupting? Many pardons. This must be the father-daughter talk. Don't stop on my account. I'd love to hear the version you give Maia. Though, I suspect it's quite different from the one you gave me earlier."

A tic appeared in Xavier's cheek.

Erik leaned against the door frame. One leg crossed over the other at the ankle.

"Every last one." Xavier knocked twice on her vanity. "I'll expect your first correspondence upon your arrival."

With the last command, he left, strolling down the aisle

dividing the bunks. She studied his back until it disappeared through the main doors.

"Charming." Erik pushed off the wall to stand. "I'd love to stay for another round of hugs, but it's time to leave."

She didn't imagine the faint bitterness in his tone. Whether intended towards her or Xavier, Maia didn't care.

"Xavier's right — leave the cuffs. No reason to provoke my father more than necessary."

He trailed his finger down her inner arm, leaving a path of goosebumps. The cuff loosened on her wrist, sliding off easily into his waiting hand.

"I don't require your help." Maia took a step back. It wasn't a retreat.

"My delightful sire has eyes everywhere." He gripped her waist. "If your plan is to succeed, you must act as the besotted lover, both inside and outside my chambers. Now, give me your other wrist."

Maia counted to five before she raised her hand.

"Perfect." He removed her other cuff, stashing both in the back pocket of his leathers. "Let's go. I saddled the horses. We leave at once. You do ride, don't you?"

~

SHE DID NOT. RIDE, THAT IS.

Erik swallowed a smile as Maia clung to the horse's neck. Most humans never traveled outside their birth territory. Riding was as necessary to them as wearing a ball gown during evening chores.

"Sit up. Trust your legs to keep you upright."

"The beast keeps knocking me forward."

"Move with him in the saddle. You react instead of working together."

"Simple, is it?" She spoke out of the side of her mouth, the words strained. "I can walk. Let the beast carry the packs."

"Too slow." He halted his mount until they were side-by-side. "Give me your reins."

Her head whipped in his direction. "Why?"

"I'll tie them to my saddle. You can ride with me." He didn't work to keep the promise out of his voice.

Maia stiffened, spurring her horse forward.

Splendid. That should keep her upright for the rest of the trip.

The journey passed in silence. Even the forest was quiet, likely from his wife's constant muttering. The backs of his legs ached from riding. He was out of practice himself but wouldn't give her the satisfaction of mentioning his discomfort.

They crested the final ridgeline. The Castle jutted out from the mountain, a monstrous stain on the peninsula's otherwise majestic landscape. Home. It was as welcoming as a dragon awakening from slumber.

"Hideous, isn't it?"

"It's... impressive," Maia hedged.

He chuckled, imagining all the descriptions rattling around in her head.

"Before we slip in..." he said, nodding to the front gates. "Hand me your dagger."

"What—"

"Your dagger, Kitten." His gaze traveled down her leg. "The one you have hidden in your left boot."

She hesitated but didn't deny carrying the blade. It would cost her, relinquishing the weapon.

"Take mine." He pulled his out, extending it handle first. "Consider it a trade. Another wedding gift if someone asks. Whatever you need to call it, just... take it."

It was a peace offering. Or something to assuage the lump in his throat.

He gulped and added, "My father or the elders might recognize Xavier's crest."

She slid the dagger out of her boot and exchanged the blades with deliberate care. Erik took perverse pleasure knowing she wore another piece of him. His eyes shot to her neck.

He needed to play this carefully. Too much attention and his father might conclude she meant more to him than she did. Too little and the vultures at Court would descend, making her life miserable.

Erik had no intention of leaving her unprotected. She was just a pawn. A willing pawn, but a chess piece between two power-hungry leaders, all the same.

In some ways, Xavier was as cruel as his father. Who the hell sends an innocent into the Castle?

Erik never voiced his objection to Xavier's plan. Perhaps if he'd protested... maybe if he'd explained the full extent of his relationship to his father, Xavier might never have considered sending her undercover.

Erik ran his hand through his short hair.

This was why he avoided relationships. The back and forth. The burn in his chest he couldn't massage away when the illusion of control evaporated. But it was too late for doubts. *Or wants.* His desires never mattered. At least not since his mother's disappearance.

The trail gave way to an arched stone bridge. Almost there. Fifty paces to the gates. Another hundred through the courtyard to the doors concealing the bowels of the fortress.

The clang of armor drew louder, a warning and a signal that it was too late for regrets.

Erik felt the moment Maia stiffened without the necessity of looking in her direction. He *knew* what he would find. Determination cresting her lower lip. Narrowed brows, sizing up her opponents.

But he wasn't prepared for the slight wobble in her voice when she called out, "Good evening."

"My Lord?" The leader of the Red Guard contingent broke apart from the group. His scowl deepened with each step.

Erik ignored the unspoken question and grinned. Might as well have some fun.

"My good man, our horses require food and water." He dismounted, flinging the reins to the guard. It was an insult. Stable lads took care of the animals. "Run along now and lead the beasts to their stalls."

"But my Lord." He reached as if to grab Erik's arm but must've remembered his station, suddenly jerking it back. "Your companion. She's human."

"Aye, Lieutenant," he drawled, dusting the shoulders of the man's tunic. "Can I call you that? The light from the torches is not enough to identify your rank. I'm aware she's human."

"But they are not allowed—"

"And a gorgeous one at that." Erik ignored the irony that the guard was human. The servants were human. The prosperity of this entire realm rested on the backs of *humans.*

"Her beauty leaves many mortals speechless. I can see you suffer from the affliction."

"But my Lord—"

"Don't fret. You won't be the last man to fall under her spell." He ran his palm up Maia's leg and gripped her around the waist.

She leaned down, steadying her weight with both hands on his shoulders, slid out of the saddle and down his body.

"Eyes up here, my good man. It's rude to stare."

"Outsiders require proper invitation," the guard sputtered. "I cannot allow her admittance." *Even for you,* hung between them.

"She does not need a proper invitation." The playful tone vanished. Erik tucked Maia into his side, draping his arm across her shoulders.

"Your father—"

"She. Is. My. Wife." His finger toyed with her collar. He moved the fabric just enough to reveal his mark. "You forget your place."

The news would spread throughout the Castle before morning. His father's minions would corroborate the tale. Too bad he wouldn't witness the reaction.

Maia gripped the back of Erik's tunic.

He turned into her touch, resting his forehead against hers. It didn't bode well if she lost her nerve the first night. Lucky for him, she was easy to rile.

"Come," he purred. "It's time for bed."

~

THERE WAS HOPEFUL. THEN THERE WAS DELUSIONAL.

Maia was hopeful she could complete her task without being discovered. Sure, she must stay in his chambers. Her ruse wouldn't be convincing otherwise. But Erik was positively delusional if he thought they would share more than sleeping arrangements.

His room was at the end of a long maze of tunnels. Thankfully, there was a small balcony that opened to the night sky.

She ran her hand along its ornate iron railing, peering over the edge.

Water lapped at the Castle's foundation and created a layer of froth visible in the moonlight. Maia wasn't claustrophobic, but she wasn't keen on the idea of being trapped in the mountain without an external escape route, either.

Erik tended the fire at her back, taking some of the chill out of the damp room. He leaned against the mantel and studied her. There was no heat in his gaze. Maybe a hint of resignation.

His air, his posture blended seamlessly with the ornate surroundings. He wore his nobility as easily as she wore her favorite olive-green leathers.

She averted her eyes.

The space was exactly as she imagined on the journey here — cavernous ceilings and plush rugs and intricate tapestries. Fit for a Faeblood Lord's heir.

Then there was the bed.

More than double the size of hers back home, it engulfed the far wall. She padded across the room and sank into the velvet covers. Her callouses snagged on the purple threads, an unnecessary reminder she didn't belong among such finery.

A log crackled in the hearth. Embers swirled in front of the grate. Her arms grew numb, but when she rubbed them, the skin was warm to the touch.

"Come," he said. "Let's put this day behind us. Did you pack a nightgown, or do you require something of mine?"

He pinched the back of his tunic and pulled it over his head.

Her eyes flicked to the tiered chandelier above.

She'd glimpsed his bare chest and bare feet more times than she could count, but here, it was an intimacy that sent her gaze darting around the room. Maia packed a small satchel with a few items. Another pair of leathers. Extra tunics. Her sleeping gown, the one with the blood red flowers Jade had embroidered on the hem.

But she couldn't summon the words to tell him.

Erik crouched down in front of her, resting a hand on her knee.

"You can wear mine," he said in a voice often reserved for frightened animals. Erik handed her his tunic. "I'll commission the seamstress for several sleeping gowns when she fits you for the rest of your wardrobe."

It was still warm. She rubbed the soft fabric between her thumb and forefinger. The mattress dipped behind her, and she quickly buried her nose in the garment. She loved his scent — a mixture of pine soap all the fighters used and a trace of what she now recognized as spicy cloves.

Dear gods, she was a mess.

She willed her fists to relax. A long sleep would barely calm her warring thoughts, but coupled with a bath in the morning, she should settle enough to form a plan.

At least that's what she told herself as she exchanged her tunic for Erik's longer one. Her leathers were next. She peeled them off, draping them across the footboard.

The socks stayed. No matter how warm the weather, Maia's feet were always cold. She would rather wash a week's worth of linens than slide her toes between cool sheets.

"Maia." Not Kitten. Erik must've sensed she could take no more of his provocation. "You need rest. Come to bed."

"I sleep on the right." She nodded to where he sat.

Her voice sounded petulant even to her own ears. She could fall asleep in an itchy hay loft with a leaking roof and not wake for hours. But it was always like this with him. A challenge. Even before he was her enemy.

"Not with me." He climbed under the heavy covers. "I sleep nearest the door."

Her tired body sank into the soft mattress. She wasn't obeying him. A soldier took rest when they could. She pulled the blanket up to her nose. It wasn't hiding, either. No, her chin was cold.

"The desk holds a stack of blank parchment. You'll find a quill and ink in the drawers. Pen a letter tomorrow. Xavier will want to know the location of my chambers and the guard's numbers."

She waited for him to say something more, but soft snores replaced the heavy silence.

Erik was right, of course. It didn't stop her from bristling at his know-it-all directives.

A bark of laughter bubbled free. Or was it a sob? If only her father could see her bundled in such finery. He would get a kick out of it — his daughter, the spy.

She regretted that he never witnessed her promotion to Xavier's most esteemed fighters.

It had been his dream for her to join the ranks. Her father had lived and breathed the militia, imparting the singular obsession to his only child. She hadn't failed him as a soldier all the years since he'd departed her world.

She wouldn't now.

CHAPTER FIVE

"Where is she?" Erik asked.

At six bells, he slipped into the kitchens and cornered a maid. She was new, timid. He took a step back and softened his voice. "Where is Demelza?"

Pots and pans clanged to his right. Servants scurried around him, vanishing into the labyrinth of hallways connecting the sleeping chambers. Few nobles rose before midday. Still, there was plenty of work to keep the Castle running smoothly. Plenty of invisible tasks to keep the Lords and Ladies from looking too hard in their direction.

He'd left Maia sleeping in his bed. She was softer in slumber, the suspicious bend of her brows relaxing. Erik woke in a tangle of limbs, arousal driving him from her arms.

"She's in the pantry, milord." The maid curtsied. To her feet she said, "Taking stock for meals, directing the butlers."

He nodded, dismissing her. Words of thanks lodged in his throat. A reflex born from years of suppressing gratitude.

Six months had passed since he set eyes on the head housekeeper. One hundred and sixty-three days. It took all his self-control not to find her as soon as they arrived at the Castle. He wanted Maia settled, else he would have snuck into Dezee's personal chambers regardless of the hour.

No one ever accused him of being selfless.

His long strides ate the distance to the rear of the kitchens. A Red Guard sentry kept the smaller chamber locked when not in use. His father's precaution. Wouldn't want the servants eating more than their allotted rations.

The door hung open and voices drifted his way. He followed the sound of her throaty commands, winding around a tall stack of grain and jars of canned vegetables.

"And we need more gooseberry jam for Lord Bierling." Dezee scratched notes on a piece of parchment. The feather quill fluttered in front of her face. "He went through the last jar in three days, slathering four teaspoons per biscuit. Send word to Lukas. Perhaps he can barter for some more next time his patrol takes him to the Farming territory."

Barter, not demand.

After the annual tithe, the populace had little for the rest of the year. This summer's drought threatened the razor thin edge of survival. A single jar of preserves could mean the difference between a family eating for a week or going hungry.

Women and children suffered the most, their bodies and faces whittled away during the colder, unforgiving months while the Faeblood Lords grew rounder and rounder each winter. Greedy bastards. Far be it from them to eat a dry biscuit.

"What good comes from starving them," he'd asked his father once. *"Their work suffers with bodies near death."*

"A hungry body works harder to feed its masters."

He never brought it up again.

Instead, Erik, with Dezee's help, prepared small packages of round breads and cured meats and hard cheeses. Surplus produce from his gardens. He deposited them on doorsteps at night, more often at the cottages with the smallest children. Or the ones without parents working the family trade.

Aye, he was selfish. Those gifts did little to ease their suffering. Long ago, Erik accepted that he left them to unburden his conscience.

"Ma'am." The young serving girl's head whipped toward him. "Ms. Dezee..."

"What is it?" Dezee asked the maid. She looked up from her parchment. "Oh, Erik, my boy."

She handed her notes to the girl, picked up her skirts, and launched herself at him. They wrapped their arms around one another.

"Oh, Erik, my boy," she repeated, this time her voice shook as she squeezed. "I thought I'd never see you again."

She leaned back and brushed an invisible tendril of hair off his forehead, the gesture so familiar it nearly brought him to his knees.

His gaze snagged on her left hand where her smallest finger should've been. He grabbed her wrist and brought it closer to his face for inspection. The end of the nub was clean. The skin healed in a grotesque pattern common with a slow, non-magical method of removal.

"Don't." She cupped the side of his cheek. Erik dimly registered the maid slipping out of the pantry. "Don't fret."

Erik swore.

"I'm sound. It healed..." She turned away from him and rearranged tins of oiled fish on the nearest shelf. "It healed... eventually."

"I'm sorry," he said, his voice gruff.

When Erik's initial reports from the militia compound lacked incriminating information, his father threatened Dezee as punishment. Lord Siodina wanted to dismantle Xavier's regime and needed proof for the High Table to overthrow the territory leader. When subsequent letters lacked evidence of subterfuge, he imprisoned her in the dungeons.

Then took her finger in a fit of rage.

Erik lived with the weight of his failures ever since. While Dezee, with her too kind heart, would forgive him, he would never forgive himself.

"Don't worry so." She pulled her shoulders back. "There is no reason to apologize. 'Twas not your blade that struck me. It's a finger. I possess nine more. Besides, he would never hinder me enough to interfere with my duties."

He — his power-hungry but practical father.

Dezee sent him a false smile.

"Who needs their little finger, anyway?" She winked. "I only miss it when I drink tea. The others stare when I wiggle it with each sip."

She may have jested about the injury, but Erik added it to the list of his father's transgressions. The long, long list he dreamed of avenging. While it was too risky to challenge his father, the mental tally served as an outlet for his rage.

"When did you return?" She smoothed her hands over the front of his tunic, lingering on his middle.

"We slipped in a few hours after twilight." He inhaled her sweet scent, a blend of cinnamon and sugar. A phantom pain radiated down his stomach with her probing.

"Heard you took a blade to your gullet." She leaned in and whispered, "Heard a commoner, a human with Faeblood powers, healed you. The news burned through the Castle like an elemental fire on the southern ridge."

"She did. Saved my sorry hide at significant risk to herself." He refused to use Ember's name. These walls had ears.

"Then I am in her debt. Blimey. A Faeblood raised in the territories. How? I have never heard such a story." Dezee gripped the front of his tunic. "Where did she come from?"

"As for how… the magic carries from her mother's line, but she doesn't know her family name." He wrapped his fingers around her wrists. "She's a powerful sorceress. Perhaps stronger than me."

"Another healer in my time..." Dezee shook her head.

It was rare. Historically, Faebloods produced one healer per generation. His mother was one. He was the next.

With his return, the Lords would fill Erik's days demanding potions for hangovers, while the Ladies would request face creams and tonics for non-existent wrinkles. For all their magic, Faebloods aged similarly to humans.

"Your father will attempt to silence her."

"She knows and commands the militia's loyalty. They will start a civil war if harm befalls her."

"Pray it doesn't come to that." Dezee paused then bit her lip. "Now, about this *we*. Don't think I didn't catch that."

Erik grinned. Or was it a grimace?

How could he explain Maia? While he wished to reveal the truth about their relationship, it would put everyone at risk. Still, Dezee knew he despised marriage and would see through their ruse. But there was no other choice than to continue with the lies. For her sake. And Maia's.

"I met someone," he hedged. "She's a militia fighter."

There. Simple. That was straightforward enough.

Dezee pursed her lips, the gesture making him feel ten years old again. She waited.

"We became close." Was the room growing smaller? The towering shelves closed in on him. Erik ran a finger around his collar, unable to loosen the fabric. "Ah, in training. We became close in training."

She cocked her head to the side.

"And wefellinloveandgotmarried." The words tumbled out, one on the heels of the next. "We got married."

"You got married?" She grabbed his upper arms as if to shake some sense into him. "What were you thinking? Your father. He..."

"I know. I *know*." He ran his hand over his hair, at a loss for words.

"You've never shown interest in a wife. Your father will see the union as another step toward you settling down into your role as a future High Lord."

She dropped his arms and started pacing the aisle.

"You took me by surprise. That's difficult in my old age."

Dezee was not yet fifty. She raised him when she was barely old enough to start a family herself. Never married. Never took lovers, though not for a lack of admirers.

She was stunning with long auburn curls and violet eyes that made painters pull their hair out for failing to replicate the exact shade. They were soulful, with a touch of compassion that drew in everyone who met her.

His father harbored an unusual amount of resentment toward her, especially for someone who treated humans no better than the furniture scattered throughout the great hall.

Erik often wondered if the intense hatred had more to do with unfulfilled longing as opposed to ire over the close relationship he and Dezee shared.

"Faeblood purity above all else, even personal desires." One of his father's favorite mantras.

Mating with humans was forbidden, but that didn't prevent the more lecherous Lords from taking them as lovers. Unwanted offspring of such unions met a terrible fate. Considered dirty, their magical parent banished them to the servants' quarters. With cursed blood running through their veins, many of the humans shunned them, too.

If any magic manifested, the High Table smothered it during the Rite of Ortus. Forever.

"And your bride? Where is she now?" Dezee bunched up her skirts as if she might take off down the corridor and rouse Maia.

"She's sleeping. I will introduce you once she wakes."

"What does she need? We must fit her for a new wardrobe.

Morning dresses and riding outfits and formal gowns for dinner."

Dezee held her fingers in the air, ticking off each item. She paid him no attention.

"And matching stockings and new corsets and silk slippers."

"Night shirts. Lacy things," he said. The corners of his mouth tugged up in a grin.

"Of course, of course." She produced a quill and another scrap of parchment from her apron's deep pockets, scribbling notes so quickly Erik could barely make out the words. "I'll inquire if the seamstress has something ready for her now. She cannot dine in the great hall without a proper gown."

"I don't care if she has one or not." But it would make her transition easier, so he didn't protest Dezee's fussing.

"She'll need hair pins and your mother's jewels." More ferocious scribbling. Her voice hitched. Tentatively she added, "If... if you'd planned on sharing them with her."

Erik swallowed, then nodded. He wrapped his arms around her and squeezed, conveying his gratitude without words. He needed this... this contact.

He wasn't prepared for the burn in his gut at the thought of someone else wearing his mother's baubles. Foolish. Mama never cared for fancy things, preferring to spend her days in the greenhouse instead of the solarium for afternoon tea.

"I'm getting ahead of myself, aren't I?" Dezee sagged against him.

"You take on too many tasks. Maia will need a maid of her own."

"Nonsense. I will tend to her myself." She leaned back, studying him. "If she is important to you, then she is important to me. I'll not assign another when I'm fully capable."

"Only a fool would think you incapable." He held up a hand to silence the objection surely dangling from her lips. "But there will be times when your duties pull you away."

"There's one who might work. A newer girl." She clucked her tongue. "Excellent work, but I catch her wandering the Castle. Perhaps this will keep her busy and out of trouble. Listen to me prattling on like some ill-disciplined gossip."

Erik rested his forehead against hers and closed his eyes. He thought he would never hear her voice again. Now, she could yammer on about crop rotation, and he would listen for hours.

He leaned back and opened his eyes. As if she knew what he was thinking, the edges of her lips tilted downward. He cupped her ears and brushed a kiss across her forehead. "Thank you."

"Anything." She rubbed her thumb along his brow, tucked his pendant back in his tunic, and repeated, "Anything for you. Now, what about earrings? Does she have her holes?"

"No. She doesn't," a deep voice answered from behind.

Erik whirled around. *Mikel.*

No surprise there. Xavier wouldn't send Maia without protection — someone he trusted.

"Faeblood frivolities," Mikel scoffed.

"I'm seeing a ghost," Dezee said, interrupting the tension in the room. "Dear gods, you've grown up."

Dezee brushed past Erik. She reached for Mikel, her hand suspending in midair.

"Is it really you?" Her arm dropped to her side. "I never thought I'd see you again. It's been..."

"Two decades, one year, and one summer," Mikel said.

Erik studied the fighter.

His golden blonde hair, normally left loose around his shoulders, was gathered in a severe knot on the top of his head, highlighting the close-cropped sides. A uniform of all black replaced his customary tan leathers and cream tunic. Long sleeves covered the arms responsible for countless knockout blows. And at the ends, matching black leather cuffs hid his wrists.

Even in training, the cuffs never came off.

Of course. Mikel was born at the Castle.

The revelation hit him like a solid uppercut. All those months. He never guessed. But seeing him here with Dezee...

Mikel was older than most of Xavier's inner circle. Erik did the math in his head. If he was correct, Mikel would've been at the Castle when his mother disappeared.

His fingertips brushed the edge of his belt where Maia's dagger rested.

"I'm Lady Maia's guard," Mikel said, responding to Dezee's unasked question.

"You two know each other."

"Aye," Dezee said. "This one, this charmer, I knew from my youth. He vowed to escape this place. Beguiled half the staff and several Faeblood Ladies on his way out. He could talk the skirt off anyone with a pulse. Never thought I'd see the day he returned to the Castle."

"Forget I'm here," he snapped.

"It's wonderful to see you," Dezee said, ignoring the warning in Mikel's tone. "I thought of you every day. We have much to catch up on."

She patted his cheek.

"If you'll both excuse me, I need to find a gown for my new mistress." She rushed out of the pantry before Erik could give her a proper goodbye.

Mikel shot Erik a look he couldn't decipher then followed.

Dezee's depiction of Mikel did not match his behavior at the compound. It was as if she remembered him as a rake.

But that couldn't be correct. Mikel avoided all amorous overtures thrown his direction, even going so far as turning heel at the first sign of a flirtation. Xavier's sister, Ada, was the only exception. It was clear Mikel desired her, though he did not act on her many, very loud propositions.

Loyalty. There it was again, the pesky emotion. Xavier inspired a deep, unwavering loyalty in his men.

When he'd first arrived at the compound, Erik hadn't recognized it. As a young man, he'd rationalized his intense feelings for Dezee as a child seeking a parental figure. He'd felt a glimmer of the same with his first mentor – the grizzled Red Guard who trained him in combat, providing an outlet for his teenage rebellion.

Now, after spending months alongside the seasoned fighters in the militia, he spotted it immediately. If Mikel swore never to return to the Castle, only his deep-seated loyalty to Xavier would bring him back.

Luckily for Erik, Xavier commanded such simpleminded devotion. Mikel might yield a clue to his mother's disappearance.

CHAPTER SIX

My Dearest Jade,

Erik lives in the grandest home. I must confess I did not realize the Castle hid such treasures. Our chambers contain luxuries of the finest craftsmanship found throughout Morvak.

His status affords him rooms with a balcony, a mere two windows from the fortresses' southern aspect. We fell asleep last night listening to the lap of the lake four stories below. Over three dozen Red Guard greeted us when we arrived, each eager to make a suitable first impression.

I'm excited to start matrimony in such splendor while homesickness hasn't yet chased away the cheer. Write when the time allows. I look forward to the news from the compound.

Yours in Friendship,
Maia

P.S. Erik declared I must have an entirely new wardrobe. I cannot contain my enthusiasm!

EARLIER, A SERVANT DELIVERED A WRAPPED PACKAGE CONTAINING a dinner gown. Maia sent the charismatic girl off with Jade's letter and a promise of stolen dinner sweets if the child sent it via carrier falcon straight away.

She eyed the new dress with all the respect she paid the rattlers in the reeds by the stream.

Afternoon sun poured through the open windows, the rays highlighting its intricate embroidery. Rich amethyst satin stared back. The offending garment hung on the front of a tall armoire, taunting her.

She stretched and padded over to the balcony, sticking to the perimeter of the room. A warm breeze fluttered the hem of Erik's tunic and flattened the goosebumps on her bare legs. She closed her eyes and tilted her head skyward, seeking more heat.

Maia willed her muscles to relax one by one, following a technique she taught the second-year recruits. Soldiers must conserve their strength in battle. Tensed limbs spent too much energy and would wear a fighter out.

She sighed. 'Twas a dress. She could wear a dress. Had worn plenty of dresses to the bonfires at the compound.

Sure, light, simple summer numbers. Nothing as fine as the one back in Erik's chambers.

Their chambers. She must remember.

"Do you like it?" Erik's deep timbre carried to the balcony.

She opened her eyes and leaned against the railing. He looked ready for battle.

Dark brown leathers tucked into heavy utilitarian boots. Two bandoliers crisscrossed his chest. At least a half dozen throwing daggers nestled inside the cleverly crafted loops on each. He unfastened the buckles and deposited them on the trunk at the foot of the bed.

"The dress." He gestured to the gown. "Does it suit?"

Her bare feet echoed on the cold floor. She held her head high, aware of her near nakedness.

"Who would object to something so fine?" She kept her back to him and ran her fingers over the long skirts.

Perhaps if she thought of it as armor. If she considered the uncomfortable finery as her new uniform for a different sort of warfare, it would be less intimidating.

A ballgown was a small sacrifice even if it made her skin crawl.

Maia was… nervous. It wasn't anticipation that hit her but… a bout of nerves. Such a skittery and edgy nervousness that she didn't hear Erik's approach.

"I didn't ask what others prefer." The heat from his chest grazed her back. "Do *you* like it?"

"It's an improvement from my wedding gown." She flattened her palm on the bodice.

"The color of royalty." The words caressed the shell of her ear. He covered her hand with his. "You are beautiful in any hue — sweet pinks or bold reds, or your favorite, too serious greens."

His other hand settled on her hip. If he thought she would be the one to lose their bet…

Maia's back arched, pressing more firmly into his hard lines. She could play, too.

"If it's not to your tastes, I will scour the Castle to find another." He ran the tip of his nose up the column of her neck and whispered, "You are mine. My wife. You deserve the best."

Easy words. Careless words.

They lived in an unkind world — a select few got what they deserved. At the heart, that was why Xavier fought for them.

Her father had warned her. *"Watch. He will lift this territory out of poverty, then move on to the next."*

Xavier had built the training barn. Then the compound. Now, he looked to his neighbors in the peninsula's heart. Subtle changes, but noticeable if one paid attention. Perhaps Lord Siodina wasn't wrong to send Erik undercover.

"It's breathtaking." Not a lie. She would leave it at that. He didn't need to know the rest. She turned in his arms and said, "And for you, my husband, do you drape yourself in luxury or attend as a warrior?

The lust clouding his eyes vanished.

"The battle outside these walls requires different tactics. Words cut as easily as the sharpest blade."

She may be simple, but Xavier taught her that lesson long ago. Undersized, she often relied upon quick thinking and an occasional well-placed barb to goad her larger opponents into making a mistake.

Maia ran her thumb across his lower lip. The pad snagged in the thicker center before continuing to the corner of his mouth.

"You mistake my question." She turned, her backside brushing against his front, and strolled to the vanity, forcing a sway in her hips. "I merely wanted to coordinate my accessories."

Maia sat down on the plush stool. Its soft fabric tickled the back of her thighs, an unnecessary reminder she still had no pants.

"Slippers send a message of a docile, complacent wife." She combed her hair, snagging on the tangles near the nape. "But boots are more practical for holding a man by his throat."

"Wear what you want. Sturdy boots or matching slippers, I don't care. But keep my dagger on you at all times. Don't hesitate to draw it."

"Even if it's your neck that has my hand reaching?" She set the brush down.

"Especially if it's my neck." A feral grin split his face.

What kind of dinner was she attending?

Meals at the compound were loud and messy. Full of camaraderie. Younger fighters boasted of their new skills. Older ones rolled their eyes, slapping them on the back of the head when warranted.

They dug into greasy meat passed around on platters and drank fresh spring water straight from the jug when Cook ran out of goblets. Everyone bumping elbows, everyone rubbing shoulders. But an underlying current of affection bonded the lot, making the dinners enjoyable instead of dreadful.

And nobody threatened to kill each other.

Knock. Knock.

Erik frowned.

"Who is it?" she called out in an unfamiliar squeak. Maia straightened and placed the brush on the vanity.

"It's Demelza, milady, head housekeeper. Lord Siodina sent me to assist with your preparations for dinner."

The last thing she wanted was a High Lord's servant helping her, reporting her every movement. What if she slipped and broke character? It was better to be left alone.

"Lord Siodina insists."

"She means me," Erik mouthed as she stood. Right. He was Lord Siodina to these people. She must remember.

"Dezee." Erik sighed as he opened the chamber door. "I told you to send another."

A short, middle-aged woman wearing a cream apron over a drab gray gown, entered. Clothed in simple attire, she was still stunning. Even more so when she gifted Erik with an indulgent smile, patting him on the cheek.

Maia looked away from the pair and caught a man slipping inside.

"Mikel," she gasped. He never mentioned—

Dear gods, it was wonderful to see his face.

"When did you..." Who cared if he was here because Xavier doubted her. "How did you..."

"I left before the wedding." Mikel crossed his arms over his chest. His lips formed a flat line.

So many unspoken words in that simple statement. Occupied with Erik, she hadn't noticed Mikel missed the ceremony.

She recognized the look. It was the same one that came over him moments before he stopped playing with his opponents in the fighting ring.

Aware of their audience, Maia strolled across the room in what she hoped was a dignified pace. She hugged him tight. He stiffened, but after a few awkward breaths, he allowed her affections. Even went as far as patting her on the back.

"I'll be at supper." He set her at arm's length. "Nearby. At the edges."

"How long are you staying?" *How long until you leave me,* she wanted to ask. Instead, she held his forearm as if he might disappear.

"Don't stab anyone," Mikel said in lieu of an answer.

"I will make no such promise."

"Demelza, this is my wife, Lady Maia." Erik cleared his throat. Or was that a growl? "Dezee will assist you tonight until she can assign a Lady's maid."

Maia relinquished her grip on Mikel.

He slipped out of the chamber as quietly as he entered.

"My thanks." It would take a miracle to look presentable enough to blend in with the Ladies. "I could use the all help you can spare."

Demelza curtsied and emptied her pockets on the vanity. Pins and ribbons and small combs cluttered the surface.

"'Tis my pleasure." Demelza wrapped Maia in a hug, wringing out a surprised yelp. She tilted her head, assessing. "Now let me take my fill of you. Beautiful. No wonder you stole my Erik's heart."

Her Erik. Maia tugged the hem of the tunic lower.

"I knew the boy just needed the right partner." Demelza leaned in and whispered, "The Ladies at Court are all back-stabbing, bird-brained biddies. More concerned about their appearance than honing their magic, providing a commodity for the Castle."

The housekeeper ran her hands up and down Maia's arms.

"But look at you. Fresh and confident. Not tainted by their society."

Maia could barely keep up with Demelza's rambling, nodding when she seemed to need a response, sometimes taken aback by the familiarity of her words. It was clear she and Erik shared a relationship unbecoming a servant and a Lord.

"You'll need that backbone for dinner tonight." She patted the stool. "Sit. Let's transform you for the part."

She gathered Maia's hair off her nape, twisting it this way and that. The ends flopped forward on her crown. Demelza arranged them in a pattern only she could see.

Long locks were a hindrance in the grappling pit. Most days, she kept them tied with a leather band. On rare nights when she didn't require something practical, she left her hair unbound.

It was interesting to see them through someone else's eyes.

She inherited her mother's rich color, the sun failing to kiss the hue during the time she spent outdoors. Straight as a seamstress's pins, she never attempted to press curls into the mass.

"Holler if this is too tight." Demelza stabbed combs into the back. In the looking glass, her simple locks transformed into an elegant twist. She caught Erik slipping into the adjacent bathing chamber, scowling in her direction.

Sure, she may not resemble his usual companion, but she couldn't look *that* hideous.

Demelza wrapped a small section around her pointer finger and held it in place for half a minute. When she released the strand, the curl bounced on her crown.

"How?" Maia asked. Her eyes flicked to Demelza's rounded ears then to the bangles on her wrists. They didn't completely conceal the skin underneath. Human.

"A servant who cannot serve is of no use to the Faeblood." Demelza held her hand aloft. The sleeve of her gown fell to her elbow, exposing thick scars. "They bind a hint of magic in the wounds. Enough for us to complete our duties. No more. No less."

"That's cruel." Maia gripped the front of the vanity.

"That's our destiny." Demelza's eyes flicked to the bathing chamber. "Don't. I can feel your pity. It's a hard life but more comfortable than anything outside these walls."

She curled another strand. Then another. Maia sat in silence while Demelza finished the style.

True, life in the territories was harsh, but they were free. Maia's fingertips grazed Xavier's tattoo on her neck. As free as a citizen could be with the tithe looming.

"Let's pour you into your gown." Demelza rested her hands on Maia's shoulders, the fingertip on her right still warm. "It was the best Erik and I could find on short notice. Tomorrow, I will escort you for your fitting."

Escort. Prisoners and wayward children were escorted.

Instead of walking toward the wardrobe, Demelza moved Erik's bandoliers to the bed, opened the small trunk, and pulled out a set of undergarments.

Lace. Too much lace. Maia's cheeks heated. And silk. She shuddered, wishing for her simple linen underwear and the long binding she wrapped around her chest for sparring. Both lent themselves to comfort and ease of movement. Form and function. Not flattering, nor frilly.

"They're not so bad." Demelza's eyes twinkled. "Erik had the same expression as a young lad every time I chastised him for romping about the Castle with nothing under his trousers."

She couldn't imagine Erik as a child. Carefree, raised in luxury.

Maia dragged in a breath and pulled his tunic over her head. It pooled at her feet. She slipped on the panties first, then the chemise. Demelza was right — they were soft against her skin but did nothing to support her chest. The gown would need a stiff bodice, or the nobility were at risk of suffering more than the tip of her blade.

"Turn around." Demelza carried over the purple monstrosity, holding it aloft so the voluminous skirts didn't drag on the ground.

Maia faced the vacant hearth, searching the ash as if it contained the Castle's secrets. She was vaguely aware of raising both arms. Of the slide of the dress over her head, down her body. Small hands trailed down her arms, pressing them back to her sides.

The corset tightened at her waist, constricting her next breath. What was she doing? More shallow breaths. Who was she kidding? She would fail.

Her stomach rolled again. She was a fighter. Not a Faeblood's wife. They would see right through her. Through their farce.

A flake of ash stirred in the corner. Her eyes tracked the spiral until it floated to the stone floor near her feet. Something cold wrapped around her neck, draping over her collarbone. Hesitant fingertips investigated the new addition.

Jewelry. Another layer. The weight of the necklace did little to improve her breathing. Nor her hearing.

"Dezee... kitchens... later..."

Curious, calloused hands replaced the soft, respectable touch. They rubbed the pad of her ear and traveled down the sensitive column of her neck, dipping to trace the jewels.

She bowed to the pressure and stepped back into a hard chest.

A warm palm wrapped around her neck, tilting her head to the side. Her snarl lodged in her throat. Erik's scent was overwhelming. Stronger now, the heat from his bath amplifying the aroma.

Too many memories flooded her at once. Nights at the

compound when everyone else tucked into the barracks. Out on patrol, walking side by side. Pinned under him in her room when he tied her up…

Pain bloomed on her neck. It was sharp. Quick.

And followed by the caress of his tongue.

CHAPTER SEVEN

It appeared as if they'd both had a terrible afternoon. Maia had woken up his wife. Erik had received his father's summons for dinner.

After leaving Dezee in the kitchens, he'd climbed the clock tower staircase leading to his rooftop gardens, only to discover his plants half dead. Decades of careful tending ruined while he was away, obeying his father's whim. Someone had kept them watered, but the more difficult cultivars had withered.

The library had been no better.

He'd spent near two hours poring over ancient tomes, searching for a potion or spell that could break their marriage oaths. Book after book on Faeblood lineages but not a single hint of anything useful. He'd heaved the last volume onto a cart and headed back to his chambers, finding her half-naked and catatonic.

Then she'd hugged another male.

Forget dinner. He wanted to escape to the armory where he could throw daggers until his arm dangled uselessly by his side. But his father would send a Red Guard minion to drag him to the great hall so avoiding the invite was futile.

His bath calmed his temper. But then he spotted her by the fireplace. She looked small and fragile, gazing into the empty hearth.

Erik needed her alert for dinner, not in this ghost-like stupor. Compliments and reassuring words wouldn't wipe that look off her face.

So he bit her. For her own good.

Too busy savoring the mark, he missed the small shove to his shoulders. The leg wrapping around the back of his calf.

The hard stone floor forced a breath from his chest as he landed with a thud.

Maia clamored on top of him, pinning his arms with her knees.

Later, he would marvel at her maneuverability in a ballgown. Now, he tried not to enjoy the sensation of her body on his. Tried and failed.

"Good evening, Kitten." He grinned. "You look splendid in that dress. It highlights your—"

Ow. Ow. Ouch.

Her knees dug into the sensitive underside of his arms. If she kept them there too much longer, he would lose feeling in his hands.

"Your eyes," he said on a wheeze. "It highlights your lovely eyes."

"My eyes?" She smirked but shifted her weight off his arms.

"Admittedly, I deserved that." Erik wrapped both hands around her waist.

He picked her up, settling her on his stomach. It put her delicious heat far from his mouth but not close enough to rub against his arousal. He tucked a face-framing tendril behind her ear. Better.

Erik enjoyed seeing her unguarded expressions. A carryover from a childhood filled with love. She would need to lose those for dinner, too.

He ran his hand up her legs, telling himself he searched for her dagger. His errant thumbs rubbed small circles on her inner thighs, and she rewarded him with a flash of fire.

There it was.

"Demelza spent the better part of an hour on my curls." She patted the underside of her twist. "Eyes up. Are they all still in place?"

"Not a single hair dares to peek out." He cupped her knees. "Those lecherous Lords will be jealous that I get to remove each comb one by one. You'd like that, wouldn't you? You will drive them mad and enjoy every minute."

She looked away, but not fast enough to hide her uncertainty. So that was it — she lacked confidence in her appearance. Well, he had something that might help.

"Up." He patted her leg. "You wear my necklace. My mark on your throat. I have one last gift."

She bunched her skirts in her hand, stood up, and strolled over to the vanity. He hid his smirk when he caught her checking and rechecking the bodice of her dress.

"You look *fine*. Stop fussing." Erik's hands hovered in the air above her shoulders, declaring his intentions. "May I?"

She nodded.

He tugged her earlobes between his thumb and forefinger, massaging a line to their rounded tops.

"I won't kiss you first." Her lips parted, and the swell of her chest rose with each breath.

"The nobility love their status symbols," Erik said, ignoring her protest. "The seating order in the great hall… the style of dress for the season…"

His thumb caressed the spot in front of her ears. She was so soft. Not the suppleness of her skin, but the way she melted from his touch. As if she were indeed feline and he discovered the secret to make her purr.

"And the jewelry we place on our lobes."

Her eyes widened. "You will not pierce my ears."

"You forget who I am. My magic. You will suffer a moment's pinch before I heal the wound."

He rested his hand on the base of her neck.

"And after, if you dislike my gift, I shall heal the marks, removing any trace of scarring."

She stared straight ahead.

What he wouldn't give to see inside her mind. Did she fear the pain? Not likely. She never balked at a fight. One might even call her reckless. Perhaps from a desire to prove herself. This was another mark binding them. Surely, she didn't feel betrayal to Xavier.

Or was she simply appalled by the ritual?

Faeblood adorned their ears for as long as Erik remembered. Longer, according to their written history. When their ancestors scattered across the Strait of Vian, the location of the posts denoted the wearer's birthplace. More loops inferred a higher status.

Now, the elaborate earrings were a mere decoration.

Several heartbeats passed while she held her own gaze. An eternity. Finally, she nodded.

He grabbed the small velvet box on the vanity. His mother's. A set of earrings nestled inside the padded interior, arranged in a manner to prevent tangles. They consisted of nine posts separated by eight hoops, all connected by a fine metal chain.

Forged from her favored rose gold, they were a betrothal set.

Had his mother felt the same trepidation as Maia did now? His parent's marriage was not a love match. Elders, who coveted the sanctity of pure Faeblood lines more than their children's happiness, arranged the union.

It wasn't a secret — both parties had been miserable.

Erik's childhood memories of his mother faded each year, so much so he could barely recall her features without visiting her portrait in the gallery. He remembered her scent — a mixture of ripe cherries, her favorite stone fruit, and Crimson Gillyflowers. He remembered her voice, soft and instructive.

And he never forgot how it changed whenever his father walked into the room.

Your father felt the same sense of ownership, marking his property.

He averted his eyes.

Under different circumstances — if Maia had chosen him of her own will — he might savor this moment, as with the bite. But he never wanted a wife. Erik enjoyed his freedom. Who would want someone to track their every move? He resisted the urge to chuck the box on the vanity.

"Quit stalling." Maia twisted on the stool. "Let's get this over with. You still need to finish dressing. Though, I'm certain the Ladies of Court would not object should you decide to arrive without your tunic."

"It's faster if I place the posts at once." He clenched his jaw and cradled the first in his palm. "But I will insert them one at a time if you wish."

"Do it." She rolled her shoulders. Her knuckles gripped the edge of the vanity tight enough to blanch. "A shot of pain is preferable to drawn out torture."

His magic pooled in his hands, warming the metal. A sour taste coated his tongue. Different. The posts glowed, a signal they were ready to pierce her skin.

"Take a deep breath. On three…"

"One," she whispered on an exhale.

"Two." He braced himself for the pain.

Erik might be a bastard, but he didn't enjoy causing her harm. Plus, he didn't trust her to voice the truth. She would swallow the discomfort and lie about how much she suffered.

"Three," they said together.

The earring pierced her flesh, and his magic quickly sealed off the wounds. A saccharine sweet flavor replaced the nasty taste. He couldn't decide what was worse, the tears pooling on her lower lid or the fact she didn't let out a sound.

Her skin turned pink, the blood pooling to the injury despite the edges of the flesh knitting around the metal.

"Go on." Maia nodded to the other set, her voice hoarse. She grabbed his wrist. "The wait is worse."

No counting down this time. He plucked the mate from the box and guided it in place. A small whimper nearly buckled his knees. Her breathing evened out as he drained heat from the wound.

Erik studied the rare design.

The Ladies at Court would fawn over them, exclaiming Maia's luck at owning lavish jewelry. Of ensnaring a Siodina. Despite their significance, Erik couldn't help but see two tiny cages.

"Excuse me." She rose and left him there, staring at her back.

He wanted to follow her to the balcony but stopped short. It would have been better if she screamed. Or at least yelled obscenities at him.

He cupped his hand over his mouth. To hell with tradition. Maia might want to blend with the nobles, but he would wear something comfortable. And if it drew some attention from her…

Erik donned a pair of black wool socks and laced his training boots. He rummaged through the chest and found a leather holster. The straps crisscrossed his upper back, a stark outline against a simple white tunic.

Dinners in the great hall required formal attire. His father would be… displeased.

Let him say something. Let him witness what Erik had become. He buttoned his cuffs and left his collar open.

Maia returned more composed, her brows furrowing as her gaze raked him from head to toe.

"Do you not approve?" he asked.

"Don't be ridiculous." Her head snapped up. "Of course I approve. Why are you allowed to wear fighting clothes while I'm trussed up, hindered by layers of skirts?"

"It didn't slow your takedown earlier."

"True. They may prevent me from running but should hide my blade well."

"Tonight," he said as he took a step closer. "Choose violence instead of submission."

"I'd rather eat in peace."

He scoffed. "Then we will need a tray delivered to our chambers."

"Don't tempt me." Maia blew a wisp off her forehead. "I want to curl up in your unreasonably comfortable bed, but we must attend the meal as husband and wife. I will not have them think me a coward."

"Or we can stay right here. Find something else to occupy our time. No one would balk at newlyweds hiding for a week or two."

Maia was the furthest thing from a coward, but she would lose sleep if they skipped the meal. He placed two fingers under her chin and tipped it up.

"No kissing, though, unless you beg me."

She had that look again. Another punch would make her feel better, but she must be hungry. When was the last time she ate? Dinner before the wedding ceremony?

"Come." Erik grabbed her hand, straightening the smirk toying with his lips. He looped her fingers under his elbow, tucked her into his side, and led her down the central corridor. "The Lords and their families take breakfast in their private chambers. At least the ones who wake before noon."

Erik slowed his steps as Maia picked her way around the damper areas. He should've insisted on boots.

The state of the corridors reflected the Faeblood's mentality.

One would think with their magic, they would keep their

home dry, free from mold. But none could be bothered. Why would they? Servants fought the losing battle. Drying out smaller hallways while exchanging runners in the heavily trafficked areas. An entire team spent their lives cleaning and polishing the nobility's footwear. What a waste.

"They serve lunch in the quainter gathering spaces." He gestured to an antechamber filled with small tables. Several settees lined the perimeter. "Small groups break off and spread out, keeping the servants hopping for several hours with their requests."

"Am I to join you for nooning meals?"

"No. I eat in the greenhouse. Alone." He softened his voice and said, "Tonight, I will introduce you to the most prominent families. As my wife, you will not lack in invitations."

He nodded toward the two Red Guards who stood sentry next to the entrance of the great hall.

The original Faeblood had buried the chamber deep within the mountain. Carved from a natural cave, it was the size of the training barn back in the Militia territory.

"Evening, lads." Time for some fun. "Fine work, keeping the Lords safe from..." He made a show of looking up and down the corridor then said, "Themselves. Must be the highlight of your career, gentlemen. All those summers of training..."

Humans had to make tough choices. Erik respected everyone's role in society. But these sycophants relished the cruelty their position afforded, encouraging the worst in their ranks.

He patted the guard on the cheek, stepped back, and led Maia inside.

"Are we late?" Maia peered around him. "Where are the Ladies?"

At the back of the hall, the Lords mingled in groups of threes and fours. They snagged fare from passing trays while sipping Fae wine. He could feel Mikel in the shadows.

"They take their drink and gossip in the solarium, a favorite spot to enjoy the setting sun." He bent down, brushing his lips along her earrings. "They will join us soon."

Her shoulders remained around her ears.

"Dinners are often a boring affair." He massaged her palm with his thumb. "Draw your blade on one of these fools, and I'll ask Dezee to find some of your favorite truffles. The chocolate ones you sneak into the compound."

Not long after he'd joined the militia, Erik had noted her preference for the decadent treats.

Once a month on her afternoon off, Maia relaxed in the courtyard with her friends. The females shared smiles and gossip. And when they thought nobody was looking, the rich chocolates. Erik wanted to remind her of her family, of happier times.

She would need the memories tonight.

CHAPTER EIGHT

"Let us rejoice," Lord Siodina addressed the Court. "My son returns, and I see he brought his whore."

The Faeblood were insane.

Maia stared at the handsome man. There was no question as to his identity. His features were so like Erik's, it was akin to looking in the future. How did Xavier not make the connection sooner?

Though, knowing her leader, he likely did, allowing Erik's unrestricted movements at the compound as a test of sorts.

Whore.

What a splendid welcome to the family. So kind of Lord Siodina to shout it across the great hall. Now, the other nobles could add it to their list of insults. Human. Dirty Blood. Whore. It took effort not to roll her eyes.

She'd been called worse.

Every new class of militia soldiers contained one or two fighters who refused to recognize her authority.

"Did you spread your legs to the top?" they'd asked. *"A pretty thing like you can't fight."*

Small-minded. Unoriginal. Especially since she had not

welcomed a partner to her bed since... well... it had been a while.

Maia took great pleasure cutting their legs out from under them. She knocked the worst on their arses in front of their friends, pinning their throats with her knee. Sometimes, an idiot kept at it. Usually a bloke from the mining village to the east, their cores as rotten and black as their territory.

Xavier handled those.

Erik placed his palm on her lower back, subtly applying pressure until she melted into his side. He grinned down at her in his near-feral smile. There he is.

She braced for whatever nonsense he was about to spout.

"Aye. She may whore for me in our chambers," Erik said, holding her gaze. For a heartbeat, it was just the two of them mashed together, sharing the same air with her murderous thoughts. "But to the Court, the populace, she is Lady Siodina."

Maia missed the outrage sparking around the room — a combination of hushed whispers and audible gasps and crashing dinnerware.

Erik shielded the hall with his body, cupping her chin with both hands. A show.

They needed to put on a performance, one that didn't involve her kneeing him in the—

His thumbs rubbed the underside of her jaw, lazily stroking their way from the tip of her chin to the shell of her ear. He hesitated then claimed her lips. Unlike his caress moments before, he didn't start off slow, exploring her mouth.

Erik Siodina devoured her like a man eating after a week-long fast.

Small sparks lit the base of her skull where his fingers tangled in her twist. His lips were soft, demanding. Maia wanted to nip at the bottom one, but she couldn't keep up with him.

He angled his head while his tongue swept inside.

Maia closed her eyes, savoring his taste — his usual spicy cloves. Now, with a tinge of mint. Half of her body wanted to shove him off, the logical part that recognized him as her attacker.

The other half? She didn't want to dwell on that traitorous sliver of her soul. Her senses shrunk to their embrace. The noise of the hall, the spectators a distant memory. Somewhere, her body had ceased acting and gave into its needs.

Her hands explored his chest. They looped around the back of his neck, tugging him impossibly closer. She wanted to drag him to the nearest alcove.

More, her body chanted. *More. More. More.*

It took every ounce of willpower not to rub herself against him like a barn cat in heat. Somewhere in the recesses of her mind, she *knew* the show must end. Only, it didn't feel like acting.

If a simple kiss had her clinging to him in the great hall, how far would a bit of affection take them in the privacy of his chambers? No. She must stay away from Erik. Xavier needed information. And she needed to leave here with her dignity intact.

It wouldn't be good to entertain this attraction. For Erik's sake.

Maia took lovers — seasoned fighters intent on returning home after they graduated from the militia training. Easy. Safe. Discreet. She snuck them into her private chambers in the barracks.

These men knew the score. Mutual satisfaction. For the homesick, a comfortable place to rest. Others took their fill, leaving her bereft. They soon realized that sleeping with one of Xavier's family members did nothing to further their rankings.

Erik was different.

Not once did he attempt to seduce her, despite plenty of

opportunities outside of training. It was just as well. Their situation was... messy.

He might be handsome and intriguing and a phenomenal kisser (stop thinking about his tongue), but he was her enemy. His father was directly responsible for suffering throughout the kingdom.

At last, she wrenched her lips free and rested her forehead against his chest.

Unlike with Erik's earlier announcement, you could hear a mouse squeak. It was as if everyone held a collective breath. Waiting for what? The first clap of congratulations? Lord Siodina to recognize the union? Handshakes and fierce hugs from the nobles?

Gods, she missed home.

"Doesn't count," Erik whispered as if she needed a reminder.

A caustic remark lodged in her throat. These were not her people. Better to let him handle the crowd. Plus, she must play a submissive wife, not a militia soldier.

Erik, she begrudgingly admitted, was smart. The kiss was convincing. Even her traitorous body thought it was real. No one would doubt their chemistry, and with the new adornment on her ears, no one would doubt her status.

Lord Siodina parted the crowd, a bored expression carved on his face.

"A jest for allowing the boy to sow his oats." Erik's father slapped him on the back and mirrored the Lord's grins. "My son thinks with his prick instead of his head. Come now. Let us dispense with such nonsense. You girl," he continued, pointing to Maia. "You can dine with the servants in the kitchen."

"She stays with me," Erik said, his voice a near growl.

"The wine." Lord Siodina clapped his hands above his head, signaling the passing butler.

Dozens of servants weaved through the crowd carrying trays laden with full goblets.

A distraction. Lord Siodina dropped the matter too easily for it to be anything but a simple distraction. As expected, the nobility dispersed, returning to their respective gossip circles.

Maia wanted to sigh, but Erik's father regarded her down the tip of his nose. He leaned in then did the last thing she expected.

Lord Siodina sniffed her.

It wasn't the slow inhale of a lover. Nor disdain as if he stepped in rot. No, he smelled her as a bloodhound searches a trail.

"Foolish boy," he hissed. Lord Siodina took a step back and wrinkled his nose. "You marked a human."

"Aye. And before the night's out, she will have my seed in her belly. Again."

"Forever the disappointment." Lord Siodina's brows narrowed, his eyes flicking to her middle. "Your mother would suffer shame."

"Leave her out of—"

"First, your weak magic." He nodded to someone across the room. "Now, diluting our line with human scum. The Court will banish any offspring, a punishment befitting their tainted blood. Enjoy your dinner. It shall be an entertaining welcome home."

He dismissed them and strode across the chamber. Overzealous nobles stepped forward, vying for his attention. Lord Siodina ignored them all and disappeared through a hidden door in the back wall.

"Smile." Erik squeezed her hand.

"Marvelous," she said out of the corner of her mouth. Maia forced her cheeks higher. Without the aid of a looking glass, it might resemble a sneer. "Your father is exactly how I imagined."

"Sip. *Slowly.*" Erik snagged two goblets from a passing tray. "I need you alert."

So he felt it too. Something was amiss. Something more than her presence. A sheep in wolf's clothing.

"It couldn't possibly be your father referring to me as your whore?" She swallowed, hiding her wince behind the goblet.

It looked like wine. It smelled like wine. But her drink tasted of unwashed wool socks. She rarely consumed alcohol, not relishing the sluggishness of her body the next day. But when she did, Maia preferred the sweetness of mead.

"That," Erik said, sweeping his arm wide, "is his usual form of entertainment. Humiliation is a favorite of his. All the better in a large crowd."

Maia struggled to find her words. When she disappointed her father, he kept his admonishments private, using them as a lesson, not an opportunity to insult her character. "Your father… he is…"

Erik shrugged and emptied his drink in one swallow.

"Worried?" He placed his goblet on a nearby tray. "Don't trouble yourself. His tongue no longer harms my ego."

But his tone implied there was a time when it did. Maia wanted to ask him more. Instead, she set her goblet next to his and feigned irritation.

"You mistake my observation for concern."

Gong.

Mercifully, the dinner bell provided an excuse to look away.

Tens of dozens of finely-dressed Ladies entered through the front doors. They chatted amongst themselves, encircling the tall tables in the back. Some broke away from the herd and mingled with the Lords. Most paid her little attention, though the hair on her neck rose when a few curious glances slid her way.

They wore elaborate gowns of ruby red, sapphire blue, and emerald green. The chamber transformed into a wealthy Faeblood jewel box.

While the cut of her dress matched the latest fashion trends, its royal color stood out.

"I should've been with the Ladies." She needed to adhere to their bizarre customs.

"On your first night? I would not throw you to those vipers without establishing your position in Court."

"So that was your intention." She flicked her chin and clarified, "with your father."

"My sire is a shape-shifter, in manners and magic." He wrapped an arm around her, gesturing to the Ladies with his other. "Those are vipers in glittering skins. Pretty on the outside. Venomous when they strike. In some ways, they hold more power than him."

"Sounds... delightful." She pasted on a smile, sagging against him. "I can handle myself. Tomorrow, I'd like to socialize before the meal."

"Allow me to introduce you, then." His long fingers wrapped around her side. "It appears they are just as eager to make your acquaintance."

A group of three broke off from the rest and sauntered their way. The one in the middle kept a half step in front of the others. Their leader.

The train of her dress trailed obediently behind her like a gaggle of suitors following her every whim. It swished back and forth, accentuating the gentle curve of her hips. Here was a true Lady. Feminine. Graceful. Confident the world revolved around her every breath.

Indeed, the Lords in the room followed her progress. As did most of the servants.

Like them, Maia couldn't tear her eyes off the beguiling creature. Her companions could be naked, skipping in rhythm and yet... yet she could not force herself to look away.

Her flawless tawny skin stretched over sharp, high cheekbones, framing bee-stung lips. The candlelight flickered off gold flecks in her eyes, a feature she shared with Erik. Naturally curly hair escaped the twist atop her crown, wisps softening the severe knot.

Maia stilled her hand from checking her own.

The Lady wore no necklace. No earrings. And she never took her eyes off Erik.

At last, the trio halted. Instead of greeting them both, she lay a hand on his wrist and purred, "My Lord."

"Stella," Erik said, unable to disguise the smirk in his voice.

So he thought this was amusing. It was as if someone delivered a jest and withheld the punchline from Maia. Perhaps she was the joke.

"The stench from the human territories followed you home." She curled her upper lip. Her nostrils flared. "Your bath failed to rid you of the oily residue of poverty.

The Lady placed a hand on her chest and faced Maia.

"Oh, I didn't see you there."

"Lady Stella," Erik said as if she hadn't insulted her. "Allow me to introduce my wife, Lady Maia Siodina."

Maia kept her spine stiff. Does one curtsy? Shake hands? What greeting befits a Lady? An elbow to the nose? Gah. What did it matter if she showed deference?

Lady Stella's mouth parted. The shard of time before her next words was the crack that fractured her indifferent facade.

"Wife?" she asked, her voice high-pitched. "Erik, you can't be serious."

"As serious as you are about your powdered rouge, your eye kohl."

A generous black sweep extended a thumb-width beyond the edge of Lady Stella's upper lids. Shiny powder highlighted the inner corners before arcing under her brow. Blush dusted her cheeks, an unnecessary enhancement to their severe lines.

This time, Maia could not prevent her fingertips from grazing her naked skin, her clean face.

Erik bent down and whispered, "Stop. You look ravishing without all the war paint."

"He's as serious as he is when sharpening his blades." Maia patted Erik's chest, refusing to meet Lady Stella's eyes. She smirked and added, "As serious as he is about sleeping unencumbered by clothing."

The two companions rewarded her with small gasps.

"What can I say?" Erik bent down and feathered kisses on the column of her throat. "She's bewitched me."

Obviously not one to relinquish the last word, Lady Stella dropped Erik's wrist and cupped the back of Maia's arm. To those in attendance, the gesture might appear welcoming.

"Keep his bed warm for me, human. Since you cannot cast, it's the extent of your value."

"Green is not your color."

The companion on the right whipped her head to the side, studying Lady Stella's dress. Her very tight, very *red* dress.

When neither responded to the taunt, Maia clarified, "Jealousy clashes with your gown."

"Why you little—" Lady Stella balled her fists.

Do it. Throw the punch. Maybe it made her twisted. Simpleminded. Maia would trade a week of washing militia uniforms for the *Lady* to take a swing at her. On instinct, she went to the balls of her feet.

Stella seemed to realize they had witnesses. She ran her hands down the front of her gown, smoothing out her skirts.

"My Lord." She curtsied, her companions mimicking the gesture. Under her breath she said, "Human."

"I'm disappointed your blade didn't grace the side of her neck." Erik angled his shoulders, blocking their departure.

Maia swallowed, too heated to speak.

Aye, insane. Faeblood were all mad.

CHAPTER NINE

The dampness from the underground passage settled into Mikel's bones.

It had been decades since he took this route, but his feet carried him along the maze of corridors like it was only yesterday when he prowled through the fortress, a young man intent on torching the Court from underneath.

He stayed along the edges, hiding in shadows when available. Mikel kept his target within earshot and guessed Lord Siodina's destination the moment he slipped out of the great hall.

The second dinner bell would ring in twenty minutes, granting the High Lord plenty of time to complete his errand and slink back into the hall without anyone noticing.

Well… anyone except Erik.

Mikel didn't know what to think about the Faeblood heir. He trained alongside him for months without suspecting his true heritage.

Foolish now, considering his resemblance to his father. But with Erik's shorter hair and his brusque manner, it was easy to overlook the connection. Or Mikel could stop lying to himself.

His hatred for the Castle blinded him to reason.

By the time everyone discovered Erik had bound Maia in her chambers, retaliation felt hollow. The Faeblood heir had taken a blade meant for Xavier's family that same day.

Plus, it was clear Erik didn't fit in with Court life. Mikel almost chuckled when he showed up to dinner in fighting clothes and announced Maia as his wife. Aye. Mikel didn't know what to think.

Though his opinions didn't matter. He was here on assignment, fulfilling Xavier's command to protect Maia. Something he would've done regardless.

But Xavier was ignorant of the battlefield within these walls. Mikel couldn't simply waltz in the middle of afternoon tea and put the Ladies in a chokehold for landing verbal blows on his adopted sister.

In hand-to-hand combat, Maia could best the most skilled militia soldier. But here, words mattered more. They packed a heavier punch than a well-placed fist. On this battlefield, Maia was as green as the first-year fighters.

Lord Siodina halted at the next corner and spoke to the Red Guard sentry. He beckoned the soldier to follow. The pair disappeared down the next wing.

Mikel quickened his strides, trailing a finger along the damp walls. At the next bend, he crouched and waited, shifting to his heels.

"I won't be long." Lord Siodina opened the door to his private laboratory. He flicked his wrist and said, "See that I'm not disturbed."

Nothing good came from that room. Full of nasty potions and spell books and animal carcasses, nothing good ever went in either.

As a teen, Mikel had spent months trying to breach this inner sanctuary, convinced he — a human without magic — could discover something, *anything,* inside to unbind the servants from the Castle.

"I can't find a way in," he'd confessed to Dezee. *"It's been months. Nothing. And what if I succeed? It would likely take three times longer to find something to free us all."*

But that was when he was young. Naive. Unaware the servants remained in the Castle by choice. Better to stay with the Master you knew.

Mikel didn't stick around much longer after that. Dezee had. Despite his pleading and begging, she claimed her duties kept her at the Castle. He was hot-headed. Angry. But he respected her decision.

The Guard nodded and pressed his back against the wall.

Later, Mikel would need to find a quill and parchment to sketch a map. Most passages he could pen from memory. Details of the smaller corridors were hazy. He would spend his spare moments painstakingly drawing every nook and cranny.

Maia could fill in the chambers inaccessible to servants. And Mikel would help her find that blasted book. Together, they could infiltrate every area except Lord Siodina's private laboratory.

He rubbed his wrists. The heavy leather cuffs twisted over the scarred skin.

The Red Guard shuffled his feet.

Footsteps echoed down the corridor as Lord Siodina exited his chambers. Mikel couldn't gauge his expression, but there was surprise in his voice as he addressed the three Ladies.

"Stella, how lovely to see you. I trust you are returning to the great hall."

Lord Siodina ran a long finger down her bare arm.

"You shouldn't be late for my son's first meal back. I arranged for you to sit next to him. See that you keep his head turned from the scum he tracked home on the bottom of his boots, hmm?"

"As you wish."

"And who are these doves?" Lord Siodina cocked his head to the side. "I don't remember seeing them at Court."

"This is their first season."

"Delicious." Lord Siodina crowded the Lady on the right.

She couldn't be over eighteen. Mikel's stomach churned. It was sick — Faeblood Lords marrying their friend's daughters. Breeding mares when they were barely out of leading strings.

"She's from a lower line." Lady Stella wrapped an arm around the girl.

"Hurry along, then." Lord Siodina's lip curled as if he stepped in horse dung. He straightened the collar of his robes. "Take them to the great hall. Make sure she sits at the proper table."

"My Lord," Lady Stella repeated, curtsying. She gathered the Ladies under her arms and ushered them down the corridor.

Right toward his hiding spot.

Mikel ducked into the nearest unlocked chamber and closed the heavy door so a hair's width remained open. He counted his breaths and willed his heart to slow.

"Stay away from Lord Siodina," Lady Stella whispered as the trio passed. "He will..."

Good. At least Lady Stella had enough sense to warn off her companions. He didn't have time to watch the younger Lady. Mikel loosed another breath and angled his ear to the crack.

A pair of heavier footsteps followed.

"Place a full dropper in Lord Bierling's goblet." Lord Siodina passed a small vial to the guard. "Before I address the Court."

The Red Guard halted and bowed.

Lord Siodina, a leader who ruled with the confidence his minions would carry out his demands without fail, didn't slow or even acknowledge the gesture.

Mikel waited for several minutes, ensuring they were far enough down the corridor, then he slipped out of his hiding spot.

Whatever Lord Siodina had planned, it couldn't be good. He

must warn Maia not to drink anything at dinner. Who knew what was in that vial?

It certainly wasn't a health tonic.

IF ONE MORE LORD LOOKED DOWN MAIA'S DRESS, ERIK WAS going to pluck their eyelashes for entertainment.

He could see it clearly. Lord Bierling, distracted by the enticing swell of her chest, wouldn't sense him sneaking up from behind.

A simple arm across the throat would work. More satisfying if the Lord kicked and struggled. A swift leg sweep would take them both to the cold stone floor, where a solid forearm across his throat would hold the cad in place.

Then Erik would pluck every eyelash, one at a time.

He would start on the upper lids. Perhaps compelling the councilman to recite an apology before moving on to the next. Then, he would switch to the lower ones, forcing the Lord to acknowledge Maia belonged to him.

Erik shook his head and struggled to keep the scowl off his face. What were they talking about?

"Thank you for the kind offer, but my husband has agreed to show me around the Castle tomorrow." Maia rested a hand on Erik's chest. "Perhaps another time?"

"She's busy." Erik wrapped an arm around her shoulders and steered them in the opposite direction. "Lecherous cretin. Stay away from him. Stay away from all the Lords."

Erik surveyed the hall. He couldn't trust the nobles to keep their hands to themselves. They may not want her to further their line, but that didn't keep them from lusting after her.

He took a half step back. Perhaps he was no better.

"I have my orders," she hissed. "It will be difficult to

complete my mission if I'm forbidden from interacting with members of the Court."

"Interact?" Erik scoffed. "You think he wants to converse with you? Lord Bierling is a rake."

"You think me ignorant of his intentions?" Maia gripped his wrist and tugged him closer. "I can handle innocent flirtation."

"Aye, Kitten," he said, using her nickname more for him this time. "You are ignorant if you believe he will stop at witty banter."

He spun to face her.

Perhaps ignorant was too harsh. She grew up surrounded by a pack of brothers who could knock out a suitor with a single glare. Sheltered was better. Erik wouldn't always be around to rescue her.

He backed them into the shadows. Servants and guards scattered in their wake.

"Stay away from Lord Bierling," he repeated.

"Listen." She jabbed a finger in his chest. "You can't accost every Lord who dares speak with me. I know what you are doing. I have no designs on ruining your honor by showing affection to another. Keep your murder eyes under control."

"Murder eyes?" He captured her finger, bringing it to his mouth.

"Your lids get twitchy. Scary murder eyes. Though, Lord Bierling was impervious. He didn't know you were close to torturing him."

"This is my normal face," he deadpanned.

"Your normal face is too much." She yanked her hand away. "I have an assignment. The sooner I accomplish my mission, the sooner I'm no longer your problem."

Good. *Fine.* She needed to remember she was an inconvenience. The sooner she found whatever Xavier required, the sooner he could resume his solitary existence. Alone with his plants. His mother's mystery.

"All the better," he said. Fine. *Just fine.*

"Really, Erik?" Lady Stella's voice crawled along his neck. Too busy staring at his wife, he didn't hear her approach. "Rutting in the shadows like an animal. Run along now," she said to Maia. "Lest you spoil our meal with your stench."

At Court, every Faeblood had a role to play. Erik had known Stella since childhood, but they were strangers now. How much remained an act? Had she internalized her viciousness?

One thing was certain. If she continued with these insults, any affection he carried from their youth wouldn't save her from his wrath.

"You have something on your lip," Maia said, dabbing her own. She tilted her head and plastered on an unconvincing look of concern. "Perhaps that is what you smell. On the corner. There."

"Clever. My advice... keep that sharp tongue in your mouth if you want to keep it at all."

"Erik enjoys my tongue." Maia batted her eyelashes at him. "Don't you?"

"I am partial to it." Erik kissed the side of her neck. Maybe Maia could handle herself. To Stella he said, "Excuse us."

Erik threaded his fingers through Maia's and led them toward the front of the room. She didn't deserve to be subjected to Stella's presence any longer than necessary.

He sighed. Court life was never straightforward.

Unfortunately for them both, he might require Stella's help. For all her other follies, she was a gifted caster. If anyone knew a way to erase the marriage oaths, it would be her. It was a balance — protecting Maia from her insults while coaxing Stella to help him break their bond.

But he knew Lady Stella's secret.

Everyone had one.

Erik cataloged every Faeblood's dirty deeds. Their desires.

Weaknesses. While he toiled in his gardens, his Castle spies collected the information.

It was a different currency. One more valuable than gold and silver. He wasn't above blackmail. Perhaps that made him a cad of a different sort.

He rested his hand on Maia's back and guided her to the two open chairs at the head table.

The servants brought out dish after dish, creating a lavish display for the senses. Boards of cured meats and cheeses, flanked by bowls of fresh fruit and pickled vegetables, ran the span of their table. Varieties of imported olives encircled jugs of Fae wine.

"Try one." Erik pulled out her chair, nodding to the green olives. "My father imports them from farmers across the Strait. Their flavor pairs well with Crocotta cheese."

Maia picked up a larger olive. She popped it in her mouth, closing her eyes.

"Delicious." She licked her lips. "I'm famished. How many of these may I eat without appearing gluttonous?"

"I'm glad you like them." Erik placed an arm on the back of her chair and grabbed the small pick next to the third fork with his other. He worked to keep his tone conversational. "Use this to spear the smaller foods."

"Oh. I didn't..." She glanced around the room, shifting a little in her seat.

"Look at me." His voice dropped. "Laugh as if I said something amusing."

She covered her mouth with her hand as if to stifle a giggle.

"Weak, but it will do." He stroked a knuckle down the column of her neck, enjoying the glare she cast his way. "The nobles are a pretentious lot. Fussy with their cutlery. Follow my lead tonight."

She nodded, picked up the small utensil and stabbed another

olive. Her tongue swirled around it before she swallowed it whole.

"You're a quick study." Erik cleared his throat.

Someone shouted near the entrance, the words too muddled to decipher. One Lord held another by the collar, high enough his tiptoes dangled above the floor. At least the attention was off them. For now.

"Don't drink the wine," a raspy voice whispered in his ear.

Erik stiffened but didn't dare turn around. *Mikel.* He dipped his chin, acknowledging the directive. What the hell was going on?

More Lords joined the scuffle, some cheering the two men who traded blows. Others pushed and shoved against the crowd in order to gain vantage.

Fights weren't common in the great hall. But sometimes even a two-story vaulted ceiling couldn't contain all the massive egos in one room. Erik suspected clever Mikel had something to do with the latest.

Between his father and Lady Stella and worry over Maia's performance, Erik lost his appetite.

"No more drink tonight. Not even water," he whispered in Maia's ear.

She inclined her head but remained silent.

"With the main course, eat extra fruit with the meat." He leaned into her, snatching her next bite and discarding the pick on a small plate. "It will help stave off thirst. We will leave before dessert and sneak off to the kitchens."

Maia squeezed his thigh.

Clink. Clink. Clink.

The sound of a fork striking a crystal goblet rang from his left.

"It's time to celebrate and nourish our bodies." His father raised his glass. "But first, a toast. To the return of my son and his acceptance of a seat on the High Table."

Gasps filled the awkward silence.

So that was his father's play.

Erik had declined a position on the High Table the last time one became available. He had no intention of ruling. It strained the already tenuous relationship with his father.

He gnashed his teeth. Refusal in front of the Court would cause trouble. He would wait until he cornered his sire in private.

His father held each of the Lords' stares as if to challenge them to speak out. Everyone took a sip, their eyes bouncing back and forth across the rim of their drinks. Some averted their gaze entirely, gulping down the wine without pause.

"Lord Siodina," Lord Bierling called out at last. "The High Table has no vacancies. The seats are full—"

Foam gathered at the corners of Lord Bierling's mouth. The rest of his statement remained unsaid.

After a few gasping breaths, his head hit the plate in front of him with a resounding thud.

CHAPTER TEN

Death claimed a Faeblood Lord.

The great hall transformed into a stampede. Red Guards rushed to the head table, while nobles at the back pushed and shoved one another as they fled. Chair legs scraped along the stone floor. Others crashed to the ground, toppled over in their occupant's haste.

Toddlers. They acted like a pack of rabid toddlers.

Maia's fingertips ran along her lower lip, the touch not registering over the din.

"Find Mikel," Erik said.

She startled at his clipped tone.

Erik didn't wait for her response. He jogged to the scene, shouldering his way between the guards, and placed two fingers on the Lord's neck.

Dead, his lips mouthed and scanned the hall.

What was he searching for? Ah, his father. Erik wore a vacant expression, but Maia did not imagine the heat in his gaze the moment it landed on Lord Siodina. She took a half step back, bumping into the table.

"Time to go," Mikel said.

Never in her wildest imagination did she think her first dinner would include a death. Sure, she expected the insults and the slurs, the cattiness of the Ladies. But no one prepared her for this.

Servants scurried around collecting dinnerware and food, erasing all signs of the meal. As the hall emptied, a handful of High Lords surrounded the dead councilman.

"Murderer!" the one closest shouted.

"You did it."

"It was you. We all saw you arguing."

"Maia," Mikel said with an urgency that plucked her nerves. "Come with me."

Mikel wrapped an arm around her, and she leaned into her friend. Who cared if someone witnessed the embrace? The rough fabric of his borrowed servant's uniform scratched her cheek.

Long tapestries flanked a narrow door near the kitchens. Mikel looked both ways, then yanked her through.

Blackness swallowed them whole. Acrid smoke tinged her nostrils. Someone must have snuffed the torches.

After several heartbeats, her eyes adjusted to the dark. Another tug on her wrist propelled her farther into the bowels of the fortress.

"Wait." She yanked on Mikel's hand. "Stop."

"Not here," he ground out and continued.

Two rights. A left. Another right. Fifty strides down a corridor where the ceiling scraped the top of his head.

Mikel hunched down but didn't slow.

After the next several turns, she lost all sense of direction. Maia was ready to pinch the sensitive skin on the back of his arm, but he halted. She tipped forward, grabbing the back of his tunic to stop her momentum.

"I want some answers." Where was he taking them? The wine — did he suspect? How did he know where to go? "Did you hear me? I'm trying to remain calm, but you aren't helping. Mikel—"

He turned around and grabbed her shoulders, squeezing in answer.

"Please." Her voice sounded small. "Where are we?"

"Outside the north tower."

She considered her next words. Was this her new life? Escaping when the unexpected occurred? She never cowered in the training barn. So why now? No matter the role — even as a human playing dress-up in the Fae Court — underneath the veil of finery, she was still a fighter. A soldier.

If she couldn't survive something as simple as her first dinner, how would she accomplish her mission?

"Take me back." She raised her chin. Louder, she repeated, "Take me back to the great hall."

"We go to your chambers. Erik wants you safe."

Safe? She loosed a bitter laugh. *Safe* was relative in the Castle. She tossed the illusion of safety the moment she left the compound. But she bit her tongue, swallowing her retort, if only for Mikel, who followed her here. At significant risk to himself.

"Escort me to the great hall." She cupped his elbow. "Please. We need to stay close to the Lords. This is exactly the kind of information Xavier wants."

"What's your plan?"

"The same as it should have been. I will stroll into the hall, wearing this fancy gown and these ridiculous earrings, and treat the death of a High Lord as just another evening in Court."

"It was murder," Mikel whispered in her ear.

"I know." At least, she suspected. Either way, she should assume the worst.

"Fine. But I'm staying with you." He opened another hidden door. Sconces flicked every few paces, bathing his scowl.

A few dinner guests filed past, their heads bent in conference. Morbid, but it was a relief not to be the topic of gossip.

Their journey through the main corridors was significantly quicker, the routes more direct than the ones the servants used to stay out of sight. They kept to the outer edges, careful to avoid the larger crowds.

When they arrived, the great hall was near deserted.

A sense of déjà vu overcame her. Her mind replayed the evening, retracing her steps through someone else's eyes.

The entrance doors were identical to the ones she passed before the meal, but she had difficulty connecting the solid panels with the ones from earlier. The Red Guards were absent. Just as well. She didn't want to converse with them without Erik.

They snuck inside and ducked into the nearest alcove.

The servants finished clearing food from the head table, working between and around the remaining nobles. There was no priestess reciting Lord Bierling's Last Rite. No clergy giving a final blessing. Instead, two guards hauled his body away, his fingertips dragging on the stone floor.

This is how they cared for their dead? How they honored loss of life?

There weren't many funerals at the compound. For decades, Morvak avoided war. While training left fighters with bruised lips and sprained shoulders and swollen limbs, it never resulted in death.

Funerals in the village lasted three days. Time for the family to grieve. Time for the community to celebrate a member. The body laid to rest on the third, the soul crossing the Veil.

The Faebloods' behavior tonight was appalling. Death herself chased the entire Court from their meals, hot on their footsteps as if they were next. As if they could outrun her touch.

"Stay hidden." Mikel rested a hand on her shoulder. "Now is

not the time to catch the elder Siodina's attention. Allow Erik to handle his father."

A lot of words from a man who hoarded them like a magpie.

For him, the choice to stand aside must be easy. Mikel likely never doubted where he belonged in society. He was smart. Fierce. A natural leader who commanded a room with a simple entrance.

As a male fighter, no one bet against him. For Maia, the spectators at their weekly matches still showed surprise when she won. And won again the next week. And the week after.

She started forward then paused.

Would Erik even welcome her presence? At the compound, she wouldn't hesitate to join him. From what little she observed of the Court, the nobles kept some outdated views on a Lady's place.

He was Faeblood. Soon to sit on the High Table if his father had his way. And she was a human female.

But what if he *weren't* the sole heir to Lord Siodina? Her heart stuttered. What if… what if he were who he pretended to be? A simple militia soldier, completing his mandatory four years of training. Her a simple lass, nursing her first serious crush.

As soon as those thoughts crossed her mind, she discarded them.

She should focus entirely on her mission, on her strategy for obtaining information for Xavier, but her anger was still so… raw. It ebbed and flowed, and Erik, with his abrasive demeanor, rubbed up against it with every encounter. One minute she wanted him to suffer for capturing her, for abandoning her. *For not confiding in her.*

The next, she wanted to tackle him to his bed and kiss off his arrogant smirk.

Worse, she couldn't decide what irritated her more. Her

failing to subdue him when he tied her up in her chambers. Or the undeniable truth: their marriage could never be real.

He lived in a Castle surrounded by opulence and table manners. She grew up burying fake treasure in the grappling pit and starting food fights with her brothers in the mess hall.

No. Erik Siodina was not for her.

And therein lay the problem. With every touch, every simple gesture, her anger faded, gradually replaced by insufferable longing. And yet… she refused to forgive herself for not recognizing his deception.

"Maia." Mikel patted her hip. "They left."

"What?" She searched the room. Tables lay empty. Chairs returned to their rightful place. As if the gruesome events of the night had never happened.

"Come on." Mikel led them through another hidden door.

How many were there? She'd counted five, but those were the ones next to the alcoves scattered around the hall.

"He keeps quarters near the dungeons." Mikel slowed. "A singular set of steps leads to the lower levels."

Dungeons. Right. Who didn't prefer prisoners adjacent to their en suite?

"I will help you find this book." He hesitated. "But don't go down there alone. And stay out of Siodina's laboratory. I'll show you its entrance tomorrow, so you know which chamber to avoid. Promise me."

"I promise." Easy. She trusted Mikel's instincts. "But… let's not miss this chance to catch Erik and his father."

"Don't entirely trust your new husband?"

"Something akin to that. Aren't you the least bit interested in hearing this exchange?"

"I do love it when they bicker among themselves."

While she didn't miss the hint of malice in Mikel's voice, she was too interested in shadowing Erik's father to stop and confront him. There was no love between the humans and nobles, but Mikel's reaction to this place was somehow more. More anger. More bitterness. More.

Later. She would force him to talk later.

The stairs wound around a central stone pillar, and the air grew thicker with each step. Near the bottom, Mikel thrust his hand out, flattening her against the wall.

At first, she didn't recognize the raised voices floating toward them.

They crept down another half-dozen steps. A trickle of water provided background noise for the otherwise heated conversation. As with Ashmere Falls, her favorite swimming hole, there must be an underground source deep in the mountain. It would explain why the walls stayed perpetually wet.

She squished her toes in her slippers, wondering if she would ever feel dry again.

At last, they reached the bottom. A dozen glass lanterns illuminated a small landing. An open door beckoned to the right. On the left, a dark hallway tunneled into the abyss.

Mikel shook his head.

So, it must lead to the dungeons. Where were the Red Guards? While it was fortunate they didn't run into another sentry, someone should be down here.

A chill ran through her. This time she couldn't blame the mountain.

There were two reasons a leader would forgo bodyguards — either Lord Siodina was confident in the Castle's defenses. Or he didn't want any witnesses to what transpired in his lair.

They crept forward and flattened themselves against the wall.

"What the hell are you playing at?" Erik said. His voice carried the reproach of a teenager continually disappointed in his parent.

"I'm waiting for words of gratitude. The seat is yours."

"If you think I'll blithely accept a position on the High Table, you forget who you sent to spy on the militia."

"I work to secure your future, ensuring the Siodina line remains in power."

"I have no interest in politics. Find someone else."

"Just like your mother. She would dirty her hands toiling in her gardens but never wanted to soil her conscience fulfilling her duty to the Court."

Maia had never given Erik's mother much thought.

When pressed for information about his family life, he lied and told everyone at the compound she died in a farming accident. Easy to take at face value.

Maia's mother returned to the gods when she was a babe. Any memories were her father's stories. He kept a small portrait of his wife tucked in his breast pocket until his last breath. An older replica of the reflection she saw in the looking glass.

Maia inherited her mother's looks. Her father's temperament. His dreams.

"Aye." Erik scoffed. "What a terrible affliction to share — a gift for growing medicinal plants and healing Faeblood ailments. For someone so concerned about pureblood lines, I assumed you would have a greater appreciation for keeping the Ladies healthy for breeding."

"Don't be crass, boy. You speak like a servant."

Huh. Whore was acceptable for conversation, but pregnancy was not.

"I'll take that as a compliment."

"Cease this nonsense. It's time to claim your place by my side."

"My place? The one you conveniently emptied of its predecessor?"

"Lord Bierling was no martyr. He claims no heir."

"Despite siring several with the servants."

"As such," Lord Siodina continued, "the remaining council members decide his successor."

"The High Lords won't vote for another in our line." Erik's footsteps echoed in the hall, their rhythm suggesting he paced. "They'll consider it a play for more power."

"They will do as they're told."

"Or else," Erik supplied. "Or else you will poison their wine. I know your style. Your magic left a trace."

"How fortuitous then, you are the sole healer in residence. The only one able to detect both the cause of death and my print."

"Your arrogance shows. Did you forget Lady Stella is gifted with potions and poisons?"

"That nitwit. Nothing but a pair of ample tits, a pretty face. She couldn't find her way out of a trunk. Too busy planning her next ball gown. This won't concern her. Once you tire of your human, you can fulfill your betrothal to her."

Maia covered her gasp. *Betrothal.* He never said. Why that... that... gib-faced hornswoggler.

Perhaps she should be more furious with Lord Siodina's threats, but her stupid heart lurched. Of course Erik was engaged to the most beautiful Faeblood courtier. Who else would his father pair with his only heir?

What was wrong with her? This marriage was temporary. She needed information on their plans for the peninsula, not a life partner. But if he so much as thought he could crawl under the sheets with her then fall into bed with the glamorous Lady Stella...

Mikel sent a subtle shake of his head and cupped her fist, prying her hand open one finger at a time.

"If you touch my wife, I will end you."

"Do as I command, and we won't have an issue. She's not a part of my plans, so I'll allow the dalliance. For now."

"Plans? What plans? The ones where you poison everyone

who disagrees with you? Or how about the ones where I end up stabbed in the arena, bleeding out for entertainment?"

"An unfortunate accident. Unbeknownst to you, one I avenged this very eve. Go to your whore. The council convenes tomorrow at noon. Your presence is required. Now, get out of my chambers."

CHAPTER ELEVEN

If Erik had a gold coin for every time he wanted to punch his father in the face, the bounty could lift the territories out of poverty.

A quick jab to the eye wouldn't suffice. Nope. He would throw a dominant hook, savoring the snap of his father's head.

"Physical retaliation is a last resort." His mentor, the former leader of the Red Guard — the last honorable man in the position since his father promoted Commander Lukas — had taught him that.

Words. Cunning. Magic. All preferred methods of dealing with overwhelming rage.

Erik curled around the endless spiral staircase, exiting one landing from the top.

He should spend some time in the library. It might be his last chance to do so. The pending appointment to the High Table would erode any free time he spent outside his gardens.

Except if he started researching old texts, he likely wouldn't resurface until midday tomorrow. It would serve his father right if he showed up at the council meeting wearing fighting clothes from the day prior.

Gods, he was tired. He needed his bed. *He needed her.*

No. That wasn't correct. He needed to ensure Maia made it safely to their chambers. At least, that's what he told himself as he lengthened his stride.

A Red Guard nodded as he passed. He didn't return the gesture.

As usual, the main hallways were busy. The nobles weren't ones to let a little death interrupt their evening. The Court kept late hours, something his body never adjusted to even in childhood. He already missed the early morning training schedule at the compound.

Groups of Faeblood huddled together on the settees lining the larger passages. Whispers teased him as he passed. The Ladies threw coy looks his way, invitations he might have accepted a few years ago. Now, they were too much trouble.

"Erik," someone hissed.

His head whipped around.

"In here," Lady Stella said, her small hand beckoning.

"It's late." He shut the door behind him and leaned against the cool wood. "I had hoped to have this conversation tomorrow."

"Too bad. I'm avoiding Lord Tiabaut's wandering hands, so it's a perfect opportunity for some answers." She brushed a lock of hair out of her face. "What were you thinking? A human? Your father will bury her at the bottom of the lake before a fortnight passes."

"He wouldn't dare touch her." Erik crossed his arms over his chest. "I realize breaking the betrothal puts you in a predicament. Though I never held the impression you wanted to marry me."

"True." She sent him a false smile and said, "But the union had its advantages."

"Now you are free to choose another."

"Me? Choose?" She swore under her breath. "It was never

my decision. Father will arrange another match by nightfall if he holds his wine long enough to corner an acceptable Lord."

"Demand the choice," Erik said, regretting the words as soon as they left his mouth.

He and Lady Stella were not dissimilar. Both single heirs to High Lords. Both suffocating under parental rule. Perhaps he had it easier — males were allowed more freedom in their choice of pursuits. Tradition denied Ladies a chance to earn their own gold, a chance to travel.

Still, Stella clung to the glamour of Court life and thrived in its intrigue. He never had the impression she was dissatisfied. She may never rule a kingdom, but that didn't stop her from ruling the Ladies. Another Faeblood grabbing power.

"A favor for a favor," Erik said.

He must choose his next words with care, staying in her grace. Lady Stella was a deft hand at potions and spells. He didn't lie when he told his father she could detect magical prints.

"I'm listening," she purred.

"I hold sway with your father." He leaned back against the door, crossing one ankle over the other. "Give me a suitor's name. I'll see that he arranges the match."

"I'll think about it." She tilted her head to the side. "What do you desire in return?"

"I require a spell or a potion to break an oath."

"You think to poison your father?"

"Tempting but no." He smirked. "I need something to erase a vow written in the stars. As you heard in the great hall, my days are no longer my own. I won't have time to search the library." At least not for this. He needed to focus on finding clues to his mother's disappearance.

"I've never known you to concern yourself with politics."

"I'm not." He shrugged. "I'll play along with my father's charade, but I have no intention of participating. I'll listen to their drivel and raise my hand when required, ignoring them the rest of the time."

And pass along information to Maia. Hopefully hastening her departure from the Castle.

"Must be nice — the luxury of thumbing your nose at power," Stella said, slinking toward him and licking her lips. When he didn't react, she side-eyed him. "Very well. I'll find your potion."

It was her tell — Stella feigned attraction for him when she worried her motives would show. With this piss-poor attempt at flirtation, she was apt to agree to his bargain.

"Give me a name. When you are ready."

Lady Stella closed the distance between them, toying with the chain around his neck. She frowned at the inscription on the back of the pendant.

His skin crawled. He wanted to bat her hand away.

"Still?" she asked.

In a moment of weakness, or maybe loneliness, he'd confessed to his fervent search for his mother. They had been young — teenagers who smuggled a jug of Fae wine and escaped to the banks of the lake. No one had paid them notice, the cloak of betrothal allowing their unfettered movements.

Stella hadn't laughed at the admission.

"Not a day passes when I don't wonder what happened to her." He lifted the charm from her grasp and tucked it into his tunic. "Not a week goes by when I don't wonder why she left. If she thinks of me."

Lady Stella opened her mouth, but nothing came out, her cunning replaced by... what?

He couldn't read her thoughts. Perhaps he paid her a disservice, never looking behind her sneer. Maybe he was selfish and didn't want to confront what he uncovered. What good would it do? She was content at Court. Wasn't she?

He sighed.

The events of the night spiraled out of his control. While Erik thrived on chaos of his own making, he struggled to shrug off his father's threats. He despised this feeling. Like he couldn't grasp the handle of his weapon when the enemy closed around him.

As if he was one false step away from causing Maia harm.

What could he do? He knew he must distance himself from her. Already, his father suspected Maia was something more than a lover. He couldn't comprehend Erik's allegiance belonged to Xavier. An eye for an eye. In his case, a life for a life. A debt he couldn't ignore.

He ran his hand over his mouth. Enough of this self-pity. He must stick with the plan. Help Maia find what she needed then send her home. Far, far away. As far as possible from the Castle. From powerful, spiteful Faebloods.

Maybe then he could stop thinking about her.

Stella would find a way to sever their vows, then he could return to his solitary existence, ignoring the Faeblood.

For now, he must play along with his father's political grandstanding. Erik could no longer avoid it. If they were desperate enough to make him a High Lord, then they could suffer his indifference.

"I'll do it," Stella said, interrupting his thoughts. "Might even know a way. Last week, I found a new text while searching for an antidote to the stomach sickness that ravaged the Castle. Nasty. Took out half the staff and all the younger Ladies at Court. How soon do you need it?"

"As soon as possible. I don't want to wait."

She grinned. "Consider it a deal."

~

"MAIA? YOU GOOD?" MIKEL ASKED.

Good? She swallowed a scoff. She was fine. Who cared if Erik had a fiancée? Everything was *just fine.*

"Mmm-hmm." She nodded.

Mikel opened the door to Erik's chambers, ushering her inside. Fire blazed in the hearth. A maid dusted the mantel above. Pampered Faeblood had their servants cleaning well into the night.

The young woman jumped, her eyes darting back and forth between them. Freckles dusted the bridge of her nose. Odd for someone who spent their time indoors.

"Pardon me?" She bowed. Strawberry blonde hair curtained off her cheeks. "I dinna expect anyone to return so early. If you like, I'll arrange the covers and place warming stones between the sheets." The explanation came out in a rush.

Maia was weary but summoned the last dredges of patience.

The maid didn't deserve her anger. She crossed the room and raised a hand, aware of the boundaries she would violate if she placed it on the servant's shoulder. Maia let it drop.

"Rise." The command made her skin itch. Back home, she led training but never controlled another's every move. Maia softened her tone and added, "In these chambers, do not apologize for doing your duties. A warming stone sounds delightful after the night I experienced. If you show me where you keep the tools, I will grab it myself. I imagine you have enough to worry about without me lolling about like a pup chasing its tail."

Mikel cleared his throat.

"I will stand sentry. Until Erik—" His gaze flicked to the maid and he corrected, "Until Lord Siodina returns."

He left, the door closing behind him with a soft snick.

"By what name are you called?" Maia asked, studying the oak slats as if they would reveal Mikel's secrets.

"Bree." She curtsied this time. "Dezee assigned me as your Lady's maid."

"Alright Bree. You may call me Maia."

"I couldn't milady." She rested a hand on her chest. "It would be improper."

A battle for another day.

"Would you help me out of this dress? I understand the hour is early by Castle standards, but I'm exhausted and eager to turn in for the night."

Maia turned around.

Nimble fingers unhooked the row of tiny buttons snaking down her spine. The weight of the luxurious ball gown fell away, cascading in a pool of satin on the floor.

She crossed the room, stole one of Erik's tunics from the trunk, and slipped it over her head.

"Please sit." Bree gestured to the vanity. "I will remove your twist and fashion a simple braid for sleep."

Bree plucked the combs. Thick sections of Maia's hair fell down her back, and she closed her eyes.

Erik could return at any moment. With him, the events of the night. A High Lord murdered in front of the entire Court, nobody rushing to his side. Not a single noble raised alarm. Instead, excited chatter had danced around the great hall.

She hadn't recognized the Lord, hadn't learned the council members' names and faces. Perhaps he wasn't important. Or well-liked, for how little concern everyone showed in his death.

Bree massaged the back of her scalp, rubbing a path of overlapping circles from the base of her skull to the back of her ear. Too soon, the tines of the brush replaced thoughtful hands.

Erik's reaction was the only one that made any sense.

But why did he refuse a seat at the High Table? He'd never shirked responsibility at the compound. Not your typical first-year trainee, Gavyn assigned more and more duties as the months passed. Erik shouldered extra tasks, still finding time to spy on them.

Didn't every male, Faeblood or human, wish for more influence? As a healer, maybe he didn't agree with his father's tactics.

The transfer of power was never a peaceful succession. Ambitious rulers built kingdoms on bloodshed. That was what made Xavier's rise so remarkable. He claimed an abandoned territory, developed a loyal following, and united geographically distant regions over the years. All with fellowship, not fear.

It was another reason she went along with Xavier's plans. Perhaps the information in her letters could save innocent lives.

Many would not agree with him for sending Maia to this hellhole. But she had a choice. An honest-to-gods choice.

She may never know Xavier's reasoning — his entire rationale for sending her undercover, his motive for retrieving the book, or ordering her entrance into the Grimoire Games. But it didn't matter. He was her leader. She trusted him.

And it was still her decision.

A subtle distinction from Lord Siodina ordering Erik to spy on the compound. One she didn't fully appreciate until this moment.

His father would've groomed Erik to sit the High Table. As his sole heir, what other choice did he have? He might prefer to tend his plants, but surely, he was not naive enough to think his sire would allow it to continue.

The High Table couldn't be that bad. Boring. Tiring. How hard was it to sit in a chamber with wheezing Lords debating the course of Morvak?

He might even accomplish some good. If he tried. *If he cared.* At least he could provide information she could pen in her letters.

If Maia could set aside her fighting leathers and squeeze into some itchy gown, he could lounge in comfortable pants, casting a vote when required.

Bree ran her palms along Maia's shoulders, coaxing them down from her ears.

She opened her eyes and studied the maid's reflection in the looking glass.

Up close, the smattering of freckles extended to her temples. Green eyes, the color of variegated Liriope grass in late summer, stared back. For a heartbeat, Maia swore their darker emerald edges glowed, but thick lashes concealed them as Bree looked away.

Flat strips if leather spanned the lower third of the maid's forearm.

Most servants concealed their mark, choosing to adorn their gnarled skin with sleeves or bracelets. She couldn't help glance at their wrists, her eyes moving on their own. Cruel. Brutal. She would never get used to the practice. Tomorrow, she must ask Bree what magic the Lords granted her.

Mikel. His cuffs.

Gods, she was slow. He never took them off.

She stilled. How did she not put it together? Mikel was a servant. That explained his knowledge of the tunnels. Why Xavier sent him and not another. It wasn't because he doubted her abilities.

No, her leader wanted someone familiar with Court.

"Milady, are you alright?" Bree asked. "Did I snag a tangle?"

"No. I've only just remembered something."

The militia soldiers who stayed in Xavier's village after their mandatory four years received a tattoo on their neck and cuffs on their wrists. Most fighters removed the symbolic straps for training, but Mikel never did. She thought little on it back home, assuming it was an oversight on his part.

But what if... what if he wore them to conceal his heritage?

Mikel was not one for words. She doubted even Ada, their resident gossip, suspected his upbringing.

He was at least a decade older than Erik, which would explain why Mikel didn't recognize him at the compound. If she was correct, Erik would have been a small child when Mikel showed up in Xavier's territory.

"Thank you." She turned on her stool, facing Bree. "I shall

wear my hair loose tonight. Please find your bed. I'll see you in the morning."

"As you command." Bree dropped to a curtsey. "You'll find the iron tools for the fire hanging on the wall to the left. The stones in the clay jar on the right."

Maia inclined her head, escorted Bree out, and whispered, "Mikel? A word?"

He allowed Bree to pass, shutting the door behind her.

Maia yawned and considered how to broach the subject. In the end, she blurted out, "You're from the Castle."

"Aye."

"You were born here." Her eyes flicked to his cuffs then quickly back to his face, as if seeing him for the first time.

He nodded.

"That's it? That's all you have to say? Why didn't you tell—"

"Left as soon as I could." He rolled his shoulders. When Maia opened her mouth to question him further, he grinned a soft, sad smile.

She hesitated because she saw it then, his smile. For what it was. What it wasn't. And a glimpse into what it hid. But for his sake, and hers, she returned it.

The chamber door opened with such force its handle banged against the wall.

"Am I interrupting something?" Erik asked, leaning against the frame.

"I will return for you in the morning." Without a glance for Erik, Mikel left their chambers.

How could she be so foolish? Worried about gowns and Ladies and proper utensils, she hadn't even stopped to consider. Mikel, her friend. Her brother. His childhood must've been horrific.

Her time here was temporary. She couldn't imagine months, endless years, with these people. She didn't want to imagine.

They would talk tomorrow. And somehow, when this was all over, Maia would make it up to him.

"The wife of a future High Lord does not entertain unaccompanied men in their chambers."

Prick. "Mikel is not some random stranger."

"Don't be simple. As my wife, you will conduct yourself in a manner which does not reflect poorly on my honor."

She was done. So done with this night. With this... this... this Faeblood arse. All her earlier sympathy for him evaporated. Maia savored the heat eddying under her fingertips. She wanted to slap the arrogance off his face.

But she was Maia Braenough.

Daughter of a loving father.

Lieutenant in Morvak's militia.

Sister to a loyal pack of brothers.

And Erik Siodina could go kiss a fish.

"I'm going to sleep," she muttered instead. Because in the morning, everything would be *just fine.*

CHAPTER TWELVE

A messenger shoved a lilac envelope under their chamber door.

Maia stretched. She covered her yawn with the back of her hand and retrieved it with the same leery respect she paid anything Ol' Eight Fingers handed her.

A transplant from the Mining territory, Ol' Eight retired from the harsh life of carving new tunnels in the mountain, preferring to sit on his front porch while regaling any lad who would listen with his harrowing tales. And occasionally tinkering with black powder in small clay jars.

While the correspondence likely wouldn't explode, Maia wanted to chuck it off the balcony all the same.

"What is it?" Erik asked, his voice deep with sleep. He rolled onto his back. The covers fell to his waist.

"A letter." Maia swallowed, unsticking her tongue from the roof of her mouth.

"So it begins." He swung his legs over the side of the bed and yawned.

The envelope was no bigger than the size of her palm. She

slid her finger underneath the wax seal and read its contents out loud.

My dearest Lady Siodina,

As Erik's new wife, it's an honor to extend an invite for afternoon tea in the solarium at three bells time. I shall be delighted to introduce you to the Ladies at Court. All are eager to make your acquaintance, myself included. Your husband and I are great friends, and I imagine we shall be the same.

Sincerely,
Lady Stella Raekova

Splendid. How... progressive to seek friendship with your husband's ex-fiancée. She didn't miss the casual use of Erik's first name, either.

She gritted her teeth and counted. *Ten, nine, eight...*

"Perfect." Erik tugged a white tunic over his head, blissfully unaware she was moments from lashing out. "You shall be in your sparring ring as I shall be in mine."

At least he didn't offer her false assurances. Tea would not be tea. *Seven, six, five...*

His pants came next followed by a pair of dressier boots. With each piece of clothing, he looked less like the fighter she slept beside and more like the High Lord he professed to despise.

He raked his gaze over her nightshirt. His shirt.

Four, three, two...

Her toes curled. Maia shook her head, failing to clear her thoughts before she made it to *one.*

"Put on some clothes." Erik gestured to her bare legs. "I can't think with you half naked. You need to pen a letter to Xavier. My father made his move. Sooner than expected."

Maia bit the inside of her cheek. Erik was right, of course. She donned her olive-green leathers and borrowed a pair of his thick wool socks. Even though Xavier didn't expect another letter, he would want to know about the incident.

She padded over to his desk and sank into the chair.

As much as she was loath to admit, Erik's account of the events was exactly what she needed. A smidge of guilt settled in her stomach. The Lord's death, while tragic, brought her one step closer to leaving this place.

This assignment was turning out to be a piece of lemon loaf, as Jade would say. Light, simple, and consumed too fast to be satisfying.

Maia needed to figure out frilly couture and fussy cutlery. Add another upheaval or two and she would be out of here in a month, tops. Quicker, if she could find that blasted diary.

"What does Xavier know about the High Table?" Erik grasped the back of the chair and leaned over her shoulder.

"The names of the High Lords but little else." Maia slid a fresh piece of parchment off the stack. "What is the selection process? Who holds the most power? Maybe we should start there."

Erik grunted.

"Over three hundred Faeblood live in the Castle. But only the strongest male casters sit on the High Table. Those nine individuals govern equally but factions form. Perhaps you should leave out the pecking order until after my first meeting. The alliances may have shifted while I served in the militia."

Served, not spied. If she bit her cheek any harder, Maia would draw blood.

"Then what can you tell me about your magic?"

"Every Faeblood harbors a trace of elemental powers. Besides our main line of casting, we inherit the ability to manipulate fire, wind, earth, and water. I'm a healer but can also light a candle or blow one out."

Erik snuffed the nearest.

"A few nobles harness the elements in greater strengths. For instance, Lord Wulffrith is a strong water sorcerer. He could drain the lake and send it down the mountain, commanding it to drown a territory."

Maia's mouth parted. Dear gods—

"I've a deft hand with plants, but I'm not an earth elemental," Erik continued as if he didn't reveal the ease with which his kin could destroy hers. "My success stems from a mother who cared enough to teach her young son basic horticulture and a healer's desire for cultivating useful specimens."

"Can you develop a secondary line?"

"No. Faeblood inherit the trait from the most powerful of our two parents. Stella's father, similar to mine, is a shapeshifter, an uncommon power and the reason he sits on the High Table. But she favors her mother's magic. Neither of us has a drop from our sire."

Don't ask about her. Don't ask about her.

"What is Lady Stella's talent? Besides her other-worldly beauty." Gah.

"Stella is a strong Nares." Erik leaned forward. The sleeve of his tunic brushed against her as he steadied himself on the chair's arm. "She's able to sniff out traces of casting."

Maia wrinkled her nose.

Erik mistook her reaction and said, "I suppose *sniff* isn't the best way to describe it. Detect. Sense. I'm not sure how it works. There are books of casters describing the sensation in the library. It translates to potions and brews."

"Books? Library?" Maybe a bit on the nose but what better place to start her search for Lord Siodina's journal?

"I can hear your eagerness. Remind me to take you soon." He snagged a second sheet of parchment. "Make a list."

Erik named off the eight members of the High Table and their primary magic. Together, they came up with an idea to disguise the information. Maia paused after she wrote the entry for Lord Idhelm, a weak air elemental who could shadowstep.

"What is shadowstepping?"

"An ancient form of magic allowing the caster to hop, or step, between two locations. It requires a great deal of power and passes down to first-born Faeblood. Aside from Lord Idhelm, it is extinct."

Erik scoffed.

"Though I've only seen him step twenty paces at most. His power is a diluted version of the original. Then there are other lines — the ability to commune with animals or create beautiful art — talents our insular society deems... inconsequential. Thus not represented on the council."

Maia ignored his last comment. She was more concerned with the Faeblood's ability to disappear and reappear. It would be devastating on the battlefield.

"How does it work? The shadowstepping?"

"The prevailing thought is the magic catapults the caster through invisible time rips in our realm. It's the same dark pockets powerful Faeblood access at will. My father isn't a Faber. Though he's long sought someone who could create magical blades. The sword he conjured for Gavyn's fight came from the armory, transported through a pocket or seam."

"Can it be taught?" A stupid question, considering he answered it earlier. But in this she must be certain.

"No." The corner of his lips turned down. "I've tried for years. I can access them, but conjuring something, let alone stepping into the rip, eludes me."

Maia gnawed on her lower lip.

Lords shadowstepping. Elementals harnessing nature to kill hundreds at a time. Erik's father hunting for a Faber of his own.

All the information a spy needed. The exact kind that could change the outcome of any conflict between the nobles and humans. But nothing prepared her for the sheer overwhelm of what they faced.

Where would Erik stand in this? It was clear he held no affection for his father or for most of the nobles. The servants, sure. If he could sit on the High Table… influence the laws and governance… perhaps with enough time, he could sway the other High Lords to pass decrees benefiting the territories.

"You father seems convinced you will assume Lord Bierling's position."

"I have no desire to rule."

"Fair." She twisted in her seat to face him. "I wouldn't want to spend my days with his cronies either. But this is an opportunity. You've traveled the realm. You've met the people. Glimpsed their lives and substandard conditions. Think of the good you could do. Imagine if you could influence—"

Erik held up a hand. "Let me stop you right there. Honest Lords do not rise to the High Table. Not a single individual will listen to my words. They have no desire to change their ways."

He straightened and rolled a sleeve over his elbow, revealing a dusting of dark hair on his forearms.

"I will be in the greenhouse. My work will keep me there until noon at which time I will head to the council. I suspect you will stay busy with your fittings this morning."

She'd pushed too hard.

Her customary directness wouldn't sway him. Maia sighed. A problem for another day. Now she needed a new wardrobe. Dresses for afternoon tea. Gowns for evening feasts.

Pretty things for her husband, the man who failed to mention his betrothal.

What she really needed was a couple of black tunics, another pair of leathers, and an arm guard for her bow. In the aftermath of their wedding, she forgot hers at the compound.

If she was to win the Grimoire Games, she must practice.

Maia was an expert archer who spent her leisure time in the forests surrounding the compound. All children of huntsmen learned to shoot as soon as they could toddle. Her father even hung a bow from her cradle the moment she was born.

Spying, she supposed, was akin to archery. Hours of practice. Hours of patience. All culminating in a single shot, striking the target.

Besides, she needed a distraction.

Erik cleared his throat.

But not that one. Not him.

"Whatever it is you are considering… be smart." Erik didn't look at her with his parting command.

Just as well. She didn't know how to act around him, either. This thing between them was easier when she was enamored. More when he pissed her off. This cool indifference left her empty.

Maia read her note one last time, trying and failing to see it through the gaze of a Castle spy.

My Dearest Jade,

I TRUST YOU READ MY FIRST LETTER. MY APOLOGIES FOR SENDING THIS posthaste, but I write with exhilarating news. Lord Siodina nominated Erik for a seat on the High Table.

Can you scarce believe it? I am beside myself with nerves.

The whole thing happened under terrible fanfare. It was my first foray at Court, and I was ever so excited to wear my new ballgown. You will never guess what happened next.

Lord Bierling died in his soup!

While I never met him, his constitution must have been poor. Erik confessed the Lord suffered from an unhealthy heart. It is my hope you do not judge me too harshly, but I confess I cannot bring myself to mourn his passing for long.

The High Table shall vote to approve Erik's seat in a fortnight, a formality I'm assured.

The realm shall henceforth know me as High Lady. What say you, my dearest friend? Did you ever imagine I might live in the Castle, the wife of a ruling Lord? Fate is a generous matron indeed.

Yours in Friendship,
Maia

P.S. Enclosed you will find a list of the members of the High Table. As Erik's wife, I desire to make a positive first impression. Next to each name, I included the Lord's preferences. Would you be so kind as to request Xavier's help in acquiring gifts for each? I wish to present them with something unique from our home. At taste of the territories, if you will.

(Page Two)

Lord Cantwine and Lord Nanscott are Sortileges who enjoy building structures by teleporting materials in place. Perhaps they would enjoy a book on architecture. Erik doesn't recall any such volume in the Castle's library.

Lord Idhelm has a penchant for air and wind and enjoys scaring the maids with his shadowstepping. Lord Wulffrith an affinity for water. Do you remember those charming statues from the Woodcutter's territory? The tiny gnomes with funny hats? I know Xavier fell out of favor with their leader but maybe he would make an exception for this. Maybe he could commission the talented crafters to chisel ones representing their talents.

Did you know Faeblood can cast illusions? Imagine. Erik informs me Lord Scarbough can craft an entire play on the arena's stage with his powers. I do not know what to gift someone so creative, but I'm sure you will figure out something clever.

Lord Tiabaut enjoys imported cigars. He's able to light an entire box at once with his fire magic. Xavier doesn't maintain foreign contacts but perhaps he could find a local merchant peddling pipe tobacco.

Lords Siodina and Raekova are shapeshifters. I'm pleased to inform you my new father-in-law is the more powerful of the two. Of yet, their magic restricts their shifts to human forms. Do you think they would enjoy a well-preserved skull or feather for inspiration?

~

She signed her name with a flourish. Who knew how Xavier would use the information? She was a mere soldier, but she'd done her job.

CHAPTER THIRTEEN

"Who is it?" Maia asked, answering the knock. She padded over to the chamber door, thankful the thick carpets warded the chill.

"It's Bree with the seamstress, milady. May we come in?"

After last night's feast, Dezee must be tied up. Her Lady's maid greeted her with a charming smile. An older servant followed, carrying bundles of fabric in her arms.

Bree picked up the discarded invitation and frowned. "From Lady Stella, I presume?"

"Aye."

"These notes have the power to strike fear or elation among the Ladies of Court. Sometimes both." Bree sighed. "It's sooner than I expected, but I suppose you are an anomaly. Able to win Lord Siodina's heart when all the others failed."

"Do you know the details of his engagement to Lady Stella?"

Bree seemed a safe person to question. It was wise to prepare for her first foray with the nobles. The fewer surprises, the better. It wasn't morbid curiosity. More of a practicality.

"Perhaps not as much as the others. But it's my impression their parents arranged the union when they were infants."

So not a love match. Still, he should have warned her. A tactical error on his part.

The seamstress cleared her throat.

"Milady, your measurements." She laid her spools on the bed and pulled a section of measuring rope from her belt. "If we hurry, there is a gown I can alter for this afternoon. Grab some parchment and a quill."

Bree obeyed, opening the vanity's middle drawer and producing the items from its depth. The benefits of cleaning — the servants knew where everything was kept.

The seamstress looped the rope around Maia's hips and rattled off numbers.

"By what name are you called?" Maia raised her arms, giving the servant easier access to her middle.

"Jille, milady." Her lips formed a flat line.

"It's a pleasure to make your acquaintance," Maia said, despite the lack of warmth in the woman's tone. "Do you know Madam MaLota?"

Madam was a seamstress from the Castle who wandered into the Militia territory five or six summers ago. Xavier offered her refuge. When his relentless conversations on safety finally convinced her to stay, he built her shop and home at the edge of the village market.

They were fortunate to have her. Not only for her skill. As a surrogate motherly figure, the crew of orphans from the compound often found themselves smothered in her embrace.

"Marisa is a childhood friend. She left after her parents died. We correspond to this day."

A ghost of a smile teased Jille's lips.

"It's easier for us, those handy with needle and thread, to earn an extra copper or two. Marissa's embroidery kept her sewing from sunup to sundown. A week to the day after we lay her parents to rest, she marched right up to the High Table's exchequer and paid off her ledger."

"Is that common?" Maia asked, thinking of Mikel. "How many servants does the Castle house? How many choose to leave?"

"The servants outnumber the nobles three to one," Bree supplied. "What would you say, Jille? A dozen or so leave a year."

"And half of those return." Jille wrapped the rope around Maia's hips. "Another half dozen from the territories come seeking work. Happy for a warm meal, warmer bed."

"So the numbers don't waver. How do the Lords keep track?"

Bree scoffed. "Lord Siodina, the father not your husband, appointed the current Red Guard Commander as overseer of the tithe collection, the servants' accounts, and the balance of trade. The nobles do not concern themselves with petty accounting or keeping track of our numbers."

"One of us is as good as the next." Jille patted her side. "I have everything I need. Do you require anything else?"

Maia hesitated. Was this Xavier's spy? Jille, with her ties to Madam, would be perfect. She had access to the nobles and a reason to correspond frequently with someone in the territories.

She wanted to ask, but it was too soon, too risky. Though there was one thing Jille could provide.

"Are you skilled with heavier fabrics? I would like to enlist your services for additional work. For coin, of course. And only if it doesn't interfere with your other tasks."

Jille paused, glancing toward Bree, who simply nodded in their direction. "I am here to serve. Whatever you require, I shall see it done."

"I would like a sheath for my dagger and a band to wear it on my thigh." Maia traced the inside of her forearm and said, "And an archer's leather guard if you can source the hide."

"Of course," Jille said, the words rushing out. "I will deliver them with the rest of your wardrobe. If you'll excuse me, I must finish your gown for tea. 'Tis the most delicious pink. It will work well with your coloring."

Pink. Again. She held back a groan. Fate, it seemed, had a wicked sense of humor.

~

MAIA INHALED AS DEEPLY AS HER DRESS ALLOWED.

Why in all the realms would the Faeblood choose to spend their evenings underground when their magic created this wondrous place?

She twirled in the small forest sprouting from the crags of the Castle.

Light bathed the solarium, encouraging the collection of trees below to reach for the peak of the four-story glass dome.

She recognized many of the same specimens that grew in the Militia territory. Even more were foreign to her, perhaps able to flourish in year-round warmth. Understory plants dotted the ground. Flowers flanked paths winding through the garden.

It was as if Mother Nature picked up a clump from the surrounding woods and deposited it randomly on the eastern rampart. And someone added personal touches, whimsical pops of color.

Did Erik maintain this sanctuary, too?

The hem of her soft mauve skirt brushed against her ankles, its color coordinating with the two-toned petals of the blooming roses. Pots of flowering vines and showy bushes and demure flowers surrounded a large marble table set for a small army. Jille was right — the pink complimented her coloring. Perfect for tea.

She raised her arms, letting the heat meld into her palms.

"They turn white at sunset," a small voice said. "When the moon shines through the clouds, the entire chamber glows. Like the firebugs down by the lake."

"Oh." Maia pressed a hand to her chest. "I did not see anyone here."

"You're early." A young servant girl emerged from the shadows.

She shared Erik's warm olive skin and wore her curls in a row of poofs spanning her forehead to her nape. A warrior's style, one kept from being too serious by the different color ribbons securing each. The ends swayed when she walked, adding a whimsical quality to her gait.

Not over six or seven summers, she curtsied or attempted what Maia believed to be a curtsy. It was closer to an exaggerated skip followed by an overzealous bow, the motions synchronous with awkward hand flapping.

Maia bit her lip, preventing a smile. She didn't want the imp to think she laughed at her.

"One does not arrive early for tea," the child said as if instructing a misbehaving pupil. "You miss the chance to make an entrance."

"Can I tell you a secret?" Maia beckoned her closer, picked up her skirts, and bent down. "I'm new here and was afraid I would get lost."

The girl giggled and pointed to Maia's feet. "Ladies don't wear boots, either."

Bree mentioned the same, but Maia refused to force her toes back into slippers. They were still cold from last eve.

"This Lady does." Maia straightened and winked. "Would you be so kind as to show me where I sit?"

"Your place is near the front."

Maia held out a hand.

The girl hesitated. Her eyes darted to the shadows as if checking for permission. Or an audience. She must have decided it was proper because she latched onto Maia, dragging her to a seat on the right.

"My thanks." Maia inclined her head. "I would appreciate it

if you told me what to do. This is my first time taking afternoon tea. Back home we flopped down on comfy chairs and sprawled on lounges, sharing refreshment and gossip."

A smile bloomed on the girl's face, revealing a missing lower tooth.

"You are supposed to wait to be seated." She motioned for Maia to come closer. In her ear she whispered, "Don't loose a belch. Dezee says it's unladylike."

"It's sound advice." Maia deepened her voice, and with the seriousness she reserved for training first-year militia, she added, "You give me wise counsel."

The girl inclined her head then scampered back to her post, her collar bouncing around her face.

Maia counted three forks, four spoons, and two long picks gracing either side of the three stacked plates. Two crystal goblets, plus a teacup with matching saucer, anchored the top of her place setting.

Exactly how long was tea?

Noise from the corridor interrupted her tally of chairs.

Pairs and trios of Ladies funneled into the solarium, chatting and speaking with their hands. All conversations halted when they set eyes on her.

"You found it." Lady Stella parted the crowd and kissed the air next to each cheek as if they were childhood friends. "I am parched."

On cue, near two dozen servants emerged from the shadows. They pulled the chairs back and poured the tea. The young lass from earlier attended the Lady across the table.

She met the girl's smirk with a small smile. Something about the child reminded Maia of her friend Ada from back home.

Ada, who would've breezed into tea and declared it too stuffy, kicking her feet up on the table for dramatic effect. She would've known exactly what to do with Lady Stella's false welcome. And likely sampled wine from her teacup and tea from her goblet. All while entertaining the crowd with her ribald exploits in the Artisan's territory.

Maia sighed. She was not Ada.

"Lady Newhiel," said someone farther down the table. "Your dress is a delightful shade of clay. Where did you find a color to rival the water stains of the mountain? I've seen wheat sacks more appealing."

Maia, mid sip, swallowed too much of the piping hot drink. Ow. Ow. Ow.

"Your husband mentioned something similar. Although, he didn't share your exact description. Pray tell... what were his words?" Lady Newhiel tilted her head to the side as if searching for the exact phrase. "That's right... he claimed the color highlighted my eyes right before I came around his cock."

Maia set down her teacup. Safer, to leave it on the saucer.

The two Ladies glared daggers at one another. Whispers floated around the table. Others hid their laughter in linen napkins.

"The color is perfect for the approaching season," Maia said with a faked confidence, her fingers toying with her earrings.

"Who asked you, human?" Lady Newhiel sneered over the rim of her teacup. "I suppose you delight in a palette reminiscent of pig pens."

"Now, Ladies." Lady Stella popped a ripened cherry in her mouth, clearly delighted by their banter. "Maia is my guest. Be civil."

Civil. Not kind.

"*Lady* Maia." The statement came from the shadows. Louder, the servant girl said, "Her title is *Lady Maia*."

"Why you insolent little—" Lady Newhiel flicked her wrist.

The servant girl stiffened. Her little body suspended in midair. She floated toward the table as if imaginary ropes pulled her by the ankles.

"No. No. No," she cried, fighting against invisible bonds. Her face scrunched. "Please..."

To hell with this.

One minute, the handle of Maia's dagger was in her palm. The next, it wobbled in the air, its blade pinning the sleeve of Lady Newhiel's dress to the back of her chair.

"Release her, or my next will pierce your black heart." A fabrication, as she carried only one blade. "Pity. My husband is too far away to hear your screams. How long do you think it takes a Faeblood to bleed dry?"

Lady Newhiel lowered her arm. The lass dropped to the stone floor, straightened, and ran her hands down the front of her tunic. Around the long table, mouths opened and closed like lazy pond trout.

"You're a heathen," Lady Newhiel spat. "Lord Siodina is out of his mind."

"Out of his mind...?" Maia strolled around the table. She braced her heel on the wooden arm of Lady Newhiel's chair and grabbed the dagger's handle. "To marry me? To bed me? Or to bring me here?"

Lady Newhiel flinched. If she leaned away any farther, she would end up in her neighbor's lap.

Maia pushed the chair with her foot, pulling the dagger free. She slipped it in her boot and fluffed her skirts in place.

"Isn't she a delight?" Lady Stella clasped her hands in front of her lips. "All this excitement. I'm famished."

"I'm afraid I lost my appetite. Come, lass." She gestured to the servant girl. Best remove her from notice. "Show me to my chambers."

No one stood. They said nothing. Their idea of manners was as backwards as their idea of friendship.

Maia flashed one last toothy snarl at Lady Newhiel and remembered to sway her hips as she sauntered out of the solarium.

CHAPTER FOURTEEN

"Did you see their faces?" The young servant girl shuffled alongside Maia, taking two steps for every one of hers. "I thought Lady Newhiel might faint on the spot."

Idiot. Why did Maia let them get under her skin? Of course they wouldn't welcome her, a human.She expected their barbs, not their abuse of a child.

Maia needed to blend in with the Ladies at Court, not slice them to pieces. It wasn't likely they could provide intel for Xavier, but she wouldn't dismiss the possibility. They would never accept her if she didn't stop provoking them.

She must try harder.

"Ooh. I despise when Lady Newhiel does that." The imp shuddered. "My mind knows not what my legs do. My arms are as heavy as a sack of flour."

"It's happened before?" Maia asked, struggling to keep her voice level.

"Aye." She halted Maia with a hand on her wrist, looked down, then dropped it as if it were a hot coal. "Mistress Dezee says I need to stand as still as a statue. As quiet as a ghost. I am to keep my mouth straight like the game I play with my friends where we pull goofy faces, trying to make each other laugh."

The girl grinned.

"'Tis difficult sometimes," she confessed. "I must be proper if I want to stay in the Castle."

What a terrible way to live. To curb one's instincts so sharply, you became... invisible. Maia wouldn't want it for herself or anyone else. Let alone a spirited child.

"Hurry. I want to show you my secret place." The lass ran ahead.

Maia quickened her stride, catching up a few moments later. The twists and turns disoriented her. She must remember to bring a quill and parchment. It would be prudent to map the interior. For herself then Xavier.

They climbed another set of spiral stairs, the stone steps a redder clay than those leading to Lord Siodina's chambers. Narrower, too.

The air grew muggier the higher they climbed. At last, the girl tugged her through an arched entrance and into a three-story vaulted chamber.

A cavern, more like. The far end opened to fresh mountain air.

Maia closed her eyes, sampling the breeze blowing over her heated cheeks. Once her heart rate slowed, she cataloged the room.

The stone walls and ceiling were jagged, save for small alcoves lining each side. It was as if Mother Nature carved the first. Magic the latter. Given the rustic ambiance, the nobles likely spent little time here.

On her approach, torches flared to life, illuminating row after row of weapons. Long broad swords. Smaller rapiers for fencing or close range. Daggers and maces of varying sizes.

Maia picked up the closest blade, slashing a satisfying arc in the air. It was heavy and carried her half a step forward before she regained her balance.

Faeblood forbade weapons of warfare in the territories. The decree signed during her grandfather's time. Militia fighters trained in hand-to-hand combat, never once picking up a sword.

That didn't stop Xavier from forging weapons in secret. While it was simple to hide dozens of blades, it was near impossible to train with them.

The next alcove housed an array of throwing knives and six-pointed stars. Interesting. She pulled one off the wall, spinning it around the hole in its middle.

"Stand back," she said as she squared to the target in the far corner. Maia let the star fly, but instead of sticking in the hay bale, it bounced off the floor ten paces in front.

"Here," the lass said, handing her another. "Try again."

Maia shook her head. While she appreciated their size — perfect for hiding several in the lining of her skirts — she would need hours of practice before she could throw one properly. If she wasn't mistaken, they were in an armory. Surely they kept—

There. Three alcoves on the left, she located hooks with bows and quivers full of arrows. More her style.

The lass ran over and grabbed the smallest bow. Before Maia could ask what she was doing, she'd selected a similar-sized quiver with several arrows.

"You shoot?"

"Every day." A grin split her face. She put her finger to her lips. "But you cannot tell anyone. I'm not 'posed to be here. I finish my chores then sneak up before the sun sets."

"Show me." Maia flicked her head toward the target.

The lass inspected the arrows with the seriousness one might give to picking out a new doll. She brushed her fingertips over the fletchings, selecting the smallest. Her little arms shook with the effort to draw the string, but she held true, exhaling whispered words as the arrow flew from the bow.

It struck the center of the painted bullseye. The tip buried a hand's width into the straw.

Dear gods, it took Maia an entire decade to make that shot. With more power, it would fell a deer at seventy paces.

"Can you do it again?" Perhaps it was luck.

"Yup," she said, popping the *p*. Her tongue stuck out the corner of her mouth, and she nocked another arrow.

This time, Maia didn't imagine the words the lass whispered before release.

The second arrow split the first in two, its feathers vibrating from impact. How in all the realms?

"That's wonderful." Maia struggled to keep her voice even. "Can you show me how you shoot?"

"The arrow must be in the center of the string. Like this." She rested the bow on her leg, aligning her last. "And then you pull back as hard as you can. Sometimes, it's too hard and you shake your arms out. Like this."

She eased the tension in her bow, rested it between her knees, and flapped her wrists.

"Other times, I blow on my hand for luck." She drew back the string once more. Without taking her eyes off the target, the lass said, "And the most important part… you gotta tell it where to strike. Arrow of my bow. Fly true and join the heart of your brothers and sisters."

A gust of wind swirled around the cavern, whipping Maia's hair into her face. She batted the strands obscuring her vision as the third arrow split the last, lodging far enough into the bale that plumes of hay filled the air.

Magic.

"Aye. My magic."

Maia didn't realize she'd spoken the word out loud. "How? You… you are human."

"Some of us are born with it. Others get theirs during the Rite of Ortus." At Maia's confused look, she continued, "When I turn seven, the High Lords will perform the spell to tie me to the Faeblood. They give me a home and food. Others, magic. And we gotta serve them until we pay our debts."

Demelza. She had spoken of this magic when fixing Maia's hair. How many servants were born with powers? And how many had magic seared into their flesh? Her eyes darted to the smooth skin on the girl's wrist.

"When did it appear?"

"A few moon cycles ago." She shrugged. "Maybe longer. I came here like always. My arrows kept missing the target like always. I bargained with the gods that day. All I want is to serve in the Red Guard. Like my father. He died in a raid on a mercenary camp."

"That's very brave," Maia said, satisfied the words didn't come out strangled. Misplaced loyalty, sure, but no less admirable. "They would be fortunate to have you. Fighters in my village arrive for militia training the summer of their eighteenth year. You will have a decade of target practice if the Red Guard follow a similar timeline."

"You don't understand, milady." The girl hung her head.

Maia understood little about Court. She must've missed something for the child to fret. While she wanted to suggest an alternative to joining the Red Guard, Maia wasn't lying. The child would be an excellent archer when she came of age.

"The Red Guard do not train females," she recited as if someone else continuously threw *that* truth in her face.

The militia didn't either. At least, not until Xavier petitioned the High Table to allow Maia's entrance. A compromise. Not a change to the draconian view of females fighting.

The Red Guard — with their proximity to the Court politics — weren't likely to make concessions for a young lass even if her father served. The elite squadron of bodyguards held a long-standing tradition of only allowing their sons to join the academy. With one exception — the winner or team of winners of the annual Grimoire Games.

The competition rules limited who could enter. While there was no age restriction, contestants required a formal sponsor. Faeblood Lords made bargains with human servants for future favors, future loyalty. Territory leaders nominated their own contenders, but they almost never won.

The Games were rigged. No one wanted a territory spy among the Red Guard ranks.

"There's an older lad. He's new and big. Really big and really mean. He caught me repairing an arrow in our dormitory. He told me not to bother. My place was in the kitchens."

Stubborn fools existed in every walk of life. Maia never once considered she couldn't join the militia.

By the time she was ten, she could heel hook a fighter three times her size. At thirteen, she choked out her first opponent. When she turned sixteen, her grappling skills mirrored those who completed their training.

"Keep practicing," Maia repeated her father's mantra. "Don't let anyone tell you what you can't do."

"But the Lords will steal my magic and replace it with something more practical. Dezee says we need more cooks. I don't mind helping, but I don't want to chop vegetables for the rest of my days."

"Don't despair. Share your name. I shall speak to Lord Erik. He holds sway with the High Table." She hoped. Maia cuffed the back of the girl's neck. "Show me the trick to throwing this star. I'd love to see Lady Newhiel's expression when I whip one out during tea."

"I'm Leatrix Langhieme, Lea for short." She giggled. "As for the star… you hold it wrong…"

"I propose we move the vote to today." His father's voice remained bland. "The standard fortnight is unnecessary. All those in favor of appointing Erik Siodina, son of Emsworth, to the High Table, say *aye.*"

Erik ran a hand over his mouth.

Angry shouts echoed in the four-story circular chamber, the High Table. A bit of a misnomer — there was no table. Only an elevated sense of importance.

Council members lined the outer walls, requiring speakers on the sunken floor to rotate a full circle to address everyone. Like circus monkeys pandering to a crowd.

Light from cutouts near the ceiling illuminated the upper levels while sconces every few paces took care of the lower half. Rows of plush chairs spiraled upward. Today, the ones beyond the first level sat empty.

The chamber also hosted tribunals. Then, the nobles filled every seat, never ones to miss public humiliation and punishment. Fitting, really. The courtroom responsible for unjust hearings, unjust sentencing, doubled as a regular meeting place for the nine High Lords.

"This is not the way of the council," said Lord Scarbough. "Since when do we cast aside the death of a member to rush the appointment of his replacement?"

"Hear, hear," several Lords murmured.

Parchments shuffled. Someone coughed, the sound dampened by the sleeve of their robes. His father remained silent.

"The stability of the High Table, thus the peninsula, depends on a ninth member," Lord Nanscott countered. Not an ally of his father, but the nobleman never missed an opportunity to argue with Lord Scarbough. The two were at each other's throats for as long as Erik could remember. "We cannot change the past. A new Lord must be appointed. Who better than Emsworth's son? He is of age and fulfills the marriage requirements."

Another archaic rule — those who sat on the High Table must marry. It was an attempt to prevent courtiers from influencing a Lord's rule. As if mistresses' desires halted at the entrance doors.

"My nephew—"

"Your nephew is a fool with weak magic." Lord Scarbough waved his fist at Lord Wulffrith. "He's more concerned about last year's vintage than ruling over the populace."

Lord Wulffrith's face turned an interesting shade of puce.

Lord Scarbough wasn't wrong. The nephew would make a terrible addition to the High Table. At least Erik could admit he, himself, was no better suited to the position. Not with his father's threats on his mind. Not with his father's blood coursing through his veins.

He caught his sire's sneer, the subtle flick of his chin. It didn't suit Erik's purpose to sit on the High Table, but he owed Xavier to go through the motions and feign interest.

"If I may—" Erik cleared his throat, waiting to gain everyone's attention. "I return home from a tour of Morvak with ideas on how to control the populace and maintain our rule."

They didn't know his father ordered him to spy on the militia. The Lords believed Erik traveled the territories to gauge the morale of the humans. To force compliance with the annual tithe. Only Lord Scarbough knew he spent an extended amount of time at the compound.

"But what of Lord Bierling?" Lord Wulffrith vaulted to his feet. "What about his murder?"

"Enough." His father climbed the steps and placed a hand on Lord Wulffrith's arm. "Sit. Down."

Since when did his sire issue orders to another High Lord? Had he amassed more influence over the months Erik was away from Court? He didn't care for any of the nobles. But Erik worried about his father's intentions most of all. The other Lords were... predictable. Easily manipulated if necessary.

"The death of Lord Bierling was tragic but not unexpected," his father said. "He had a penchant for wine and a weak heart. If I cannot convince you of his expected demise, then perhaps I will gain your favor with news he conspired to murder my son."

Whispers flew around the chamber.

"What lies do you speak?" Lord Scarbough asked. "A human attacked your son in the stands of the arena while all nine of us sat on stage."

"He sent his men." The corners of his father's mouth tipped upward. "My guards apprehended them when they fled in the chaos. A little truth serum was all it took to coax their tale."

Truth serum was illegal unless sanctioned by the High Table.

He could tell by the Lords' expressions that his father acted without their approval. Erik didn't know what was worse. That his father kept a supply or the ease with which he admitted to using it.

"Where are they now?" Lord Scarbough slammed his fist on the arm of his chair. "I shall question them myself."

Their lack of outrage answered Erik's earlier unease — his father's actions were above reproach.

Erik ran his hands over his hair. Dammit. He grew the ingredients for the serum's antidote in his greenhouse. He would need another favor from Stella.

"The men are… indisposed," his father said. "The fact remains, my son not only meets the requirements for a sitting High Lord, but we should grant him recompense for the attempt on his life."

"See here, Emsworth," said Lord Scarbough. "I regret your son suffered because of Lord Bierling's scheming, but it should have no bearing on the due process for appointing a new member."

Several Lords nodded their agreement.

"Per our laws, each High Lord may suggest a candidate of their own. The council will conduct interviews. We will hold a vote in fourteen days." Lord Scarbough gestured to Erik. "You may plead your case as your father's candidate."

Erik smirked. Time to play the part.

"Siodinas do not *plead*. I shall speak to the chamber as you demand. Far be it from me to thumb my nose at tradition. Gentlemen, I will take my leave as I'm no longer required for this meeting."

He didn't wait for their acknowledgement, striding down the steps and out of the chamber. He didn't look back at his father. Didn't slow in the corridor.

Didn't scream his frustrations for fear if he started yelling, he would never stop.

Was this his future? Days and hours spent in the company of greedy Faeblood? Erik had no more right to govern than those parasites. Still, in a fortnight, he must present a convincing argument for ruling alongside them.

Erik never wanted power, responsibility. Even less since he traveled the peninsula and observed the consequences of the heavy tithe on families. Sure, some prospered, like Xavier and his territory. More suffered.

And the Lords wouldn't benefit from his example. True leadership took time. And trust. And honor. Day two at home, they already disgusted him with their antics.

It didn't used to bother him.

Erik's skin crawled, a simmering restless energy. He needed a fight. A release. He needed Maia. But she couldn't be that for him. So he did the next best thing.

His feet moved on their own toward the armory.

CHAPTER FIFTEEN

"Another," Leatrix said as she produced a small, deformed apple from her pocket.

"What do you wish me to skewer this time?" Maia smiled.

"The parchment in the corner. I don't know what it says, but Jasper always wrinkles his nose when he reads it."

Jasper, Maia learned in the two hours they spent in the armory, was a boy four summers Lea's senior. He ran around with her at night. The pair snuck down to the lake when Demelza paid them little notice. By the wistful way she said his name, Maia suspected a childhood crush on Lea's part.

"Perhaps we should leave a mark of our own. On the count of three." Maia drew back the bow's string.

"One." Lea cocked her arm behind her head, the apple in her hand. "Two."

"Three," Maia said as Lea tossed it in the air.

Her arrow speared the red flesh, pinning the fruit to the offending parchment. They threw their hands up and whooped.

Clap. Clap. Clap.

Maia spun around. Another arrow found its way into her palm.

"Bravo." Erik nodded to the bow. "I came for some practice. Lo and behold, who do I find in my armory? Two mischief-makers up to no good."

His words bit, despite their teasing nature. Maia couldn't be certain if Erik aimed his irritation at her, the destruction of the parchment, or Lea, a servant who dared to leave the shadows.

She didn't care.

"Milord." Lea curtsied, a slight tremor in her voice.

"Run along." Maia hugged her with one arm. The child didn't need to witness this. "Help Demelza with the evening meal."

Lea bowed to her, then to Erik, and scampered off without meeting their eyes. Once she was out of earshot, Maia whirled around.

"What's wrong?"

"What?" He crossed his arms over his chest, the muscles straining the sleeves of his tunic. "I can't congratulate you on an impressive shot?"

"Don't play ignorant." She placed her arrow back in the borrowed quiver and hung them both on a hook.

"Nothing's wrong." His fingertips trailed over a row of daggers, selecting three from their holsters on the wall. "I came for practice. An activity I enjoyed regularly before my assignment to your compound."

"It's not *nothing*. I can hear the lie in your voice."

Something happened since his meeting with the High Table. She was still upset Erik didn't disclose the betrothal, but if he came here instead of his gardens...

Well... it was just good sense to stay informed. That was the only reason she pushed.

"Perhaps I should make myself clear. Nothing that I need to confess."

He threw his first dagger. It sliced the ends of Lea's arrows, lodging in the hay bale.

Alright. He'd spent the last couple of hours with the Lords, with his father. Likely not a pleasant experience.

Erik never bristled even when given the least desirable commands in training. Quite the opposite, he seemed to relish the hard work required for improving his combat skills. He was unflappable. Reliable.

It was unnerving — seeing him this irate. She should respect his privacy. Erik wanted to let off some anger. That was what brought her here too.

Maia sighed. At some point, she must confess her actions at afternoon tea. Perhaps when he calmed down. Or after dinner. Maybe before they fell asleep.

Or never.

He cocked his arm back and let another dagger fly. Before it thudded next to the first, the last one left his palm. His chest heaved. His eyes went a little wild.

She handed him another, keeping the last one for herself.

Erik held the blade by its tip, closed his eyes, and tapped the handle against his forehead. He pivoted on his heel, throwing it over his shoulder. The momentum from his spin carried him a few paces forward. Bullseye.

She bit her tongue.

He stalked the target and wrenched Lea's arrows from the center. They dangled in his grip. His other hand paused midair in front of the target.

"My turn," she said, breaking whatever thoughts held him in a trance.

"Have dreams of chucking blades at my head, do you?" The edges of his lips curled in a snarl. "While fascinating, I don't trust your throwing abilities. Summon patience."

He turned his back on her and pulled his first dagger free.

Prick. Stubborn, arrogant... prick.

Her insults weren't original. Satisfying though. Before her

mind registered her intentions, Maia's blade flew. It turned end over end, nicking the shell of his ear and lodging into the bale.

Right next to his head.

"Watch your temper. You are too easy to rile," Xavier had told her again. And again. *"The smarter fighters know how to exploit your weakness."*

Pride. Willful pride served as Maia's constant companion through years of grueling training.

When she wanted to quit, it never allowed her surrender. When a task seemed impossible, it kept her focused until she discovered a solution. Over the years, it grew and grew, becoming a beast of its own.

It nipped and circled and hunted her until she'd earned her cuffs.

Erik didn't appear to share this shortcoming. Either he never had others question his station (a Faeblood heir to a powerful High Lord), or he learned to set it aside to accomplish some of his father's more ethically dubious tasks.

He rubbed his ear and inspected his fingertips.

"You have something to say, Kitten?" He tucked the daggers into loops on his belt, his motions deliberate. His eyes never left hers.

"Your ear was in the way." She shrugged, unable to hold his stare.

"And here I thought you aimed for my head." He prowled toward Maia, stopping when his boots aligned shy of hers.

"If I aimed for your head, we wouldn't hold this conversation now."

He took a step forward.

She tipped up her chin. It was either retreat or get knocked over. Maia stepped back. Better to have this conversation standing.

"Fair." Erik never doubted her. Sure, he may poke and prod, but he never once questioned her skills. "You want to talk? Let's talk, hmm. Why don't you tell me about your afternoon?"

He grabbed her hips and walked them backwards.

"I enjoyed a spot of tea with the Ladies." Her back bumped against the rough stone wall. Its chill seeped into the thin bodice of her dress, a startling contrast to the heat of his chest at her front. "The solarium is delightful."

Was she whispering?

"I enjoyed the roses. They don't grow near the compound. I'm told the soil isn't hospitable." Stop yammering about flowers. "Ada bartered for them. For the altar. Our wedding. The ceremony. Mar–marriage."

"Roses, huh? I never noticed. And a spot of tea?" His cheek brushed against hers, his lips a hair's width from her ear. "Is that what the Ladies are calling it?"

He knew. How?

Erik angled his body so her chest smashed against his tunic.

She was trapped, her legs nestling between his thighs. Her gaze shot to the shadows outside the chamber's entrance.

Mikel, the traitor. He must have informed Erik about her mishap with Lady Newhiel.

"Refreshments with a spirited discussion?" she asked, her voice raising an octave.

She should push him away. Instead, she ran her tongue along the underside of his jaw. His skin tasted salty. If they were lovers, she might take a bite where it curved near his ear.

Her hand bunched the fabric of his tunic. She wanted to pull him closer. Better leverage to shove him on his back.

"Would your blade find its way to my neck?" *Would you enjoy it?* he didn't add.

"Why do you presume—"

His hand encircled her wrist, applying featherlight pressure. The dagger clattered against the floor.

"Ask me to kiss you."

So that was his game. He wanted her to lose their bet. Perhaps thought it wise to strip her of her ire, her weapon, first. Her hands cupped the back of his neck, and she rested her forehead against his chin.

"Did you kiss Lady Stella?" Dammit. She should've let it go. The question left her raw, exposed. Something she couldn't allow. But Erik had a knack for confusing her. Aye, it was his fault.

He was the one that lied.

Erik tilted her chin up, waiting until her gaze stopped searching the chamber.

"I never kissed Lady Stella." More waiting. "I never will."

She craned her neck to the side. Did they have an audience? Nope. Still alone.

Maia should push him for more. Maybe she was weak, too, where he was concerned. Because she didn't ask another question. Worse, she knew she would forgive him for not divulging his betrothal sooner.

Perhaps it was for the best. They had more important matters.

"Ask me to kiss you?" The lines around his eyes crinkled.

Dear gods, she wanted to beg him to claim her mouth.

Her husband. Was that the source of this need? She consumed his potion, so the oath to the stars didn't bind. Though there was something primal about the title. He may be heir to his father's line. Lord to the Court. But for a few moments, he was hers.

Erik dipped his head, pressing forward and forcing her legs to wrap around his middle. Soft, demanding lips trailed a path up the column of her neck.

A manic self-preservation kept her from grabbing his head and guiding his mouth to hers.

Maia enjoyed kissing — the push and pull — a conversation without words. Hard to resist. Harder to lie.

He ground his hips into hers. Heat pooled between her legs. Perhaps it was good their relationship was in name only, because if Erik teased like this when they were reluctant partners, she would forgive every transgression if they became lovers.

He pinned her wrists above her head with one hand. Fingertips trailed the inside of her arm, tingles lingering in their path. Curious. So curious. They dipped into her bodice and skimmed the swell of her chest.

"Kiss me first, and I'll relieve your ache," he said.

It would have been better if he asked for her blind trust.

"No," she managed.

Erik tilted his head to the side, studying her.

Was that regret? She didn't doubt the heat in his eyes. It matched the arousal pushed against her core. Was he angry? At her? At his father? *At his lack of control?*

Too busy worrying, she missed the warning growl before he dipped his head and bit her neck. A small whimper escaped, too late to swallow down. This was not her. She was not a besotted fool, unable to keep up.

"What am I going to do with you?" Erik ran the tip of his nose along the shell of her ear. He nipped the lobe. Not hard enough to draw blood. A reminder of how she'd pushed him over the edge in the first place.

His cut may need salve. She reached for his ear, eager to inspect the damage, but her hands stayed pinned.

The pressure on her wrists vanished. She tugged. Once. Twice. Something anchored her in place.

"What did you do?"

Throwing stars tacked the sleeves of her dress to the stone wall. Six in total. Three per arm.

While he'd distracted her with his tongue, his magic had lodged the tips deep enough to support her weight.

"Why you," she snarled. "Get me down from here. Release me right now."

"Tsk. Tsk. Tsk. Turnabout is fair play." A feral grin bloomed on his face. He bowed low. "For the ear."

ERIK WIPED HIS LIPS WITH THE BACK OF HIS HAND.

"Let her stew for a bit," he said to the shadows. "Before you take her down."

"What did she do?" Mikel asked, a rasp in his voice as if he had failed to use it today.

"She threw a dagger at my head. Nicked my ear." The bleeding had stopped, a thin crust forming on his skin.

"What did *you* do?" Mikel grunted. "Show your temper? Challenge her?"

The hulking fighter had her measure. Erik's silence might as well be a confession.

"I'll wait. Give you a head start."

Now, more than ever, he needed that potion to cleave his vows. They couldn't give the stars a reason to believe the union. How much longer would Erik last before he threw her over his shoulder and took her to bed? Their bet be damned. He'd pinned her for both his amusement and his sanity.

Erik wanted to corner Mikel and interrogate him about his time in the Castle. But he needed to pay Stella a visit. So he left the fighter, a potential link to his past, and went to find her.

Stella had chosen a suite in the western wing, far from her father, from his wrath. But close enough to dozens of younger courtiers.

He knocked twice on her high gloss door, relaxing his expression in its reflection.

A willowy Lady answered. The faint golden undertones of her rich umber skin contrasted with the white sheet wrapping around her body. She gestured him inside, climbing back into bed next to Stella without announcing his arrival.

"Lord Siodina, have you come to join us?" Lady Stella asked. Her lover must be new. Otherwise, she would've never extended the offer. Her use of his title was another hint.

He must watch his next words.

"With such beauty before me, it's tempting. Sadly, I must decline. I inquire after the progress of your research."

Another Lady exited the attached bathing chamber and snuggled under the sheets.

To her lovers, he said, "Lady Stella is kind enough to offer her services. I tend a fickle plant and need some guidance. Some sort of magic rot is devastating its roots."

They yawned.

He sat on the edge of the oversized bed.

Stella kept an array of lovers. Young females who blossomed under her tutelage at Court. One or three at a time. Anyone she could sneak under her father's nose. Males, if he became suspicious.

If pressed, it was the one thing Erik admired about Stella — her ability to foster a genuine connection with anyone she desired. It had taken him the better part of a decade to mask his jealousy. His resentment toward Stella's straightforward relationships fizzled over the years. Mostly.

The willowy lover kissed the column of Stella's neck. So intent on her journey, she never slowed. Even when Stella's hand dove under the covers.

"I spent the morning in the library, poring over spell books."

The courtier's head fell back against the pillow. Her hands clenched the blankets.

"I discovered a reference to a potion that would… ah… solve your dilemma. Your problem. With the plant."

The Lady's mouth parted in a soft *o*.

"But not the actual incantation?" Erik asked, rising.

"No." Stella closed her eyes.

The courtier on the other side, a curvy fox with bright orange hair and a wicked grin, tweaked Stella's nipple.

"I shall resume my search tomorrow. As for payment..." Stella's lids fluttered. "I'm still pondering my options."

"Very well. Good eve, Ladies."

"My Lord," Stella called after him. "Perhaps your wife would care to join me for a tour of the grounds. We had such an invigorating time at tea today."

Her laughter followed him down the corridor.

CHAPTER SIXTEEN

Maia woke to an empty bed.

It was a good thing, too. She hadn't calmed from Erik's antics in the armory.

Mikel had freed her, his quiet eyes sparkling. She'd dined in Erik's chambers last night, alone. Exhausted.

She wasn't a coward. She could only handle so much Faeblood.

The sheets beside her were warm. So, he slept here last night. She straightened the covers instead of doing something foolish... like snuggling in his scent.

The dress from yesterday hung on the hook next to the wardrobe, ready for the servants to clean and press. It really was beautiful, and for a moment, she felt beautiful wearing it. It wasn't a hardship to wrap herself in such finery, but she doubted she would ever feel comfortable in the frilly couture.

Someone had laundered her tunic. It sat on top of the trunk next to her leathers. She donned both. Until the seamstress produced more gowns, she would wear her own clothes. Maia stuck out in the Castle regardless.

She strolled to the vanity and combed out her hair.

Knock. Knock.

"Who is it?" Her hand stilled.

"It's Bree, milady."

"Come in." Maia set the brush down. "I didn't expect you so soon with the rest of the Court still in bed."

The maid entered, carrying a small package wrapped in simple brown parchment.

"Lord Siodina informed me you prefer to rise at dawn." Bree hurried across the room and lay the gift next to a crystal bottle of perfume. She pointed to the brush and said, "Allow me."

"May I have a simple braid?" The Ladies of Court favored elaborate updos and knots. Severe coifs with no room for softness. But in the quiet light of morning, she couldn't seem to muster enough care to instruct Bree to fashion a twist.

It was too soon for homesickness. She just wanted to look like herself for a few hours.

"As you wish." Bree nodded to the parcel. "For you, from Jille. After yesterday's tea, I encouraged her to finish it before your gowns."

Maia untied the twine binding the wrapper. She set both aside.

The seamstress sent a small leather belt, complete with a delicate rose-gold buckle and a hand-tooled, fawn-colored sheath.

She traced the pattern of the stitches. Two simple rows of hunter green outlined a design of Gillyflowers on both sides. Exquisite.

"How did she find the time?"

"It's her gift." Bree cleared her throat. "From her Rite of Ortus. She tells me she always had a deft hand with needles, with thread. The High Lord who performed the ceremony granted her the ability to stitch at a faster pace."

Maia pulled Erik's dagger from her boot and slid it inside its new home, strapping both to her thigh.

"Thank you for yesterday." Bree clarified, "With Lea. It could have been worse. Has been worse..."

So the maid was in the solarium. Did Lea seek Bree in the shadows? Jille had done something similar yesterday morning when they came to take Maia's measurements.

"You're welcome," Maia said simply. "This is where I say something flippant. Like *it was nothing.* Or *anyone would have done the same.*"

"Then you'd be wrong on both counts." A flash of gold ringed Bree's eyes.

There. Maia hadn't imagined it before.

"It is my hope you do not judge me too harshly. For not interfering, that is."

Bree ran the brush through Maia's locks. Several moments passed before she set it down, apparently satisfied Maia's hair was free of tangles.

"Mistress Dezee forbade us to intervene."

"And you don't wish to go against her?" Maia didn't require confirmation, so she continued, "What magic did the Lords grant you?"

"None." Bree parted the hair, gathering three separate sections on the side. When Maia didn't press, Bree added, "I arrived at the Castle later in life. As an adult. Since I came here without debt to my name, the Lords spared me from the Rite."

Maia's gaze flicked to the intricate leather bracelets.

"I keep them covered in case they spot the unscarred skin." *In case they change their mind,* fell between them.

Bree wove the strands together. The braid hugged Maia's temple then her ear. She finished, tied it with a piece of ribbon from her pocket, and started on the other side.

"Have you ever wondered who you could be?" Maia asked, uncertain where the question stemmed. "If circumstances differed?"

She'd never given it much thought herself. Still, it was difficult to fathom Lea's quest to join the Red Guard. Perhaps more than Bree's willingness to spend her life in the Castle.

"Perhaps when I was younger." Bree tied off the end of the second braid. "I dreamt I would marry a prince in a faraway land. He would rescue me from my treehouse, fight my brother."

Bree bit her lower lip.

"My brother played the role of a Spartan conqueror in our childhood duels." She pinned the tails in the back, creating a simple crown. "The imaginary savior would come and whisk me away to a land where my sister and I could play with our dolls."

"Play with your dolls?" Maia chuckled and met Bree's reflection in the looking glass.

"We were very young. Silly girls with silly dreams. My sister..." She hesitated, and then her voice dropped to a harsh whisper. "We snuck away from our chores and hid in the forest near our home. Grandfather turned his eye, telling Baba, my grandmother, we would grow up soon enough. The chores could wait."

"Where are they now?"

"My grandparents crossed the Veil together," Bree said, her tone implying it wasn't peaceful. "My brother and sister stayed in the territories. Enough of the villagers knew our parents, our line, and allowed them to apprentice in the family trade."

"What is your birth territory?"

"We hail from the lumber mills."

"But you came here?"

Did Bree know Kiehl, the current leader? Surely, he would find a home for her too. His influence was not as strong as Xavier's throughout the peninsula, but his community respected him. Lads from his village who showed up for militia training consistently received some of the highest marks.

"If that will be all, milady." Bree gathered the discarded

parchment and twine, shoving them in the same deep pockets where she stashed her pins.

Oooh, Maia struck a nerve with the last. She didn't want to be alone with only her thoughts for company, so she held up her hand, studying Bree. "Wait."

Here was someone who needed a friend.

Maia wanted to take back her earlier question, regretting that she'd pushed too much. While Maia may never appreciate Bree's reasons for seeking a position in the Castle — nor Lea's for yearning for a spot in the Red Guard — in the end, it didn't matter.

Perhaps Maia had started her search in the wrong place. Sure, she must establish relationships with the Faeblood Ladies. But her time might be better spent forming friendships with the staff.

"Spend the morning with me," she blurted out. Maia rested her hand on Bree's leather bracelets. "Come explore the Castle. I have yet to discover all its passages."

Bree titled her head to the side, regarding Maia through those long lashes.

"I fear I will get lost without help." The words rushed out. Truth. Admitting a weakness went a long way in building connections.

She forced a giggle to sell the tale. Too much, if the look Bree gave her was any sign. She dropped the act.

"I'd like to map the corridors. Learn the common routes." Maia rummaged in the smallest vanity drawer. She produced a folded piece of parchment. "Mikel and I started last night."

It had provided an outlet for her anger after the armory incident.

Maia could retrace her steps later and note the various offshoots in the early hours when the Court slumbered. Mikel mentioned he would complete the task, but he undertook too much.

"Let me find a quill," Maia continued on without Bree's agreement. She snagged Erik's leather satchel off the post at the foot of the bed, tucking the items inside. "We have time before afternoon tea. Though, it might be prudent to skip it. One day won't cause alarm."

She spoke the last more for herself.

"As you desire." Bree curtsied, her head dipping to the ground, but not before Maia caught a smirk. "What route interests you?"

The route to the dungeons. Lord Siodina's chambers. The library.

"Can you show me the way to the greenhouse?" Maia slung the bag's thick strap over her shoulder and tucked the folded map into her back pocket. "I have yet to visit my husband in his sanctuary."

Bree nodded. "Might I suggest learning a path to the barracks as well?"

Maia stiffened.

"If you require help and your husband is not around, of course."

"Of course." Her tongue lodged in her throat, so she flicked her head, gesturing for Bree to exit Erik's chambers ahead of her.

She closed the door behind them, fumbling with the small pouch of sand she kept hidden in her boot. Maia sprinkled a pinch on the handle. Her chamber didn't have a lock, a useless defense against magic. If someone wanted to search her rooms, she couldn't keep them out.

But she would know if they entered.

She had been lax, relying on Erik and Mikel to accompany her into the rooms. But they wouldn't always be around. Mikel needed rest. And Erik needed… well… he had his duties. Just as she had her tasks.

Bree looked away, studying the tapestries lining the hallway.

Her gaze landed on everything else except the door. Maia wouldn't be surprised if she started whistling.

"This way," Bree said.

She secured the pouch and followed.

They passed another two dozen chamber doors, all bedrooms for the nobles, apartments for their families. Bree pulled her into the shadows at the end of the hall and grabbed her hand.

"Here. Do you feel the outline?" Bree asked and guided Maia's fingers along the stone. A thin vertical crack ran up the wall. Too fine to be mortar. "This passage leads down to the lake."

Bree grabbed the nearest torch, shining the light in Maia's direction.

She unfolded the map and drew a hasty sketch of the corridor, writing the number *24* and an *X* at the end. Perhaps, when it was time to leave, she needn't escape via her bedroom balcony after all.

She waved the parchment in the air until certain the ink had dried.

"Another two rights takes us to the clock tower." Bree set off.

When Xavier announced his plans for her to marry, Maia asked Ada, the compound's keeper of written things, to borrow a history book on the construction of the Castle.

The original inhabitants built the structure on the side of Morvak Mountain, angling it so three turrets jutted from the depths. Where one might place a fourth, the outer wall plunged deep inside the stone.

Two generations ago, the Faeblood added a clock tower.

Up close, it was easy to spot the differences between the original foundation and the newer addition.

Smooth gray stones, distorted with veins of blues and greens, curled in stacks at least ten stories high. The blocks alternated, winding in a circular pattern, and narrowing at the top where a large copper bell hung.

Maia squinted.

Light snuck through windows under a vaulted roof, highlighting the bell's aquamarine patina.

There were no ropes. No sprockets or gears. Nothing suggesting how it rang. The silo's only other structure was a rickety wooden staircase, leading to the top. Perhaps for cleaning or maintenance.

Surely, the servants didn't climb it on the hour — and more often for dinner service — to ring the bell.

"The others tell me that your husband's grandfather commissioned the clock tower after his daughter's gifts with plants emerged." Bree gestured her forward toward a smaller set of stone steps hidden in the shadows. "These lead to Lady Siodina's greenhouse."

Now Erik's. Maybe that's why he spent so much time up there. It was a connection to his mother. Or maybe she read too much into the maid's nugget of gossip.

Two flights above, an archway opened to a landing. Another staircase. This one was also absent of torches.

Several thudding heartbeats passed before Maia's vision adjusted. Even then, she could only see several paces in front of her outstretched hand.

"At the end of the passage, a door opens to… you guessed it. More stairs. Seven stories up, they lead to the greenhouse. They are steep but candles line the walls."

Silence settled around them. Somehow more comfortable in the dark. Instinct told her not to fill it. Perhaps it was because they couldn't see each other's faces.

And then she realized — why someone would abandon their family. Would work as a servant to the Faeblood oppressors directly responsible for their suffering. She wanted Bree to say the words, if only to acknowledge the grip they had on the maid.

Maia straightened, and in a tone reserved for leading the younger militia fighters, she asked, "Why are you here, Bree?"

More silence stretched, interrupted by the scrape of Bree's slippers along the floor. At the end of the passage, a door squeaked on its hinges, revealing dozens of lit candles, their flames bathing Bree's outline.

"What else could it be?" Bree asked, her voiced returned to normal. "I've come for revenge."

Bree's eyes flashed. Golden and bright.

Her confession eddied out of Maia's mind, leaving a tiny kernel of truth, a sour taste on her tongue, and a warning not to probe further.

CHAPTER SEVENTEEN

"Will you show me the library after the greenhouse?" Maia asked, some unknown power compelling her.

She glanced down at the crude map in her hand. Huh. How did that get there? She stowed it away, her movements slow. "What did you say?"

"Nothing, milady." Bree climbed the steps. "I'd be happy to take you to the Faeblood library."

With her promise, Maia followed. One hundred and forty-three steps led to Erik's greenhouse. The trek was seven stories to another world.

Constructed of the same strange stone as the clock tower, the greenhouse was six times the size of the solarium. Larger, when you included the outside gardens and terrace overlooking the sprawling forest.

"Breathtaking, isn't it?" Bree asked. "Dezee sends me up here to harvest herbs and vegetables for meals, flowers for bouquets. Lord Erik packs baskets of his best for the nearby villages. Delivered every second and fifteenth day of the moon cycle."

"And when he was away?" Erik never mentioned...

"We took turns tending the garden." Bree trailed her fingers over a squat potted palm. "Only killed a few plants. The deliveries never stopped."

Bree meandered ahead.

Maia followed, halting every so often to admire the individual blooms. Soon, she lost sight of the maid.

Rows and rows of raised vegetable beds occupied one half of the greenhouse. Placards on each end labeled the different varieties. She recognized tomatoes and peppers, bold produce shouting their variety. Cucumbers dangled off vines, some as large as her forearm. Others perfect for pickling.

She scrunched her nose.

Hundreds of eggplants littered the soil. At the compound, Cook found about two dozen different ways of disguising the vegetable. For Maia, it wasn't the somewhat bland taste that bothered her. She couldn't abide the texture.

But a hungry belly wasn't picky. By the looks of the plants, the villagers would receive enough mushy purple squash to last until the next delivery.

A collection of pots contained cooking herbs and spices, their soil a lighter color than the rich loam in the beds. Next to a tower of old cauldrons, a large potting bench — with its dinged top and fading paint — held clay jugs and glass bottles full of dark brown liquid.

No wonder he stayed up here for hours. A garden this size… it would need a small crew to maintain.

She wandered to the end of the next row, trailing her fingertips along the fronds daring to hang over the edging. The path widened, opening to a small stone table directly under the peak of the dome. Shadows, cast from metal frames securing panels of glass, formed an intricate pattern on the crushed stone.

A large succulent commanded the center. Cursed Itchweed.

Maia shuddered, unconsciously scratching her neck.

Its distorted stem supported a large pod that opened and

closed like a clamshell. Perfect for snaring flies and mosquitos, but if one rubbed up against it, the sap caused instantaneous hives. And many milk baths. Ask how she knew.

At the farthest curve of the greenhouse, Maia stumbled upon a patch of Crimson Gillyflowers. Named for their drooping buds, they bloomed overnight in a glorious display of deep reds. The hip-high bushes sagged under their weight.

An elaborate wooden arch opened to a maze. The layout enclosed a small sandstone bench, and if the hedges had been taller, a secret garden of sorts.

As she strolled to the center, loud reds gave way to sharp whites and lush violets and soft pinks.

She sat down and savored their heady scent. Unlike the Cursed Itchweed, Gillyflowers were not rare. Hardy little plants. Villagers with cottage gardens claimed they were invasive and fought a losing battle to keep them from their yards.

Maia traced the pattern on her new sheath.

She pulled out her quill and a fresh piece of parchment. Not to sketch the greenhouse layout — that felt too much like an invasion of Erik's privacy — but to pen a draft of a letter destined for home.

~

My dearest Jade,

ERIK ESCORTED ME TO HIS GREENHOUSE TODAY. WHAT A WONDERFUL place to survey the surrounding forests. The passage travels through the clock tower. It is not well lit — something I complained about to my husband — and I confess I will not likely go there on my own.

He spends much of his time in the sanctuary, often forgoing meetings with other Lords in favor of toiling in the dirt. I am worried that he is adrift, confessing as much to my Lady's maid.

I can hear your censure now. Of course, I should hold my tongue.

Or at least, keep from wagging it in front of the help. But the poor dear is all alone. She hails from the lumber mills and has no family to speak of. I know Xavier forbade contact with those from Kiehl's village, but I can't help enjoying our simple rapport.

Write with all the news of the compound. Give everyone my love.

Yours in Friendship,
Maia

XAVIER CONSIDERED KIEHL — THE LEADER OF THE TERRITORY responsible for harvesting the kingdom's timber — an ally. For appearances, the two leaders staged a feud. Extra trade halted. Normal correspondence cut off. And to Ada's dismay, they forbade travel between the neighboring territories, too.

But the leaders still communicated in secret. And Kiehl sent extra lumber, through hired mercenaries, for the construction of a new watch tower, as promised.

Hopefully, Jade would recognize her ramblings for what they were — a ploy to uncover information about Bree's history. When her assignment was complete, it would be wise to stay in contact with someone inside the Castle. Another reason nudged the crevices of her mind, but she couldn't remember it now.

Maia closed her eyes. Maybe it was the tranquility of this hidden spot — or the warmth of the sun captured by the dome's glazed windows — but her thoughts drifted to her mother.

What would she think of her child?

For so long, Maia had only considered her father's opinion. Only sought his good grace. Would her mother be proud of her accomplishments in the militia? Or ashamed of her nontraditional path?

Her mother had been a gentlewoman. Fair and sweet and fun. Or so her father had told.

Maia's opposite.

In the years since his passing, her thoughts centered on their time together. On what she would give for one last hug. One more kiss. Final words of encouragement.

In this peaceful spot, absent of responsibilities or assumptions, Maia wondered if she'd made a mistake accepting Xavier's mission.

And for the first time, she yearned for her mother's counsel.

Her father would tell her she'd done the right thing. The marriage to Erik a smart one. She was a soldier. Her role was to obey Xavier, following his lead without question. Even if the battle included too many forks instead of weapons. Too many frilly dresses instead of utilitarian chain mail.

Maia lingered on the bench, suddenly unsure of her place. She clutched her letter in one hand, swiping the solitary tear with her other.

"I walked the grounds," Bree said. "Your husband is not here."

Her eyes flew open. Maia cleared her throat, hoping to pass off her melancholy as allergies, and stood.

Either her acting had improved or Bree understood she didn't wish to talk because the maid pasted on a smile and said, "Time to head to the library."

"I'll be down in a moment. I need to gather my things... "

Maia folded the letter, her hands busier than the task required. She refused to look up and verify Bree's departure.

A splotch of ink stained the top corner of the note. Her quill must've rested there when she wasn't paying attention. She tucked both inside Erik's satchel.

The letter wasn't due for another two days, but she could send it tonight, misdirecting any Castle spies who monitored the frequency of her correspondence.

It took half the time to return to the main corridors.

"The Faeblood library is near the solarium." Bree pointed left. "You'll want the third alcove down. A polished gold plate etched with a picture of a book indicates the door. If you find nothing to your tastes, the servants keep a separate stash of novels in our dormitory."

Bree inclined her head.

"Your blood keys the lock. Hold your hand in front of the plate until you hear it unlatch. I must take my leave. Dezee will wonder otherwise. Can you find your way back to your chambers on your own?"

"Wait." Maia's hand shot out.

What if the library was one of places Xavier mentioned? A room locked to his human spies. Since Erik's elixir nullified the marital oath, her blood wouldn't work. But if Bree could enter...

Surely, the servants cleaned the chamber. Something whispered for Maia to ask. Better that than trying and failing to open it herself.

"I don't think my blood will work. Since I'm human." Maia hung her head. Easier to lie to her feet. "Do you have access? For cleaning and... and whatnot?"

"Aye," Bree said, sending Maia a look she couldn't decipher, and led the way.

Two large torches flanked an oiled door. Someone had stained it to blend in with the alcove's paneling. As Bree mentioned, the gold plate boasted an etching of a book. And underneath, two simple words.

Caveat Lector

Caveat was a warning. What did "Lector" mean? She must remember to ask Ada. The first part was accurate. The entire Castle should be a warning.

"Why are you here?" Bree rested her hand on the lever.

"What?" Maia whirled to face her.

"Why are you here?" Bree glanced up and down the hallway. "What's in the library?"

Maia searched her mind for a plausible excuse. As much as she trusted Bree, she wasn't ready to divulge her mission. The map was easier to sell. But Xavier wouldn't want anyone to know his interest in Lord Siodina's mysterious book. It might prompt someone to make it... disappear.

"I need an etiquette guide. Rules of engagement. For Court. Supper and such." Dear gods, she made a mess of this, yammering about the first thing that came to her mind. And because she couldn't seem to stop, Maia added, "I don't know what fork to use."

"Just so I understand..." Bree put her hands on her hips. "You don't mind throwing daggers at heads during tea, but you are worried about cutlery choices. An interesting line you draw."

"I have a temper," Maia explained.

"An understatement."

"It gets the better of me."

"I disagree."

"And I don't want to cause trouble."

"It was an appropriate response."

"Or bring shame to my husband."

"I don't buy your nonsense, Maia Siodina. But I owe you for Lea." She raised her hand to the gold plate. "My distant ancestors possessed a drop of Faeblood. Baba told tales of our line descending from the lost city of Atlantia. If you could believe it."

"Mmm-hmm," Maia muttered. She bit her tongue, unsure of a more appropriate response.

The door opened. Bree pushed her way inside, Maia on her heels.

A large worktable anchored the room. Scrolls and pieces of parchment strewn on its surface. And on one end sat—

"What is it?" Lady Stella asked. She didn't bother to look up from the heavy tome in front of her. "I am not to be disturbed."

"I'll take my leave." Bree gestured widely. "You can deal with... them."

"Excellent." Lady Stella flicked her wrist. "Now, we must contend with the stench of a single human."

Her companion — a willowy Lady who Maia recognized from tea but couldn't recall her name — teetered on the edge of her seat and snickered. Lady Stella paid her as much attention as she did Maia. That didn't stop her from leaning closer.

"My thanks," Maia said to Bree, ignoring the taunt. "I shall see you before supper."

Bree left. The sound of the door shutting was as loud as a bear's sneeze.

"What do you want?" Lady Stella lifted her head. "Can humans even read?"

Another snicker.

"Read. Fight. Ride." Maia let innuendo seep into the last. "Erik sent me for some references on plant cultivation."

Better if they thought she came at his direction. If she ran across something on herbology, she could carry it with her then use it as an excuse to return. Though she must find a time when Bree could let her back in.

Maia glanced around. The space was smaller than she expected. Similar in size to the shops in her village. Books covered every available space. Her best estimate — a few thousand lined the walls and shelves.

"Interesting. Plants, you say? Your *husband* asked the same of me."

Lady Stella sat back, a gleam in her eye. She dismissed Maia and studied the proprietary hand on her forearm. A silent command passed between the Ladies.

After several tense seconds, long enough for the minion to decide whether to object or follow orders, Lady Doesn't-Add-Much-To-The-Conversation stood. She bowed low to Stella and left without so much as a farewell.

"Ah." Maia smirked. "Bootlickers inhabit every layer of society."

"Watch yourself."

"Or what? You'll insult my heritage?" She swept her arm downward. "My clothes? Surrounded by so much knowledge, it's a shame you can't come up with something clever, original."

"Envy is unbecoming." Lady Stella stacked the loose parchment and rolled the larger scrolls, securing them with leather binding.

"I don't envy your companion."

"I wasn't talking about *her*." Stella closed her book, tucking it under her arm. "Tell Erik that I'll see him later."

With that last insult burrowing into Maia's side, Lady Stella sauntered out of the library.

Maia allowed herself one swear word before she haphazardly pulled down journal after journal. Book after book. Asinine tome after asinine tome, off the shelves.

She read the first few pages of each, muttering as she went. After ten books, her furious skimming snagged on the word *Ortus.*

Maia turned it over.

Faecraft: A Handbook of Binding Curses and Summoning Rituals, 3rd Edition
Author Unknown

On the title page, someone had drawn an elaborate house crest. Underneath, in sprawling cursive, was a signature.

Property of Emsworth Siodina

Erik's father. Huh. Maia returned to the section that caught her eye.

In the year of thirteen dragons, ancient travelers from Toplith crossed the Strait of Vian. They discovered an abandoned stronghold in Morvak, the once prosperous military civilization of winged Spartans.

Legend claims the gods smote the mighty warriors, wiping their existence from the realm.

Centuries passed. The Castle lay forgotten. Our ancestors — whether from tales flying across the water or an ability to detect magic deep in the mountain — claimed the stronghold.

For decades, non-magical humans and those who harbored Faeblood lived in harmony. It wasn't until the strength of casting declined with each birth that the King's advisors turned to forgotten writings on the origin of magic and its limitations.

Faeblood powers passed down through blood but occasionally sprouted in barren families. For every new caster, the magic of the exiting generation weakened. As if stemming from a finite well.

It was the first ruler, King Reimar, who instituted the Rite of Ortus. A brilliant solution for preserving the lines. He cursed humans who exhibited powers in childhood, binding their magic in wounds on their wrists. The scarring was symbolic — a permanent form of shackles.

After the death of the King and collapse of the monarchy, the knowledge of the Rite went to select ruling families.

The chapter cut off half-way down the page. Maia flipped to the next. Blank. The one after held an incantation for truth serum.

She started again at the beginning of the book, skimming each paragraph. Dozens of curses and rituals filled the rest of the pages. If the author would not explain the cast, why include this history? Perhaps the details stayed with those select families.

One thing was clear, the High Table had fed the territories a bunch of Faeblood propaganda.

Her father shared stories of the first settlers. How the magical nobles fought against invaders, saving the humans. It was a washed version of events, of why the territories served the Castle. A debt inherited from their great-great grandparents.

Ember. Dear gods, no wonder her story was so remarkable. Not only did her magic appear outside the fortress walls. But her powers rivaled those within. She *was* a threat. Though not in the way Xavier predicted.

And Lea. She would need to question the child. Was she a product of a dalliance between a human Red Guard and a noble? Or did her powers stem from the mountain? Though did it really matter?

Regardless, Maia would find a way to spare her from the Rite.

~

"MILORD," BREE SAID THROUGH THEIR CHAMBER DOOR. "I CAME to assist Lady Maia with preparations for dinner."

Erik frowned and shrugged on his tunic.

He returned from foraging in the southern forests twenty minutes ago. Enough time for a hasty bath and quick change of clothes. He assumed Maia left earlier for pre-dinner drinks in the solarium.

"I thought she was with you," Erik said in greeting.

Mikel rounded the corner and must've caught sight of Erik's expression because his pace quickened. "Maia?"

"She didn't return?" Bree asked. "I left her in the library at ten bells. That was—"

"Nine hours ago." Erik ran his hand over his hair. "And you haven't seen her since?"

"Dezee stationed me at tea then with Lea in the kitchens." She turned to Mikel. "I assumed you would find her."

Maia had ordered Mikel to sleep after night watch. By the looks of the dark purple smudges under the fighter's eyes, he'd disregarded it.

"Where have you been?" Erik growled, not caring if Mikel was her family. The fighter had a singular mission.

"Which one?" Mikel cupped the back of Bree's arm.

Which one? Which one what?

"The Faeblood library," was all Bree said. "Time probably slipped away from her, 'tis all."

That wasn't like her. Maia thrived on routine, following a rigid schedule.

Erik took off at a sprint.

Please be safe. Please be safe. He'd tie her to their bed if that's what it took.

Please be safe. Please be safe. Until she listened to reason. Aye. He would give her an earful.

Please be safe. Please be safe. Then a timepiece. Do dresses have pockets? No matter. She liked pants better.

Erik dodged groups of nobles gathering in the halls. He almost plowed into Lady Stella emerging from the solarium. Mikel stayed close behind. Bree farther back, clutching her skirts.

They reached the library. He waved his hand in front of the gold plate, opening the door with his other.

His heart dropped at the sight before him.

Maia slumped on the worktable. Her head lolled to the side. No blood.

A firm grip clamped down on his shoulder.

"Sleeping," Mikel whispered.

Erik padded around the table. His hand trembled as he

brushed the curtain of hair off her cheek. He noted the subtle rise and fall of her chest. The healthy complexion. His heart didn't slow.

Bree skidded to a stop in front of the door, her hand flying to her chest.

"Bollocks." She stepped into the room. "Go on. I'll clean up in here and send a tray to your chambers."

"Wait." Erik gestured to the small stack of books. She spent all day in here. These must be important. "Bring them with you."

He pulled back her chair and scooped her in his arms. Mikel scowled, grabbed the books, and trailed after Bree. Good. Erik wasn't happy about this either. Anything could have happened. If his father…

She snuggled into the column of his throat and sighed.

He tightened his hold. Best not to drop her. Erik spent the journey back to their chambers calming his temper.

He bent down, careful not to jostle her, and yanked back the covers.

She stirred, muttering something under her breath that sounded suspiciously like *prick*.

That he was. She may not like him, but Erik would keep her safe until she left.

"Maia," he whispered as he set her down. When she didn't wake up, he tried again. "Kitten."

More muttering.

He unlaced her boots and tugged them off. The dagger and sheath came next. He paused, appreciating the intricate design. No surprise, she'd already charmed the staff.

"Wake up," he repeated, louder this time. "You can't sleep in your leathers."

Her lids fluttered. She fumbled with the cord binding their front. Eventually, she untied the knot and shimmied them down her legs. They caught on her ankles. She fell back against the pillow, a snuffle snore escaping her lips.

He should wait for Bree, but it could take ages to put together a tray during the supper rush. Erik averted his eyes, yanked off the leathers, and covered her lower half with the blankets.

The trembling in his hand stopped.

What was he going to do with her? She couldn't be left alone during the day. Couldn't follow him around. If he spent any more time in her company, he was bound to do something foolish — like bed her. Or worse, kiss her.

Knock. Knock. Knock.

Bree returned with a tray of food.

"Stay with her." He didn't miss the flash of ire in her eyes. Nor did he care enough to smooth out his harsh tone. "If she wakes, make sure she eats. I'll speak with Dezee."

"Where are you going?" She didn't bother with civility either.

"Out." He shut the door. It was an effort not to slam it. To the shadows he said, "I don't care how it comes to pass, but figure out a schedule with Bree. Maia is not to be left alone."

Erik set off for the great hall, not waiting for Mikel's response. It was just as well. He would've been more irate when it never came.

CHAPTER EIGHTEEN

A tray of breakfast meats and biscuits lay on the bed in Erik's spot. Beside it, the book on Faecraft.

Maia rubbed her eyes. That blasted thing. So intent on her search, she must've fallen asleep in the library.

Dawn crawled through the open balcony doors. Bollocks. She'd missed dinner. Faeblood hours were terrible. Used to going to bed early and waking up before the roosters, her body would need more time to adjust to the Castle schedule, it seemed.

She must remember to thank Mikel for carrying her back. And for the tray he ordered. Her stomach grumbled its agreement.

Maia dressed and slathered butter on a flaky biscuit. The first bite melted in her mouth, and a hint of cinnamon hit her palate. She swallowed a groan.

Yesterday, she'd scoured the library for hours. Rows of texts revealed no other mentions of the Rite of Ortus or other curses that bound magic. Worse, she didn't discover anything that might be Siodina's mysterious book.

She should find Bree and spend another day there. But

instead of setting off for another failed attempt, she leaned back against her pillow, her thoughts straying to Leatrix.

Raw hunger simmered in the girl's eyes. Most would see a spirited lass.

But when Maia had looked — when she'd stopped and studied the girl in the armory — she'd seen herself.

"Girls don't serve in the militia." Her father's words. *"That doesn't mean they can't."*

His support made all the difference.

Oh, he was a strict taskmaster, demanding perfection.

She was grateful for the extra work. The endless repetitions. Grateful that he pushed and pushed when even her pride wanted to yield to fatigue and soreness.

Dread and disappointment twisted her gut as she dressed in her militia attire. There wasn't anyone who could fill that role for Lea.

Erik was busy doing who knew what. Soon, the High Table would take up more time. Mikel could help, but Xavier ordered him to protect her, not play bodyguard/nursemaid/weapons master.

I could do it, a quiet voice whispered.

So she would train the lass. Then what?

She could sneak her out of the Castle. Or Erik could balance her ledger. Xavier would agree to it. Maybe the girl could stay with Ada until Maia returned to the compound.

These were dangerous thoughts... reckless thoughts... and yet, she couldn't stem them once they took root.

An image took shape in her mind: Train Lea. Keep her from the Rite. Dissuade her from joining the Red Guard. Guide her toward the militia.

She would worry about the last later. Maia possessed the skills. Time is what she needed.

That and her husband's blessing, his coin. It rankled — more than she would admit out loud — begging for something so simple.

She peeked into the hallway and beckoned Mikel, wishing for a friend to lend her strength.

His head filled the crack, but his body remained in the corridor.

Maia swallowed a snarky retort. It wasn't the time to chastise him for bowing to Erik's tirade about entering their chambers. Not when she needed him to help with her plan.

"Do you know where Erik went?" she asked, hoping he wasn't in a council meeting. Or worse.

Mikel grunted. "Greenhouse."

"Will you accompany me?" she asked, not quite concealing the relief in her tone.

Maia wasn't sure what she would have done if Mikel had named a Lady's chambers. Most of the Lords kept mistresses. Since their marriage was in name only, it would be churlish if she denied Erik that basic need.

Still, a treacherous part of her was glad he tended his flowers, not another noble at Court.

"Why?" Mikel asked.

"Why, what?"

"Why do you need to see Erik?"

"I have a request for him. Why the inquiry?"

"I see how you look at him." He shifted his weight.

A subtle movement, one her training noticed. The real question was — why did Mikel assume his fighting stance? When he didn't elaborate, she shrugged it off.

Yesterday had been a long day. Today might be even longer. Maybe she was mistaken. So she added a bit of levity to the truth. For his sake.

"How? As if I'm one breath from punching his lights out?"

But Mikel just gave her a look. It wasn't the exasperation he so often reserved for Ada's antics. Not pity, either. Close though.

"They aren't meant for us."

Layers. Mikel had more layers than even Xavier suspected. She would let it go for now. It would've been better if he just shouted, *Be Careful.*

Dark circles ringed his eyes. How long had he been awake?

She knew the answer without asking just as she knew it would be pointless to push him. When this was over, she would repay his kindness. Perhaps lead the scouts, so he could sleep for a few days. Or better yet, a week straight.

He pivoted and took off toward the clock tower.

~

ERIK DONNED A PAIR OF THIN, DEER-HIDE GLOVES.

Helispore was a delicate plant. Hard to keep alive, it required precise soil conditions. Faeblood valued it for its magical roots. One nibble produced a relaxed state.

This particular specimen was a gift from his mother when he was five, a mere week before her disappearance. The last of its kind.

He dug up a small offshoot, careful of its anemic stalk, and snipped a tip of root. Bits of soil fell to his potting bench as he inspected the cutting.

A white powder coated the sample. Not again. He must ask Dezee for more botanical soap. Erik repotted the original plant in a bigger container and placed the offshoot in its own bowl.

He fell into a rhythm, his mind clearing with the simple tasks. He was more centered in the greenhouse than anywhere else in the Castle. It was one of the few places his anger did not threaten to consume him.

As a child, he'd shared this refuge with his mother. More precisely, she'd shared it with him. His earliest, most vivid memories of her were here, covered in petals and dirt and smiles, working at this same battered bench.

As the years passed, it was difficult to recall her features. Her hair was several shades darker than his, an inky black similar to the rich loam of the marshes deep in the northern forests.

He couldn't recall her voice. Or her laughter. But her scent lingered in his memories. Most days, the smell of damp moss overpowered her signature mixture of ripe cherries and Crimson Gillyflowers.

As with his recollection, clues to her disappearance dried up a decade ago. 'Twas as if she never existed.

Nobody spoke of her. Nobody acknowledged his father had married. Lost in his own sorrows, Erik didn't remember if his sire even grieved.

And when Erik died, her memory would, too.

What would she think of his choices? Would she be proud of him? There were days when he could not hold his reflection in the looking glass.

And what about Mikel? Did he know her? Did he serve his mother? Where was he when she vanished without a note? As if conjured from his thoughts, the fighter climbed the ladder to the greenhouse.

Mikel was not alone.

"Good morning." Maia's gaze lingered on his pendant. "I have a favor to ask."

From the stunned expression on Mikel's face, the bodyguard didn't know her plans.

"I'm listening." He removed his gloves. "And intrigued. It must be important."

"I wish for you to pay off a servant girl's debt."

"Is that all?" He scoffed.

"Aye," she said and took a step forward. "Humans have a choice. Do they not? To serve the Castle or take their chances in the territories?"

Mikel's face darkened.

Indeed, the fighter was unaware of his wife's intentions. Otherwise, Mikel would have corrected her assumptions.

Freedom was an illusion, a facade crafted by the Faeblood to keep a steady supply of workers. The option to stay after one's eighteenth birthday was no choice at all.

Sure, for a steep price, humans could leave.

They had to pay the equivalent in gold for every year the Castle housed them. For every meal they ate in the kitchens. Ledgers balanced by midlife, a time when most humans had married, had children. Their ties to the system harder to break.

"The servants may leave when they are of age." He wiped his hands on his pants. The gloves kept most of the soil from coating his palms but not all. "After they undertake the Rite. After they pay for their keep."

"And if they purchase their freedom prior to their eighteenth summer?" She crossed her arms over her chest.

"Do not waste your breath." Erik pried his eyes back to her face. He was a bastard for staring, especially since this conversation meant something to her. "My father will not allow it."

"Convince him." Maia grabbed his wrist. "Convince him to spare her, at least, from the Rite. She is a gifted archer. And she desires to enter the Red Guard academy. If they take that from her—"

"You ask too much." He turned away, studying the heavy clouds. Last night, rain lashed the Castle, leaving behind a blanket of fog.

"If it's about the coin... Xavier will pay you back. I'm sure of it."

"My actions are not my own. Soon, I will belong to the High Table, the Lords. I suggest you forget this nonsense and remember to whom you belong."

He couldn't look at her.

"Please." The simple word hung between them, curling over his shoulders and lodging in his chest.

He stiffened and said, "No."

MAIA BRUSHED PAST MIKEL, HER FOOTSTEPS LIGHT AND QUICK ON the stone floor.

She didn't look at him. Didn't speak. It was as if her hurt blinded her to everything else.

He should follow. If she stayed in her head, she presented an easy target. It was his duty to keep her safe, but his feet rooted to the greenhouse floor as she climbed down the ladder, out of sight.

"You find me in the wrong," Erik said. Not a question.

"No." Wrong wasn't the correct word. Harsh, maybe. But the Faeblood heir couldn't change decades of tradition for one child. The Lords would use the soft-hearted gesture against him.

This situation with Leatrix was... complicated. And familiar. He adjusted his cuffs.

Mikel's gifts manifested when he was a toddler. Instead of a bow, he favored an axe. At five years old, he could sever a branch twenty paces away with the small-handled ones the Red Guard looped in their belt. At six, he could hit a bullseye at a hundred paces with the longer blades designed for splitting logs.

End-over-end they sailed, weighing no more than a feather in his palm and obliterating hay bales in the armory. He knew it then, even if he never told a soul that an inkling of magic flowed through his human veins.

Mikel had picked up a second axe the spring before he'd turned seven. In the Castle's shadows, he'd studied the Red

Guard, practicing their stances and movements late into the night.

Aided by his powers, he transformed into a deadly weapon before he needed to shave.

"I would say the same," Mikel added.

"Then we are both heartless for the right reasons."

Erik ran his hands through his close-cropped hair. Something the Faeblood heir did more in the last few days than all the months at the compound.

"I cannot ask my father for this, no matter my wishes. My appointment to the High Table is not secure. In the event I win the vote, I cannot beg favor as my first order of business. It is unwise to start in their debts."

"Why not say that?" Mikel asked. "Defend your position?"

"You know Maia." Erik stacked and unstacked some of the smaller pots on the bench. "She does not see the bigger picture."

"You're shortsighted." He smirked. A small part of him enjoyed Erik's irritation at this discussion.

"She would argue until her face turned purple. Or until she held a dagger at my throat. And for what? A single life? The child is in no danger. I cannot alter her destiny."

Lea was a threat, but Erik was too busy bickering with his father to see it. The High Lords would silence the child's magic. Same as his.

Erik was right about Maia's tactics — she preferred brute force to honeyed words. But he made an incorrect assumption about her motives.

"Perhaps." Mikel shrugged. "She values the individual. Makes her an excellent trainer."

Erik studied him.

"She sees people. Often when they don't see themselves."

"Here I thought you a pretty brute out to toy with his opponents for sport."

"Think I'm pretty?" Mikel's smirk widened to a grin.

"Since you are chatty this morning, satisfy my curiosity." Erik inclined his head towards Mikel's cuffs. "What's your story?"

"Couldn't wring the truth out of Dezee?" he asked, baring his canines. His reprieve was over.

"I'd rather hear it from your lips." Erik unsheathed a dagger.

Mikel tensed.

Erik turned and pruned the brown fronds on the underside of the nearest fern.

"Same as Lea's." It was easier talking to Erik's back. "Except I favor axes."

"What happened?"

"I wanted to impress the High Lords, hoping for a recommendation to join the Red Guard academy early." Mikel released a bark of laughter. "So I entered the Grimoire Games."

"The competition is designed for young adults." Erik paused. "How old were you?"

"Shy of seven summers."

"A lad." Erik shook his head and sliced a branch. "And to be defeated so publicly."

"I won the tournament." Mikel paused. "I won too well, humiliating favorites of the current Red Guard. The Lords snatched me from my bed that night. Performed the Rite of Ortus in our dormitory. My magic — gone. No replacement."

He swallowed, clearing his throat.

"I plotted my revenge. Dezee kept me out of trouble. Kept my head on my neck. And when I had the chance, I paid off my debt and left."

"How old were you?"

"Nineteen." He ground his teeth.

"Where does a nineteen-year-old servant find enough gold to settle their ledger?" Erik whirled around.

A foolish question, one to which Erik should know the answer.

There are many ways a servant could earn extra coin.

Gossip was the easiest. A hazard of the job. Why not make a few coppers selling what fell into his lap? It wasn't difficult to keep track of the inclinations of courtiers. Who coveted whom. Which marriage contracts were close to completion. What partners met behind closed doors before the ink dried on the parchment.

Secrets on lineages paid the most. Almost as much as rich Ladies paying young, virile lads to service them.

Erik knew all of this, but the bastard still pressed. He turned on his heel, and over his shoulder he said, "You know how. Story time is over."

"Wait," Erik called out, a hitch in his voice. "Humor me with one more question."

Mikel halted and rested his hand on the doorframe.

"My mother, Lady Siodina, did you know her?"

How much did it cost Erik to ask that? The young Lord surprised him — revealing his cards so early. Perhaps he was not as cunning as his father.

"How much does a servant know a Faeblood?"

"Don't play with me." Erik took a step forward, his fists balling at his side. "The servants know all that transpires within these walls. You must've heard something."

Mikel considered his options.

He truly didn't know Lady Siodina beyond observing her from afar. Unlike other high-ranking Faeblood, she kept to herself. She stayed in this very greenhouse, nurturing her plants, her young son.

He never held the impression she enjoyed Court life, but then again, he viewed everything at the Castle through the lens of adolescent rage. He learned nothing Erik would find useful.

But he wouldn't waste this opportunity.

"Sponsor Maia in the Games."

Xavier had pulled Mikel aside and confided his plans. His

leader wanted information on the Red Guard. No better way to acquire it than as a recruit. Besides, it was a better use of her time than attending tea parties.

Everyone knew contenders from the territories never won. It wasn't in the Castle's interests. But... if a High Lord's heir sponsored her, maybe she had a chance. Or at least a fair fight.

"I wondered if you dared ask. Xavier and his scheming..." Erik shook his head. "Foolish, but who am I to question."

"Question? No. Help? Sponsor? Aye. If you want the information, that is."

"Don't play with me." Erik sheathed his dagger, a fine tremor making the task more difficult.

Mikel had him. Perhaps the viciousness of Court left its mark.

"Everything has its price. You, of all people, should understand. This is mine. Sponsor Maia. My information is yours."

Mikel held his stare. He nurtured the reputation of a jester at the compound, a carefully crafted mask. It was easier to allow everyone to see an irreverent brute, so he forced another grin.

"Even if she places in the competition, they may never accept a female into the academy." Erik tossed a browned frond onto a pile of refuse near his bench.

"Your time away from the Castle has weakened your tongue. I never stipulated the outcome of the Games. Merely that you sponsor Maia."

Betting on Erik's honor was risky. Mikel was loath to admit it, but a part of him expected the Lord to step up and protect Maia. And if he was wrong, well... Mikel would take care of it himself.

Erik straightened and held out his hand. "A deal, then."

CHAPTER NINETEEN

"Again," Maia instructed Leatrix. Her tunic clung to her lower back. "Shift your weight to the center. You favor your front foot."

After a fruitless hour in the library, Maia convinced Dezee that she needed Lea's services. They skipped afternoon tea. Again. She was busy, not hiding.

They returned to the armory to gather supplies. Mikel carried their haul. A few daggers and a wooden bullseye later, the trio found themselves in a small clearing outside the fortress's gaze.

The second event in the Grimoire Games, after archery, featured throwing daggers. Might as well keep her skills sharp and teach Lea at the same time.

Mikel leaned against the nearest tree, content in the sliver of shade. Content to hoard his advice.

"Steady your breath. Don't trap it." She placed her hands on either side of Lea's ribs, trying very hard not to obsess over Erik's decision in the greenhouse. Selfish, insufferable prick.

"But my center—"

"Use your belly muscles to stabilize your body, not your

lungs." Maia squeezed, picturing Erik's handsome head on the target. "Push against my palms. Do you feel it? Exhale on the release."

Maia stepped back.

Lea nodded and threw her blade. The small dagger hit the bullseye but didn't lodge into the straw. If that were Erik's face, it would've nicked his irritatingly straight nose.

"Gah." Lea stomped over and picked it up. "They won't stick."

"Give it time." Maia bit back her smirk. "Your aim is true. You need a little more meat on your bones."

She crouched down, resting a hand on Lea's shoulder.

"You know, Cook from back home says fighters need to eat their favorite dishes so they grow big and strong."

"Like Mikel?"

"Like Mikel. Chocolate cake is my favorite. It's so rich it makes my eyes close when I take a bite." Maia paused, glancing at the dagger in Lea's hands. "What if I... we... could offer you something else, something other than the Red Guard? Something better?"

Lea's lips tightened.

Too soon. Too quick. When she didn't respond, Maia added, "I could send you to my home where you could grow big and strong. Far away from the Ladies at Court."

The lass took a step back. Maia let her arm drop.

"The others... they whisper about your leader," Lea said to her feet. "I don't want to leave the Castle. Or Mistress Dezee. She gives me warm milk at bedtime and tucks teddy in beside me."

She never considered the Lords might poison the servants against the territories. Just as she underestimated the bond the servants shared with one another. Maia opened her mouth to protest, but she caught Mikel shaking his head.

"Don't," he mouthed.

A simple request. And if anyone else had asked, one she would disregard. Maia stood, brushed off invisible dust on her leathers, and forced a smile.

"Then let's make you the best dagger thrower in the Castle." Maia lined up beside her, blade in hand. "Ground yourself from your feet to your arms. Exhale on the release."

They threw in unison. Maia's dagger buried in the target while the tip of Lea's dug enough to stay in the straw. They raised their arms in the air and whooped.

"Excellent work." Erik strolled into the clearing.

Lea whirled around, her smile faltering, and bowed. "Lord Siodina."

He was shirtless. Sweat slicked his skin. A broad sword hung in a scabbard at his side. A smaller rapier in his outstretched hands.

Why was he here? *Where was his shirt?*

"Pull the blades and join me." He flicked his chin to the straw bale.

Maia helped Lea with the daggers. They left them with Mikel and strolled over to Erik.

"Assume first position," Erik said. He handed the smaller rapier to Lea and pulled the larger one for himself. Both hands wrapped around its hilt. His knees bent into a fighting stance.

Maia studied his foot positions. *Don't look at his chest.* Her eyes betrayed her and flicked up. Gah.

Lea mimicked his posture, checking and rechecking until she adjusted every limb to her satisfaction.

"This is the Rhiya Strike, a combination named after a diminutive Fae warrior from a millennia ago. She was cunning and crafty and fearless."

Erik demonstrated the sequence, taking extra time for each transition.

"Parry right. Slice right, then drop low and jab the midsection. Use the momentum to roll across your opponent's front, popping up on their blind side."

Lea replicated the strikes, albeit slower and a little disjointed. Her tongue stuck out of the corner of her mouth. The blade was too long. Her arms shook under its weight.

"Keep an angle." He corrected the height of the tip then stepped back, allowing her room to move.

"She's a quick study." Erik's shoulders brushed Maia's. He handed her the broad sword and said, "Your turn."

Too stunned at his sudden appearance, she took it without comment. Maia wrapped both palms around the leather handle, adjusting her grip.

Erik curled behind her, and his signature scent of spicy cloves wafted off his warm skin.

She leaned back. What was wrong with her? *Prick.* She must remember he was a prick.

"Choke up on the hilt." He moved her hands. "I spoke with the blacksmith. He will have a sword for Lea tomorrow. You can use the one she has now."

He dropped his arms and gestured for her to join Lea.

They moved through the combination together. Maia's body shook from the effort.

"Good," Erik said. "Feel the transition. Let one flow into the next. Change your level."

They dropped. Maia's thighs burned from balancing the sword in a crouched position. She glanced over. It was the same for Lea.

"A slice to the leg hinders your opponent. In a battle with more than one opposition, you cannot linger down there. Roll out and pop up as soon as you are free of their counterstrike. It's not enough to memorize the forms. A good soldier understands why the sequence works."

Maia tucked her head to her chin, following the path of her

blade. The soft grass cushioned her somersault. She was grateful they practiced outside instead of the armory.

She shot to her feet, assuming a ready stance. Huh. Not so different than striking.

It would take time for her body to memorize the pattern, but she could do this. She must do this. That is... if she wanted to win the Games.

For the past two decades, sword forms were the last event. Ada had sent a book detailing the twelve combinations, but Maia preferred to learn through *doing,* not reading.

She'd be a fool to ignore his instruction. Not that she'd admit that to Erik.

"Excellent." He clapped. "Again."

Maia and Lea fell in sync.

It was difficult to keep up with her smaller partner, and soon the blade became unbearably heavy. Lea smirked and launched into another round. Surely, they must be close to the end. The tremors in her arms transformed into full-blown wobbles. Sweat poured from her brow.

"Together. In sequence," Erik said. "First position."

Her body responded without thinking. Her mind emptied of worries. How to keep Lea safe. Gone. How to blend into society. Gone. How to find the journal. Gone. How to avoid stabbing Erik.

Well... that one stayed.

She kept a steady count in her head, focusing on her breathing.

This was her happy place — where her muscles took over on instinct. She didn't need to glance over to know it was the same for Lea.

Erik commissioned a sword.

Maia's stomach fluttered. It was a practical gift. Erik might not spare the girl from the Rite, but it was... something. Not an apology. She wasn't even sure if he knew the phrase, *I'm sorry.*

But it was something.

"Excellent form." Erik rested his hand on Lea's shoulder and bent down. "Return to the Castle with Mikel. Make sure you rinse off before Dezee sees you."

"Thank you, milord." Lea bowed, presenting the rapier in her outstretched hands.

Erik took the blade.

"You're still a prick," Maia said, waiting until Lea was out of earshot. She handed him hers.

"I know."

"Though at times even pricks can be nice."

"Is that what you tell yourself?" He re-sheathed the broad sword and took three steps, crowding her space. "You want to think me a decent male? Go ahead. I won't waste words trying to correct the assumption."

"Then why are you here?"

Erik shrugged. "I'm bored."

Maia waited. She crossed her arms over her chest, her foot tapping out a rhythm.

"I will not interfere with the Rite or balance Lea's ledger." Erik held up a hand, warding off her protest. "But the child wishes to join the Red Guard?"

"That is her desire."

"Then she should practice with more than her bow. In another decade, she can compete with the others in the Games for a spot in the academy."

Maia's lips pressed together. Why *was* he here? Surely, it was for something other than boredom.

"… and since I'm in a gracious mood, I'll even sponsor your bid this year."

"But I thought Xavier—"

"Ah, Kitten, I caught you unawares. You are my wife. As such, your allegiance and your actions and your *body*…" He paused, grinning. "They all belong to me. It's our way."

Erik rested the small blade against his shoulder and turned on his heel, cutting off her retort.

"Come with me. I want to show you something," he added as he strode deeper into the woods without glancing to confirm she followed.

Curiosity calmed her temper. The walk and fresh air helped too. Their path wound between towering pines and prickly Windroot, ending at the edge of the bluff.

One of the lake's larger fingers spilled over and crashed on the boulders below. A river grew out of the base, carving the territories downstream. The water led right to the barracks. To home.

"This way." Erik pointed to the right and disappeared behind a wall of vines. His hand shot out of the vegetation, clamped on her wrist, and pulled her through.

What—

She wanted to tell him to stop tugging her around like a rag doll, but the censure died on her lips.

Maia blinked, dumbfounded. She stood in a cave the size of the solarium. A large pool spanned the entire width. A very large, very deep pool.

A very neon pool.

Her eyes adjusted. A trickle of light from the forest illuminated the front bank while an eerie pink washed the water's surface.

Why was it always pink?

Some primitive instinct shouted for her to run, not walk, to the Castle. Energy hummed across her skin. An ancient voice screamed for her to leave.

"Come feel it." Erik knelt and propped the rapier against a boulder. He swirled his hand in the water. "This is one of many pools that carve a home in the mountain. Protected from the summer sun, the water stays consistent year-round, both in temperature and volume."

"What is the source of the glow?" She padded over to him.

"The Navitas crystals? They are scattered throughout the tallest peaks of Morvak, marking the graves of ancient Fae trapped in the mountain's maw. The nobles don't consider them a precious gem, so they leave them lodged in their home. Dead useful when exploring."

Creepy. Why were Fae stories so... creepy?

First the wedding ceremony, which etched bonds in the stars and tethered souls across the Veil of Matrimony. Then there was the tale of the rebuffed Fae damming a water source and trapping his beloved in stone when she turned down his proposal.

Maia didn't even want to think about the outlandish rumors of the Nightwalkers — ancestors who drank the blood of their enemies. Legend claimed the gods were so disgusted with the ritual, they banned them from living in the sun.

He stood, removed the belt holding the broadsword, and untied the bindings of his pants.

Her gaze lingered on scars on his back. Before she registered his intentions, Erik undressed and dove into the pool.

"Come. The water will help with your sore muscles."

Her shoulder chose that moment to throb. A consequence from wielding his heavy sword. She could refuse and return to the Castle, chancing a meeting with Lady Stella and her cronies. But he was right, soaking would help.

Death stones and naked Erik it was.

"Turn around." Maia peeled off her clothes. The cavern's cool air singed her overheated skin.

A short trek from the militia compound, there was a hot spring hidden on the edge of the Xavier's territory. She could swim in the aquamarine pool at the base of Ashmere Falls for hours, longer if the girls accompanied her for a picnic, some gossip.

She dove. The ice-cold water stole her breath. Hot springs, this was not.

Maia broke the surface, sputtering. "Why you—"

She swam to the center where Erik lazily treaded water.

His eyes widened when he realized she wasn't stopping.

Maia put all her weight on his shoulders and shoved him under. The pool swallowed her, too.

They resurfaced together, a tangle of wet hair and slippery limbs.

"Hellcat," he said, wrapping his arms around her.

They bobbed together. His chest rumbled against hers with suppressed laughter. He tightened his hold. Her nipples pebbled.

Light from the crystals bounced off his cheekbones. Not so eerie in the water.

"This was our secret when I was a lad."

Erik whispered the confession so softly she nearly asked him to repeat the words. His copper chain floated between them. It was easier to study its engravings than look him in the eye.

"Our?"

"Mine and my mother's." Erik stared at a spot over her shoulder. "During the height of summer, when the drama at Court became sweltering, she rescued me from my tutors, claiming she would finish the lessons herself. The noble my father blackmailed into the role didn't think twice about letting me leave with her."

"And she brought you here." A statement — a chance for his choppy words to steady. "As an escape."

"As a lad, I enjoyed the reprieve from my boring studies. Happy to take a break from learning the ancient tongue. As an adult, I see this grotto for what it meant to her. A refuge from my father. More than the greenhouse."

"Perhaps it was a chance to spend some time with her only

child," she supplied. And guide him away from the negative influence of Court.

A tic appeared in his jaw. It was an effort not to reach up and smooth the flutter.

"Perhaps... though she left when I was five. So much for mother-son bonding."

"What happened?"

"Not much to say. Woke up one day, and she was gone. No note. No goodbyes."

Erik never spoke of his childhood. Back at the compound, he fabricated a story involving the Farming territory to satisfy passing curiosity. There was more than a hint of bitterness in his tone.

"Surely, someone heard something. Your father?" she asked, unsure of what to say.

Was he responsible?

"My father never cared for her. Not in a way a husband should care for his wife. They suffered an arranged marriage."

He dipped his chin and cleared his throat.

"Over the years, I sent inquiries into the territories. Interviewed servants. Tracked every lead, no matter how far-fetched. Nothing. A hunter would say the trail was dry. An experienced one would say there never was a trail to follow."

Erik tugged them to an underwater ledge. He perched Maia on the lip then sat next to her.

"When I was older, I slipped truth serum in his evening wine." One side of his lip curled up. He rested his head against the hard wall. "My father insists the guards sample his food and drink in the great hall. But he thinks our blood connection is stronger than my desire to poison him."

Maia scoffed.

"He never needed a reason to strike me, but when he discovered what I did..." He laughed darkly. "Well, that was plenty an excuse. He didn't stop at my face."

Erik dropped her hand.

"I didn't protest the belt. I was bigger. Stronger. Besides, questions prolonged the punishment. I remember the coppery tang of blood. My failures between lashings to heal the strips of flesh. The hatred in his voice when he spat, *Suffer like a human.*"

He took a shuddering breath and rubbed his shoulder blades back and forth against the rough stone wall.

"Later, I discovered he conjured old magic. Dark magic. The scars sealed a curse in my flesh, forever preventing me from tending myself. He left the rest of my power untouched."

"Faeblood or commoner, no child deserves abuse." She raised her hand to offer comfort but dropped it as fast.

"Feeling sorry for me?" His voice deepened. "Don't."

"You? Never. Past you? Child you? Aye."

"Don't look at me like that. Spare me your pity. Dezee and the Ladies at Court are bad enough."

"I don't pity you." Maia schooled her features. She did. A little.

Her mother died in childbirth, so there was no mystery as to her location. Perhaps the closure, the finality of it all, was better than not knowing.

Erik had been a wee lad left to the whims of a monster. Her father had never figured out how to braid her hair and often forgot to purchase new pants when she sprouted over the summer. But she'd never wondered if he'd loved her.

Maia skimmed her palm on the water's surface.

"I never met my mother. Complicated birth." Her babbling filled the heavy silence. "Short of betraying Xavier or my adopted family, there's not much I wouldn't do — beg or barter or steal — to spend a day with her." *Or father.*

She leaned back against the cold stone wall.

"Theirs was an epic love story," Maia said. "Our family hails from the clan of huntsmen on the western edge of Morvak. My parents were best friends in childhood. Lovers when youthful dreams transformed into adult longing. One night, when father had one too many pints of mead, he confessed to running away to join the militia. After her death, he couldn't stay in their home, seeing her ghost in every room. When I was big enough to travel, we left."

"Not everyone gets their epic tale." Erik's forearm brushed against hers. "Not everyone finds their happy ending."

"Is that what you believe?"

"That's what the world has shown me. Marriage is society's construct for the continuation of the next generation. Love is not required for children."

His father's words? Maia cupped his cheek, turning his face to hers.

"You're right. Love is not a requirement. Doesn't mean it can't be a dream."

Maia pushed off the ledge and swam to the front bank. When her feet found purchase in the shallows, she glanced back and inclined her chin.

"Thank you for bringing me here. And for Lea."

CHAPTER TWENTY

My Dearest Jade,

Today my husband joins the High Table.

I am beside myself with anticipation. Erik would never confess, but pride overwhelms him. And why should it not? Why shouldn't he revel in the satisfaction of claiming his birthright?

My newest ballgown arrived this morning. The skirts are the palest pink satin trimmed with lace of rich raspberry red. My favorite. And the bodice — the seamstress, whatever her name is — she outdid herself with the neckline on this one. The rules of the council do not permit Ladies to witness the vote, but I shall wear it to dinner in the great hall. To please him.

Though I must remember to eat beforehand. The Faeblood Court convenes late, three strokes before midnight, without fail. A sight to behold. All the nobility in one place. At one time.

Listen to me blathering on. No wonder my penmanship suffers. I look forward to your reply. May it contain many congratulations on my new title. High Lady. Oh, I love the sound of that.

Yours in Friendship,
Maia

Maia's words haunted Erik.

"Love is not a requirement. Doesn't mean it can't be a dream." Not only did Erik not have a heart, but it was also foolish for her to assume his still worked.

He crossed an ankle on the top of his thigh and studied her sleeping form from the wing-backed chair near the hearth.

The choice to sponsor her in the Games was simple. Straightforward even. He needed information about his mother's disappearance. Mikel wanted some sort of second-hand revenge. If the servant lass benefited, good. It was great.

But he didn't enjoy lying to Maia. Perhaps the omission was the reason for his bad luck.

Nothing had gone right these last two weeks.

Erik's plants were slow to respond to his care. Neither he nor Lady Stella found a spell or potion to erase their marriage vows in the stars. Maia ignored him.

At least Stella had brewed an antidote to truth serum. He'd divided the vials, giving a portion to Dezee and Mikel, and kept enough for Maia and himself.

His father was up to something.

He could feel it like he could sense the first winter frost from the charge in the air. Instead of spending time these past weeks preparing Erik for the vote, he left him alone.

Erik patted the parchment in his pocket. His speech.

He practiced earlier in front of the looking glass while she slept in his bed. It took all his discipline not to curl behind her, using her luscious body to chase his unease.

Every morning, it was the same. Her glorious hair spread out, soft and messy. As soon as he rose, she snuggled under the blankets, burrowing into his side and hugging his pillow for warmth. She was cold at night, succumbing to the Castle's unnatural chill. So Erik made a habit of adding extra logs to the hearth before bed.

He ran his hand over his mouth and counted her next few breaths.

She was a dreamer. On the outside, Maia strapped daggers to her thighs instead of jewels around her neck. Shot a bow better than the most skilled marksmen in Morvak. Swaggered with a confidence earned, not inherited.

But deep down, she harbored innocent ideals.

Erik didn't want to change her clothes. Her manners. He didn't need a demure damsel. Maia was perfect as she was except for one, not so small, problem.

He wished to rid her of the notion that love was necessary for happiness.

Erik was selfish. He wanted to strip her bare. Cover every inch of her with his tongue. Make her beg for release. He wanted to force her to admit the pesky emotion didn't exist.

Sex and lust, those were assured.

He could make her body sing, hum with desire. But Erik didn't dare act. He wouldn't lose their bet.

"Think to stab me while I sleep?" Maia asked, her voice heavy with the last dredges of slumber.

"Too messy." A half-hearted grin tugged at the corners of his mouth. "Extra work for Bree. Blood is hard to clean out of cotton."

"What are you doing?" She sat up. "What time is it?"

"Late. Never known you to sleep past seven bells. You train too hard."

"It's the dinners." Maia yawned and pinned her arm across her body in an awkward stretch. "Service begins so..." Another yawn. "Late."

"What's wrong with your shoulder?" He stood before he realized his intentions. Erik climbed into bed beside her and tipped up her chin.

"I tore it out of socket as a youth." She rolled it backwards. "It pops in and out with heavy training. At the compound, I visit Ember every few days for a bit of gossip, a bit of pain relief."

"Hold still." The command came out harsher than expected. He massaged the area with both hands, his magic searching for the source of pain. "There's a fair amount of scar tissue."

"That's what Ember claimed." Maia closed her eyes. "She couldn't fix the damage from the initial injury."

"Healers' magic only works on fresh wounds." His palms warmed. "I need you to relax."

The sweet taste of a cast filled his mouth. Erik realigned the joint, stealing as much pain as he could. He drained the last and leaned against the headboard.

"Why are you up so early?" she asked by way of thanks.

"I wanted to review my speech before council." Erik pulled out the folded piece of parchment. "I may not want the position, but my father will punish me for a poor show."

"Is there a possibility you won't gain the votes?"

"No. The other candidates are unsuitable. I'm just going through the motions to ensure my performance is convincing."

"Just because you find them unworthy doesn't mean they won't secure the backing to win." Maia tapped the parchment and added, "Show me what you have so far."

They practiced his speech for the next hour. She made suggestions on words to tweak and reminded him to slow his delivery. The changes were trivial, but they seemed important to her.

Bree interrupted with a tray for brunch. She took one look at them, placed it on the side table, and left, claiming, "I shall return. Later. Much, much later."

"Meet me in the clearing at half past four bells." Erik cleared his throat and refolded the parchment. "I can help with your sword forms. If you want..."

He ran his hands over her shoulder, missing the hitch in her breathing. With the swelling reduced to an acceptable level, she should be fine to practice today. Erik donned his boots and crossed to the chamber door.

"Oh, I almost forgot. As you are my wife, etiquette will spare you from bowing before me."

"The day I bow before you, Erik Siodina, is the day they pave the way to the Underworld in Crimson Gillyflowers and dwarf dust."

~

ERIK PUSHED THROUGH THE THICK DOUBLE DOORS LEADING TO the council chamber, ignoring several nods thrown in his direction.

The din washed over him in waves.

Red Guard filled the upper levels, their armor clanging as they shifted into position. An entire contingent spread out in a circle, observing the gathering from above. Protocol dictated no humans in the chamber during official business. Inquisitions were different. The vote must be different, too.

Erik pinned back his shoulders.

His father occupied the center stage and leaned on a podium. An unexpected addition, one normally used for tribunals.

Over two dozen carrier falcons perched in windows, ready to spread the announcement throughout the territories as soon as voting finished. High Lords filled the seats in front. Lower-ranking nobles trickled in from the corridor, one by one. Some were in pairs, their heads bowed, sharing confidences.

His father strolled over to Lord Scarbough with his arms spread wide. He grasped the elder in an unexpected hug, whispering something in his ear.

The color drained from Lord Scarbough's face.

Erik ground his teeth. Looked like blackmail wasn't off the proverbial table.

His time was up. Erik had hoped his appointment to the High Table would come later in life. Much, much later. He didn't realize until today, he'd counted on his father serving another ten or fifteen years, at least.

More, since he appeared to age in reverse since Erik left for the militia.

These lazy cowards. No doubt fearful of his father, they'd rather fill the vacant seat than investigate Lord Bierling's suspicious demise.

Not a favorite among the Court, the dead noble was, at best, an ailing Faeblood with little magical talent. At worst, a powerful High Lord with a penchant for Ladies who didn't return his affections.

His father resumed his position in the middle of the chamber. He brought his hands together over his head and clapped.

The Lords murmured and took their seats.

"Silence." He struck the podium with a gavel. "Let us begin."

"What's the meaning of this?" Lord Nanscott gestured to the guards stationed on the outer wall. "Emsworth, the humans must leave."

Heads nodded in unison.

"An historic day. They shall bear witness."

The Red Guard widened their stances. Several Lords looked over their shoulders. An heavy silence descended.

"Lord Erik, you may take the floor and present your petition," his father said. "The other candidates will follow."

Right. His speech. Erik pulled the dog-eared parchment out of his pocket, reciting the first line under his breath. Even after practicing with Maia, it took him three tries to arrange the words in the correct order.

Two younger Lords entered the chamber, swaggering

despite their tardiness. They split at the staircase, each choosing to stand behind their family members.

Someone cleared their throat.

Decades of this nonsense stretched before him. Infighting among old Faeblood. Young challengers waiting their turn to rule a kingdom.

Erik wanted to thumb his nose at them and return to his greenhouse.

He unfolded his speech, smoothing out the crinkles on the scarred surface of the podium, taking extra care to cover the deep gouges in the wood. Claw marks from the last defendant?

Erik grabbed the edges, took a deep breath, and began.

"I stand before you, requesting a seat at the High Table. I represent the future of Morvak. Our kingdom is a land of prosperity, cultivated from a careful balance between humans and Faeblood. But that dream is slipping away. Every year, more and more families cannot meet the tithe. Our crops suffer. The luxuries once afforded to the Court now rationed. Too many turn their backs on the Castle, thus our lifestyle erodes."

He paused for effect.

"Aye. I dare criticize this council." He hammered his fist. "It's time to wake up. I lived amongst the humans, traveling extensively in the territories. I know what must be done. Cast your vote for my name, and I will guide us out of these dark times."

The last line was Maia's addition. They argued. He claimed there was nothing *dark* about the Lords' cushy life. She called him naive, alleging Erik must pander to their perceptions.

He stepped around the podium and held the gaze of all eight sitting Lords. This entire performance was a waste of precious daylight. He could be harvesting the bumper crop of split peas.

"Our generation needs to claim what is rightfully ours. I believe in an exceptional Court." Erik waited. "I believe I am the candidate to bring it about."

The young Lord to his right scoffed.

What was his name? Erik never cared for Faeblood males his age, never learned their family lines. They belonged to one of two factions — those who bullied everyone around them for entertainment. Or those who cast against the servants, claiming one insult or another.

Since he spent half his time with his plants, the other training in the armory, he never formed friendships with his peers.

Around the room, Red Guard passed out wine. So focused on staring down the members of the High Table, Erik missed them uncorking bottles, filling goblets.

"A toast to my son," his father said. Everyone took a sip. "May you—"

A Red Guard thrust a drink in his view, cutting off the last.

"Your wine, milord. For the toast," the man added.

His father met his eyes.

Erik raised the goblet to his mouth, letting the crimson liquid slosh against his closed lips. They were fools. Didn't they learn from Lord Bierling's death? There were potions worse than poison.

He climbed the steps, claiming a chair in the second row.

Lord Scarbough gestured the next candidate to the podium.

After a pretty speech, the sitting council members peppered the younger Faeblood with questions about his beliefs, his magical talents. None paid attention to the Red Guard refilling their wine.

"Excellent." His father raised his glass to the candidate. He must need the Lords to consume the entire contents of their goblet because he chanted, "Hear, hear."

Idiotic parrots. They took another sip.

Erik mimicked the action, scanning the crowd over the goblet's rim.

His father sneered and clapped, nodding to the sentries stationed at the chamber's entrance.

They closed the doors. Every guard unsheathed their broad swords.

"Splendid." His father placed his goblet on the podium. He took a pull from a flask hidden inside his robes. "Let's begin."

"But what about my speech?" asked the other candidate.

Erik resisted the urge to shake his head. That one was dense. Though confused expressions around the room meant he wasn't the only one.

"Silence. You will all kneel before me."

As one, the Lords gasped.

"I, Emsworth Siodina, declare this council absolved of its duties to Morvak. The High Table is an antiquated form of governing. I stand before you as your new sovereign ruler. Today, you will pledge your allegiance to me."

He paused.

"I shall henceforth be known as King Siodina."

Dear gods, this was insane. Too busy worrying about his appointment, Erik never considered his father might seize power for himself. Dammit. He should have seen this coming. The threat against Maia was a ruse, a cleverly-designed ploy to focus his attention elsewhere.

Six months ago, Erik might have chuckled at the play. He would've snuck into the kitchens for a snack and a laugh with Dezee.

This was bad. The relief of not serving on the High Table never came. Dread weighed in his stomach. This was bad. Bad. Bad.

His sadistic sire. King of Morvak. The entire realm would suffer.

The silence was deafening. His heart pounded against his ribs, the beat thudding a rhythm of bad. Bad. Bad.

"You're delusional," Lord Scarbough said, clutching his throat. "This is treason."

Several of the Lords raised their fists in agreement. A few

eyed their goblets, setting them down on nearby tables and sliding them as far away as possible, a gray pallor already washing out their faces.

"Under the old laws." His father shrugged and clapped twice. "But today marks the dawn of a new rule. A new empire. My son is correct — the peninsula needs a leader who sees the future, fixes the Castle's mistakes. Someone to restore our powers to their former glory."

Restore our powers, an interesting turn of phrase.

Except for Ember, the magic in the peninsula ended with those in the Castle. The expression nudged something deep in the recesses of his mind, but he had more pressing matters.

Such as the steel at his neck.

He glanced around the room, careful not to make sudden movements. Red Guard blades rested on the shoulders of the High Lords. His father didn't spare the lesser Faeblood, either.

"Do nothing foolish," the guard behind him said, his tone suggesting the opposite as if he relished the opportunity to act against Erik. "Your father wants you alive. He didn't say unharmed."

"You can't kill us all," Lord Scarbough ground out. "The rest of the Court will not support your reign. A monarch without a populace. You will lose everything."

"I expected your... reluctance. Change is never easy." His father gestured to the Red Guards. Then the falcons.

The birds flew away, their legs empty. Interesting. His father intended to keep his seizure of power quiet.

They lowered their weapons.

"You will swear fealty to me." His father clapped again.

The sentries dragged a heavy chair to the center of the room. Did they practice the routine? One clap for the wine. Another for the swords. The next for a throne.

"Free will is an illusion. Who's first?"

His sire was always one for theatrics. If Erik weren't so

pissed, he might enjoy the Lords' gaping mouths, looking like surprised fish nibbling on a worm to find out they swallowed a hook.

"The Red Guards may answer to you, but I refuse to bend at the knee." Lord Wulffrith raised his fist.

"As you wish," his father said, sounding almost... bored. "Perhaps the rest would appreciate some clarity."

He waved his hand, and a small leather pouch appeared in his palm.

"Inside are vials of antidote to the poison in the wine. Your fealty for the serum."

Lord Wulffrith collapsed to his knees, foam bubbling at the corners of his mouth. His eyes rolled back in his head. He planted face-first on the floor.

"Pity. It appears as if Lord Wulffrith consumed his portion and another's." His father pulled a timepiece from inside his robes, studying the face. "Might I suggest haste when making your decision? Tick-tock."

Erik rushed to Lord Wulffrith's side and turned him over.

No heartbeat. The body was unnaturally cool to the touch as if he'd died hours ago. Or the poison froze him from the inside out.

His magic wouldn't be enough to save the rest of them. Nor to slow the spread. He could stitch most wounds. Heal lungs riddled with cough. Mend broken bones. But this... whatever this was... worked too fast. Worse, his father had expected him to drink the wine too. Blood relations be damned.

Two dead. One psychopath. That left six council members between Morvak's populace and his father's reign. Terrible odds.

As expected, the remaining Lords bent at the knee, their heads hanging to their chests.

He listened, as if observing from a distant land, as they

repeated oaths of fealty. The words filled the chamber, slowly at first. Then faster as the poison leached the first strands of life.

"… And transfer the power of the High Table to Lord Siodina. Freely. Without coercion," the chorus of voices called out.

"Erik, my heir." His father beckoned him to the podium. "I require your oath as well."

His feet moved on their own. Down the stairs. Past his father. All the way to the chamber doors.

He left without a backward glance. Let them think what they wanted. Let them believe he either walked to his death or took a chance on his abilities as a healer.

Despite remaining upright, he never felt so small. How would he explain this to Maia? More than ever, he needed Lady Stella to find a potion to erase his marriage oath.

She must leave. She shouldn't be anywhere near his father now that his power went unchecked. Erik would pen a letter to Xavier himself if needed.

He balled his fists. As much as Erik wanted to punch the stone wall, he refrained and gritted his teeth. It wasn't as if he could heal his own broken knuckles.

The bastard took that from him, too.

CHAPTER TWENTY-ONE

"It's the other fork," Lea whispered in Maia's ear as she filled the teacup with steaming water.

Hushed conversations drifted around the solarium.

Of course. The smallest one to the left of the knives was for... what did they call these little morsels? Right, appetizers.

The next smallest utensil was for the salad. The biggest for the main course. Though she doubted they would serve anything substantial at afternoon tea. The final one, the fork at the top of her plate, was for dessert.

Maia was ravenous. She was always a big eater, the mess hall one of her favorite places. Back home, Cook smushed everything together on the same plate. Perfect for a single fork.

The Ladies picked at their food, their eyes darting nervously to her. This was her first tea since the incident with the dagger.

She'd been neglecting her duty to spy in favor of training.

Bree rested a hand on Lea's shoulder and pointed to the kettle.

Maia didn't miss the way the older servant instructed her younger charge on the needs of the table, nor the disdain Bree wore when she thought none of the Ladies looked in her direction.

She crossed one leg over the other, her skirts rustling with the movement. These blasted gowns were too big. Too much fabric. She would rather sit half a day in a tree stand, patiently waiting for prey to approach, than spend an hour stuffed into her latest.

Still, she must keep up the pretense of a Lord's wife. Soon to be High Lord, if they already finished the vote.

Though the longer she stayed in the Castle the more she realized Erik didn't care what she wore. He didn't dwell on their social standing. Nor the opinions of others. But she would appear less threatening to this crowd if she showed up dressed like a flamboyant flamingo.

Maia swirled the contents of her teacup.

Swamp water, her father called it. Snippets of soggy leaves clung to the sides as she took a small sip of the putrid drink. Perhaps she should swing by the kitchens for a proper cup of coffee afterwards.

"Did you hear Lord Scarbough took a new lover?" Lady Stella asked no one in particular. "That old crone. He couldn't find his way under a Lady's skirts with a map and torch. There's not enough gold in the realm…"

"Who?" Lady Newhiel asked.

"I don't have a name yet." Lady Stella sipped her tea, leaving the cup in the air longer than necessary. "Poor chit. She must be desperate."

By design, the Ladies hung on every word. Well… all except the young Lady near the end of the table. Stella's companion from the library. She kept her eyes averted.

What games did Lady Stella play now?

"His lips." Lady Newhiel shuddered. "His breath."

"I suppose she wants to stick around for his demise." Lady Stella set her cup on its saucer. "He must be near the end. No other reason to share sheets with the old codger. I'd pay a hefty sum of gold to see his wife's face when she learned he willed a portion of his fortune to his mistress."

Maia resisted the urge to glance back to the Lady in question. If the others didn't know of whom Stella spoke, Maia didn't want to clue them in.

She took a bite of the stuffed mushroom, washing it down with tea.

"Enough of that old bat." Lady Stella gripped the edge of the table and leaned forward. "Did you hear about the changes to the Grimoire Games?"

The next bite of mushroom paused in mid-air.

"Ooh, such fun." Lady Newhiel clapped her hands together. "Sword forms are so droll."

She must've misunderstood. Did Lady Newhiel say *sword forms?* Maia toyed with her earrings.

"Could you repeat the last?" Maia placed the bite on her plate, forcing a giggle. "I didn't hear you. My mind is elsewhere this afternoon. With the vote and all."

"Lord Siodina replaced the boring sword forms with actual sparring." Lady Newhiel's eyes lit up. "The contestants will wield wooden swords, but it shall be more entertaining than forms."

Two weeks of practice. Wasted. Six weeks remained, a blink compared to the years required for proficiency in battle.

"They fight with swords?" Maia asked in a high-pitched tone. "In a duel or..."

"It's a free-for-all." Lady Stella pursed her lips as if she smelled something rotten.

"With wooden weapons?"

"Aye. Don't you listen? What's the point of determining a new Red Guard recruit only to have them incapacitated before they undergo proper training? You whore for the militia, but surely you can appreciate the logic."

"How do they determine a winner, then?" Maia asked, ignoring the slur. Let them think she was ignorant. She needed to keep them talking.

"Who knows?" Lady Stella leaned back in her chair. "It will be exciting. Erik can heal broken bones. Most contusions. I suspect he will stay busy during the competition."

The color drained out of Lea's face. While Maia appreciated the lass's concern, she would be fine. It would all work out. Nothing to lose sleep over. Aye, she would be fine.

"Though accidents happen. Even in the Games." Lady Stella glanced back and forth between them, smirking. "What chance might they have in the territories if one cannot fight with a wooden weapon?"

"Indeed." Maia took a hasty sip. "What about shields?"

"What about them? My, you ask the most ridiculous questions."

"Do you know—" Maia cleared her throat. "Do you know if the rules allow them?"

She struggled to hide the thread of panic in her voice. Maia didn't care if the Ladies thought her foolish. Their derision was a small price for more information.

"They won't," Lady Newhiel said confidently.

Lady Stella's mouth tipped up. "How did you discover that gossip?"

"Commander Lukas let it slip. Lord Siodina visits the Red Guard barracks most nights."

"Still spreading your legs for the help?" Lady Stella asked. "You'll never find a proper husband at this rate. Why do you sully yourself with humans? They are all the same. Ignorant. Barely more than savages. Though I would make exceptions for the new Red Guard."

"He isn't a guard," Lady Newhiel supplied.

"Hush. What's his name again? Maia..." Lady Stella inclined

her head. "You know the human. He came from your territory. The man who follows you around like he's lost."

Clever bait. She never gave Lady Stella enough credit. This time, Maia didn't need to bite the inside of her cheek to avoid lashing out.

Perhaps she'd learned to fit in after all.

"Oh," she said, feigning confusion. "You mean Mikel."

A giggle.

"He's an officer in the militia." Another giggle. "I think he prefers redheads."

She let ice frost her voice. Mikel was in love with Xavier's little sister, Ada. Though he never admitted to it. Or wouldn't allow himself. Even if his heart didn't belong to her friend, he wouldn't touch a Faeblood.

"Interesting." Lady Stella smirked. "I heard he prefers gold. And occasionally works for silver."

"What—"

"You didn't know? Your Mikel was a palace whore. The stories the older matrons tell... How else do you think he paid for his freedom?"

"You're lying," Maia spat, beyond caring to disguise the vehemence in her voice.

"Am I? Look around. Humans are only good for two things — soiling the linens and changing the sheets." Lady Stella gestured to the room at large. "Sometimes both in the same night."

With that, she turned back to her plate, popping a mushroom into her smug mouth.

She knew. The realization hit Maia in waves. The change in the Games. Mikel's history with the nobility. Maia's bid for the Red Guard.

Ironic. Lady Stella, coveted for her beauty, was a more competent spy.

All Maia had accomplished was penning useless ramblings

on the number of guards. Magic classification and the Court's schedule. The locations of some of the most important rooms.

She failed as an informant. She failed as a friend to Mikel too.

"Another thrilling afternoon." Maia rose from her seat, tossing the napkin on her plate. "My thanks for your gracious invitation, but my husband requested my presence at half past four bells."

No one stood. No one returned her small wave. She sent a subtle shake to Lea and Bree. They needed to stay and finish the service. And Maia needed to hunt down her husband.

Erik would know what must be done.

~

AFTER A SEARCH OF THE CLEARING, SHE FOUND HIM IN THE armory, pounding the straw bale used for target practice.

His hair was damp at the edges, darkening to a near black. Beads of sweat rolled down his back in rivulets.

She tracked their path to the waistband of his leathers.

There was a rhythm to his strikes, even when he dropped his guard and sent a sloppy hook to the side.

She stood there for who knew how long, studying him. It was clear she wasn't the only one who suffered a terrible afternoon.

"Keep up your right." She leaned against a column, savoring the cool stone against her heated temple. "You leave your face unprotected after your left."

"What do you want?" Erik asked without taking his eyes off the bale.

Thud. Thud. Thud.

He landed another two jabs, followed by an uppercut. When she didn't answer, he repeated, "What do you want?"

"We don't have time to list all the things I want." She couldn't prevent the harsh laugh that escaped. "As for why I came, Lady Stella took immense pleasure in informing me your father changed the rules for the Grimoire Games."

Maia pushed off the column, straightening.

"We need to change our tactics. I mean..." she said with her hands. "Forms are a good place to start, but we must add sparring. Perhaps with a shield. Maybe you can figure out from your father if he intends to allow shields. Lady Newhiel says otherwise, but I want to be sure. It would require a new strategy."

"Seems like you have it all figured out. If you will excuse me, I'm busy."

"You promised to help." Her eyes darted between the destroyed hay bale, the bloodstains on his wraps, and the set of his shoulders. "I know hand-to-hand combat but need your guidance for swords."

It was the wrong thing to say. She barged in full bore and had overlooked how pissed off he was. Typical. She couldn't take it back now.

"I promised to sponsor you. Not instruct." Erik ran his hand over his hair. "Besides, there's not enough time. You'll never be ready."

A single-leg takedown would've been less shocking.

"I deserve your best." Maia grabbed his arm, her fingers slipping to his elbow. Erik looked down his nose, but she didn't let go.

"My best?" Erik swung his arm free and unwrapped his hands. "You need more than my support. I am naught but a nobleman, good for healing minor injuries and providing Ladies with their precious face creams."

"Stop. I don't have time for self-deprecation. My territory's future is at stake."

"Haven't you heard a word I said? It's too late."

"If you won't help with training, perhaps you'll reconsider bringing up the possibility of female recruits to the High Table."

She took a step forward, adding, "I know it's a lot to ask for a new High Lord. Perhaps when this is over—"

"I lost my bid to join the High Table." Erik chuckled darkly. "As I mentioned, your husband is naught but a courtier. I have no more sway with the laws than I have with dinner arrangements."

"They voted for another?" How? It made little sense. There were two other candidates but gossip around the Castle indicated they didn't have the support.

"Nope," Erik said, popping the *p*. "My dear father dissolved the High Table, appointing himself sovereign ruler of Morvak. Instead of nagging me, perhaps you should run along and pen a note to Xavier."

Maia counted to ten in her head. This was good. Not the dissolution of power, nor his father's play for more. Those were terrible. Erik's obvious anger meant he cared. Even if just a little.

She glanced again to his battered hands, the sullied wraps on the floor. How long had he been here, working off his anger?

"I'll add it to my list of duties," she said. Maia didn't have time for this tantrum.

"Looks like I won't have to play at being High Lord after all." He studied a leaf carried on the breeze. "Still the heir apparent — good for breeding and maintaining appearances."

"And sword trainer extraordinaire."

"Don't bother." The haze in Erik's eyes cleared.

"We will meet you at the usual spot," Maia said, ignoring him. She scanned the alcoves but didn't find what she needed. "I'll speak with Mikel about acquiring wooden practice swords."

It wouldn't be the only thing she spoke with Mikel about.

"There isn't enough time. It would be best for you to drop out." Erik buried a left hook into the bale.

"What?"

"Give it up, Maia." Not Kitten. "You have no chance of

winning. Do you want to suffer that kind of defeat? That kind of humiliation?"

Jab. Cross. Jab.

"Is that what this is?" She balled her fists at her side. "You're worried about me embarrassing you?"

"Don't be naive," he spat. "I don't care if you enter. You need more realistic expectations though."

"Since when do you roll over and play possum?"

"You stubborn, illogical fool. Did you hear what I said? My father abolished a functioning government with little resistance. None of this matters. You think I enjoy this outcome? You think I want his unchecked reign? That sadistic bastard who I'm positive killed his own wife once she produced an heir. Truth serum be damned. I just can't prove it."

"Erik—"

He pulled out of her reach.

"You think he killed your mother?" She let her arm drop.

"Does it matter? Does any of this matter when he declared himself king? The truth will not change a damn thing."

"Of course it matters if it means getting closure for her death."

She wasn't some simpering fool. She knew that tone. His defeated posture. He could lie to himself, but she wouldn't swallow this nonsense.

"The only closure I seek is a stake shoved through his dead heart."

Maia didn't miss the subtle reference to the Nightwalkers. Their kind, if they even existed, vanished long before their Fae ancestors' powers dwindled. Rumored to roam free, a wooden stake to the heart was the most efficient way to kill them.

If she thought about it, Lord Siodina possessed striking similarities to the creatures.

Faeblood lived the same life span as humans. Perhaps a little longer, given their access to healing potion and cushy lifestyles.

But Erik's father was in his sixth decade, appearing twenty years younger. Plus, he shared their pasty coloring and penchant for late hours.

She rubbed her eyes. A Nightwalker. Gah. She was being fanciful. Erik was right about one thing — his father owned a black heart.

His shoulders sagged. Erik kept his back to her, his head tilted to the rafters.

Maia resisted the urge to run her hands along them. Let him stew. She pivoted on her heel and went in search of Lea. Let him wallow alone.

She had a competition to prepare for.

CHAPTER TWENTY-TWO

Maia picked at the raspberry lace decorating the edge of her cuff and washed down the roasted yams with a swig of Fae wine. The lump stretched her throat. An uncomfortable reminder to take smaller bites.

"Are you finished?" Erik asked as he leaned back in his chair, ignoring his full plate.

It took all of Maia's will not to reach across him and spear his uneaten potatoes.

She'd skipped afternoon tea in the solarium in favor of training with Mikel and Lea. A hard session and no snack left Maia a hungry goose, as Jade would say.

Dinner in the great hall was an awkward affair.

She half expected Erik's father to announce his ascension, but the elder Siodina skipped the meal entirely. A quarter of the former High Lords were absent, too. Chatter carried on the tongues of the inebriated nobles, except their overall tone tended toward hushed whispers instead of the customary gossip.

"Are you going to eat that?" She pointed to his heaping portions with her fork then sucked the tines clean.

"We're leaving."

A simple *no* would've—

He stood, cupped her elbow, and hauled her to her feet.

She attempted to rearrange her skirts, but Erik didn't wait, tugging her through the door leading to the kitchens. He bypassed the chaos of supper service, took a right at the buttery, and led them along a servant passage behind the residential wing.

"What is wrong with you?"

"I need you back in our chambers." He dropped her arm and laced his fingers through hers, muttering. "I need—"

His pace increased, forcing Maia to add a shuffle step to keep up with his longer strides.

Typical. Erik didn't know what he needed. She wasn't in the mood to guess. Maia was tired of being yanked around in these impractical slippers. She pulled. Hard.

Erik whirled and took two steps forward, caging her against the wall. He searched her face. His own expression was unreadable, emotions flickering across his brows too fast to pick out. A tic appeared in his cheek, the only constant.

Her back pressed against cool stone. She cupped his jaw with one hand, steadying herself against the wall with the other.

They stayed in that position for a long, long time.

The first day Maia saw him, she'd somehow overlooked his arresting features.

Now, in the dim corridor with the destiny of an entire kingdom weighing on their conscience, she couldn't help but revel in their appearance. She loved his thick lower lip, the crook of its corners when he spouted absurdities. The bend of his smirk when she caught him looking at her.

She loved the way his brows furrowed in amusement. The way they drew together if he cared. And how they spread, relaxing when he listened. When he gave her his full attention.

Their world, full of demands and duties and deceit, was reduced to two of them.

His chest crowded her, putting him close enough that his breath caressed her ear.

"Maia, I want—"

Cool air rushed her front. Maia lurched forward, catching her balance before she fell to the floor.

"What is that?" He took another step back and pointed to the wall behind her.

An imprint of an inverted hand glowed, flickering twice before reducing to a faint glimmer. Maia glanced down at her palm then back at the wall. Then back down to her palm.

Erik encircled her wrist and guided her hand back to it, flattening her fingers with his own.

The outline of a door appeared.

He pushed against its center, and the stone wall recessed a foot then slid to the side. Erik — absent the healthy dose of mistrust that kept Maia's feet grounded — grabbed the nearest torch and entered.

Creepy chamber or creepy corridor. She didn't like her options. Her stomach let out a yowl. Trust her gut to protest at a moment like this.

"Don't just stand there. Come on."

Maia stepped inside. "If you think you can order me—"

An eerie hum crawled along her skin. Her skin tingled as she passed through. She could live for decades and never get used to magic.

"Wow." Her mouth parted.

The passage closed behind her. A faint circle in the shape of a knob glowed halfway down the right side.

Her eyes darted around the chamber. The size of the great hall, it was constructed of the same stone as the clock tower.

This couldn't be right. If her memory was correct, the

Faeblood's personal apartments lined the corridor. How could a room this size fit between them?

"There are rumors that magic lives in the mountain." Erik rested a hand on her lower back. "Like a beast trapped in its den. This chamber must be of its making."

In one corner, dozens of barrels rose from the floor to the ceiling. Too far away to read their label, there was a faint picture of a plant on the front. Grain or seeds. Trunks lined the opposite wall. Black powder dusted the tops of the nearest, spilling to the ones below.

Shelves and apothecary cases lined the middle of the room. Some in neat rows. Others at odd angles. They were full of jars and cans and tins — a disordered pantry with enough staples to feed a territory through a harsh winter.

Or an army through a long siege.

Food. Blasting powder. She craned her neck. There. Along the back wall, hundreds of swords hung from hooks. More arrows stacked in piles, bundled with thick rope.

"Xavier is not the only one who prepares for battle," Erik said.

Maia nodded, unable to find her voice. Not a stranger to combat, she'd devoted her entire life to training as a fighter. Hours and days and years in the ring and grappling pit. Still, nothing prepared her for the reality of war.

Dear gods, the death toll would be unimaginable. She resisted the urge to close her eyes, afraid of the seeing her loved ones fall.

"Did you know?" she asked, the accusation barely above a whisper. She didn't want to hear his answer, but she would never forgive herself if she didn't push him.

"No." The denial was swift. "You have no reason to trust my word, but I didn't know he..." Erik ran his hand through his hair. "This level of preparation..."

She believed him. Erik might be indifferent to politics, but he wouldn't lie about this.

Maia strolled along the rows, trailing her fingers across the various shelves. She halted at a pile of timbers stacked haphazardly to one side. On their outer rings, sap oozed between curls of thin bark. They had milled a few down into boards and stained them the same dark red of False Ash trees.

Erik tilted his head to the side, searching. For what? Before she could ask, he crouched down and reached between boards near the bottom.

"I'll ask the carpenter if he can carve wooden swords." Erik straightened, holding three splintered pieces. "You can practice your forms with steel. Spar with these. It's the best I can do."

The hair on her nape stood on end. It was this room. She couldn't put her finger on it, but something set her on edge. Perhaps it was witnessing his father's scheming. Each barrel represented a loved one who might die. Every jar could feed an enemy who would cut down a brother.

She should find some parchment to take stock. Xavier would want to know quantities. Ada, who had a sharp mind for numbers, could use the information to help her brother make strategic decisions.

"We must leave. Dinner is almost over."

She bristled at his tone. He was right, of course. They'd stayed too long. She could always return with Mikel when there was less of an opportunity for someone chancing upon them.

Erik led them back through the maze of shelving and hesitated at the door. His mouth parted as if to say something, but he shook his head and opened the passage with his palm, ushering her through first.

"You lead." He flicked his head toward the residential wing and tucked the wood under his arm, following several paces behind as to not poke her in the back.

The rest of the journey was uneventful. Mikel greeted them at their chamber door.

"Dezee waits with a tray." His arm thrust between them, blocking Erik from entering.

"Go on. It appears as if Mikel wishes a word."

An understatement. An entire lecture likely rattled around in his mind, but he wouldn't give Erik the satisfaction.

She was tired. And hungry. She wanted to crawl into her bed and sleep off her nightmare. But these two… they needed a reminder of why—

Movement at the end of the hall drew her attention. A servant. Bollocks, she was jumpy. The man disappeared around the corner, his wide shoulders scraping against the edge. It was rare for male servants to walk the halls at this time. After the supper cleanup, most assisted with bedding the animals down.

Maybe a family promoted a new butler.

"Don't wait up." Erik left her without a backward glance. Mikel followed, his gaze burning a hole between her husband's shoulders.

"Not like I ever do," she said once they were far enough away.

It wasn't Bree who greeted her. Demelza tended the fire. A tray of appetizers awaited on the vanity.

"Figured my boy stole you away before you finished. Sit. I can hear your stomach yelling from here."

Bless her. Maia didn't even attempt to stifle her moan. They were just as delicious cold. Maybe more since she didn't worry about hiding her reactions.

Demelza unwound her twist, tucking the pins in her endless pockets. Clever fingers massaged small circles on her scalp.

Maia closed her eyes. She'd worn her shoulders around her ears for weeks. Careful of her words, forcing her face to relax for the sensibility of others.

Perhaps it was because of Erik and Demelza's unique relationship, but the housekeeper's voice changed to something wise and solemn. Her words were not exactly friendly.

"Losing a parent never gets easier. Especially when you carry the blame. Real or imagined."

Erik must've told her about Maia's past. "My father—"

"I do not speak of your father." Demelza let the words settle.

Maia regarded her through the looking glass. Then it hit her.

If circumstances differed — if her mother had access to proper healers, if Demelza had been born outside the Castle — they would be roughly the same age. *Mama*. Her beautiful, selfless mother who sacrificed herself to bring her daughter into this world.

She sagged on her stool and thought of her father. Did he resent her for the death of his soulmate?

Maia never asked. He never said. Maybe the answer was between them all along. Maybe it was why she worked so hard to earn his approval. She didn't work for his praise. She worked for his forgiveness.

No. That wasn't right.

The militia was her dream. Her choice.

"Don't let their expectations be your sole purpose in this life," Demelza said. "Erik lives for his mother. His search — it consumes him. He will perish within these walls, never having lived. A part of him died that day. The weight of the past will crush his future."

Demelza gave her a knowing look.

"You should know that about him. A pity if you committed the same."

Was that what she was doing? In the militia? First for her father. Then Xavier. Now wasn't the time to—

And then it slammed into her like one of Mikel's famous takedowns. Demelza *knew*. She must've figured out Maia's presence in the Castle was at the direction of a territory leader, not for some... forbidden love story.

Demelza sectioned hair for a braid, her deft fingers combing through her crown in silence, letting Maia shift uncomfortably underneath her ministrations.

Oh, how she wished to confide in Erik's adoptive mother. She wanted to unburden her thoughts. Seek her advice on the best way to handle her husband. Xavier's tasks. But it was too risky. In the end, she said simply, "I know not of which you speak."

CHAPTER TWENTY-THREE

Clack. Clack. Clack.

"Pivot on your right heel. Slice through the turn," Maia said to Lea, demonstrating the move.

True to his word, Erik commissioned wooden swords. He must've woken up the carpenter before dawn because Mikel strolled into the clearing with three, crafted in the same shape and size as their steel counterparts.

Sparring. Dueling. Fighting. If she thought about it for too long, Maia would make herself sick. While Lady Stella meant to scare her yesterday at tea, she was grateful for the warning disguised as a taunt.

Leatrix wiped the sweat on her forehead with the back of her hand. She lowered her guard and lunged forward.

Maia knocked the sword from her grip before she could take another step.

"You signal your attack. Don't dip your shoulder before the strike."

"I didn't." Lea picked up her weapon and dropped into her fighting stance.

"Aye, you did. On your left." Maia grinned. "A skilled opponent will notice. Choke up on the handle. It will shorten the arc, making the swing faster."

"Like this?" Lea adjusted her hands.

Maia nodded and lunged. The tip of her blade speared the air as Lea spun to the side, out of her range. Maia parried the next blow, allowing the child to take the inside position.

Their swords met in a flurry.

Maia defended each strike, leaving her right side vulnerable. Take the bait. *Take the bait.*

Lea pivoted at the correct moment, turning under her guard and slicing the back of Maia's thigh. She spun out as instructed, a smile splitting her face.

"Excellent. Rest. Drink some water."

The girl trotted off to where Mikel leaned against a tree. She traded her sword for a flask and guzzled its contents.

Maia paced, twirling her blade in a figure eight. She stopped and speared the air.

Swords extended the fists. At least, that's what she told herself. And Lea. And Mikel, though he never asked.

Jab, jab, cross became *thrust, thrust, parry.*

Her world shrank to the competition. To Lea's fate. She wanted to prove Erik wrong. A single life was worth the fight. It had to begin somewhere. What better place than Lea?

"You need a larger opponent," Mikel said as he raised the wooden blade to her throat.

And they were off.

The clearing became a whirl.

Maia choked up on the hilt. Gods, he was fast. He sent strike after strike after strike. She forgot to breathe. Her vision blurred around the edges.

For a split second, the weight of invisible expectations vanished. It was just Maia and Mikel, battling in the clearing, her straining muscles louder than the voices in her head. She was meant to be here. Not in some frilly dress, sipping tea and gossip. She might be a terrible informant, but she could do this.

Clack. Clack. Clack.

Swords extended the arm. Mikel, using Lea's smaller blade, was at a disadvantage.

They shared a feral grin. Then they *sparred*.

Who knew how long they tangled? It could've been two minutes or two days. Her arms wobbled like a heaping of gooseberry jam on its way to Lord Scarbough's mouth. At last, Mikel signaled a draw.

She flopped down, too tired to bow. Her legs fanned out on the ground still attached. Or so she thought.

He joined her. Maia rolled to her side and plucked a strand of grass out of his hair.

"That was brilliant," Lea said, the only warning before the lass launched herself on top of them. She straddled Maia, squishing her cheeks between her small hands. "Teach me to fight like you. Wystan says girls can't hold a sword."

Lea scrunched her nose.

"She will, little one." Mikel chuckled. "We both will. Who is this Wystan?"

"A newer servant. He's as mean as a dragon with a torn scale but Mistress Dezee never catches him being bad."

"Sounds like a bully," Maia said, tugging one of Lea's poofs. "You know what would make this day perfect?"

"What?" Lea asked.

"A dip in Ashmere Falls." When Lea's brows drew together, Maia added, "Near my home, there is a *huge* waterfall and swimming hole. The water is warm year-round. Perfect for a soak." She hesitated. "You should try it."

"Oh, I don't think—"

"Time to return you to Dezee." Mikel rolled to his feet and extended a hand. "Maia?"

"Go ahead." Maia clasped it and pulled herself up. She sniffed the air, attempting to add levity to the conversation. "You reek of defeat. Find a bath."

"Aye." He grinned a true grin. "The stench of your loss blankets me."

There it is. She didn't know she needed to hear his taunts until now.

She hadn't spoken to Mikel about his past. After she'd cooled down yesterday, she'd realized it would do no good to push.

He would confide his story when he was ready. If ever.

To the Castle, the flat line of his mouth and his furrowed brows might resemble a bent of seriousness required for his bodyguard role. But the more time she spent with him, the more she realized his pretty smiles and teasing grins were the mask.

Lea crashed into her, wrapping her little arms around Maia's waist.

"Thank you," Lea mumbled and took off.

A hulking Mikel followed, leaving Maia alone in the clearing with only her thoughts for company.

She should go for a swim in the lake or a bath in her chambers. Instead, her feet carried her toward the bluffs hiding Erik's pool.

The same eerie pink glow greeted her when she pulled back the vines. There was a charge in the air, frying her already tingling skin.

Her presence felt like an intrusion, so she slid down the boulder and stared off into the horizon.

Maia owed Jade another letter tomorrow.

It was strange. Lord Siodina... now, King Siodina (she must remember) chose to keep the announcement from the territories. She'd need to disguise the news somehow and add her discovery of the war room too.

Jade responded to her last letter with word that her family would attend the Grimoire games. It was difficult to decipher, but there was a hint Xavier might extract her from the Castle that night. Perhaps he was dissatisfied with her progress.

She pulled the correspondence out of her pocket, reading and re-reading the paragraph in question.

I BEAR ILL TIDINGS. WE HAD HOPED XAVIER'S SISTER WOULD JOIN US for the Games, but Ada wishes to remain at home. You know how she is. Her fear of the territories keeps her at the compound. After the competition, you can show me the view from your balcony. You spoke so highly of the lake's tranquility at night. I simply must experience it for myself.

LIES. ADA LEFT THE COMPOUND WITH EVERY OPPORTUNITY SHE chanced upon. More than Xavier was aware. And humans, while permitted at the Games, were unwelcome in the Castle proper. There was no chance Jade would set foot in Erik's chambers.

She studied the note. *After the competition...*

Did they mean for her to escape that night?

Maia didn't relish the idea of jumping from her window. Plus it was too soon. She still hadn't found the book.

The warmth of the stone at her back bled into her tired muscles. Four more bells until supper, plenty of time to rest her eyes before she needed to get ready. She had an hour, an hour and a half at most, before Bree expected her return.

She could close her eyes for a bit...

ERIK FOUND HER SLEEPING OUTSIDE HIS MOTHER'S GROTTO.

His Kitten curled up in the late summer sun. A faint burn already dusted the tip of her nose. Her head slumped to her shoulder in an angle sure to cause a crick when she woke. His magic stirred.

When she hadn't returned with Mikel after sparring, he'd assumed she wanted some quiet. When one bell sounded, he moved from his greenhouse to the library, listening for her footsteps.

At two bells, his worry drove him from his books.

By three bells, Mikel joined the search.

When the bells chimed four times, a fruitless hunt around the lake's banks ended in full-blown alarm.

He worried his father or the Red Guards apprehended her while searching for the room of hidden things. Or whatever it was called. He had no idea the chamber existed. His father must've stocked it when Erik spied in the Militia territory.

Thank the gods that its contents distracted Maia from her ability to open the door. He needed that elixir from Stella. Now. Yesterday. A week ago. Maia was bound to figure out their oath was still intact.

"What am I to do with you?" He tucked a strand of hair behind her ear, willing his fingertips to stop shaking.

"I'm still mad," she mumbled, turning her cheek into his palm. Soft snuffle-snores followed.

"I know." Erik wrapped one arm around her waist, the other under her knees. He hoisted her up and kissed her forehead. "That doesn't count."

It took twice as long to return to their rooms. The scent of jasmine hit him as he nudged the bathing chamber door open with his boot. Steam wafted from the copper tub. A welcome sight.

"I can walk," she said, her voice louder but still filled with sleep.

"Grab two towels, then." Erik set her down. He nudged her forward with a gentle pat on her hip and undressed.

"I don't need one for my hair."

"The second is for me."

She whirled around, awake now. "You—"

"Don't be a prude." He climbed in and closed his eyes. "It's late. The tub can hold both of us."

Erik wasn't ready to let her out of his sight. Not after the slight panic she caused. He wanted to yell and scream at her carelessness, but instead he asked, "Scared you can't keep your hands off me?"

"Not a chance. I worry the tub may not be big enough for your inflated head." She scoffed, the noise followed by several muttered curses and the sound of her clothes falling on the floor. "Keep your eyes closed until I'm in."

"As you wish. Though I'm still thinking of you. The outline of your curves is burned in my mind."

"Insufferable prick."

Water lapped at his chest as she settled. Erik gripped the sides of the tub, regarding her through hooded lids.

She went under then surfaced, her hair slicking down her back. A feline smile crested her lips.

"I owe you an apology." Erik swallowed.

Perhaps stunned by his words, she kept silent. Her lips formed a flat line. They held each other's stare, their breathing more labored as the seconds ticked by.

Admitting when he was wrong was never easy. The gods knew he practiced it enough as a lad with Dezee. But voicing the ugly truths to someone as selfless as Maia, someone who would march to her demise carrying the banner of a lost cause, a noble cause...

He couldn't say the words to her face.

"Turn around," Erik said, softening it with a whispered *please.*

She must have sensed how uneasy he was. Or perhaps her curiosity was greater than her aversion to him because she obeyed and scooted backward. Her shoulders brushed his chest. He looped an arm around her middle and hauled her against him.

"What are you doing?" she asked, a hitch in her voice.

"Washing away the evening." He poured a dollop of soap in his hand.

Dezee purchased it from the Artisan territory. The liquid created a rich lather, perfect for her thick locks.

"Stalling for time. Trying to figure what to say." Erik slathered her crown, massaging it into her scalp. He rinsed his hands and allowed his magic to heal her sunburn, her shoulder. When her spine relaxed, he continued, "My father mistook you for a Faeblood."

"What—"

"At the compound," he clarified. "When news of a caster in the Militia territory reached him, he wanted to see for himself. So he arrived unannounced to fight night, with an entire contingent of his Red Guard goons, and tried to determine who it might be. I don't know why, but somehow he assumed that you, not Ember, harbored Faeblood."

A small lie. It didn't take long for Erik to figure out why his father focused on Maia. Even in the chaos of the training barn — an evening filled with entertaining battles and riotous betting and flowing drink — he watched Erik.

And Erik had been watching Maia.

"I confronted him before he left. He threatened to harm you."

His hands moved from her hair to her shoulders, gliding along her collarbone.

"You must understand. I didn't know his intentions. He never confided his plans."

"I can take care of myself."

"In a fair fight, sure." Erik stroked her arms. A trail of tiny bubbles sprouted on her skin. "My father is many things. Honorable, he is not."

Erik never gave his father much credit for creativity. Most of his schemes were of the *torture now, ask questions later* variety.

But his father had planted an illegal weapon at the compound. Rallied the High Table to sanction Xavier, demanding he produce a follower to fight to the death in the Castle arena. A punishment and a distraction.

In a fit of insanity, Erik had tied Maia up in her chambers. His actions had kept her home. Kept her safe.

And took a knife in the gullet as a souvenir. A fair trade.

"I didn't trust Xavier. And you had a proverbial target pinned to your tunic. I knew you wouldn't listen, wouldn't stay behind, not with the rest of your family in danger. So I did what I thought best."

Maia dunked under water and ran her hands through her hair, rinsing out the suds.

"You did what you thought best." She vibrated. "Tying me up in my chambers. Leaving me to ponder my demise. Worrying about my family. That was the worst part. I couldn't save myself. *I couldn't save them.*"

He hesitated. She was right. And if their roles were reversed… if she tied him up, taking away his ability to protect his loved ones… well, he wouldn't be sitting in a tub patiently waiting for the tale.

Shame stole over him. Not a simple acknowledgement of wrongdoing with a dose of embarrassment. No. This feeling was raw, acidic — burning him up from the inside. His memories were so vile that he feared voicing them would hurt too much. Still, he owed her this. Not because she was selfless. Not because he tied her up.

She deserved to know why he broke her trust. So he busied

his hands washing her, a part of him grateful she allowed his fidgeting, and told his story.

"My mother was the only one who gave a damn about me. When she left..." He cleared his throat. "When she left, I wanted to follow her across the Veil. She was the only good thing in my life."

Maia leaned her head into the crook of his shoulder.

"After she disappeared, the entire Castle ignored me. It was Dezee who kept me fed and alive. I spent months curled under my mother's portrait. She brought meals to the gallery. She never spoke. Never pushed me to rejoin the Court. One day, it could have been four weeks or four months, she brought me to the armory and introduced me to the commander of the Red Guard."

Erik added more soap to his palms and ran his hands over her ribs. His thumbs lingered under her chest, stroking a path down to her belly button then back up again.

"Commander Lachlan had no patience for spoiled Lords. He took one look and told me to grab a weapon. I was small for my age, my pants loose from infrequent meals. That beast of a man challenged me to a sword fight. Right then and there."

He couldn't prevent the smile tugging on his lips.

"My pride gave me strength. The other Faeblood lads were keen on ganging up on a High Lord's heir. I learned to defend myself against two, sometimes four boys at a time."

Maia covered his hand with hers.

"He knocked me down. Time and time again. I couldn't sit for a week without thinking of him. In the end, he picked me up by the scruff of my tunic and told Dezee, *He'll do. He has fight yet to give.* Then he looked me in the eye, something no one, not even Dezee, bothered to do since my mother's disappearance, and declared I smelled like a sewer rat."

This time, Erik chuckled.

"Clean off in the lake, he'd said. *I don't allow unwashed soldiers*

in the armory. It was like he lit a candle. I was humiliated. Sore as hell. Mad. So mad, but for the first time in memory, my belly rumbled. Dear gods, I was hungry. I remember thinking I could eat an entire pheasant right then."

Erik shifted, cradling her closer.

"Dezee took me to the lake, then to her kitchens. I moved my stuff into the Red Guard's barracks that night. Took meals with the servants. I spent every minute as Commander Lachlan's shadow."

He rested his forehead against her temple.

"My powers came early. The full ability to cast doesn't manifest until halfway through the change. Usually when a lad's voice deepens to match his sire's. I hid it for as long as I could, but the magic builds — becomes dangerous to deny. More than one Faeblood lost their mind suppressing their powers. My father left me alone for years, but when his guards and servants started showing up with freshly knitted wounds, he knew. He knew what I was."

"What happened?" she asked. "What did he do?"

"My father strung Commander Lachlan up in the dungeons."

Erik swallowed past the lump in his throat.

"The torture lasted for weeks. He made me watch. It was an important lesson: there were worse things than physical pain. As he flayed Lachlan's hide, my father's accusations became wilder and wilder. Not only was the commander training me like a human but conspiring to overthrow the High Table, having affairs with married Faeblood. He was unhinged."

"I understand," she whispered. "You don't need to explain the rest."

Erik ignored her. He didn't want to stop. "I should've ended it."

"Why didn't you?"

Not a challenge. Perhaps she recognized the poison leaching

from his memory and the need to express the rest, urging him to continue.

"I tried," Erik said, his voice breaking. "He spelled the locks. I called in favors from the Lords. I had enough markers to flip the entire Court on its head but couldn't convince a single noble to open a cell door. My father's influence outweighed my blackmail attempts."

Her fingers dug into his wrists.

"I begged Stella for an elixir. Somehow, she spelled it through the bars. The next morning, Lachlan was at peace. Before they buried him, I found the full vial in his pocket. I don't know what to think about his choice. Was he too weak to drink it? Was I too late?"

"You're not—"

"So when my father imprisoned Dezee while I spied on Xavier, I didn't hesitate to do everything in my power to guarantee her release. Call me a traitor. A coward. There is no winning against him."

He trailed a knuckle down her arm.

"I am not indifferent to Lea's wishes, but if I bring attention to her... if my father for one second believes her to be someone important... I refuse to let another suffer because of me."

"Erik, it's not—"

"Every person I care about has either been taken away or tortured. You judge my morals, my methods. *I never do the right thing.* But I survive. Because that's all I can do. I can't lose someone else I love."

"So you're going to let him win?" Maia straightened. "You're going to spend your life toiling with your plants? Continue your plush existence in your comfortable chambers? For what? For how long? I won't ever understand. You have so much potential. So much power."

"And who are you?" he asked quietly. "Who are you really? That family who loves you... Xavier who you worship... they sent you *here.* He sent Mikel here, knowing what this place was for him. Don't lecture me when you don't know your own desires. When you don't acknowledge how fuzzy the line between right and wrong blurs."

Dammit. He didn't mean to lash out.

Erik's chest heaved. He cupped her cheek and looked her in the eyes, studying the glint of his own reflection. It was as if he searched a looking glass and instead of seeing a man, he saw the nastiest parts of his soul.

Maia couldn't know what she was to him.

He couldn't admit it to himself, either. "Alive and safe is better than tortured and honorable."

CHAPTER TWENTY-FOUR

Maia wouldn't justify his statement with her opinion.

He wasn't ready to hear it, anyway. Erik had honor. His actions proved that. He just buried it under a mountain of sarcasm. And a heaping of questionable choices.

She needed time. Time away from him, away from the Court, to work through his confession. Despite the distinct lack of apology, she felt lighter. Not the relief of forgiveness, no... her stubbornness wouldn't allow that yet, but maybe an understanding of sorts.

Besides, she wasn't ready to consider what he said about her.

Maia knew who she was. Her self-inflicted extra year of militia training was the one time she came close to questioning her path. But that choice stemmed from a lack of confidence. Not conviction.

The water grew tepid, suds swirling around them. She was reluctant to leave. Maia crossed to the opposite side, settling back against the tub, her arms under her chest.

It seemed as if Erik was content to wallow. He tracked her but made no move to get out and dry off.

"I know what you are doing." He brushed his thumb over his mouth. "It won't work. I won't lose the bet with your little show. Keep playing, Kitten."

"I know not of what you speak."

She bit her lip and hugged herself tighter. Her chest buoyed above the surface. She enjoyed the heat in his eyes. Perhaps too much.

"If I'd known bath time was always this... stimulating for you, I would have suggested sharing sooner. Saved the servants from lugging the water twice."

Another reflection of the Faeblood's mentality. Erik's minuscule reservoir of water magic could fill this entire tub.

She heard it more than once since her arrival — servants without work were not serving. Who were the nobles to take away a chance to earn their keep? At least, that was the rhetoric preached at Court.

Erik grabbed the soap, pouring a small dollop on his palm. He rubbed his hands together then through his hair. Down his neck. Under his arms. And lower. Much lower, spending more time than necessary under water.

He was tall, with a fair amount of skin to clean, but not *that* tall.

Erik rinsed off, and when he emerged, a predatory hunger replaced his vacant expression. They both needed a distraction. She wanted to forget these past few days. For a little while. Poor decisions plagued her time here.

What was one more?

"Do you take care of other needs when you bathe?" she asked, her voice husky as she met his stare.

"No." He chuckled. "Would it please you if I made an exception?"

Erik added another dollop of soap to his hand.

"All yours," he said and handed her the bottle.

He leaned back, surveying her like a king cataloging his treasury. The corners of his lips tugged into a lazy grin. He flicked his wrist and half the torches snuffed out. The room dimmed to all but the tub.

"Go on." His hand sank under water. "Show me."

"Show you what?" she asked, playing along, wanting to hear the filthy words tumble from his mouth. Maia poured some soap and placed the bottle on the floor.

"Part your legs," he demanded, his tone a near growl. His biceps bunched, and small ripples formed in front of him. "Show me how you clean yourself. Don't be shy. Your kitten needs attention."

She willed her eyes to remain open. They wanted to close and imagine his long fingers wrapped around his length. She plucked a memory from their time wrestling in the training pit when he had been thick and heavy under her.

Her fingers toyed in her folds, gently parting the lips. How long had it been since she found release? Not since her arrival at the Castle. Long. She groaned. Too long. She might come from the first stroke.

"That's it. Insert the tip of one finger. Curl it toward your belly."

Maia obeyed, wishing she added another. Wishing it was a thicker finger.

"Deeper. Massage the front wall. We wouldn't want you stiff from today's sparring." His arm worked faster. Small waves traveled the span of the tub. "If it pleases you, I've been stiff since we arrived. Deliciously, annoyingly sore."

Her eyes met his as she added a second finger. In and out. In and out, her rhythm matching the ripples from his side. A soft moan escaped.

"Not too fast. Pull them out."

Her eyes widened.

"Aye, I know you added a second," he rasped. "You never were good at following directions."

At least she wasn't the only one affected.

"My turn," she said with a false bravado. "Close your eyes."

He obeyed without hesitation. She focused on his breastbone as if he were an opponent, squaring up in the ring. This was a different type of fight. No winners, perhaps no losers, either.

"I can hear your thoughts." Erik's eyes remained closed.

Oh, she wanted to wipe that smug smile off his handsome face. Instead, she commanded, "Grab yourself at the base. Describe your stroke."

"I'm thick, tapering at the head." His lips parted. "I can feel each individual finger, wishing they were yours. Is your hand big enough to touch on either side? For months, I wondered."

"Would they?" She asked, filling in the silence so she could plan the next command.

"At the root? No. Near the tip? Aye. Your clever fingers would touch. But would they be timid? Slow and methodical? Bold?"

"They would be… not hesitant," she said lamely. "Purposeful, learning your likes and dislikes. They would bring you to the edge — squeezing and pumping and twisting — until you begged for release."

He chuckled. "I never beg."

"Hush. This is my fantasy. There's a first time for everything. Now, stroke yourself and don't ease until I say."

Maia dipped her hand below the water. There was a certain power in leading a partner with simple words. Erik didn't need a leash. She didn't want to hold one. But this… this she could get used to.

"Take your other hand and give your nipples some attention," she said.

"Why don't you put that pretty mouth on them?" He didn't move as instructed.

Bossy. A small part despised her body's instinct to follow his instructions. She wouldn't give in so easily. If she submitted now, she might never steal another chance at this.

"I'm too busy." She ran the pad of her thumb across her nipple.

His eyes flew open in time to watch the gesture. He smirked, rubbing small circles around his dark, flat one. Erik twisted and plucked the peak, harder than she would have enjoyed.

Maia studied the line of his mouth, savoring his ragged breathing.

"Do you want me to stay like this?" His voice cracked. Another fissure of his control splintering. "Needy. Desperate."

"Depends. How close are you?" She dropped her hand and massaged the hood concealing her nub. Tiny lightning bolts skipped a path down her inner thighs. She wouldn't last much longer.

The last layer of suds dissipated, and the sight of Erik stroking himself nearly sent her over the edge.

"Say the word, Kitten." He cupped his heavy sac with his other hand and tugged.

Erik wasn't joking about his girth. Her fingers wouldn't touch when they wrapped around him.

The veins on his shaft stood out in relief.

She wanted to run the tip of her tongue along each. A reconnaissance mission if they took this to their bed. Not if, but when.

Because who was she kidding? This was bound to happen again. And why shouldn't it? As long as they avoided kissing.

Maia increased the speed of her fingers, matching the pace of his strokes. The first drop of cum leaked from his engorged head. Her hand stilled. It was an effort to pull her eyes away, but she didn't want to miss his reaction.

"Do you wish you were inside me? Pumping through your release? Do you wish it was me clamped around you instead of your hand?"

A strangled moan echoed between them. His? Hers? Didn't matter. His head fell back. The cords in his forearms popped. Delicious.

Thick ropes of white pulsed between them, suspended in the water.

Time slowed. She savored his release then found hers. Maia ground her palm, fighting through the prolonged spasms wracking her body. She wrung out every last one.

"If I'd known how responsive you are, I'd have fought harder to catch your attention in the training barn."

She couldn't read his expression, but the words hit their mark.

"Why didn't you?"

"I may employ methods you don't approve, but I take no pleasure in conning lovers, using their bodies."

Stupid heart. Worthless dumb muscle. That was how he saw her? A part of his deception. As if she had no say in the matter. She, a hapless female strung along by the handsome, all-consuming male.

She stood and toweled off, rubbing the soft linen over her breastbone. Maia strolled across the bathing chamber, stopped at the entrance, and said, "Perhaps you are right."

"Right about…?"

"Alive and miserable *is* better than tortured and honorable."

"WHAT ARE YOU DOING?" MIKEL ASKED BREE, ANGLING HIS BODY to block the door to the hallway.

The maid dropped the stack of parchment on Lord Siodina's desk.

She shouldn't be down here. The feather duster in her hand provided a plausible excuse, but rifling through his belongings was akin to asking to be locked in the dungeons.

"Dusting," she said as she raised her chin. "The regular maid feels unwell."

She took a step closer. The freckles on her nose made her appear younger than she was. She must be close in age to...

Mikel shook his head.

"What are *you* doing down here?" Her lips formed a frown as if she just realized her predicament. "He doesn't allow guards in his chambers, let alone an outsider."

He liked that about her. She didn't flash coy smiles, charming her way around him. Bree didn't blink at his snarls, nor Erik's. She would fit right in at home.

"My usual sweep of the Castle." He tilted his head to the side. Perhaps he should take a step back. His size alone frightened many.

"You're performing a perimeter sweep, here? In the dungeons? In the most secure part of the Castle?"

Nope. Definitely not scared. He nodded and cupped her elbow. A flash of gold ringed her eyes, so quick he could convince himself he imagined it.

"You're insane." She tried to pull free. The parchment in her grip crinkled. "Let me go before we are both caught."

Mikel slid his hand down her arm, encircling her small wrists. Her smooth skin.

"You're not from the Castle." He held her arm in front of his face as if staring would make the scars manifest.

She wrenched it free and folded the parchment in half. Then fourths. She tucked the resultant square in her bodice but not before he caught the slight tremble of her fingers.

"No. I was not born in the Castle if that's what you ask." She took a step back. "But it's my home now."

"Where are you from?" Why was she here? This place was a prison for humans.

"I'm from all over," Bree said as if she practiced the answer each morning in the looking glass. "My parents moved us a lot as children."

He waited, holding her gaze. Mikel had learned long ago remaining silent was more effective to get people to talk than endless questions, brute intimidation.

"I applied for a position in the Castle last spring. As for the bracelets…" She shrugged. "It was easier to cover my wrists than answer probing questions. This land is unforgiving. I have no desire to sleep in barns nor on the side of the road."

The Faeblood nobles would see another servant, never looking beyond the drab dress and ready help. Bree sold years of her life for the comfort of a dry roof, a full belly. She must be careful.

"Stay out of the Lords' beds." He glanced around, noting the general disarray of the desk. No books. No journals. "Stay away from Siodina."

Come to the compound with me when I leave, he wanted to add. Like the others, it was a lost cause. He wasn't sure he could smuggle her out of this hellhole even if she wanted to escape.

"I'm not a whore." She bunched the top of her skirts, glaring. Bree strolled out of the chamber. Over her shoulder she added, "I'm here to clean."

"Forget I said it." He ran a hand through his hair. Dammit. He was messing this up, letting his past seep between them. "Just… just be smart."

She looked as if she wanted to say more but nodded, following him up the stairs.

Footsteps echoed from above.

There was nowhere to hide. He pushed her against the stone wall and wedged a knee between her hips.

"What are you doing?" She rested her palms on his chest.

Lovers met all over the Castle. Let whoever approached think they'd stolen away from their duties for a tryst. He wrapped her hands around the back of his neck.

"Pretend you can't get enough of me." He dipped his head. The rough stubble of his beard rubbed against her soft cheek. She was beautiful, but his body didn't stir.

"Are you crazy?" She threaded her fingers behind his head, tugging his face nearer. "No one will believe us."

"You're a maid. No excuse for my presence." He angled his hips, pressing her body into the shadows.

The footsteps slowed.

"Well, well, well. Who do we have here? Lady Maia's dog. I wondered when I would catch you sniffing around King Siodina's chambers."

The distinct swish of a blade freed from its sheath resonated off the stone walls.

Mikel pivoted, pushing Bree farther behind him.

The commander of the Red Guard studied him. He didn't know the man's name. But he carried his bulk with ease, suggesting a higher level of skill than the average grunt. His dark brown hair curled at his temple. The nearest torch highlighted notes of red. A close-cropped beard of the same color covered his jaw.

There was a familiarity Mikel couldn't place. Something to set him on edge.

It didn't matter. Only a man with loose morals could climb the ranks of the Red Guard. If rumors were true, Erik's father had unceremoniously relieved the last man of honor to hold the position.

"Who's hiding in your skirts, Mikel?"

"Lukas?" Bree nudged Mikel to the side. "Lukas, did you follow me?"

"Bree." The commander exhaled her name, lowered his sword, and brushed past him as if he wasn't present.

Mikel held up both hands. He wanted no part of this reunion.

"I told you not to come down here," Lukas said and gripped her waist. "It's not safe."

Mikel climbed a few steps, adding much needed distance. He recognized the anguish in the Red Guard's voice. Lukas wouldn't hurt her or report their whereabouts. Though he might take a swing at Mikel.

"And I told you it's not your concern." She pointed to herself. "I'm not your concern."

Bree came up to Lukas's shoulders. She puffed out her chest as if to make herself bigger. A pixie confronting a giant.

The commander looked torn between strangling her and kissing her. The entire exchange might be amusing if not for their precarious location.

Mikel covered a laugh with a cough. Maybe not convincingly enough by the glare the commander sent his way. Time for some light-hearted teasing.

"Oy, lovebirds. As much as I enjoy your foreplay," he waggled his brows, "now is not the time nor place. Let's find something… more cozy, hmm?"

CHAPTER TWENTY-FIVE

Two days later, Erik leaned against a large oak tree and rubbed his back against its trunk, failing to ease the constant itch between his shoulder blades. Bark crumbled next to Mikel's leg.

The fighter ignored him. Instead, he observed Maia and Lea sparring in the clearing, grunting every few minutes at a well-timed strike. Or a solid parry.

It was difficult for Erik to keep his opinions to himself. Their footwork was off. They held their swords too low. Easy fixes.

"Maia needs to choke up more on the hilt and raise her hands half an arm's length."

Another grunt.

"Tell Lea to widen her stance. One hard blow will knock her clean over."

"Not your messenger." Mikel snapped a long piece of dried grass and wove it between his fingers. "Tell her yourself."

If it were only that simple.

There were no more baths. No more soft greetings in the morning. He longed to step in and help with training, but a part of him held back, wondering if Maia's temper would cool enough to listen to his suggestions.

The other part of him swelled with pride. Her skills in the training barn transferred almost seamlessly.

Her smiles and lyrical tone tightened something in his chest.

She spent too many hours stuffed into uncomfortable couture. At tea in one gown. Then at dinner parading in another.

Her manners were impeccable… as flawless as the smile she forced day after day. Her speech matched the cadence of Ladies who spent decades at Court, blending in as her mission demanded. But her spark dimmed.

"Chickenshit," was all Mikel said as he stood, strolled to the pair, and corrected their forms according to Erik's suggestions.

Snap.

Erik whirled around.

A servant approached. Heavy-footed and bulky like a bull prone to bloat, he stepped on damn near every twig in the oak's understory. He halted several paces away and bowed.

Up close, he was younger than Erik expected.

"Your father requests your presence in the former High Table chamber," the servant said to the ground. "I am to escort you straight there. The other nobles await your arrival."

"Very well."

Erik turned his back on the servant, missing the slight curl to the man's lips. He jogged over to the trio and waited until Mikel finished correcting Maia's form.

In the late afternoon sun, the dark circles under her eyes stood out. Fatigue etched faint lines in her forehead.

"May I?" he asked as he stepped behind her. His father could wait another five minutes.

"What are you doing?" Perhaps intended as a hiss, her tone was full of resignation.

"Correcting your hold." He wrapped his arms around her.

She didn't stiffen under his touch. She didn't relax either.

Erik ran his palms along the outside of her arms. *Slow down.* Best not to spook her. That was the only reason he took his time and skimmed her wrists, lingering on her pulse before wrapping his larger hands around hers.

"Elevate the base of the handle. You waste time raising the blade to counter someone taller."

She lifted her hands.

"Good." Erik leaned forward and whispered, "Lead with the handle's base on the parry. Up and away."

"Like this?"

"Lock your center." He spread the fingers of one hand on her lower back. Those of the other on her stomach. "Exhale when you raise it."

It took every ounce of concentration to not chuck the weapons aside and suggest they grapple for old time's sake. Her nearness drove his body to distraction. It remembered the feel of her as she wrestled for control. Of Erik flexing his hips in half-hearted attempts to buck her off.

"Like this?" Maia repeated, her voice soft.

He trailed his fingers down one arm and applied pressure to her wrists until she dropped the weapon.

Maia whirled in the circle of his arms. Her mouth parted but whatever barb she intended to throw died between them.

"My father requests my presence." He tucked a tendril behind her ear, his fingertips grazing the many posts and hoops. "I'll send a tray to our rooms. Take the night off from Court. Who knows how long he will keep me."

Erik leaned down. A trip to the High Table was never a pleasant experience. To be summoned there now that his father was the King, knowing the small check on his power vanished the moment the Lords swore fealty... Erik's lips brushed her forehead.

Maia's grip on his tunic tightened. "Erik? What's wrong—"

Erik grunted. Mikel may be onto something with his nonverbal conversations. Maia had too many responsibilities. It was selfish to add worry to the list, so he said, "That kiss doesn't count, either."

~

TWO PRISONERS KNELT ON THE FLOOR OF THE FORMER HIGH Table chamber.

Ropes bound their wrists behind their backs. Gags kept their thoughts in their heads. The one on the left wore a servant's uniform. The one on the right—

No.

Erik stared at the leader of the Huntsmen territory.

Hair, black as the stone mined deep from Morvak's clutches, curled at his nape. A single stripe of silver tucked behind his right ear. An odd birthmark, rumored to be a blessing from the gods.

In one of the many attempts to groom Erik in his image, his father had commanded him to memorize the faces and family lines of all the leaders from miniature stills. To learn their strengths. And their weaknesses.

Where the servant struggled and moaned against his restraints, Cedric Canes held his head high, his fury aimed at the false King.

Someone had rearranged the seating.

A dozen chairs encircled the chamber floor, leaving the first row empty save for a large, overstuffed chaise. The former High Lords occupied the lower seats while his father lounged above.

"Ah, Erik, my heir." His father clapped his hands. "Sit. Let's dispense with this odious task."

"My Lord? I mean… my King… my apologies… my liege…" Lord Cantwine stammered.

"Silence," his father snapped. "You will hold your tongue for my sentencing."

That was the reason for his summons. A trial of sorts. Erik took the only vacant seat.

The clang of armor echoed, reverberating off the stone walls until disappearing under the vaulted ceiling. Over three dozen Red Guard lined the upper levels. They wore customary sneers and a new gold crest on their tunics.

Erik squinted. Intricate embroidery depicted an eagle mid-flight, carrying two snakes in its claws. The Siodina family crest.

His father didn't waste any time claiming the soldiers for his personal use. Though with their aid during his coup, perhaps their allegiance shifted long ago.

Commander Lukas descended from his post two flights above. Six guards followed, the last wearing a black executioner's mask and carrying a long-handled axe. They fanned out, each one stationing himself next to a Lord.

"Attempt nothing foolish," Lukas growled under his breath. "Your father won't spare your life if you interfere."

Erik's fingers dug into the upholstery tacks on the chair's arms. He willed his breaths to slow. Soon, his magic would fight his determination to stay seated. He needed every second to prepare.

The odds of Erik stopping whatever his father planned were rubbish. Spineless Lords stayed rooted in their chairs. Bloodthirsty guards fondled their blades, likely looking for any reason to maim the nobles who humiliated them for sport.

"Interesting you should ask, Lord Cantwine." His father crossed one leg over the other and gestured toward the servant. "Do you not recognize your charge?"

"A servant?" Lord Cantwine asked. "My King… there are so many. 'Tis impossible to learn all their faces."

"Look." His father leaned forward. "Bring the traitor closer. Maybe the Lord's eyes fail him in old age."

The executioner hoisted the man by his bindings and marched him over, stopping in front of Lord Cantwine.

"Why... yes. Now that he is nearer, I seem to recall his features."

"Lies," Erik's father spat. "He is your family's personal butler. His father served yours. His sons wander the realm, scouring for material for your idiotic additions to the fortress."

"Of course. Forgive me. I wished to limit my association as it appears he has drawn your censure."

"Do you want to take a guess as to his transgressions?" His father asked with the same honeyed tone courtiers use when teasing the object of their affections.

Lord Cantwine didn't hear the trap. Or perhaps he thought more lies would spare his father's wrath. Erik received too many punishments not to recognize where this would lead.

"I haven't the faintest clue—"

His father inclined his chin.

Erik balled his fists – the only movement he allowed himself as the executioner swung his blade, beheading the servant at the same time the guard nearest Lord Cantwine plunged his sword in the noble's gullet.

Several horrifying seconds passed before Erik could swallow around the lump in his throat. His magic pounded against his ribs, fighting to burst free. Despite harnessing his considerable strength to keep it locked down, he never felt so powerless.

After one shuddering cough, Lord Cantwine's body fell forward, landing in a pool of blood next to the severed head.

"Let this be a lesson for everyone else. History demands rulers cut down their greatest contenders. I spare your lives because of the valuable magic coursing through your veins. Another monarch wouldn't have been so magnanimous. And how do you repay me?"

The Lords' lips all formed flat lines, none keen to answer the question. At least they understood his father didn't require one.

"... by sending a servant into the territories, carrying a missive containing falsehoods. The throne is my birthright. Each of you swore fealty to me. Lord Cantwine sought to spread rumors of coercion, stealing my glory and announcing my ascension prior to the Grimoire Games."

So that's why his father waited to spread the news. He wanted the entire realm gathered to make the formal proclamation.

"I expect no more interference in the matter." He tutted and took a sip from his flask. "Anybody wish to take back their oath of fealty?"

Cedric muttered against his gag.

"I haven't forgotten about you." His father stood, gathered his robes, and strolled down the steps. "Untie him. I'm curious what the thief has to say."

Cedric's eyes widened.

Surprise or fear? Erik couldn't be certain. He shifted to stand but pressure on his shoulder kept Erik seated.

Lukas squeezed then strolled over to Cedric. He untied the gag, hooked an arm around his prisoner's middle, and hauled him upright.

"Cedric Canes, leader of the Huntsmen territory, you are hereby stripped of your title. You stand accused of treason for seizing the Woodcutter territory's annual tithe. How do you wish to plead?"

His father raised his hand.

"Take care with your next. Kiehl shall suffer the consequences if you claim innocence."

Dear gods. This was no trial. His father would rid the territories of a capable leader one way or another this afternoon. Both Kiehl and Cedric were honorable men, respected by their villages for their genuine care of their peoples.

"Father—"

"Sit down. Unless you wish to take his place."

The coppery tang of blood filled Erik's mouth. He relaxed his jaw.

Cedric's chest heaved. Silence stretched, thickening the air as he hesitated. He stared at something out of the windows. And after several excruciating minutes, the leader of the Huntsmen territory tilted his head to the side, met Erik's father's glare, and said, "It was me who—"

The swish of the executioner's blade silenced the last words of his confession.

CHAPTER TWENTY-SIX

The next night at dinner, Maia stared at her plate and toyed with the small strips of parchment in her dress's pocket.

She'd found the stack of Erik's latest training advice on her vanity and spent the entire time Bree styled her hair stewing over their contents.

Jille deserved extra coin for sewing the hidden compartments. Not only did they keep Maia's hands warm in the perpetually chilly Castle, but they were useful for smuggling contraband too.

The small notes made the meal bearable. Erik was distracted, his normal taunts hollow. Lady Stella made her rounds, her insults sharp per usual. Maia considered chucking an olive at her eye but didn't want to waste tasty appetizers. Then there was Lord Nanscott who insisted on talking over everyone, pausing only to leer at her chest.

So she'd kept her hand in the pocket, folding and refolding Erik's words into fourths then eighths.

If she didn't dwell on his motives for leaving them, Maia could admit the directives were sound.

Don't allow Lea to drag the tip of her sword when rising from a roll.

Strike the lower flank after pivoting left.

Tell Mikel to find shields. It takes time to learn to balance with one on your arm.

Then there was the last...

You look beautiful tonight.

Erik repeated the same four words every evening, except there was something about seeing it written down...

Not soon enough, the meal concluded and the great hall emptied. Courtiers clogged the main corridor, breaking off in groups of three or more.

"Bree will bring up a tray," Erik whispered in her ear. He pulled her close, steering her around a slow-moving group in front. "Don't wait for me."

"You're not staying?" Maia clasped his hand, intertwining their fingers, and nudged him into a nearby alcove. She stepped between his legs, hoping to appear mid-tryst to passersby. "Where will you be?"

"In the library." He nuzzled the side of her neck, following her ruse. "Before you ask, I don't know when I will return. You must eat to keep your strength."

"Take me with you. I spent the afternoon with Lea." *Not searching for your father's journal,* she didn't need to add.

"Food first. Then Mikel can escort you."

"What's wrong?" she asked, not allowing his deflection to stand.

"Nothing." He sighed against her neck. "I'm taking care of it."

"Don't lie to me." Maia gripped the front of his tunic. "Something happened. Dinner was... subdued."

Erik dropped his head against her collarbone. He wrapped his arms tighter, pulling her flush against him.

Something terrible must've transpired for him to seek

comfort. The pain in Maia's bad shoulder receded. She let him hold her a little longer, fussing with his magic.

"Mikel left to spend the night outside the servants' quarters." She massaged the tips of his ears. "He won't return until dawn."

"Why?"

"Nightmares plague Lea. She swears someone is watching her as she sleeps."

Erik leaned back, searching her eyes. "You still need to eat."

That was the only warning he gave before tugging her in the direction opposite their chambers.

As expected, the library was quiet. Its heavy door cocooned them inside, shielding noise from the corridors.

"Stay here. I need to ensure we are alone." Erik walked the perimeter.

Maia couldn't stand still, so she trekked up and down the center aisles, listening for a third pair of footsteps. Or hushed whispers. The small ribbon she used to mark her place hung from a shelf near the back. She ignored Erik's scowl and pulled down the book next to it.

"Do you ever listen—"

The door creaked open.

Erik held a finger to his lips, his eyes pleading for silence. He beckoned her to the end of the widest bookcase.

Maia closed her book, replaced it on the shelf, and tucked into his side. Together, they tiptoed several paces forward for a better look.

"... retrieve it," Erik's father commanded. He gestured to a faded map of Morvak pinned on the wall. "No, not that one, you fool. The other."

A tall Red Guard removed the parchment, rolled it up, and handed it over.

Erik inclined his chin in her direction. A silent plan passed between them. They waited a few seconds then stalked the pair through the maze of hallways, past his father's lab, and down the tunnel connecting Red Guard barracks to the arena.

King Siodina and his minion exited the Castle through the main entrance doors. Erik and Maia through the adjacent servants' passage. They scurried to the half-wall enclosing the courtyard, dropping low enough to conceal their hiding spot, close enough to hear their conversation.

"Where is Lord Cantwine?" Erik's father asked the guard, his voice deceptively low. "I gave specific instructions to haul all three traitors here."

Maia squinted.

Moonlight reflected off the Pool of Illumination, casting shadows on the ground from a pair of headless bodies lumped at the King's feet. One in servant garb. The other, a uniform of fine black leathers. A sack rested beside them. A dark brown stain wrapped ominously around its bottom.

Her stomach lurched.

"Milord—" the guard stuttered.

"Find him." Erik's father untied the burlap's bindings and pulled a severed head free. He caressed a section of black hair, stopping to tuck a wisp of silver behind the ear. "Unless you wish to take his place."

Maia's lips parted. A rough hand covered her gasp.

"Shhh," Erik growled in her ear, saving her from a cry sure to alert the nearest sentry.

"Lady Cantwine wished for a holy man to deliver her husband's Last Rite." The guard bowed. "I shall retrieve his corpse at once. If it pleases..."

Maia studied the unseeing eyes of Cedric Cane, ignoring the guard's next.

Dear gods. Erik's father had killed a territory leader. Oh, she suffered no delusion that he delivered the fatal blows. Dirty work reserved for lesser humans. But she was certain they died at his command.

Maia's chest heaved, preventing proper breath. Her eyes watered. Two blinks before she would've passed out, Erik released his hold.

She'd known something rattled her husband last night and all day today. When she'd pressed him about it, he'd shrugged her off. But this…

This...

There were no words for this atrocity.

Just when she thought it couldn't get any worse, Erik's father dropped Cedric's head. It hit the ground with a wet thud. King Siodina crouched down next to his lifeless body and bit his neck.

She gagged. Bile burned her throat, threatening to spew out if she dared open her mouth.

The sick bastard, marking his kill like a mate marks their lover. One look at Erik's face told her all she needed to know about his thoughts on the practice.

"My liege." The guard returned. He carried a very heavy, very unalive Lord Cantwine over his shoulder. His head, thankfully, was still attached. "Where would you like him?"

The King stared at his minion. He glared until the weight of his censure forced the lackey to decide himself.

The guard unceremoniously propped the dead noble next to the others like a morbid puppet cleaved from its strings.

"The lake spills over the southern aspect, yes?" Erik's father produced the map from inside his robes, unrolled it, and frowned. He pointed toward the grotto then looked back at the parchment. "How old is this depiction?"

"I–I didn't check the date."

Maia recognized the guard's mistake at the same time Erik's father plunged his blade into his gullet.

The guard slumped next to the others, a look of shock etched on his face. Blood seeped between his fingers and stained his tunic a darker red. He fell backwards on the growing pile.

Erik's father poked the wound and rubbed his fingers together in front of his face. And sniffed.

What in all the realms—

"Imbeciles." He wiped them on the man's collar, took a swig from his flask, and flicked his wrist. "I find myself surrounded by incompetent fools."

The bodies burst into flames.

Maia didn't possess the energy to flinch.

Erik leaned back against the wall and held his arm out. An invitation. She didn't hesitate to snuggle into his side, curling into his warmth. They stayed there, each in their own thoughts, until the final embers disappeared into the night.

~

"You knew," Maia said the moment Erik shut their chamber door. "You knew what he did and didn't tell me."

"Eat." Erik gestured to the tray on the vanity.

"Eat. *Eat.* That's all you have to say. Who could eat after... after that?" Maia flung her hands up.

"You require sustenance," Erik said in a dull tone, one that made her fingers itch to slap some life into him.

Erik pulled out the chair, gripping its back hard enough his knuckles turned white. He waited.

Maia wanted to hurl words at him. She needed something... anything to relieve this pent-up rage. Tonight, Erik would be her target. She was beyond caring if it was wrong. It was clear his father's actions shook him. But she wasn't in control of her anger enough to stay her tongue.

He lied to her. Sure, it was a lie of omission. A flaw Xavier often shared. Still didn't excuse his behavior.

"What. Happened?" She sat in the chair, her body vibrating, and refused to touch her food until he began.

"This was the outcome of my summons yesterday." Erik ran a hand over his hair. "Prior to my arrival, he assembled the Lords. The Red Guard."

Erik paced. Every turn, he glanced back at the vanity, studying Maia. It wasn't until she picked up her fork that he continued his tale.

"He accused Lord Cantwine and his servant of sending letters to the territories with news of his ascension. Perhaps if that had been all… my father would've overlooked it. But the missives contained a truthful version of events, including his coercion of the other High Lords."

Maia took a bite of the cold potatoes followed by a hearty swig of water, washing down the dry lump as it appeared she could no longer swallow.

"Either they didn't find your letter to Xavier or your writing convinced my father's spies that you had little more to say than updating Jade on Court frivolities. Otherwise, I fear he wouldn't have spared you, either. My wife or not."

He halted and stared pointedly at her plate.

"Eat," he snapped and resumed pacing, not bothering to confirm she followed his command. "You didn't see it. See them. I sat in an overstuffed chair, surrounded by Lords I've known since childhood, and watched as they did nothing. *Nothing.* My father ordered the prisoner's deaths with as little fanfare as he orders an extra loaf of bread for the dinner table."

Maia took another bite. Another swig of water. It was eat or open her mouth and scream. She swallowed. It appeared as if Erik needed to confess as much as she needed to hear it.

"Over thirty guards. The highest-ranking nobles. And they sat. *Sat,* as the bodies bled out on the chamber floor."

Erik whirled and regarded her in the looking glass.

"My father accused Cedric of stealing the woodcutter's annual tithe while the purse was en route to the Castle. He granted an impossible choice. Deny the story, claiming innocence and pitting his word against Kiehl's. Or confess to the crime."

"What did Cedric do?" Maia knew the answer, but some part of her needed for Erik to say the words.

"He confessed." Erik strolled over to his desk and picked up an envelope. "Yesterday, I debated sending missives to the remaining territory leaders. They deserve to know what transpired here. Today, my reasons for waiting sound... shallow."

"Send them with Mikel." Maia swallowed another lump of potatoes and cleared her throat. "He has men stationed in the surrounding forests. If you want to contact the territories, it's safer to send the note by foot rather than carrier fowl."

Erik's head snapped up. "Mikel won't risk the safety of his men. I'll send my best hawk."

"He won't deny me," Maia said, ignoring his protest. "This is information is too important. Soon, the leaders will gather here for the Games. We must warn them beforehand."

"I'll consider it." Erik held up an envelope. "You've a letter."

It wasn't agreement but she let the subject drop. Maia crossed the room, her meal forgotten, and plucked it from his hand.

Someone had tampered with the seal.

Oh, they went to great effort trying to re-affix it, but the edge curled upward on one side. She recognized the crest.

"It's from Jade." Maia slid a finger under the wax and skimmed the contents.

"What does she say?" Erik rested a hand on her nape and peered over her shoulder.

Maia side-eyed him and frowned. She held out the parchment, pointing to the last couple paragraphs.

"I'm not sure what it means."

Despite my request for privacy, Xavier stands over my shoulder as I write to you, dear friend. He says to give you his love and wants to ensure you know this correspondence is from both of us.

We miss you. Me, for your wit and good humor. Xav, for your organization with the trainees. Think! In a fortnight, we shall be reunited.

"It could be as simple as Jade expressing excitement for the Games, or it could be a hint at their intentions to retrieve you after."

Maia stilled. First the mention of her balcony. Now this. It was too soon. She wasn't close to accomplishing her tasks. And what if she won? Why would Xavier pass on an opportunity for a spy in the Red Guard academy?

Some soldier she turned out to be. Thus far, she failed to find Siodina's book. And while her reports to the compound meant Xavier received news days, sometimes weeks before other territory leaders, his other scouts could keep him abreast of the latest. She couldn't even find Siodina's war room to determine if he added to his supplies.

"Circumstances change." Erik paused. "You should drop out of the competition."

"For a moment there, I thought *you* changed." Maia sat back down and snatched her fork.

"What? You thought I grew a heart?"

"No." She shoveled roasted pheasant in her mouth. Erik was right — she would need her strength. "I thought you grew a spine."

[illegible] through the trees. [illegible]

[illegible] would be a feat in their [illegible]

[illegible] to the attention of her [illegible] Who would [illegible] of an opportunity to [illegible] at the Red Thread Academy?

[illegible] she turned out [illegible] and [illegible]. At [illegible] her [illegible] to the competition [illegible] news [illegible] letters [illegible] of the latest. She [illegible] determined [illegible]

[illegible] of the competition.

[illegible] down and [illegible]

[illegible] in her hand.

[illegible] smile.

CHAPTER TWENTY-SEVEN

Another week lapsed, one more until the Grimoire Games.

Except for sharing a bed, Erik avoided being alone with Maia in their chambers. Easy, considering he rose before her and returned when she slept. During the day, she trained with Lea or scoured the library with Bree, stuffing herself in those ridiculous gowns in the hours between.

He hadn't heard any more rumors of her stabbing courtiers at tea. Swordplay, it appeared, kept her temper leashed.

Stella had sent a summons last night, requesting his presence in the library at eleven bells.

Erik rubbed the tip of his nose. While the servants kept the worktable and shelves in the library dust free, the entire chamber made his skin itch.

He strolled a lap around the aisles, absentmindedly trailing his fingers along various spines. So many texts. So many forgotten works. He wasn't, by admission, a scholar. Why read when one could learn by casting? Or training?

Too many Faeblood neglected their magical education,

centering their lives on parties and dalliances. But he could see the resources here. A waste, considering how few used them.

Maybe their powers deserved to fade into extinction.

Near the back, hidden behind an articulated model of the peninsula's ancient portal system, half a dozen steps led down to the older archives.

A trickle of water carved a narrow trench under the railing, adding to the general mustiness. Cobwebs framed the landing's corners. A solitary filament stretched across the width.

Erik swiped his hand, but instead of the sticky mess clinging to him, it flickered, then reformed.

An illusion. Lord Scarbough's work? Or was this cast older?

Erik skirted the model's broken arm and descended.

Light spilled down the steps from the library proper and illuminated a solitary torch mounted next to a battered door.

The sweet taste of a cast coated his tongue. His magic lit the wick, a blue flame sparking alive.

How long had it been since someone came here? In his quest to search for clues to his mother's disappearance, he never once considered digging around in the archives.

Where the stairs behind him matched the rough walls of the rest of the Castle — crude passages chiseled by a combination of hasty magic and human pickaxes — they'd built this antechamber with the smoothest gray granite. Distorted with veins of blues and greens, there was only one other place like it.

Did his grandfather commission the construction of the archives too?

Centered halfway down the door, a heavy iron handle doubled as a knocker. His palms warmed, another cast coating his tongue. He twisted it to the left. Then the right. Nothing. Locked.

Erik crouched down and studied a keyhole in the center of the ring.

He couldn't remember the last door his magic failed to open.

The interior tumblers mocked him. No matter how many spells came to mind, none nudged the tiny levers.

Faint footsteps echoed from above, close enough he didn't have time to snuff the flame. The comfortable weight of a dagger filled his palm. Erik pressed his back to the far wall.

Whoever came down would see him. But he had the element of surprise from this position.

"Before you slit my throat, perhaps you should listen to what I have to say."

Stella. Erik sheathed his blade and raised the torch higher.

"Put that away." She swatted the air. "Or at least farther from my face. I abhor the smell."

The drawback of being a Nares.

"Looking for these?" Stella jangled a pair of ornate iron keys in front of his nose.

"You've been down here." Not a question.

"More and more, these days." She breezed past, the flame flickering in her wake, and opened the door. "Let's just say, I've been… properly motivated."

Erik followed her into the chamber, careful to shut it behind them.

Small glass lanterns hung on the walls. Here, the aquamarine threads cleaving the stone ran in whirls and swoops, unlike the fractured lines outside the door.

He crossed to the nearest candle and raised the torch to light the wick.

"Don't," Stella said, a thread of urgency in the command. "Don't light them."

His arm hung in midair, the weight of her words heavier than a wooden club.

"Pray tell, how many times have you visited these archives?"

"Enough," she hedged and strolled to the back of the room.

Erik followed at a more leisurely pace.

Shelves lined the outer walls. A ladder rested against a taller one down the right aisle. The middle of the room boasted a small counter-height table. A solitary stool tucked underneath, its legs free from the illusory webs decorating the stairs.

The entire chamber appeared to be clean. No spiders. No dust.

Books lined the shelves, rows upon rows. Scrolls peeked out of clay vases in the corners. Single sheets of parchment hung on every available surface, pinned haphazardly with nails and sewing needles.

He recognized a map of Morvak. The streams and rivers differing from what he learned in his travels, as if time and human interference altered their course.

Erik must sneak Maia down here. Though perhaps he should wait to tell her about the archives. She didn't need a distraction so close to the competition. A few more days couldn't hurt.

Stella stopped at an apothecary case in the back. It was five shelves high, the lowest missing the glass panel on its door. She snagged a small leather-bound book off the top and flipped through the it.

Curious, Erik joined her, keeping the torch aloft.

Untidy writing filled the pages, the tight lettering difficult to decipher. It was too messy for a priestess with neat penmanship. A journal?

"You'll find what you seek in here." Stella caressed the front cover. "It took me ages to discover it. I had just finished my search upstairs when fate nudged me. It would make more sense for valuable spell books and lost potion recipes to be in the larger volumes near the front."

She gestured to the open shelves on either side of the door.

"Something about this little book caught my attention."

Huh. Perhaps her ability to sniff out threads of magic extended beyond potions.

"It took a week of late nights." She pulled out a ribbon

dividing the pages, letting it dangle to the side. "Read it for yourself. You will find what you require."

"I don't have time to read it for myself," Erik said.

"That is the magic of the spell." Stella smirked. "In order for it to work, the caster must interpret it in their own manner, choosing the ingredients to break a vow. Clever, really. As each bond written in the stars is unique. Everything has a beginning, a middle, and an end. Oaths and casts and vows are not immune."

"You speak in riddles." Erik ran his hand over his hair.

"Work backwards. That's what took so long. It is a personal spell book disguised as a journal. Or the journal of a tinkering genius. The voice is..." she tapped her finger to her lips. "Not drivel, per se, but the author is a dreadful bore. Honorable Fae always are."

She shrugged her shoulders.

"Not enough back-stabbing intrigue and harmful gossip for you?"

"What's the point of writing something so droll? They should keep it between their ears." She flicked her hand and strolled toward the front. "Enjoy."

"Wait, that's it? Did you discover anything else down here?"

"I haven't had time to look. Since I've finished with your little errand, I plan to devour everything in this room." She snagged a small navy journal out of a collection of at least twenty matching volumes, tucking it under her arm.

Should he ask her about his father's journal? It was a risk. But the more he considered, the more he realized Stella might not favor his sire's unobstructed rise to power.

"Stella?" Erik asked, forcing a hint of vulnerability in his voice. "My father is up to something. He wouldn't abolish the High Table unless it suited some greater scheme. I can't help but wonder... all this..."

He opened his arms, gesturing to the Castle proper.

"All these changes began when he sent me into the territories." Erik leaned in and whispered, "After the disappearance of his personal journal."

"Say the words." Stella had known him too long to fall for his poor performance. She tapped a foot. "What else do you require?"

"His book — a journal." He nodded to the volume in her hand. "Small. Navy."

"I'll consider it."

He would press her about it later. For now, it was enough to plant the seed.

"You still haven't given me a name." He dipped his chin. "For payment. I shall speak with your father tonight."

"I changed my mind." She looped the ring of keys around her wrist and gathered her skirts. "I have another task that will settle your debt."

"We didn't—"

"Smuggle Talia from the Castle." Stella closed her eyes. "I don't care where you send her. Just... just get her out of here. She'll require a full purse. And I require a promise. Don't tell me where you send her, not even if I'm of sound mind when I ask."

Lady Talia Owenspaete. Stella's willowy lover. An unpredictable complication. Mikel would take her, no questions. But would the courtier willingly leave with a militia fighter?

"My father's spies are everywhere. What am I to do with a simpering Lady? It's not so easy as—"

"I'm not asking," Stella said. Her eyelids flew open. "She has no family, if that's what stays your hand. No one will care. No one will retaliate. Find a way. That is my price."

Stella was right — he owed her. Erik dipped his chin, his protest dying on his lips.

The book in his hand was small. The weight of its contents pressed into his palm. He should feel relief. Shouldn't he? It was what he wanted from the moment he concocted that fake potion for their wedding ceremony. Now, he wasn't so sure.

They always had a countdown on their marriage. But it was as if the clock jumped forward.

It was selfish for him to want to keep Maia by his side.

For one, her entire life was at the compound. She had a loving family with all their messy trappings. They fought beside her. Cared about her happiness. Their support was unwavering. He shared something similar with Dezee, with his first commander. But Maia had an unending supply of love.

He would never keep her from that life. Even if the ball of dread in his stomach felt more like possessiveness. Less like jealousy.

Besides, Maia needed to follow her own path.

She enjoyed a freedom so few in Morvak had. Xavier's wealth and power afforded her that luxury. Her pride and hard work maintained it. She was unencumbered by the responsibilities of a monarchy. She never had to work a family trade. Never had to scratch out a living in the territories.

She could simply… choose.

Between the backstabbing Ladies and the lecherous Lords, Court was not where one thrived. No, she was better off at the compound where idealistic fools grew soft in the mind while militia training honed their bodies.

"Oh, and Erik, your mask is slipping." Stella ushered them out, locking the door behind him.

"My mask?" Did he hear her wrong?

"Aye. You wear your feelings for her on your face. Don't let her discover your treachery. She'll never forgive you if she found out you lied about the oath."

"The elixir is for my father. I don't—"

She sent a haughty wave over her shoulder. "Save it for someone who doesn't know you."

~

ERIK PACED THE EDGE OF THE OUTDOOR TERRACE, THUMBING through the journal's pages so quickly he had to re-read most entries.

Stella was right. This little diary was dry. He went against her recommendation and started from the beginning.

The author was Fae, and if his history was correct, lived over a millennium ago nearby in the Northern Isles.

She hailed from a clan who dwelled in the trees, carving out homes and palaces in magically modified trunks. The land was submerged in frost, a tundra that proved inhospitable to others who didn't share their thick blood.

If the entries were any sign, the Court was... lively. Not surprising, since there was little else to do. Today, the Northern Isles, while not exactly tropical, followed similar seasons to Morvak, with a designated winter, spring, summer, and fall.

Most of the entries centered on the owner's longing for a commander in the army instead of salacious details of the nighttime parties.

Erik didn't spot a name, and the author didn't sign the pages. He could decipher she was some sort of stable master. She spoke of training horses, though she didn't call them that. But they were four-legged beasts bred to carry both civilians and soldiers.

The entries ended abruptly around the time of the War of False Prophets. It was a decades-long civil war between the Seven Courts. The bloodshed decimated over ninety percent of the Fae population.

Most scholars attributed the demise of their immortal ancestors with the conflict.

Three pages from the end, there was a small entry at the bottom, written in a different hand.

You may call it binding and resolute
But it is an oath, not absolute
As breakable as a circle with a beginning.

Instead of dotting the last *i*, the author drew a small cross.

Erik flipped the pages. Was it too much to ask for Stella to mark them? It took him three scans to find the next cross.

There. A little over halfway from the middle, a second verse stood out. It was subtle — this time the different slant buried within the text.

A simple Draught of Forgetfulness
Consumed on the fade of twilight
Reverses the words at the stroke of midnight

He lodged a finger in the page and flipped to the last part. Then back again. The dates at the top of each entry were the same.

Samhain, the end of September.

Another clue. Casts required a combination of practice and patience. Potions needed the correct ingredients, the proper time to brew. Or a specific date of the lunar cycle to mature.

This one would be potent for three days, when the calendar rolled over from September to October.

The days before, during, and after the Grimoire Games. Fate was a fickle friend.

Erik thumbed the front half, spotting the cross faster this time.

If my intentions are good and true,
And I must take back what I spoke anew
To give up something of my own
Be it blood or hair or bone

Same date. Same crooked slant to the letters.

A Draught of Forgetfulness was simple. Easy, even for him. Ingested for its calming effect, he brewed it regularly for when he healed nastier traumas. Erik grew most of the ingredients in his greenhouse. The rest bloomed this time of year in the forest surrounding the Castle.

He studied the penultimate line.

To give up something of my own.

The strength of potions depended on the quality of the ingredients. The marital oath was one of the strongest vows a Faeblood or human could make. A lock of hair or a drop of blood may not work.

And if he was correct about the date, they had one shot. At least until next year. But too many things could transpire in that time.

What could he give...

What could he give...

Blood wouldn't work. He'd spilled too much of it in his life for it to mean something. Bone was out too. That suggestion reserved for those already dead.

What could he give...

What could he give...

Erik strolled inside the greenhouse, tapping the diary against his hand as he went. His mother's locket could work, easy enough to melt but ingesting copper...

He shuddered. Metals and magic didn't mix. He threw the book on his potting bench, hitting a sack of fertilizer.

Crumbs spilled over the bag's lip, coating the surface. Dammit. He didn't need more work.

The clock tower bell clanged four times.

Erik swept the rich granules in his hand, careful to not spill any on the floor. He brushed them into the nearest pot and froze.

Helispore.

Of course. He ran his hand over his mouth, no doubt smearing streaks of black on his chin. It could work.

He studied the fledgling specimen. A cutting would kill the plant. He never had success propagating it from the root. And if he stripped the last leaves from the stem…

His heart thumped in his chest. He had his answer.

But Erik wasn't prepared for the cost.

CHAPTER TWENTY-EIGHT

Erik was late. He hadn't returned to their chambers to escort Maia to the solarium for pre-dinner drinks.

She stood, running her hands down her new silver dress.

Unlike the flouncy design of its mates in her wardrobe, the skirts molded to her curves, narrowing well past her knee. Halfway between a ballgown and a form-fitting nightshirt, it was as if the seamstress couldn't decide on the style, fashioning a blend after drinking too much Fae wine.

Maia loved it.

She paced in front of the hearth, widening her path until it encircled the entire room and balcony.

Chocolate truffles called to her from the bedside table. Dezee, or maybe Bree, was always leaving them around for her to find. She popped one in her mouth, savoring the rich flavor.

Her fingertips drummed a tune on her bodice. Maia recognized the jitters. Not their cause.

It wasn't the Grimoire Games. Her confidence with a sword grew every day. Combined with her archery skills and throwing accuracy, she had an excellent shot at winning the competition.

The rest of her time blended together into one giant failure.

She penned letters home, took afternoon tea, and searched the library for the journal when Bree could let her in. Despite her attempts, the book continued to elude her.

Then there was the magical storage chamber. Siodina's war room.

She and Mikel spent every morning for the past week scouring the underground tunnels, looking for clues and other secret passages but found nothing. They even asked Demelza, playing ignorant and taking care to disguise their intent.

The head housekeeper just gave them a funny look and claimed no knowledge that such a thing was even possible. And if it was, she would've discovered it by now.

Maybe it was her husband? More specifically, his absence that made her restless.

Since the bathtub incident, they spent evenings at Court where his soft hands grounded her and his sharp words kept the vultures away. Then... poof. He vanished until bedtime. As much as she wanted a repeat of their bathtub tryst, it was clear he didn't.

So she feigned sleep when he eventually climbed into bed.

It was her favorite part of the day. She struggled to stay limp when he pulled her to him, his chest aligning with her back. It was torture when he brushed aside her hair and burrowed into her nape. Whispered words never followed, but a protective arm draped across her waist until he snuck out in the morning.

Aye, a repeat of the bathtub would be a welcome distraction. But sexual tension is not what burrowed under her skin tonight.

Maia rested a hand on the balcony railing, slowing her breathing to match the lap of the lake against the foundation.

With distance from the compound, she could appreciate how much of her life Erik had infiltrated. It had started off small. In the training barn, he'd partnered with her more often than not. They had taken meals together in the barracks, sharing glances over the antics of the exuberant first-year trainees.

Then there were grappling sessions when the rest of the compound slept.

They were both talkers when they sparred. Maia rambled about mundane things to frustrate her opponents. Erik likely just enjoyed the sound of his voice. An unconventional exchange but they ended up getting to know one another.

Erik Siodina had been… her friend.

Stubbornly, she would've denied the relationship even before he locked her in her rooms. But now, as he actively avoided her, his absence forced her to admit that she missed him.

Instead of waiting in their chambers, her slippers wearing a hole in the rug, Maia requested Mikel accompany her to the greenhouse.

To her surprise, Erik wasn't there either.

She dismissed a frowning Mikel and wandered over to the Gillyflower patch.

The stone bench was cool beneath her hand. Maia sat and leaned on the arm, tracing sun's plunge under the horizon.

Thus began more waiting.

In the sparring ring, time slowed, allowing Maia to plan her next three moves. A clarity borne from experience, it was effortless. Comfortable.

Here, time slowed for a different reason. It wasn't from boredom nor impatience. The energy that hummed through her, guiding her in battle, was absent.

This… this was a messy, uncomfortable slog through her thoughts.

ERIK PUSHED THROUGH THE GREENHOUSE DOOR, READJUSTING THE journal at his back.

His father searched his sanctuary once a week. Sometimes more. He needed a better place to hide it. Until then, he kept it on his person.

Mikel had intercepted him outside their chambers, claiming he left Maia up here.

Erik scanned the potting bench, his eyes landing on the anemic cutting of Helispore.

She wasn't in the vegetable rows nor in the herb garden. He pressed his face to the glass. Not on the terrace either. He wound around the berry patch, their upright stalks creating a thorny wall separating his worktable from the Gillyflower maze.

He stopped in his tracks.

She sat on his mother's bench, angled so the fading sun caught the trail of dampness rolling in front of her ear. The lighting, her dress, her sadness — hit him like one of Mikel's match-ending left hooks.

All he could see was his mother.

This was her favorite spot. His memories, normally a hazy child-like grasp on reality, rushed back. She favored bold metallics, too, his mother. Their bright tones complimented her olive skin, her dark hair. She would escape the Court, finding solace on this very bench. Silent tears streaking down her face.

Like Maia, she was warm and loyal and beautiful.

Unlike his fiery wife, she spoke softly, her actions louder than a raised voice. A part of him wondered… no, wished that they could've met. His mother would've enjoyed her entrance to society. The way she conducted herself at tea.

He ran his hands over his hair.

And unlike Maia, she never had the comfort of an entire family waiting for her safe return. An out, an escape.

His mother never had a chance at happiness.

Perhaps there was no hope for him either. Court was where he belonged. At least until he could solve the mystery of her disappearance. And if he thwarted his father's plans, then that was a bonus. But his happiness was never a consideration.

He didn't know if it was her pose. Or her presence in his sanctuary. Or her tears. But Erik couldn't stop the longing that lurched against his chest.

Maia was his equal in temperament. They both had a sharp tongue. A call for thrills. A keen sense of loyalty to those who returned it. If they had met in a different time — under different circumstances, as different people — he would've made her his.

But Erik would only ever be the Heir. A title he couldn't shed, no matter how much he desired to follow Maia home. He never wanted power. Never wanted to descend into whatever monster his ancestry produced.

He stood by what he said to her in the tub. It was better to be alive and miserable than dead and honorable. His only chance of salvation was to do as little harm as possible on his way to the Underworld.

"May I sit?" He approached the bench, dragging his boots to make his presence known.

"Oh." She wiped her cheek with the back of her hand and cleared her throat. "I came to enjoy the view."

Liar. She always was a terrible liar.

He once assumed everyone was born with the nature to deceive. The Ladies lied to themselves, their husbands, each other. The Lords fabricated tales of bravery, of pure blood, of more power. It was humans who showed him something different.

"A better husband would ask, *what troubles you?*"

She sniffled.

He handed her a piece of binding from his back pocket. A bit of linen to bandage limbs, nothing as fancy as a handkerchief.

She took it all the same and dabbed the corners of her eyes.

He waited, comfortable in the silence. More so when her arm brushed against his. He held his breath, relaxing as she leaned into him.

"I came here to find you."

She smelled of chocolate and cinnamon. So she enjoyed the truffles he left. Good.

"But I found my way to this bench, wondering about things I'd long since buried, wondering about my mother."

He wrapped an arm around her waist.

"What was she like?" Maia asked herself as entwined her fingers with his. "Did she enjoy the rare pickled peppers at the end of summer like father? Or prefer the sweeter red ones, perfect for dipping in savory cream like I do?"

"Did your father ever speak of her?"

"No. I used to think it was because it was too difficult to share her memory. But I never inquired, either. I was too busy chasing the next goal, learning the next submission. Improving my speed, my aim with a bow. He buried his grief in the militia, following Xavier's cause. Me… I'm not sure I ever allowed myself to mourn the other half of my soul. To simply miss her."

"She wouldn't want you to waste your life wondering what never came to pass."

"What if your mother wished the same?" Maia sat back, twisting out of his hold.

Erik picked the nearest flower. Its petals would brown overnight. Gillyflowers were fast to blossom, faster to perish. Flashy. Showy. It made them easy to adore. Easier to forget since they spread as fast as weeds.

He often wondered if his mother enjoyed the variety of colors, their ease of care. Who wouldn't desire a break from tending more difficult plants?

"The Violet Orion." He held it out. "Dozens of pods swell in the late summer, so heavy, many fall to the ground before their bloom. The leaves grow, collecting sunlight. The roots gathering nutrients, until one day they come to life. All that work for twelve hours of fuss."

"Still exquisite." Maia plucked the flower from his palm.

"There are days when I believe her life was the same. Bright, blinding even, but too short. She burned with passion for her plants, with music in her ear. With dancing in her soul. As a child, I felt it. The magnetic pull of someone so special, all you could do was hold on and enjoy. And when she was gone, when the light winked out, she took that spark with her."

"I imagine it was the same for my father." Maia picked the petals one-by-one, letting them twirl to the stone floor. "It drove him from our home. A widower, fleeing his supportive village. He was a simple man, my father. Hard-working, determined. Stoic."

Erik chuckled. "If you speak the truth, then I assume your temper stems from your mother."

She sent him a soft, sad smile.

"What must they think of us?" Erik knocked his knee against hers. "Two lost souls struggling in the rot of the Castle. Would they tell us to face the sheer impossibility of our situation? Or command us to separate and regroup with our kin?"

It was his turn to smile. Erik sat back and cupped her cheek. His thumb caressed the dried tears.

"In another life, I would face the wrath of my father and fight to stay by your side." His lips brushed her forehead. He couldn't bear to look at her. "But I am not the male for you."

He was glad when she didn't pull away. Glad — he told himself — when she sagged against him, keeping her thoughts to herself.

She squeezed his hand, the only sign she understood his words.

Not accepted. Not agreed with. But she wouldn't fight him on this. And if she did, if she so much as breathed a word of protest, his resolve would crumble. So before she could fill the uncomfortable quiet, he said, "I could use your help with something."

He didn't give her time to decline as he tugged her up from the bench and over to his cupboards.

"Here." Erik handed her a small set of pruning shears and pointed to the Black-Eyed Polecat bushes. "Snip six branches the size of your index finger and meet me at my potting bench."

He located his pewter cauldron. Heavy for its size, the walls were thick and unreactive to most potions. Next, he found its metal feet and his Elderwood stirring stick. He clutched everything to his chest and deposited them on his work surface.

Above his bench, a tap stuck out of the thick stone wall.

Erik had installed it as a teenager, harvesting a supply of rainwater from one of the terrace's shade pergolas.

He turned the spigot. A few drops splashed to the bottom. His palms warmed. The sweet taste of a cast filled his mouth as water filled the cauldron.

He crouched down, pulling out a small tin he kept hidden on the underside of the counter.

Everlasting Flame — a gift from Stella when she was in one of her more generous moods.

Unlike a traditional candle or lantern, it burned until the user's magic snuffed it out. The Draught of Forgetfulness must simmer for two sunsets to reach maturity.

He lit the wick and pulled out the diary.

There were no instructions on when to add the bit of himself. He wouldn't take any chances. The longer the Helispore brewed, the better.

He unsheathed his blade from his belt, slicing off the plant at its base before he balked. He stared at the stub, an emptiness settling over him.

"I cut seven. Just in case." Maia approached, eyeing the journal. She handed over the bundle.

"These are perfect." His voice sounded hoarse, but if she noticed, Maia didn't comment.

Erik arranged the cuttings in a six-point star, their ends sticking out of the water in equal intervals. The first time he brewed the draught, he'd singed his eyebrows as it bubbled up, a misfire from a haphazard arrangement.

"What are you making?" Maia leaned over the cauldron, her shoulders brushing against his.

"Elixir of Elation," Erik lied, tossing the Helispore cutting into the center. It sank to the bottom. "For after the Grimoire Games. It instills euphoria in the drinker. More than a bottle of mead, but the magic allows you to keep your balance, your wits."

The small hairs on the Helispore glowed an eerie pink.

"I thought you might enjoy it after your performance, regardless of the outcome," he added.

"Look." Maia grabbed his arm. "It's the color of the Navitas crystals from your pool. What else do you require?"

"A few more ingredients."

Erik led them to the herb patch, gesturing to the massive vine weaving between the stalks. It curled around his pots and climbed the walls, reaching for the dome's peak.

"Its white flowers open at midnight, curling up as the sun rises in the east. Strip three leaves. I'll add the buds later."

Maia knelt down and grabbed a section near her slippers. She held it up. "Will this do?"

"Aye." He inclined his head toward his mother's garden. "The potion requires Gillyflowers. You can choose the color."

She ducked behind the hedgerow.

Maybe one day she would forgive him for his lies.

Maybe when they lay awake in their beds — him in the Castle, her in her chambers back at the barracks — she would remember this night and how they brewed the potion to free her of their oath.

She might think it an indulgence. Or worse, a terrible prank. But magic was more than complex spells and complicated words. A thread of the wielder wove through every cast.

His mother had taught him that.

Erik experienced it with every wound he healed. Every time he cared for his plants. A piece of himself intertwined, guiding the magic to do his bidding. Maia might possess human blood in her veins, but she was the other half of this oath. It was only fitting she took part.

She returned, her arms laden with blooms of every color.

"You didn't say how many you needed, so I brought some of each."

"The choice is yours." He grinned. "Cover the surface. Their blooms must conceal the bottom."

She arranged the crimson reds with the loud purples and severe whites, forming alternating rings of color.

He could've said it didn't matter. He could've said he normally dumped them without thought, creating a raft of soft petals. Instead, he asked, "Do you have enough to complete your pattern?"

Her tongue jutted to the corner of her mouth. She pinched a pink flower, the only one of its color, and placed it in the very center.

"There. I had plenty." She cocked her head to the side. "I don't dislike it."

He closed the distance between them, and when she didn't stiffen, he wrapped his arms around her waist, resting his cheek against her crown.

"I don't hate the pink," she whispered.

He gripped her shoulders, nudging her to face him.

Her chest rose and fell, faster now that they shared breath. She trailed a finger over his lower lip, snagging in the center. The tip of her tongue darted out, then she repeated, "I don't hate the pink."

Before she could raise on her tiptoes, before she could meet him halfway, he crashed his lips to hers, swallowing the words. She tasted of sugar. His Kitten. He deepened the kiss, cradling the back of her head.

Maia pushed up, molding against his body.

He could bend her over right here, consuming her soft cries and driving her to a frenzy with his clever fingers. Then his tongue. Erik could worship her until night extinguished the last rays of dusk.

But he relinquished her lips, untangling her hands from the back of his neck, and took a step back. Then another. He willed his hands to the side.

"That cannot happen again."

Maia brushed invisible soil off the bodice of her dress. She blew on her outstretched palm, sending a saucy air kiss. He might've bought the act, but there was a slight wobble in her voice when she said, "You owe me a favor."

He strode toward the door, holding out the crook of his arm. They would be late for dinner.

Maia looped her hand through, and her mouth parted.

Before she could argue or pull away, Erik said, "I've done worse things than owe someone like you a favor."

CHAPTER TWENTY-NINE

The morning of the Grimoire Games arrived. The opening ceremonies would start in two hours.

Erik had snuck out of their chambers at twilight, finishing the final preparations for the oath-breaking elixir.

The flame reduced the mixture so it fit into a single vial. Two swallows worth. One for each of them. He hid it away in her vanity next to the antidote for truth serum. One more crisis from owning a small apothecary.

After returning to their chambers, he tossed and turned in bed, unable to find sleep. At three bells, he finally gave up and moved to the wing-backed chair.

Ironic, Erik never succumbed to nervousness. It was easier to fix a problem or avoid it altogether. Or make an inappropriate jest. Sometimes all three. But he couldn't deny the flop of his gut when he studied her. Foolish. He wasn't even the one competing.

Maia curled into his side of the bed, clutching his feather pillow to her chest. Her long locks covered the lower half of her face.

A leather suit lay on top of the trunk.

Crafted from deerskin, the hide allowed movement and flexibility. Pig might've been a better choice, but Jille assured him it would deflect a wooden blade.

The waistband was thicker than the legs with leather strips crossing in a herringbone pattern. An additional layer that protected vital organs while supporting built-in sheaths for daggers. Four in total, their location would allow two blades to be drawn at once.

He purchased a new olive-green tunic to wear underneath the strapless bodice, paying extra gold for the stitching on the front. Jille fashioned a matching wrist protector for the archery event.

Her new boots, a gift from Mikel, laced just below the knee. The fighter insisted on the custom fit, claiming the thinner soles would keep Maia lighter on her feet.

"It's too early to frown." She stretched, her hands grazing the top of the headboard.

"I have a surprise for you." Erik rose, grabbed her suit, and sat next to her on the bed. "For the Games. Jille worked late nights to complete it on time. You should have something practical for the occasion."

"I hope you paid her handsomely." Maia traced the pattern of gold thread on the tunic. Her eyes shot to the replica on the pendant around his neck. "It's exquisite."

"My mother's family crest." He held it aloft. "I thought you could wear something that wasn't from the Siodina line."

"It's beautiful, Erik. I'm honored."

He cleared his throat. "Either way, as your sponsor, it's customary to wear my crest."

"Don't." She lay a hand on top of his. "Don't diminish the significance."

"If you're going to scandalize the populace, do it in style. Yours..." he continued, rubbing the sleeves of the olive-green tunic. "Not theirs."

Erik cupped her cheek, waiting until he commanded her full attention, and tapped the chain connecting the loops on her earrings.

"You never asked me to remove them."

"They were no bother." She averted her eyes.

Erik slid off a post's backing and set it in her outstretched palm. He removed another. Then another, until all nine were clear. He gently freed the entire piece from her lobe.

"Leave them," she said. Maia licked her lips. "Leave the holes."

Erik's nostrils flared. The warmth in his palms dissipated. And he nodded, unable to find his voice. She would change her mind. He could heal them later.

He massaged the outer shell then started on the other ear. This time, she didn't avoid his stare.

"They expect Xavier in the crowd," he said hoarsely. "Our rules… Faeblood tradition… differs from the territories. Pay him little deference. Once a Lady marries into a line, the expectation is to cut ties to her past. If you show affection or spend too much time in his presence, it will draw my father's notice. A nod or curtsy will suffice."

She dipped her chin, the only sign she understood.

"They will announce the prizes first. The contenders and their sponsors next. Then the parameters of the competition. Sponsors last. Prepare yourself for the crowd's reaction. Even with my support, you are the only female contestant ever to enter."

He swallowed and methodically removed the other earring.

"Stay focused. Stay strong for them. The Master of Ceremonies will provide the weapons, ensuring no arrows or daggers imbued with magic find their way into the competition."

"So let me understand. I am to ignore my family who I haven't seen for months. Stand still like a good girl while the

Court and crowd jeers our presence on stage. Leave my dagger — your dagger — behind. Anything else?"

"Don't interact with the other contestants, no matter what they say." *Or do.*

"Right. Forget sportsmanship. Is that all?"

"Don't injure yourself. I won't be with my father in our family seats. I can heal many injures but will be farther away than normal."

"Where might you be?" she asked, her voice raising an octave.

"I will be in the stands. With Xavier and your family."

"I thought you said—"

"*You* should not make a statement." He grinned. "I said nothing about myself."

THE ARENA ANCHORED THE NORTHERN ASPECT OF THE courtyard. Stone stands descended to a sunken stage. Tunnels behind the back wall served as a place to gather between scenes in a play. Or for contenders to rub shoulders with one another before a competition.

Maia forced a blank expression. She kept her stare straight ahead, her spine ramrod.

If she balled her fist any harder, she wouldn't be able to feel her fingertips. Under her breath she murmured, "Relax."

In this wing, a dozen contenders lined the walls. Some talked to their neighbors. Those must be the pairs. Others kept to themselves.

Know thy opponent — the first rule in combat.

Mikel had befriended a Red Guard. He wouldn't tell her the man's identity, but the informant fed him information on the other contestants. Who was the strongest. Who was the meanest.

Overall, Mikel and his source expected five or six teams. And another ten or twelve competing on their own.

She recognized a few they discussed yesterday.

Every year, a handful of male servants near eighteen summers competed. Easy enough to find a willing Lord to sponsor them. Or the occasional Lady if the entrant possessed certain, ah, qualities. Several prospects from the territories entered, those too young to apprentice in the family trade.

As with the first-year militia trainees, most contestants were gangly, their bodies stretching with growth spurts and the occasional skipped meal. A couple were softer with stocky builds and childhood clinging to their cheeks.

An older male leaned against the wall near the front of the line. One leg crossed over the other, he chewed on a piece of... Maia squinted. Was that straw?

Similar in height to Erik, the contender carried a stone's more muscle than her husband. Who was he? His face was smooth and young. Many would consider him handsome, but there was something about his eyes that kept Maia from describing him as such. In the dim hallway, they were almost black. Almost dead.

Had they been anywhere else, she would've given over to a shudder.

From what territory did he hail? Did they allow one of the current Red Guards to enter?

He must've sensed her attention because he straightened, spit out the straw, and met Maia's stare.

"Line up." The Master of Ceremonies peeked around the corner.

He was a short Faeblood with severe features and pockmarked skin. His entire body vibrated, and the ends of his floppy hat quivered.

"Line up," he repeated, clapping his hands. "We enter the arena as a group. On the stage floor, you will see markers. Find an X and stand there until your name is called. You will assemble in front. The contenders from the other wing in the back."

He clapped his hands again.

"On my mark."

Gong.

The Master of Ceremonies ushered them out. His sneer caught her off guard as she passed. It shouldn't have.

Maia jogged to the farthest unoccupied X, waving to the crowd. Might as well stir them up. She competed better with the thrum of an overexcited mob.

Where were they? Maia scanned the stands, searching for her family, careful not to linger too long on any one location.

"Get off the stage, Kitten, before you get hurt," a deep voice said, loud enough for both rows of contestants to snicker.

She stiffened at the nickname.

The Red Guard patted her down while his cronies checked the other contenders.

"A pretty little treat like you shouldn't be in the Games." He wrapped an arm around her waist. "Bow out now. Nobody will think anything of it."

The snickers turned into jeers.

"Watch out for Wystan, the big lad at the end." His close-cropped beard scratched the side of her cheek. "Ally with the brothers behind you. Don't look now. Two spots from the far left. I slipped a blade in your boot."

He pulled back, smacking her backside on his way to check the next.

"Get your hands off me, you filthy lout." This must be Mikel's contact. For good measure, she added, "Do you know who I am?"

The Master of Ceremonies spared her from his answer.

"Lords and Ladies and humans. We gather today to celebrate the seventy-fifth annual Grimoire Games. Originally held in honor of our liberation from the Northern Isles, the competition has evolved to serve a higher purpose. A noble purpose."

He spoke into a wooden wand no longer than her forearm.

"The winner today earns a coveted spot in the Red Guard academy. Let us..."

Maia's head swiveled, searching for the source of his amplified voice.

There. In the scraggly trees over-hanging the stage and perched on top of the columns of the upper wall, the beaks of dozens of Blackbirds opened and closed with his words. Their voices were the same high pitch.

A Namir Faeblood, a caster who controlled animals.

"It is my greatest honor to introduce your newest monarch. Everyone kneel for Morvak's hymn. For your King."

The crowd gasped as one.

Maia spotted Kiehl and the leader of the Farming territory in the crowd. They stood with arms crossed over their chests, their lips forming flat lines. No surprises there. Erik's missives must've reached them in time.

The spectators were slow to kneel. As if frozen upright with the news.

In the center rise of steps, an orchestra played from the first three rows. A fiddle mixed with the upbeat harmony. Before the end of the first chorus, the entire stands went to their knees.

Erik's father sauntered across the stage, holding his arms above his head, palms turned skyward. At the final percussion triplet, he clasped them together.

"Rise, my Court. My territories. Today marks the dawn of a new beginning. My first peninsula-wide event after the High Table's unanimous vote to rule as your King. I'm honored, not only to stand before you this day, but also that my brethren chose me to lead our realm to greatness."

Was anyone buying this load of pig dung?

"... and I cannot think of a better occasion than the Grimoire

Games. A chance for our brave lads to compete for the honor of entering the prestigious Red Guard academy."

He strolled to the edge of the stage.

"This year, I arranged for a treat. As in the past, judges will still score each event. But I took the liberty to change the parameters to favor a more... shall we say," his arms circled the air as if to build up suspense for the next, "exciting time. I leave you with one more announcement before I turn it over to our Master of Ceremonies."

The King grinned.

"My son informs me he will sponsor his wife."

A murmur rushed through the crowd. The Master of Ceremonies patted the air. The crowd noise dulled.

"A first, to be sure. A noble Lady," King Siodina said *Lady* in the same tone he used when he introduced her as Erik's whore in the great hall. "Don't worry, my good constituents. I was just as worried about her tender heart as you must be. But..."

He held up a finger.

"I have it on good authority a Faeblood healer is in the crowd."

She followed the quick swivel of the audience's heads. Erik stood next to Xavier. Gavyn on the left. And tucked into Gavyn's side was Ember.

"Erik, my boy. Introduce us to the female."

Female.

Female.

Female.

He didn't say introduce yourself.

It was only a matter of time before his father discovered Ember's identity.

Word would've spread after her cast in the arena to save Erik. Too many saw her face. Too many would've figured out her name. Expected, but no less shocking, hearing the proof in front of the populace.

Gavyn rested both hands on Ember's shoulders. She tipped her chin high, gifting a small wave to the crowd.

A loud silence filled the arena, causing the hair on the back of Maia's neck to stand on end.

"Never fear," his father continued, "I arranged for additional human healers to take care of our valuable contestants, in the off chance an accident removes them from the event."

Or from life.

The Master of Ceremonies scurried across the stage. The small bells on the toes of his slippers jangled in his wake. He unrolled a piece of parchment, clearing his throat once more.

"Our forefathers discovered our sacred fortress high in Morvak. Generations of rulers added to the structure, creating a defensible position that favors those with accurate bows. In our first event, our judges will score the contestant's ability to hit ten targets hung in the in the surrounding treetops."

Why did they hang—

"... where the candidates will travel on horseback."

Maia wanted to groan.

"Then they will return to the arena where they will show their skill with throwing blades."

That didn't sound so—

"While battling an obstacle course. In the last event, our contestants will duel each other. First to draw blood keeps a contender in the fight. They will proceed until all but one, or a team of contestants, is eliminated."

First to draw blood. That meant steel. You could pommel someone until they blacked out with a wooden sword, but even the most honed tips wouldn't pierce the skin.

Maia glanced to the side. Several contestants paled. She swallowed.

The contraband dagger in her boot made sense. Everything made sense. Erik's father didn't need to resort to poisoning her.

He could simply sit off to the side and watch others do his bidding.

Erik pushed through the row of spectators. He reached the aisle, his eyes never leaving hers as he took two steps toward the stage.

Maia pinned her shoulders back and shook her head. His involvement would draw his father's attention.

Erik froze. He wore the same dark leathers and tunic from their sham wedding ceremony.

She hadn't seen the uniform since that day. He might not have given it much thought. But she glommed on to the symbolism all the same. For the sake of the crowd, for their families, they were a bonded pair.

Maia shook her head again. She had this. She trained for this. Well… maybe not this exact situation, but close.

As with their first ceremony, she needed to put on a show.

Everyone adored an underdog. But they were more than that. A human girl and a handsome Faeblood Lord.

Maia cocked a hand on her waist. With her other, she kissed the tips of her fingers, plastered on the sultriest smile, and blew him a kiss.

The crowd went wild.

Because the one thing that could yank these spectators to their feet… more than rooting for an underdog… was a love story.

CHAPTER THIRTY

"Ah, young love," the Master of Ceremonies cooed. He waited for the cheers to dwindle. "Our liege has prepared one final surprise. A wedding gift for his son and only heir."

Erik held his breath. The entire arena froze on a collective inhale.

"King Siodina elects to sponsor her Lady's companion, Leatrix Langhieme. Come, child. Your presence is required on stage."

Lea emerged from a sea of gray. The servants, those who Dezee spared from their duties for a few hours of entertainment, sat together toward the rear. She walked, her back too straight and her steps too stiff, like invisible strings held her upright while simultaneously pulling her to the other contestants.

"... another first... the child wishes to join the Red Guard academy... honor her father..."

Erik would kill him.

His father had been too quiet after murdering Lord

Cantwine and the others. And he'd been so busy brewing their potion that Erik had missed the most obvious play.

The bastard. He didn't care if the entirety of Morvak witnessed his wrath. Didn't give two whits if it led to his own certain death.

He expected his father's demand for allegiance to the crown. He guessed another attempt at poison. Another kidnapping and torture.

Not this blatant attempt on her life. On Lea's. He should've suspected. Erik was a fool.

Maia kept her head up and slung an arm around Lea's shoulders.

A heavy hand clamped his neck.

"Blow a kiss and smile." Xavier squeezed, his fingers digging under Erik's collar bone. "That's it. Return to the stands."

He would follow her lead on this. For now. The weight of the crowd's stares bore into the back of his head. He wove through the row of spectators, unclenching his fists.

"Trust her." Jade clasped his elbows and pulled him tight for a hug.

Gavyn slapped him on the back. The hulking commander remained silent, but the tic in his cheek throbbed.

Maia is nimble and an expert markswoman, Erik imagined Gavyn saying. *She will use her smaller stature to her advantage,*

"The Master of Ceremonies is new," Jade said, a poor attempt at drawing his attention. "He is not the same from Gavyn's fight."

"After his contender's defeat, my father relieved the former host of his duties." Relieved. Banished. Killed. Erik wasn't certain.

Ember grabbed his hand, threading her fingers through his. Her palm heated.

He glanced down. A calming cast. Not his.

"Fighters make better choices when they stay collected," she said, her eyes never leaving the stage.

He couldn't be sure she spoke the words to him. Or herself.

"I won't let him hurt you." In his panic, he hadn't forgotten his father's introductions.

It was an empty promise considering her mate, her new family. Erik's ineptitude. But he wanted her to know.

Since healing him in the arena, too many in the territories traveled to the compound for Ember's care. Then there were the fighters completing their fourth and final year of service, carrying tales of her powers back to their villages.

"It was only a matter of time before your father discovered my identity. If he didn't figure it out when I healed you in the arena, then Castle spies would carry whispers of my gift."

"I didn't tell him the truth. Your name never left my lips."

Even if he didn't owe her his life, Erik would have never used the information against her. And not because she was Maia's family.

"I know." She squeezed again. "I know."

"So a calming spell, huh..."

"I imagine it's customary to ask permission, but your aura reflected a great deal of stress."

She blushed, the pink traveling down her neck, fanning the tips of her ears. Her round ears. Human blood shaped Ember's line. He marveled at her, not for the first time. She was a miracle, a gifted caster born in the territories.

And if Xavier was cunning — a talisman for the spark of a civil war.

Magic served as the main division between the nobles and the humans. If the gods bestowed it on the populace in any great number, it would shake the very foundation of his father's rule.

No wonder he crowned himself. There was no better way to command the Red Guard. The Lords. No one more ruthless. And if he called up the entire militia...

Erik shuddered.

How many would answer his father's summons? Honor-bound to fight for a ruler who sent them to slaughter their neighbors. How many more would join Xavier, pitting friend against friend? Or worse, family against family?

He scanned the crowd.

Most followed the action on stage. Red Guards led the contenders up the stairs, through the spectators, and under the stone arches. Some in the crowd threw flowers. Others reached out, touching their favorites' sleeves.

More than one person ignored the parade and focused on Xavier.

Ember wrapped an arm around Erik. She didn't use magic, but warmth spread through her touch.

"As our champions make their way to the stable, it's time to remind everyone to keep their seats during the action." The Master of Ceremonies spoke into his ornate wooden wand. "I will provide commentary for the event. If you must wander, please do so during the scoring as to not disturb your fellow patrons."

He paused. His instructions reverberated around the arena, the Blackbirds squawking in unison.

"Put your hands together for our first champion. Gunn hails from the Mining territory. He's a strapping lad, weighing in at over eighteen stones. If he proceeds through the first two rounds, someone to watch in the last event. He chooses an Uakari horse. Slow but stocky enough to support his bulk. Perhaps some brains accompany those muscles."

The audience applauded, their shock from Lea's entrance into the competition dissipating in the face of certain amusement.

"Our next contestants are Callan and Bremen. Twins, born of Castle servants. Their leaner frames and rugged appearance are sure to make them Court favorites. They choose a matching pair of Auidann horses. Fast and agile if one can control their spirited nature."

And on and on he went, until at last he spoke of Maia and Lea.

"Our final contestants look to be in disagreement over the choice of a mount. An awful lot of head shaking and gesturing between them. Will this trouble spell disaster for our unlikely pair? I can only imagine what young Lord Siodina is thinking. Do I sense a firm hand and stern lecture in his wife's future?"

The crowd chuckled.

"Ah, they made their choice." The Master of Ceremonies paused for dramatic effect. "Ooh, I can't say I agree with that one."

What one? What is going on?

"It looks as if Lady Siodina and Leatrix will ride the Palomino Uakari. She is gesturing to the stable lad to remove the saddle. Folks, I don't see how this will assist their cause. Lady Siodina rides astride the mare, while… I can't believe it. She hoists Leatrix up. The young charge faces the wrong direction." He chuckled. "Both without a saddle."

A roar of laughter rose from the stands.

"This may be all we see of this pair. Lord Siodina, if you are listening, you have a way to go with your wife's education."

THE HORSE WAS A COMPLICATION. LEA WAS A COMPLICATION. THIS entire event… was a complication.

Maia couldn't bring herself to dwell on Lea. If she started, she feared she would send an arrow straight at Siodina's heart. *Breathe. Take a deep breath.*

Oh the mare was beautiful, sporting a thick mane of onyx. Her honey-colored hide complemented Maia's leathers. She was sturdy enough to carry them both but reacted to every shift in their weight.

The mare jerked her head. Maia heeded the warning and stopped fidgeting.

Leatrix sat with the nimbleness of a circus acrobat, her quiver of arrows across her back. Her bow at the ready.

Someone had painted stripes on the wooden shafts. Two yellow ones with a thinner red in the middle. Markers for tracking who shot what.

The stable lads handed Maia a second quiver, a larger bow.

Lea argued something fierce about sharing a horse, but she had the brilliant idea to ride backwards. Eyes and ears toward the other contestants.

Since there wasn't a time limit, Maia would keep them near the rear of the pack.

If someone snuck behind them, she didn't want to be caught unawares. Lea assured her she could shoot standing on the horse's rump. And if that failed, her magic would guide the arrow toward the target.

They lined the riders up in a chute of timbers stacked on their sides.

The horses didn't like the confinement. Many side-stepped into another contestant. Others reared up.

Their mare flung her head twice then calmed.

Gong. A bell rang from behind.

The pack surged into the woods.

She allowed those in the back to pass. Maia squeezed her legs, and their mare ran. No, not ran. What did Erik call it? Trot? Canter? Either way, the horse set a nice even pace.

Maia resisted the urge to lean forward and grasp her mane.

The first target hung from an old Elm branch. Sixteen hands in the air, only two arrows stuck out of it, neither within the center two circles.

"On the right. One hundred paces," Maia said over her shoulder. "I'll keep her steady."

Lea tapped her arm, a signal they agreed upon moments ago. She was in position.

The arrow whistled by Maia's ear and struck the target dead center.

One down. Nine to go.

Faint cheers resonated behind them.

Maia scanned the trail. There. In the forest canopy, dozens of Blackbirds perched on high limbs, staring down at them. They must report the progress to the Master of Ceremonies.

"Callan and Bremen on the scoreboard at the start. And my what do we have here, it appears as if Lady Maia and her young charge come away with a bullseye. Time will tell if lady luck stays on their side."

That's right. Let them think it's all luck.

The next two targets hung from tree trunks on the left. They were staggered a few paces apart. Lea would need to shoot the first at a considerable distance then attempt the second.

No. That wouldn't work. Even the quickest archer wouldn't have time to nock the second arrow.

"On the left. Pick one. We can't claim both."

Indeed. Four arrows stuck out from the front target. None from the back.

Another tap.

Maia kept the mare steady as another arrow whistled past.

Two arrows lodged in the targets, striking the center of each.

"How did you—"

Lea leaned against her back. "I shot them at the same time."

"Clever girl." Maia threw her head back and laughed. "The next one is on the right. It's ten paces from the edge of the trail, facing us. You will need to wait until we pass it."

Another target. Another bullseye. Four down. Six to go.

They were too far from the arena to hear the crowd noise. She would love to see Erik's reaction.

The mare kept a steady pace, following the other riders without too much direction from Maia. She would need to find an extra bucket of oats or sugar cubes. Or whatever counted as a reward for the beast.

Lea claimed two more targets. Two more bullseyes. Easy. Too easy.

"Maia," Lea shouted in her ear. "Wystan approaches from behind."

What was he doing back there? He started at the front of the pack but must've circled around. Maybe he wanted a slower pace. Less congestion. She almost believed the lie.

Lea missed the next target and cursed.

The weight at her back shifted. Maia turned.

Lea hung off the side of the horse, her ankle wedged in Maia's belt. She loosed her arrow, its path true until the last minute when it arced around, striking the target's front.

Maia didn't need to see it to know it lodged in the center.

Wystan's eyes widened. He kicked his horse with his heels, closing the distance between them.

Lea pulled herself up and wrapped her arms around Maia.

He rammed his horse into their flank. Maia kept their mare on the trail.

Wystan slowed, switching sides, and hit them again.

The mare threw her head back and sprinted.

They rode past two targets without attempting a shot. The risk of getting thrown from the horse was too great.

"Faster. Faster," Maia chanted. Either the horse listened, or Wystan slowed.

The forest opened. Near the arena's entrance, the other contestants dismounted from their rides.

One target left. It hung from a stack of hay bales twenty paces from the last bend.

"Maia," Lea said, her tone elevated. She pointed. "I lost my arrows. You need to hit it."

Lea didn't wait for her agreement, climbing in front and taking the reins.

Maia reached behind her and grabbed her bow. Then an arrow.

Steady.

Stead-y.

Her vision narrowed, growing fuzzy at the edges. The crimson red of the bullseye filled her line of sight.

She loosed her arrow. It struck the center, wobbling from the force.

Lea whooped. Several of the other contenders clapped. Their mare slowed.

A stable lad greeted them.

Lea flung him the reins and slid off. Maia followed, her legs not as sure. They turned in their bows and quivers.

Eight out of ten targets. Not bad. They were in the lead even without striking the targets where Wystan rammed them. Only two other arrows hit bullseyes.

Wystan dismounted, his eyes never leaving hers.

That's right, you brute. We won this round.

A Red Guard ushered them down the steps and back onto the stage. She found her original X and tucked Lea by her side. A Lord handed the Master of Ceremonies a slip of parchment.

"May I have your attention," the magnified voice said.

The crowd quieted.

"The scores are in." The Master of Ceremonies waved the paper. "Tied for last place and hitting no targets..."

He named seventeen contestants. She bit back a smile when he read Wystan's.

"In fifth place we have..."

Maia spotted Erik in the crowd.

His face was full of fury. The Blackbirds must have relayed the underhanded attempt to throw them off their mount.

"Tied for third…"

Jade sent a small wave.

Maia swallowed. Her family was here. She could do this. *She could do this.* She and Lea could win the whole thing.

"And in second we have Lady Maia and Leatrix."

What? What did he say? Surely…

"And our winners of the first competition," the Master of Ceremonies continued, ignoring the booing, "Callan and Bremen for striking nine targets."

CHAPTER THIRTY-ONE

Those dirty, rotten cheats.

Erik forced an unconcerned face but inside he seethed.

He'd listened to the asinine commentary, his heart lightening with each bullseye Lea stuck.

Maia was right. The girl's magic was incredible.

Another ruler would hone her talents. Spare her from the Rite of Ortus. She was an asset to the Castle's defense. But all his father would see was a future adversary.

"Nasty bit of scoring." Ember toyed with the copper chain around her neck. "I assumed they would favor accuracy."

"You assume this is a fair competition," Xavier said, saving Erik the trouble of responding.

"King Siodina won't allow Maia and Leatrix to win." Gavyn wrapped an arm around Ember's shoulders. "It's not in his best interest."

"Then why let them compete?" Jade asked.

"To punish me." Erik ran his hand over his hair. "It's a convenient way for him to eliminate her. Too soon to use poison again."

"And you allowed her bid?" Jade whirled on him. "Why?"

"Erik allowed nothing." Xavier barked out a scratchy laugh. "Maia listens to no male when she wants something."

"He agreed to sponsor her in exchange for information." Mikel shouldered his way into the group. "Isn't that right?"

Erik flinched.

When said out loud, it sounded worse. Was that what he did? Risk her safety for information on his mother?

No. Maia wanted to enter the competition. She would have found a way without his support. Now, at least she didn't owe anyone else favors.

"You and the gods know she would've entered without my sponsorship. It's safer to compete under my seal."

"How'd that work out?" Mikel slipped between Xavier and Jade, not waiting for Erik's answer, when he said, "You played right into your father's hand."

Don't hit him. Don't take a swing.

Mikel was furious because his family was in danger. He knew the stakes. Hell, the bodyguard helped them prepare.

But Erik felt it too. That gnawing sensation crawling along his skin, pecking at his patience. He wanted to do something besides sitting in the stands.

"Enough," Xavier ground out. "Maia entered under my orders."

Jade frowned. The others kept their faces neutral.

"Our next event features throwing daggers." The Master of Ceremonies gestured for Lord Nanscott to come to the stage, stopping any more argument on the matter.

He paused again, waiting for the predictable crowd response.

"Our contestants will compete while running an obstacle course. Often in combat, a soldier must release their blade from unstable surfaces. Or precarious positions. Bring your hands together and help me welcome Lord Nanscott — our architect for this competition."

Another power play.

Timbers and wires and iron bars levitated through the air. Awed silence spread through the arena.

A tower rose from the stage's center, erected piece by piece.

It was three stories tall with a platform at the top. A large water wheel, turned sideways, went on next. Long pieces of rope threaded through the channels and hung down the sides of the structure.

Four in total dangled, stopping varying heights from the stage.

A target from the forest floated over the crowd. Free from arrows, Lord Nanscott mounted it on the mountain face across from the tower's top.

To the right, a network of timbers assembled, forming two tall ladders connected by horizontal cross beams of similar size. Iron rungs spanned the width, creating a network of swinging bars.

Lord Nanscott fixed the next target to a stack of hay bales. He mounted it so the contestants would need to travel from bar to bar, dangle at the last, then throw the blade with their other hand.

A second structure assembled.

Anchored between the swinging bars and the tower, it comprised two ladders at each end.

The one closest to the tower was twice as high as the one in front. Two wooden boards — with zigzagging risers set at an angle — connected them.

An iron bar floated into place on the lower side. Lord Nanscott positioned a target next to the rope dangling from the tower. Same as the swinging obstacle, the competitor would need to travel its span to get a clear shot. Or leap to the rope and scale the tower. But how?

Gavyn scoffed. "Maia could climb that with her eyes closed."

"What is it?" Erik asked.

"A Salmon Ladder. She will hang from the bar then swing her legs. The momentum will catapult her to the next rung. The bar stays in her hands as she scales it." Gavyn pointed to a pile on the ground. "Looks like each contender will carry their own. If someone falls, the next doesn't need to wait to start."

Erik surveyed the contestants.

They would need both upper body strength and agility to complete the obstacles. Gavyn was right. Maia, with her shorter stature and acrobatic build, would not have difficulty. Wystan — with his massive chest atop sticks for legs — wouldn't either.

He craned his neck.

On the stage's right side, a rectangular box took shape. Water floated over the audiences's oohs and aahs, filling the container.

Lord Nanscott summoned one, two, three... sixteen logs total to float in the small pool. They aligned parallel to their neighbors.

A favorite sport for the Red Guard recruits, Erik had spent his teenage years sneaking down to the lake to practice balancing on spinning logs.

At the end of the pool, Lord Nanscott mounted two targets on the base of the tower. A rope dangled between them.

A third obstacle took shape.

Wooden platforms, three paces by two, formed an alternating pattern, also leading to the tower. He propped the twenty boards at an angle.

The contestants would need to jump between them to reach the end where they could throw their dagger at the target. Or scale the rope to the top for a chance at the highest bullseye.

Clever. They would expend more energy with the course than the traditional event of simply standing behind a line and chucking blades at hay bales twenty paces away.

It guaranteed a sloppy, exhausted final round. An entertaining end.

He stole a glance at Xavier.

The heat in the territory leader's gaze could scorch an entire wheat field.

MAIA DIDN'T DWELL ON THE SCORING NONSENSE FROM THE FIRST event.

"It's over." She crouched down to Lea's level. "Focus on the next."

They lined up along the stage's back wall, out of the way of summoned pipes. Ropes. And flying timbers. *Flying timbers.*

"Tell me what you see," she said.

Maia enjoyed this part of training — forcing her student to assess the situation. To look for weaknesses and figure out ways to apply their strengths. Only Lea was a child, and this wasn't the training barn.

Another log floated into place.

"The ropes dangling from the tower don't hang low enough for me to grab."

"Good." Not good. But she was proud of Lea for pointing it out. "What else?"

"We will need to work together to climb the central structure." Lea grabbed the sleeve of her tunic. "You must hoist me up. But if I gain a foothold, I can scale its height in less than thirty seconds."

"Is that so?"

The girl grinned. "The Red Guard leave out their practice ropes on the southern face of the Castle. I sneak out at night and race the lads to the top."

"We will speak of the safety risk later." Maia wanted to hug her. "Excellent. What else?"

"The swinging bars should be easy for us. Perhaps we start there." She tapped her fingertip on her chin. "The angled ramps are too far apart for me to run them. I would need to hang on to the edges before springing to the next."

Lea's eyes widened. She tugged the sleeve of Maia's tunic.

"We must split up. You take the platforms. I'll run the bars. The last ladder is the tallest. Perhaps I could grab the rope from there."

"Aye. My thoughts, too. Listen to me."

Maia cupped the back of Lea's arm.

"If you don't think you can jump to the rope, then leave it. The fall may twist your ankle. My gut tells me they will not allow a healer between events."

"What about the logs?"

"You aren't the only one who snuck off for some fun." She cupped her hand to Lea's ear and whispered, "They are better with two. One of us will straddle the timbers to counterbalance their rotation while the other will work ahead. It's risky but our best bet of scaling the tower together."

Lord Nanscott walked to the front of the stage and raised his arms. A dozen small rocks flew to him. The tower was in the way, but the crowd cheered whatever he did.

Dunn walked to the end of the line, shook his head, and returned.

"The stones are smooth," Maia said. "An easy climb to the top but my guess, many won't make it past halfway."

Maia and Lea shared a look.

In less than five minutes, Lord Nanscott transformed the entire stage into a sterile battlefield. His display was a reminder of their power. To face this magic in war…

"Brilliant, isn't he? Let's give a round of applause for our architect." The Master of Ceremonies strode across the stage. "As there are twenty-four contestants, they will compete in three rounds of eight. Each target is worth a different score based on the difficulty of reaching it."

At once, numbers appeared above each. The blood red digits shimmered, their outlines blurry in the afternoon sun.

"A true bullseye carries a multiplier of three. The inner ring has a multiplier of two. And the outer ring will count for the score above the target."

Ten points for the highest target. A handsome reward for a risky gamble.

Five for the one near the logs. Another five points for both targets on the ladder course.

The one at the end of the angled platforms was worth three.

On the stone climbing wall, the number eight appeared above a half circle peeking out from behind the tower's edge. The Lords might as well have written "trap" above the bullseye.

"And now for the groups." The Master of Ceremonies unrolled a parchment. "Our first contains all those who hail from the mining, militia, and forestry territories."

Quicker to say the mining and forestry territories. Since Xavier took over militia training, not a single lad from their village competed for a spot in the Red Guard academy. Eight contestants stepped forward.

"Our next group includes the remaining territories."

Contenders from the artisans, the huntsmen, farming communities waved. Humans from the roving band of healers never competed.

"And those hailing from the Castle will form the third and final group."

She grabbed Lea's hand, raised it above the girl's head, and took a bow. So focused on the crowd, on finding her family, she missed Wystan sidling up next to them.

"Each contestant will have nine minutes to strike as many targets as they can. They may carry only one dagger at a time. After every attempt, they must return to the Weapons Master and retrieve their next blade. Falling off the obstacle will not disqualify a contender, but they must restart at its beginning if they wish to continue."

A heavy weight rested on the back of her neck. It took all of Maia's restraint not to take out its owner's knee.

"Filthy whore," Wystan whispered in her ear. "Perhaps I shall eliminate your shadow first. Or do you volunteer in Lea's stead?"

Her stomach heaved more from the foul stench of his breath than from the unoriginal threats.

All brutes were the same. Petty words. Lack of originality. She stroked a finger down his cheek. Let the crowd think what they want. There were other ways to fluster a bully.

"You can try," she said and bopped him on the nose.

CHAPTER THIRTY-TWO

It was nine minutes of pure chaos.

Same as fight night. Maia could do this. It was just three, three-minute rounds. With no break. And a child for a teammate.

Just like fight night.

Going through the obstacle course last was an advantage. Maia studied her competitors, noting the areas they struggled the most.

Lea's commentary added lightheartedness.

Under other circumstances, she would've preferred going first. Not for glory — everyone remembered the first. But they would have more time between events to regain their strength, to catch their breath.

A man from the Artisan territory fell off a log and bashed his head on the side of the pool. No one helped him up. Why would they? He didn't have a partner. It was a free-for-all, with everyone competing for the same spot in the academy.

"Ooh," Lea said, flinching as if she suffered the blow. "That's going to hurt."

The contender shook his head a few times and climbed out of the water. Or attempted to climb. It was more of a tumble.

No chance of him competing in the last event with a head wound.

"Look." Lea tugged her sleeve and pointed to the far side of the tower. "The contender is near the top."

Indeed. He unsheathed a dagger from the loop in his belt and stabbed the target on the climbing wall. One minute he dangled by one arm, swinging his legs for momentum. The next, he fell three stories to the hard stone, a groan parting his lips.

"Big no*p*e for the climbing wall," Lea said, popping the p.

"The stones near the top must be farther apart." Maia still couldn't see that side of the tower. "Agreed. We stick to our plan."

Gong. The sound of the bell signaled the end of the round.

The Master of Ceremonies didn't reveal the scores, but Maia guessed nobody earned over twenty.

"Let's hear some applause for our brave contenders. Not so easy is it, folks? And for our last group, we have the contestants from the Castle. The handsome twins, our first-place champions, are loosening up near the rock wall. In second place, Lady Siodina and her companion huddle in the back. Another group to watch. I'm not sure they'll stay in the top three."

Maia nodded to Lea and jogged to the starting line in front of the slanted boards.

Lea sprinted to the swinging bars. Wystan shouldered his way next to the lass, a snarl on his face.

They shouldn't have split up.

"Oof, ham face," Maia said, cupping her hands around her mouth. The other contestants chuckled. "Oy. Are your chicken legs not strong enough to make the jumps? Do they skip leg work where you're from?"

Wystan cracked his knuckles but stayed at the station.

Lea took a healthy step back, allowing two contestants to fill the gaps between.

Good girl. Maia tucked her thumbs under her armpits and flapped her elbows.

The crowd joined in the laughter.

"Can't spread your legs to the top," Wystan said at a break in the noise.

"What upsets your constitution more? That a Lady will win this event? Or that none will give you and your knobby knees the time of day?"

A flush climbed up his neck and settled on the top of his ears.

"A little friendly banter." The Blackbirds' beaks opened and closed. "All a part of it, folks. On my count. Three. Two. One—"

Wystan caught the first bar, clambering to the end of the obstacle by the time Maia finished clearing six boards. Two other contenders were close behind. Lea stayed in back.

Maia leapt to the next, her left ankle giving too much on the landing.

Wystan spun around and hooked the nearest opponent with his legs, wrenching him from the bars.

Maia barely registered the yells of the spectators when he repeated the maneuver on the next man.

Lea hung on the second bar, a look of terror on her face.

Maia didn't hesitate. She ran across the final boards and hurled herself against the tower. She caught the rope with one hand, steadying herself with her toes and the other.

If she used her dagger now, she would need to clear off and get another. Better to keep it for the highest target. Plus, who knew what Wystan would do to Lea during that time? She pushed herself to the side, peering around the tower's edge.

"You waiting for an invitation?" She blew another kiss and pushed off, re-centering.

The platform loomed ahead. Just like the training barn. One pull at a time. *Just like the training barn.*

Hand over hand, she hoisted herself up. Her feet curled around the rope, keeping it from swinging. Soon, she gripped the edge of the water wheel.

Fevered screams from the crowd were the only warning moments before a shadow blanketed her hands.

A hulking silhouette looked down at her. His features blurred from the sun at his back. Wystan picked up his foot.

Bollocks. He'd scaled the tower fast. Too fast. Maia moved her fingers to the side, the stomp of his boot missing them by a hair.

He raised it a second time.

She dodged it by shifting her weight to her other hand.

"Dance for me, whore." Stomp. Stomp. Stomp.

This arse. Her grip would fail soon, hopefully not before he tired of his little game.

Wystan stumbled forward. Was it too much to ask that he might fall head first off the tower? He peered over his shoulder.

"Tag. You're it." Lea peeked over the platform's edge. She winked at Maia and vanished.

She counted to three, waiting for Wystan to return. When he didn't, she flung herself up and spotted him grabbing the rope on the opposite side and dropping out of sight.

Two daggers protruded from the highest target. One buried to the hilt on the outer edge. The other's tip lodged in the center. That was her girl.

Maia threw her blade. It landed next to Lea's. Sixty points.

She sprinted to the side with the swinging bars, grabbed the rope with one hand, and rappelled down the tower.

Her feet struck the ground. She bent her knees on impact.

Maia would worry about the burn on her palms later.

Where were they? To her left, the twins summited the stone climbing wall. One blade dug into the target mounted on the tower. Callan had another in his in hand, ready to stab for more quick points.

On her right, logs spun in the water. Several curse words flew from that direction. An opponent fell into the shallow pit, the man behind him struggling to regain his balance.

A small body tackled her from behind.

Oof. She stumbled a half step forward and wrapped an arm around Lea's neck. She must've run in a circle.

"Hurry," she said and tugged Maia to the logs.

The box containing the timbers was wide enough Wystan couldn't grab them from the side. Though the Red Guard might not stop him from trudging through the waters to snatch them. Lea would be too slow on the slanted boards. He would catch them on the hanging bars.

The logs were it.

ERIK BALLED HIS FISTS.

Maia and Lea scrambled across the first few timbers, swaying back and forth.

They lost precious time, retracing their steps when they forgot to grab new daggers. They tucked them into the holders on Maia's waist and stretched their arms for balance.

Wystan was close enough he could reach out and grab Maia's braid.

"Faster. Faster," Jade cried out as if they could hear her at this distance.

Erik couldn't tear his eyes away from his wife. If Wystan survived, he would find him in the Castle and knock out all of his teeth.

The bloodthirsty crowd cheered on the excitement. A chase and injury at the hands of another contestant heightened the show.

And that's what this was — a show. He couldn't forget.

"Forty-eight for the twins." Gavyn pointed to the pair dangling from the bars. "A mere five for the next. Maia and Lea have this."

"Leave him be, Gavyn," Ember said. "He's not worried about the score when he's plotting Wystan's torture."

Mikel grunted.

"You want to add anything?" Erik asked the bodyguard. Maia would give him hell for it later. But he needed an outlet for this restless energy.

"This worth it? Is her safety worth it?" Mikel smiled.

Later, Erik would recognize the taunt for what it was — the fighter worried too. Now, Erik balled his fists.

"Enough." Jade wrapped her hands around his knuckles. "Mikel, go stand next to Xavier. And you," she said, digging her finger into his chest. "Maia wouldn't want this. Get it together."

She released him.

Erik rolled his shoulders and straightened. Jade was right — Maia wouldn't want him fighting with her family. But she chose to compete. Maybe if he kept reminding himself, watching her would get easier.

But he was a fool for agreeing. If it had been anyone else, Erik would stride right up on stage, throw her over his shoulder, and haul her out of there. Lea, too. But Maia would never forgive him.

And somehow that mattered.

For months, her notion of good and bad irritated him. It was clear she followed some sort of code, not blind hope.

He'd thought her naive. But what if he was wrong?

What if, instead of doing as little as possible to gain his father's notice, he should've been undermining his rule this entire time? Instead of saving his own hide, he should've placed himself in the direct path of his father's wrath?

He clung to the memories of his mother. Would she be

proud of his choices? Would she understand? Agree with his actions? His inactions?

Gods, he wanted nothing more than to speak with her one last time.

He'd searched for clues of her disappearance at any cost, not once wondering what she might think of his transgressions.

His smirk vanished.

Sure, Erik's father manipulated the Games, but this... this was Maia's choice.

A subtle distinction as their machinations led them to the same outcome. But an important one. So he cupped his hands to the side of his mouth, and with the entirety of his chest, he bellowed, "Behind you! Go. Go. Go."

Maia didn't so much as flinch in his direction. She ushered Lea to the next log with a shaky gesture that belied her fears.

Four timbers behind them, Wystan swept another contender into the watery abyss.

The girls, his girls, vaulted from the last log onto the rope dangling from the tower. Their best bet was to stay ahead of Wystan, while still scoring points. The scores had to mean something. Perhaps an advantage in the final round.

Erik winced as Wystan hurled himself onto the tower. His jump precarious, forcing him to lodge his dagger into the wooden planks to maintain his grip.

Erik cupped the back of his head as Maia and Lea climbed on top of the platform.

Lea stepped forward and threw her dagger. The blade struck the center target once more. She turned, grinning. It morphed to a look of surprise as Maia stalked back to the edge of the tower.

He couldn't hear the taunt she spoke over the roar of the crowd.

Maia blew Wystan a kiss then severed the rope in one strike.

Wystan plummeted, the watery tomb breaking his fall. He

rose to his feet, regrettably uninjured, and pointed at Erik's wife.

The crowd went berserk.

Maia spun and released her dagger. Its blade turned end over end, lodging in the red bullseye. Combined with Lea's, it added another sixty points.

Erik couldn't believe his ears. The spectators chanted, their cry indistinguishable at first, but slowly transforming into one word, repeated over and over.

"Mai-a. Mai-a. Mai-a."

She wiped her brow with the back of her hand. Lea gripped the other.

And together they faced… not the stands nor the other contenders waiting at the back of the stage. No. They face his father. And bowed.

His wife. His beautiful, cunning wife. His vicious Kitten.

Oh, she knew her role. Better than him, it seemed. His father, the King, could not risk retaliation in front of his constituents.

She played the crowd, strumming them into a frenzy like a fiddler in the final thralls of a song.

That insolent bow — respectful to those who did not have the privilege of sparring with her — was a perfect message for his sire.

She might not blend in at tea, despite filling out her dresses. Might struggle to choose the correct cutlery at dinner. But she was no simple soldier doing the bidding of her general.

Today, Maia Braenough was a courtier.

"Move," Gavyn said under his breath. "Move. Move. Move."

Wystan sprinted for the bars. It took him thirty seconds to swing across the obstacle and twenty to scale the rope.

The twins hung from the side with the slanted boards.

With the rope to the logs severed, they had only one way to go down.

Maia glanced at the magical numbers wavering above the tower. Two minutes.

They must evade him for two minutes. An eternity. A lot could happen in one hundred and twenty seconds.

Too busy tracking Wystan's progress, Erik missed Maia clasping Lea by the elbow.

She flung the girl off the tower's front, dangling her above the highest climbing stone.

Lea's toe searched for the foothold. She found it and released Maia's grasp.

Whether planned or instinct, Lea clung to the wooden side then dropped straight down. She caught herself on the same stone before the crowd could gasp. From there, she scrambled down two more levels, making room for Maia's descent.

Only there was no one to dangle his wife off the edge.

He watched in slow horror as she pivoted and dropped backwards.

She missed the first rock, grasping the next.

One heartbeat. Her hold broke. Two heartbeats. She caught herself again. Three heartbeats, more of the same.

To others, it appeared as if she swung from the stones like a macaque in search of his next banana, but her descent was too fast.

Grip. Fail.

Grip. Fail.

Until at last, she held, snagging a rougher stone halfway down. Her feet found purchase. Thank the gods for Mikel's gift.

Erik didn't need to see her grimace to know what that maneuver cost her. To know how much damage her palms suffered after her uncontrolled rappel down the tower.

It would be a miracle if she could hold a sword.

Gong. The last bell chimed, its sound framing the triumphant smile on their faces.

And the murderous look on Wystan's.

CHAPTER THIRTY-THREE

Mikel appreciated a good swagger.

Those brazen enough to strut around the realm hailed from one of two camps. Either they possessed the skills to beat everyone in the room. Or they covered for a lack of confidence.

Mikel knew why he taunted his partners in the ring. Now, he took great pleasure watching Maia.

The Master of Ceremonies lined up the contenders.

About a third looked as if they could barely continue onto the last event. Another third composed themselves enough to flirt with the crowd, mimicking Maia's earlier success. The last third, including Wystan, couldn't take their eyes off her or Lea.

"Lord Nanscott," the Master of Ceremonies called through his birds as he swept his hand wide. "If you please..."

In the front row, Lord Nanscott stood. He clasped his hands together, muttering a spell Mikel couldn't make out, and bowed his head.

The tower and boards and bars vanished at once, followed by the logs. Water swirled above the crowd, dancing and twirling out of reach before disappearing over the courtyard wall.

He shuddered. All Mikel could see was how a vast body of liquid might drown fighters on dry land. Even after all this time, he feared the depth of the Faeblood's powers.

The nobles didn't train, not like the Red Guard. Not like Erik. They cultivated their talents in the privacy of their suites. But if they put effort into honing their lines, an army of humans, no matter how skilled or how numerous, wouldn't stand a chance against them.

Ember grabbed his hand.

Her palm warmed and he would swear, perhaps only to himself in the looking glass, that his chest felt lighter.

She never claimed the ability to heal more than physical wounds. Could her powers see into hearts, into minds? He squeezed, sending his appreciation down the link, then pulled away.

She should save her gift for someone else.

"Judges, the scores." The Master of Ceremonies rubbed his hands together as another Lord handed him a parchment. "This year, as you witnessed…"

The announcer paused, reeling the crowd by a hook.

"… the unique format of the Grimoire Games. Historically, our judges combined the scores from all three rounds to declare the winners. Today, the results from the first two events will grant an advantage to the top contestants. But they will not carry over to the end. The last man, or team, standing will earn the honor of joining our prestigious Red Guard."

The crowd booed.

"Hear, hear. I understand your frustration." He winked at the spectators, the expression exaggerated as if he had something in his eye. "But we have a treat for our top contenders. They will select their weapons first."

He held up a finger.

"And... will join the event three minutes after the start. Those in second will go next, entering the fray after two. Third place, at one minute. The rest will choose their weapons in order of rank, starting at the same time."

He bowed to the left side of the stands where Siodina waited.

"My King..."

Erik's father stood, hiked his robes, and strode onto the stage.

He lifted his palms over his head, his hands almost touching. As he spread them farther apart, the blade of a broadsword appeared. Followed by the hilt. He snatched the weapon out of the air and floated it to a rack on the side of the stage.

The King conjured twenty-five weapons in less than three minutes.

Altogether, Mikel counted five broad swords, ten shorter rapiers, and ten pairs of throwing daggers.

The crowd, whether from respect to their King or from the presence of weapons outlawed in the territories, fell silent.

Those who chose long blades held an unfair advantage. Their reach would make it difficult to land a strike with the much shorter rapier. Near impossible with a dagger. A purposeful choice, one that would make the competition risker for the contestants.

A slow clap started in the middle of the stands. Others in the vicinity joined. Soon, the entire crowd stood, the applause near deafening.

Erik's father held his pose, and when the noise subsided, he snapped his fingers together.

A row of shields appeared at his feet.

"Splendid, my liege. Another round for our magnanimous King."

Between the overzealous crowd and the blood thundering between his ears, Mikel caught snippets of the next.

"And... if chooses... a shield... forfeit a blade," the birds lining the uppers walls squawked.

"You trained her," Gavyn said.

A question or a statement? Gavyn must've noticed his apprehension. He needed to do a better job of concealing his concern. Mikel nodded, unable to force a grin.

"Maia is light and nimble. If Ada were here, she would lay smart odds on our girl," Jade said. "Except those in the Castle proper, the contenders likely never practice with a steel blade."

Mikel stiffened. Ada. He was glad Xavier refused to bring his sister today. One less thing to divide his focus.

"Aye, but they'd be fools not to pick up a wooden one." Gavyn ran his hand over his jaw. "The differences in the weight will impact their swing."

"But it's a competition to first blood not to the death," Jade said.

"Accidents happen." Xavier crossed his arms. "I'm sure Erik's father expects one. Why else would he plant a trained contender in the trials?"

They all turned to Erik. For confirmation? Or did they think the Faeblood heir was privy to his sire's plans?

"Wystan is a newer servant," Erik ground out. "If I had known..."

"I expected this," Xavier said. "But what I want to know, Erik Siodina, is why the hell you are in the stands with us? Have you fallen so far from your father's grace he forbade you to sit with the former members of the High Table?"

"I wanted to sit with Maia's family, and... I'm a healer." Erik glanced down at Ember, not meeting Xavier's stare. "My powers run toward knitting wounds and cultivating medicinal plants. My father wanted me as far away from that stage as possible."

"How?" Ember's eyes widened. "That makes little sense..."

"Don't you mean why?" Erik hesitated. "Why didn't I heal

myself the last time we gathered here for a round of my father's fun?"

Mikel shook his head.

Erik should've told them long ago. Ember especially, since she was the one who risked her safety to save his sorry hide.

And it all spilled out. His mother. The wounds on his back preventing the ability to heal himself. Lea's budding powers. Once Erik started, it wouldn't stop.

Erik didn't once take his eyes off Maia.

While it was clear her cared for her, Mikel didn't trust the Faeblood heir. Maia didn't belong in the Castle. If Xavier didn't pull her tonight, Mikel would arrange for her to leave at the next opportunity.

"The judges tallied the scores. In first place, we have the twins from the Castle," the Master of Ceremonies said. "Lads, choose your weapons."

They selected two swords. No surprises there.

"In second place..." He held his hand to the side of his mouth. "And a shock to all in attendance... we have Lady Siodina and her charge."

Lea ran her fingertips along the handles, pulling a broad sword off the rack. She grasped it with both hands and swung it in a downward arc.

Too heavy. The movement pulled her forward, off-balance.

A few chuckles mixed with the hum of the arena.

She replaced the blade, choosing a rapier toward the end of the rack, and repeated the strike. Her form perfect this time.

Maia shook her hands, a slight movement, likely unnoticed by the crowd as they followed Lea's selection.

Her palms must be torn to shreds. She bent down, retied her laces, and patted the side of her leathers.

Mikel swore. To the crowd, it would appear as if she dusted the bottom of her pants.

How did she smuggle a dagger into the competition? They

checked all the contestants at the start. Who the hell slipped her the blade?

Ahh. Commander Lukas, his informant, had been the Red Guard to pat her down. Mikel was grateful for his quick thinking, but they would share words about his inappropriate manhandling.

Maia rose and strolled over to the line of shields.

A practical choice. She could brace one by looping her forearms through the two leather handles, sparing her palms. Maia must be in more pain than he realized. For her to forgo a blade…

Mikel crossed his arms. "They trained for this… if one lost their sword…"

"Let's hope it's enough," Erik said, not bothering to keep the snarl out of his voice.

~

Maia's hands hurt. She didn't need to glance down to know the burns ran deep.

The rope had serrated her flesh. The rock had opened the wound.

Still, it was better than letting Wystan catch them.

She strapped on the shield and pirouetted, executing the perfect spinning kick. Its heavy weight carried her through the motion faster than normal. She landed with a thud but covered the less than graceful movement with a crouch and a grin.

The show must continue. Maia bowed.

The crowd answered with a wave of applause.

Instead of returning to the back of the stage where Lea stood, she walked along its front edge, raising her free hand and shaking her fist.

More cheers. More catcalls.

"Captivating, isn't she, folks," the Master of Ceremonies said.

"Perhaps Lady Siodina should save some of that enthusiasm for the next event. In third place…" He carried on as if he didn't insult her chances. "We have…"

The other contestants came forward, selecting their weapons. Only one other, a fighter from the Farming territory, chose a shield instead of a blade. He gave her a curt nod.

"My hands are ruined," she said to Lea. "We must fight together, front to back, as we practiced. The battle is to first blood. Aim for their legs. Stay out of Wystan's way."

"Perhaps we keep to the edges."

Maia answered with a true grin.

The girl was wasted on the Red Guard. Between her talents bolstered by magic and her intuition, she would make a fierce militia soldier. A battle for another day.

First, they needed to get through this event.

Maia straightened, scanning the arena.

There. In the far-left row, Bree waved. Then Demelza. Followed by the entire kitchen staff. Teenagers jumped up and down while the littlest perched atop of shoulders.

Who cared what the Lords and Ladies thought? Maia nudged Lea. She hadn't realized, until now, how much their support meant. Her family, sure. They were always in her corner, and after so many months without seeing them…

But this crew, these humble servants, ordered to serve her…

They cheered for Lea. But a small part of Maia wished they rooted for her, too.

If she stayed in the Castle, these would be her people. She would drop all pretense of trying to fit in as a Lady, perhaps even stop attending tea altogether.

Maia straddled two worlds, as she had always done.

To her father, she was both a daughter and a protégé.

To her family, an adoptive sister and a fighter.

To her friends, a protector and a confidante.

And to Erik, a wife and a nuisance.

If she stayed in the Castle, she could continue to train Lea and the others if they wished. She would take any who showed interest, no matter their magical talent. As for the rest, she would champion their working conditions, their living arrangements.

They sacrificed too much of their life. It was time to make some changes.

Except she wasn't staying.

"Fighters," The Master of Ceremonies called.

Fighters, not contenders.

"Our top three places line up against the back wall. Everyone else spread out. We begin on the bell."

"Look for those who don't hold a sword properly," Lea said to Maia. "We take them out first."

Maia nodded, pride filling her chest at Lea's cunning, albeit bloodthirsty plan.

Before she could offer words of encouragement, a resounding gong rattled her chest.

CHAPTER THIRTY-FOUR

Fighters scattered on the stage.

Erik's eyes locked with Maia. *Stay safe. Stay safe. Stay safe.*

She and Lea had positioned themselves on the far side, opposite from Wystan.

The brute twirled his rapier in one hand. And pointed to the nearest contender with his other, stalking his prey.

A clock shimmered overhead.

Within twenty seconds, Wystan felled his first opponent. The lad from the Artisan territory with the head wound. An ugly slice to the thigh sent him to the ground.

He should've bowed out after the last event.

Another set of shimmering numbers appeared next to the clock.

Boom. The strike of a drum sounded as the number changed from zero to one.

In the back corner, three scrawny lads danced around each other, their stances slow and awkward.

It would take a miracle for them to land a blow. Another for them to not severely injure each other if they did.

Wystan barreled into the group. He stabbed the first in the shoulder, pulled his blade free, and slashed the next in the thigh. The third one fled. Wystan sliced his back as a parting gift.

Boom. Boom. Boom.

The count rolled over in quick succession.

Fifty-six seconds in. Was time ticking faster than normal?

Dunn, from the mining village, commanded the front of the stage. Even though his scores allowed him a rapier, he chose a throwing dagger. He sliced the forearm of one opponent, ducked an uncontrolled strike to the head, and popped up, drawing blood on another's calf.

Boom. Boom.

Wystan brought down two more. *Boom. Boom.*

Blood pooled on the stage. A contender lost his footing.

Three hobbled off toward the healers, clutching limbs. One lay face down, unmoving.

Red Guards rushed to his side, dragging him back. They propped him to a sitting position while a healer shoved wads of linen against the wound.

Erik's magic rumbled beneath his skin. Even from this distance, he knew the gash was near fatal.

A heavy hand grabbed his tunic, halting him.

"Don't," Xavier said. "Your father won't allow your interference."

Erik gritted his teeth but stayed in place. Xavier was correct — not only would his father not allow him to heal the contestants, but he might take his anger out on Maia and Lea.

His magic pulled and tugged and strained some more.

Gavyn slung an arm around Ember, likely providing comfort and anchoring her at the same time.

A blank expression marred her face. Her hand wrapped around the chain on her neck, her thumb rubbing the links. The only sign she struggled to control her powers as well.

One minute, thirty-eight seconds.

The third-place contender — Erik couldn't remember his name — had already joined the chaos. The fool cleared a path toward Wystan.

Their blades met in a clash that echoed through the stands. It was like watching two ancient gladiators spar amongst toddlers who stole their parents' weapons.

The third-place contender parried each strike, but Wystan stayed on the offensive.

"He won't last long," Gavyn said beside him. "Best we can hope is for him to wear Wystan down."

A moment later, Gavyn's prediction came true as Wystan broke through his opponent's guard, stabbing him in the bicep. The man dropped his blade and held up his other hand in surrender.

Wystan — either out of spite or fury that someone dared to confront him — slashed his chest.

The crowd yelled as he crumbled to his knees.

Boom.

"Ooh," called the Master of Ceremonies. "That will keep our healers busy. Accidents happen."

Accidents happen.

The crowd — previously on their feet — rose even farther on their toes. Many shook their fists at the commentary. Others shouted obscenities.

The third contestant hailed from the lumber mills. Sure enough, a section of the crowd wearing the customary cedar-colored trousers screamed for their champion.

Careful. They must be careful.

Erik's father scanned the stands, no doubt marking the faces of the loudest offenders.

Boom. Boom.

Dunn cut down another two. The difference between his victories and Wystan's was absurd. With the smaller throwing dagger, his opponents walked away with pinpricks for wounds.

At worst, a gash that would heal on its own without Erik's magic knitting it shut.

Xavier leaned against him, whispering in his ear, "I'm taking Maia tonight. The girl, too."

"Why now?" he asked, before he could stop himself. Erik raked his gaze over Maia. He knew this day would come.

"You failed. On the High Table, you would've held sway with the other Lords. Now, you are nothing more than your father's liability. Your day of reckoning will come. I won't risk Maia as collateral."

So Erik was expendable. What more did he expect? Maia had a home. A family. For a moment in the greenhouse, he'd believed...

The clock flashed two minutes.

Erik's heart thudded against his ribs.

Someone grabbed his hand.

The warm palm gave away Ember's identity without tearing his eyes from the stage. He didn't stop to consider if Gavyn was a territorial mate. Erik wasn't letting go.

Maia and Lea entered the fight.

A quick block with the shield provided a narrow opening for Lea to somersault underneath and slice the leg of their first opponent.

Boom.

One down. He scanned the stage. Another ten to go.

The larger brawls dwindled to pairs. With over half of the competitors eliminated, it was easier to concentrate on the individual matches.

Boom.

Wystan eliminated another. This time, a slice to the upper arm sent the contender to the healers. He must have decided the risk was too great — or he was in too much of a rush to reach the next victim — but Wystan let him go without another mark.

Those remaining showed more skill, their volleys more controlled.

The clock turned over to three minutes. The twins entered the fray.

His girls took on the opponent from the Farming territory. He was taller than Maia by several hands.

At some point, he'd swiped a long blade from someone, wielding it to keep them well out of their striking distance.

Maia deflected his blow with her shield, resting it on her hip between attacks.

"She needs to maneuver him to the front." Gavyn pointed. "She won't be able to press their advantage in free space."

As if Maia heard the instructions from her commander, she blocked the next strike, but instead of circling out, she shoved her shield at him. Not once. Not twice. But three times.

The man peered over his shoulder at the spectators behind him.

Maia twirled her finger in the air, a signal of sorts. Because Lea fanned to her left.

They attacked at once.

Maia raised and lowered the shield, deflecting his increasingly frantic strikes. Lea bobbed on her toes, waiting, it seemed, for the perfect moment to execute the roll they practiced over and over.

"She can't hold for much longer," Erik ground out. "The fighter possesses skill beyond many in the territories."

Lea must have thought the same. Instead of diving into the mix, she crouched low, drawing a dagger from Maia's boot. Lea cocked her arm to the side and whipped the blade with a side-arm throw.

The blade nicked the torso in a way that only magic could control.

"She's a caster," Ember said to no one in particular. "I

suspected before, with the arrows then the daggers, but that throw..."

Boom.

The crowd went wild.

"Aye," Erik said, squeezing her hand. "Some Castle servants are born with magic. It's subtle, not the usual family lines. The Rite of Ortus strips them of their powers."

"Authority dislikes competition," Xavier grunted. "Short-sighted fools. They claim their goal is to restore magic to the realm. From this side, it appears as if they hoard it themselves."

Hoard. Is that really what his father desired? He preached purity of lines, citing old texts warning of offspring from mixed matings, dirty human blood. Teenage Erik, too concerned with concealing his growing powers, assumed his father worked to that end.

The carefully-controlled breeding — and that's what it was, not a desire to nurture children — was nothing more than a veiled plan to ensure magic didn't spread outside the Castle walls.

Ember, not her magic, was a threat to the balance of power between the nobility and the sovereign humans. As a healer, she wouldn't lead an army to battle. But if one caster sprang from the territories, another could follow.

And the next, well... the gods might gift them more threatening magic.

He could understand his father's play for more power, even as Erik shied away from it himself. But to what end? What was the purpose of—

A cry from the crowd shifted his attention to the stage's left. The twins worked as if they had been born with blades in their hands. They took on Dunn.

Erik could see the dance play out a breath before each strike occurred.

Dunn parried one blow only to turn into another. The time

between the strikes narrowed with each retreating step. Soon, the mountain wall would press against his back.

In one last surge, Dunn whirled around and pinned Bremen in place. He nicked the twin's inner arm as Callan struck from behind.

Dammit. Erik would never admit it to Maia, but he'd hoped they would go after Wystan together.

Boom. Boom.

"Bollocks," Gavyn said, as if he was privy to Erik's thoughts. "The twins were her best chance against Wystan."

Callan surveyed the contestants.

Maia and Lea squared off against a scrappy lad from the Mining territory. He was fast and erratic. They couldn't bring him down, likely for fear of getting stabbed by his flailing rapier.

Wystan battled two opponents at once. Not partners. They must've decided working together as temporary allies was the best way to handle the brute.

Erik could see it on Callan's face — the moment he decided to imbalance the odds — he threw Maia and Lea one last look then charged into battle with Wystan.

Three on one.

It should have been a certain victory, but the additional contender confused the other two.

Wystan seized on the distraction and struck the torso of the nearest. Blood spread across the man's tunic, red overtaking the white before he toppled to the ground.

Boom. Wystan smirked.

Callan and the other man spread out. Good. Divide his focus. But the strategy failed as Wystan quickly picked them off individually.

Boom. Boom.

"You idiots," shouted a man in the row behind them. He

raised his tankard in the air. Ale sloshed over the rim and splashed Ember.

"Careful," Gavyn growled, keeping a protective arm around her.

"They had 'im. Worthless louts. I lost fifty coppers on the twins."

"A pity," Mikel spat.

The wrong thing to say. Though, the fighter had a penchant for saying the wrong things to the wrong people.

"What was that pretty boy?" The drunk wiped foam from his lip and threw his tankard to the ground.

Gavyn thrust Ember toward Erik.

The man lunged, earning a meaty fist to the face for his efforts. He toppled onto them, hitting the back of Erik's leg.

Time slowed. The momentum was too great for Erik to stop their fall. He had a heartbeat to choose the safest place to land.

The din from the crowd faded to a hum.

They went down.

Erik's knees buckled. He turned to absorb the brunt of the fall, cushioning Ember in his arms.

She landed on top of him, the side of her face slamming into his chest. Ember pushed up on her arms. Her eyes glazed over. She blinked, but they didn't appear to refocus.

"Are you hurt?" he asked, concerned more for her mindset than her safety. The crowd had tousled her last time she was in the arena. "Ember, can you hear me?"

She nodded.

"Ember," he repeated her name, hoping it would snap her out of the memory.

His commander had told him stories about fighters returning from battle. How they would react to the slightest sound. Jump with the smallest provocation.

"Gavyn is next to you," Erik said, enunciating each word as he sat them upright. "He is not fighting. Gavyn is sound."

She nodded slowly as if the movement caused her pain. Ember looked over her shoulder. A charm on the copper chain swung free from the bodice of her gown.

No.

Erik grabbed the necklace, his hands shaking.

It couldn't be.

The pendant was small, depicting a staff with two snakes intertwined. More ornate than the typical caduceus, it was a mark reserved for Faeblood healers. The serpents swirled in a perfect circle. A blue green patina, heavier in the crevices, added depth to the metal.

He turned it over.

Someone had etched an inscription on the back. The lettering was the same style as the one around his neck.

"Where did you get this?"

"It was my mother's." Ember's voice was distant. "Passed down from her family. It holds no value other than—"

"Your mother?" He dropped it, pulling his hand back as if singed. "Who was your mother? From what line of casters do you hail? How long has the charm been in your family?"

The questions came one on top of the other. No time for her to answer.

"Ember?" Gavyn asked tentatively. His eyes darted between them. "Are you well?"

Gavyn picked her up off the ground. Ember dusted off her skirts, her hands trembling. She refused to meet Erik's gaze.

"Who was your *mother*?" Erik repeated, growling the last. He stood. "Tell me."

"I don't know what this is about. But back off." Gavyn raised an arm between them. "Give her some space."

"I'm sound." Ember went on tiptoes and kissed Gavyn's cheek. She stole several shuddering breaths. To Erik, she said, "My mother never spoke of her family line. She fled her home when she was pregnant with me. Her name was—"

Sharp cries echoed through the crowd.

Boom. Boom.

Erik wrenched his eyes from Ember.

It took him half a second to register the battle on stage. Lea lay on the far wall, clutching her shoulder. Blood trickled between her fingers.

Maia and Wystan squared off, her shield tossed to the side. A limp kept her within striking range. Anguish marred her beautiful face.

Wystan raised his sword above his head. Blood from a gash on his thigh ran down his legs.

"He's out!" Mikel raised his fist. "He's out!"

Why wasn't he stopping? The event was over. They won. His girls... they won the damn thing.

Maia tripped. She held a hand in front of her face.

"There comes a time in every man's life when he must choose between what is right and what is easy. What is selfish and what is selfless," his former commander had said. *"Those moments define a man's character. The decision will break you, but those singular choices define one's life."*

His commander was wrong.

Oh, Erik's entire existence was a summation of those moments. Of doing just enough to survive. Of choosing to forsake his heritage, avoiding power. He was neither a hero nor a villain in his own tale. But this decision, choosing between his past and his heart, was not difficult.

It was the easiest, the clearest choice he ever made. It wasn't a choice at all.

When Wystan took another step forward and brought his sword down on Maia's outstretched arm, when her cry filled the arena and her body curled on itself, Erik released the pendant and abandoned his questioning.

He leapt down the stairs, taking three at a time.

He shoved spectators out of the way, hard enough a few fell to the ground.

He hammered a fist on the back of Wystan's head, ignoring the pain radiating down his elbow from the knockout blow.

He collapsed to his knees, allowing his magic to consume him.

Erik Siodina, Faeblood heir to Morvak's throne — *his mother's son* — looked to the gods for forgiveness as he cradled his wife, quietly chanting one word.

Mai-a. Mai-a. Mai-a.

CHAPTER THIRTY-FIVE

Death was warmer than Maia imagined.

A quiet energy coated her skin, enveloping her body in a calming embrace. The afterlife, or whatever this place might be, was dark. Quiet. Not frigid, as she feared.

Perhaps she would soon see her father. Meet her mother.

She could feel the thudding of her heart and hear its pulse between her ears. Huh. The organ must be in there. Not that she needed it now. Last she remembered, it threatened to empty on her new tunic.

The events of the day played in her mind.

Her family. The Games. Lea. Erik crashing the stage.

Gods, she wished for the chance to say goodbye.

She wanted to hug Mikel and Xavier and her friends. Wanted to hold Lea in her arms and tell her how proud she was. Then dissuade the girl from joining the Red Guard ranks. She would have smirked if she had a body.

But above all, she wanted to kiss Erik one last time.

Maia wanted to savor his lips. She wanted to claim him without the lies and the debt and the espionage between them.

Him, as a Faeblood. Her, as a human. An impossibility. A fantasy.

Then she would confess — for her, it had been real.

Because in this warm antechamber, in the space between this life and the next, all she could see behind her eyelids was Erik. Clearer than the others, she focused on his pointed ears, his lop-sided smirk. His velvety eyes.

And before the world went black, the deep timbre of his voice as it chanted.

Mai-a, it called. *Mai-a. Mai-a. Mai-a.*

"GAVYN WAITS DOWN BY THE LAKE." A DEEP MALE VOICE RUMBLED. Loud, too loud. "Ember is there. Go. It appears as though you have much to discuss."

"They can wait. I'm not leaving her."

Erik. Clearer than the first.

Who was else was here? She searched the recesses of her mind. Recognition dawned. *Xavier.*

Someone moaned. Why was everything so loud? Her head hurt something fierce. Dear gods, her gullet was on fire.

She meant to run her arms down her front, only they proved too heavy to move. Death may be warm, but it wasn't painless. Wasn't that just a kick in the—

She pried her eyes open. Erik's mouth came into focus.

"Welcome back," Xavier said.

"Maia, it's me, Erik." Cool liquid splashed the front of her lips. "Don't move. Your injury is fresh. Small sips. The drink will help with the pain."

Either she only caught every other word or Erik was angry. Full of sly comments and flirtatious remarks, Maia never heard him speak so plainly.

"I need her awake," Xavier said.

"She must rest."

Aye. Sleep sounded wonderful, but she wanted answers. Where was she? What happened to Wystan? To Lea?

She would have said as much, but her tongue wouldn't cooperate.

Maia opened her lids more, blinking Xavier's lower half into existence.

The wardrobe with her frilly gowns and ridiculous slippers came next. Was this a sad joke? Would the gods force her to wear pink in purgatory?

"More," she groaned, hoping they understood her request for a drink.

The cup rested on her lower lip, and she took a heartier sip this time.

"Easy," Erik coaxed as the blur around his profile melted away. He placed the goblet on the bedside table and cupped her cheek. His lips brushed against her temple and he breathed, "Kitten."

"I have little time." Xavier appeared over Erik's shoulder. "Mikel smuggled me in the Castle, but you know the consequences if I'm caught in your chambers."

"You have five minutes," Erik said, his gaze never leaving hers.

"Fifteen."

"Ten. Not a moment more."

"I won't go far." Erik kissed her dry lips and strode out of the chamber.

"It's not every day a male surprises me." Xavier hooked an arm around her back and guided her to a sitting position. "One more drink."

He held the cup to her lips. She took a long pull.

"Erik is correct. There is little time."

"What do you require?" she asked, the words forced but sure.

"Ever the ready soldier." Xavier scoffed. "An error of mine. Your father's."

"What?" She ran an unsteady hand over the linen binding her torso. "My head is still woozy. Repeat the last, if you will."

"I made a mistake, allowing you to believe your only option was to follow his path."

Her rebuttal died in her throat.

"My father was a miner," Xavier said. "My Pa the same. As was his sire before him. I grew up thinking I would live my life in Morvak's caverns. Marry Jade. Our sons following in my footsteps. Our daughters in hers."

In all their years together, Maia had never once heard Xavier speak of his childhood. Plenty in his inner circle had hailed from the Mining territory. Enough that she'd pieced together his history.

Strange he wanted to tell her now. Perhaps she lost more blood than expected.

"When an explosion buried my father under a pile of rubble, everything changed. Everyone in the Mining territory knows the risks of stealing from the mountain. Accepts the possibility that our last resting place is more likely to be under Morvak herself than in a pine box in the forest."

She grabbed his hand.

"But it wasn't until my mother passed a month later from a weak heart that I envisioned a different future. Though, nothing like we have now."

He averted his gaze.

"Nothing as grand as the training barn nor the compound. Gavyn and I aimed for a few quaint cottages, thinking to barter with landowners for a slice to call our own."

"Another transplant torn from their birthright," she added.

In this, they were similar.

Trauma spurred them to a new territory. To outsiders, it

might appear as wanderlust. As taking a chance for glory and risking the safety of the known.

But to her father, to Xavier, they'd fled from a loss so catastrophic the best chance of recovery meant finding a new dream, accepting someone else's idea of happiness.

Was that what she did?

Was that how she coped with the loss of her parents?

Perhaps in the beginning. As a child, she sought her father's approval in all things. More, since it was just the two of them. As a young adult, Maia wanted to show to the world that females deserved a spot in the militia ranks.

Wanted to prove it to herself.

But several years had passed, and she'd earned her cuffs. Years in which her skills grew. Her reputation grew. The desire to train others grew.

And she didn't just enjoy it. Maia excelled at it.

She imagined most youths pondered their future, a rite of passage, so to speak. But Maia never asked herself what the peninsula held for her. Never once considered anything else. Maybe, for her, that question was inconsequential.

Oh, the distinction was subtle — the line between what her father wanted for her and what she wanted for herself was smudged. For her, the sides reflected mirror images.

Because she crossed that line every day that she woke up and schooled another crop of militia recruits. She straddled it when she trained Lea.

The line, for her, was non-existent.

"*Heavy are the shoulders that inherit an obligation.* My father's words," Maia said.

She squeezed Xavier's hand, trying to convey her gratitude without words.

"I used to think he spoke of his debt to you. The one he passed on to me. For years, you clothed and sheltered and accepted us. He died thinking he never repaid your kindness. But I'm not so certain that is what he meant."

"If you hear one thing from me today, Maia Braenough, know that your debt is repaid."

"You males," she chuckled weakly. "All your talk of balances. Of what is owed."

"If there is one thing I wish for you, my fearless leader, the man who holds the territories in his grasp by sheer stubbornness alone..." She paused, swallowing. "I wish you to act for the sake of kindness, not balancing a ledger. I won't pretend to know your heart but... it's enough. You've done enough."

"Impossible." He smirked, hesitating. "You sound like Jade."

"What would Jade say right now?"

"She would want me to admit that a woman shouldn't destroy herself for a man. No woman should tear herself apart then hand him the pieces to build his own foundation. Your father asked too much of you." His voice cracked. "I share his folly."

Maia let him sit with his confession, not because she was angry. She sensed this was the first time he admitted it to himself.

Xavier tended toward *act now, deal with the consequences later.* He met a problem with all his resources. No hesitation.

He was a leader who lived by a code so strong that his sleep suffered more nights than not. The purple smudges under his eyes confirmed it. Near permanent tattoos in this decade of life.

"I should never have sent you here."

There it was, finally.

"You did what you thought was right."

"I did what I wanted. 'Twas selfish."

"Yet here I am. Alive. Perhaps a little battered. Unsuccessful in your directive to find the book."

"To hell with the book. You took a marriage vow under the

stars. I keep looking over my shoulder, waiting for the ghost of your father to strangle me."

"Xavier, it's—"

"Worse, Jade hasn't spoken to me in weeks. Gavyn and Rowan and Zoie refuse to converse more than necessary. Mikel sends home scathing missives. Ada won't jest when I'm near. Though I'm not entirely certain that is because I sent you here or because I ordered Mikel to follow."

She patted his hand. He took a big breath. Here he went again…

"As if I didn't know. As if I didn't already figure out how badly I messed up."

"Stop." She attempted to hold up her hand, but it fell lamely to the bed. "Allow me to assuage you of some guilt. I should have told you before, but we rushed the ceremony. Then our departure."

Gods, it hurt, admitting the next.

"Before the wedding, Erik pulled me aside and offered me an elixir." She gifted him a soft smile. "At first I thought it might be poison, a way out of his end of the bargain. Erik explained it was a potion to erase our union from the stars. They do not recognize the promises we spoke."

Though… now that she thought on it, perhaps the bond was there. Weakened, maybe. But something remained since she accessed the magical storage room.

When she recovered, she should try to enter the library without Bree unlocking the door.

She wished she had time to savor Xavier's shock. Maia memorized his slack jaw, his wide eyes. One day she would regale Ada with the story.

"I won't scold you for blindly consuming a Faeblood elixir." He shook his head. "Partly because it absolves me of some guilt and makes your escape tonight that much easier."

"Xavier," she yawned and waited until she had his full attention before saying, "I'm not leaving with you. There's the Red Guard academy, and I still have to find Siodina's book—"

"I don't *need* you in the academy. And forget the book. I don't even know what its pages hold. Of course you'll leave tonight. I have it all planned. Didn't you receive Jade's letter?"

The missive hinting at her extraction after the competition.

"Why now?" Before, she would've played the good soldier. Never asking questions. But she deserved to know. Deserved to be included in the decision. "Why pull me now?

"These walls have ears."

"You are a man used to keeping secrets. Speak softly. It's time you stop shouldering this burden alone. Our troubles belong to all of us."

Xavier studied her, his lips forming a firm line.

"Not long after you departed for the Castle, I received a strange missive from the Huntsmen territory. I sent Mikel's scouts to confirm its contents, but the entire village was gone."

"What do you mean, *gone*?"

"Gone. The cabins deserted. Hearths empty. Gone."

"They had contenders in the Games."

"Aye. And those contenders gave Mikel the slip. He still fumes somewhere in the Castle. Too busy tracking Wystan and finding a safe place for Lea, he missed them. His anger is unprecedented."

Xavier rubbed his jaw.

"You still have cousins there. Distant relatives. I worried Erik's father might kidnap them to hurt you. And with Cedric's death—"

"Why didn't the Master of Ceremonies announce Cedric's alleged treachery and punishment?"

"My best guess... either Siodina didn't want anything to overshadow his grand introduction as our sovereign ruler, or he anticipates the rumors will sow discord among the territories."

"Politics make my head hurt." All the posturing. And she

hadn't even considered her extended family. They'd cut ties with her father when he left the territory.

But they shouldn't suffer because of her.

"What happened to Wystan?" she asked, buying time to think on the latter.

"He disappeared. Lea's strike was too shallow to slow his departure. After you collapsed, the arena descended into an uproar. I took advantage, slipping inside the Castle through the clock tower's access door."

Revenge, it seemed, would wait. At least Wystan was far from Lea.

"Good. I hope he goes back to whatever pit he calls home." Maia smoothed the covers then asked, "Would it benefit you to keep someone in the Castle?"

"I have other—"

"Spies?" she asked. "Sure, but can they mingle among the nobility? Do they have access to the King's movements? Are they privy to the Red Guard's strategies? I can accomplish all three."

"No, but—"

"I am not my father," Maia said, raising her voice. "I can be both a soldier and me. Plus, there might be others in the Castle who I can train. Promise you will take Lea with you. I fear..."

"It's already done." He rubbed his calloused hand across her knuckles. Xavier sighed. "He doesn't deserve your love. He's not the right partner for you."

He — Erik. Despite his faults, Xavier didn't deserve to carry this guilt any longer.

"I refuse to believe we live in a world where the gods bless us with the love we earn. Everyone deserves happiness. A mate, a family of their own. Erik is that someone for me."

She fought the pull of slumber.

"Isn't that what defines love?" she asked, more to herself as she reclined, relieved her body moved on command. More so when pain failed to surface. "Our actions speak louder than words."

Oh, it was a cliché, but that didn't make the adage incorrect.

Erik Siodina — who professed to do the bare minimum, ignored the politics of the Castle, and took the simple path in life — did anything but that. It was his one tell, saying the most flippant words then acting in opposite interests.

He was the man who wore a wheat sack over his head, tied her up in her chambers, and left her for hours, instead of simply confessing his identity.

He was the Faeblood who fought off assassins, took a blade intended for her adopted family, and accepted death all because his sadistic father stripped him of the power to heal himself.

He was the heir who refused to ascend to the High Table under his father's tutelage, shirking power.

He was the son who hadn't given up hopes for finding his mother in spite of his father's indifference.

He was her forbidden love who ignored Maia for the better part of the last couple of months instead of taking what she offered.

He was her husband — her handsome and foolish mate. Theirs wouldn't be a marriage in name only. She may never trust every word out of his mouth, but she would trust his actions.

No matter how farfetched… no matter how utterly ridiculous they may be.

"Your ten minutes are up." Erik slipped inside. "I'll escort you out."

"I'm coming too." She hadn't heard his knock. Maia swung her legs over the edge of the bed. "Let me find some pants—"

"No," they said in unison. Erik added, "Out of the question. You must rest."

The door opened again.

Erik and Xavier whirled around, their daggers drawn, their stances widening for battle.

Ember peeked inside, looking left and right as if confirming she was indeed in the right place.

Her gaze landed on Erik then Maia before slipping in the chambers with Gavyn on her heels. She rushed to the side of the bed, her focus entirely on Maia, ignoring the males and their incredulous expressions.

Maia bit her lip.

"You're awake." Ember closed her eyes and ran her hands up and down Maia's body. After several methodical passes, her lids opened and she breathed, "You should be resting."

"See," Gavyn said with the exasperation of a male on the losing side of a long-winded argument. "Maia is healed. I *told you* Erik would take care of her."

CHAPTER THIRTY-SIX

There were too many visitors in his rooms.

Erik wanted a few more minutes alone with his wife before she succumbed to the drowsiness of the pain draught.

Mikel entered, adding to the crowd, and closed the door behind him. The fighter — sometimes bodyguard, all-the-time big brother — snarled his way.

When Erik lived in the barracks, he'd thought the fighter simple. A male who knew his worth and found joy in the light-hearted teasing of others.

But this brute, the one who stalked him now, this was the real male. The man under the irreverent mask he wore at home. Rough edges and all.

As much as Erik wanted to rush to Maia's side, he must first settle the air with Mikel. He held up a hand, cutting off any barb the fighter might lob.

"She is sound. The wound healed." There. Best to lead with Maia's well-being.

Mikel grunted, but Erik didn't imagine the relief in his eyes.

"I owe you a gratitude for training them." He ran his hand

over his hair. "For your help with Lea. And an apology for pressing you for information regarding my mother."

"It was enough to see their faces." Mikel leaned against the door frame.

Aye. Mikel would appreciate her pandering to the spectators, the Court. Second-hand pride spiraled around his chest at Maia's performance.

"I should apologize," Mikel said. "I never possessed information about your mother's disappearance."

"I know." Maybe he never admitted it to himself, but he knew Mikel was another dead end. Still, Erik wanted the fighter to think he held the cards.

Mikel's eyes widened.

"My father tracks my movements. He has spies, loyal humans..." Erik tried not to gag on the word. "They would've reported my investment if I took part. I suspected he knew enough, as evidenced by the change in events. Still, I couldn't risk it. So I allowed you to think the worst."

He hesitated, worrying over the next. But Mikel proved to be a trustworthy companion.

"My father thrives on pain. I suspect it is more than a predilection."

It was as if his magic blossomed from the suffering of others.

"He keeps his guests in the cells next to his chamber. If he kidnapped you, I couldn't risk you confessing my support. Better to believe my cooperation was not without gain. He understands such transactions."

"As he whipped a confession out of me." Mikel crossed the chamber without a care in the realm until he stopped within a few paces of Erik. "You mean."

"A loose end, if you must." He forced a shrug. "Don't take it personally."

Mikel laughed. His head flew backward as he loosed the deepest belly laugh.

"What's the jest?" Gavyn asked.

"Once a Faeblood prick, forever a Faeblood prick." To Ember, Mikel said, "My sympathies."

Mikel tipped an invisible forelock and left without a backward glance.

"What did you say to him?" Gavyn started forward, frowning.

"Wait." Ember placed a hand on his chest. The simple touch, to Erik's amusement, halted the fearsome warrior. "No fighting. You promised."

"Go join Mikel," Gavyn said, softening the command with a peck on her nose. "His Highness and I have much to discuss."

About tonight, no doubt. They still needed to share details for smuggling Maia and Lea out of the Castle. With careful timing, and Mikel's knowledge of the secret passages, they could move her without further harm.

Xavier better have a mount — a cart would be smarter — hidden somewhere in the surrounding woods. Otherwise, Maia wasn't going anywhere.

Erik didn't care if they had to retrieve her at a later date.

"Gavyn," Ember said with enough censure that the big man flinched. "We talked about this. He is Maia's husband."

"Let us get one thing straight, Erik Siodina," Gavyn said. "I don't care whose blood runs through Ember's veins. If I so much as hear a whisper of your father suspecting her heritage, I'll gut you from hip to cheek, leaving your entrails across the territories as a warning."

Erik bowed. "I expect nothing less."

And because he wanted to needle Gavyn's temper more, either out of spite or misplaced anger over the fighter's misconception he would ever hurt Ember, Erik lifted his elbow and said, "My Lady."

Ember ignored Gavyn's warning growl and kissed him,

smoothing the twitch in his cheek. She hooked her arm through Erik's. They left her mate stewing by the entrance.

Erik led them to the bed and gestured for Ember to sit in the nearest armchair.

"What's going on?" Maia asked. She covered a yawn with her hand.

Erik steadied his breaths and nudged her under the covers, willing his hands to stop shaking.

He thought about this day for years. Some nights, the need for closure so raw he couldn't fall asleep, couldn't rise from bed. He glanced at Ember.

Flat lips replaced the amiable smiles.

Every emotion eddied from his mind. They churned and swirled and leaked out of his pores until an echo of his reflection in the looking glass remained.

He'd waited so long for a crumb, a tiny morsel of news.

When Ember didn't appear inclined to speak, he fished the charm from under his tunic and pulled the copper chain over his head.

"This was my mother's, handed down from her grandmother." He held it out, pendant first. "A match to the one you wear."

Ember's hands shook, but instead of grabbing his locket for closer inspection, she removed hers.

"This was my mother's. She wore it every day. I removed it —" Her voice cracked. "I took it with me when I fled our last home."

"And yours." Erik inclined his head, not ready to voice the obvious conclusion. "What does the inscription say?"

"Sed Non Amoris." She flipped it over. "It took years of searching for its translation."

"Not the end of love," Erik said, lending her a soft smile. "She insisted I had tutors who knew the old tongue."

"I thought it was a gift from the man who hunted her, hunted us."

His father. Ember didn't need to clarify.

"I assumed it was a sick, twisted gift from him that she carried as a sort of talisman. Something to keep her moving, keep us safe when it would have been easier to stay in one place and let him find us."

"No," he said as he placed a reassuring hand on Maia's hip. "It was an old wedding gift from her grandmother. I didn't realize she inherited a pair. Perhaps it was meant for her groom. Father never would've worn something so... common."

"And yours?" She latched onto his wrist, tugging it closer.

"Finis Vitae. The end of life."

"The end of life is not the end of love."

He inhaled, the breath too shallow to prevent a shudder.

"I assumed it was a clue," he choked out, not bothering to wipe the lone tear streaming down his face. He couldn't if he tried as a slight weight on his knuckles kept his hand pinned. "She left it for me in her grotto. In our place. I discovered it several summers after... after she vanished."

It was as if saying the words reopened the festering wound inside his heart. For so long, he assumed his mother not only abandoned him but life, too.

Sure, he'd told Dezee and others at Court she went missing. No one had blamed him for his dedicated search.

He scoured the Castle and questioned its occupants, traveling to the ends of Morvak when warranted. A feverish quest to prove his beliefs wrong. *To prove mother didn't die by her own hand.*

A sob wrenched free.

Ember wrapped her arms around him, and either by some sisterly intuition, or a wise guess as to the origin of the darkness leeching from his body, she didn't ask him to explain.

He wasn't sure he could. He wasn't sure this wound would ever heal.

And Erik wasn't sure could forgive himself for believing the worst of her, so instead of confessing, a near impossible task, he did what he did best — he made a poor joke.

"To I think I found you attractive when you trailed Jade into the training barn that first night."

"Gross." She played along.

"Our clever mother." He glanced at Maia, her presence steadying him. To Ember, he added, "I'd like to believe she thought we might find each other one day."

She smiled at the lie.

"You have her eyes, her nose. And I… I have a brother," she said louder as if testing the word. "Gods, your expression when my charm fell between us. It was like seeing a ghost. And me — a Faeblood born of a Faeblood line. No chance of magic sprouting in the territories. I'm not so remarkable after all."

"Gavyn would beg to differ," he replied in a tone matching her lightness.

Another moment of silence pressed down. More comfortable than the last.

"Tell me about her." He pulled Maia's hand into his lap and traced the lines on her palm. A soft snore tugged his lips into a smile. "Tell me about your life."

"You know the gist of it from your time at the compound. We moved from village to village. It was—" She hesitated. "A hard life for a child."

Gavyn crossed the room and stood sentry behind her chair, resting his hands on the back.

"She spent all her free time gazing out of open windows, locked in melancholy. Oh, she cooked and cleaned and took care of me. Taught me my letters. How to read. Basic math and history. And when my magic emerged earlier than she expected, fear extinguished whatever spark remained. I was a bit of an impetuous child. Headstrong."

"A volatile combination with magic." His grin widened, and he knocked his knee into hers, attempting to add levity.

"Aye. Your father sent a letter threatening to track the magic, to kill us both. He somehow learned she escaped while carrying me. Perhaps the pregnancy spurred her to flee. King Siodina is not my sire."

Erik froze.

"She had an affair." Ember cupped the side of his cheek, turning him to face her. "After you returned to the Castle, Xavier sent inquiries to all the farming villages where we stayed. Oh, he claimed it was over worrying about the grain supply for the winter. But Gavyn knew how much it meant to me, not knowing my father's name."

"For years, I searched for clues about her life. Ember, I swear I didn't find so much as a hint she took a lover."

"I believe you." She rested her hand on his. "Xavier's persistence paid off. A man, a Red Guard, visited us. The neighbors might've forgotten if he was a simple soldier. But they remembered the week Morvak's famed commander stayed in our cottage — a single mother and a toddler who shared enough features with him to set their tongues wagging."

In Erik's lifetime, only two humans claimed the highest position in Morvak's royal guard. The honorable soldier who trained him. Mentored him. Loved him like a father. And Commander Lukas — the male who held the position now.

"The letter mentioned—" Her voice wobbled. "Your father killed mine."

He was going to be sick.

CHAPTER THIRTY-SEVEN

"Lachlan." Erik could at least give Ember this. He wrapped an arm around her shoulders. "Your father's name was Demir Lachlan. He lived with honor. He died with honor."

She sagged against the chair.

Erik hesitated. He should tell her of their bond. She had every right to despise him. Despise his tainted blood. The guilt of spending so much time with her father when she had none overwhelmed him.

But he couldn't find the strength to divulge this truth. Not now. Maybe never. At least, not to Ember.

Maia curled around him, a kitten providing comfort even in slumber. It was more than he deserved. He would fill her in on the details later. Seek her opinion if he should reveal the relationship or let it remain hidden.

"She withered a little each day." Ember wiped tears with the back of her hand. "Our mother was a husk — a dried out, desiccated shell. But sometimes I glimpsed the memory of a smile on her lips. Perhaps she recalled her forbidden love. But now… I wonder if her thoughts lingered on you."

He didn't believe her, but somehow her words dulled the sharp pain in his chest.

"How did she die?" he asked simply.

"Oh, how magic taints our story." A bitter laugh. "A local farmer retaliated after she cast against him. He murdered her."

The logical part of his mind buried his mother long ago. It was the small slice of sanity that allowed him to grieve. Only the truth was worse. Filled with death and so… so many lies.

This day was worse than he'd imagined.

"What happens now?"

"We've made ourselves small." She leaned forward and smoothed a hand over Maia's brow, smiling when another soft snore escaped. "Mother taught me. Survival taught you. My magic… it's different. Stronger. Can you feel it?"

"No," he said too quickly for either of them to believe. Erik stood.

"You healed Maia a mere hour ago, yet here you are, alert. And earlier, you could've held your own against Mikel. Don't assume I didn't witness *that* exchange."

Erik paced at the end of the bed, ignoring the prickles on his nape, the not-so-subtle probe for information on his conversation with Mikel.

"The last time I stepped into the arena, I cast to save your life, then Gavyn's. If I believe mother's warnings, then I should be dead. You tended Maia and two other fatal wounds tonight without harming yourself."

Her eyes flicked to the door.

"Can you feel it — the bottom of your powers? Mine is gone."

"What if I admitted as much? Then what? So I can heal others faster without the drain."

"Even the endless supply of injuries in the training barn is not enough." She wrung her hands together. "The magic requires an outlet. It feels as though it will boil over at any moment."

"That's no different from when we were teenagers. Perhaps the emotional toll of that day makes it harder for you to rein it in. With time—"

"No," she said and lifted her arm, palm up.

The remaining pain draught in Maia's cup hovered above the rim. It wavered in the air, coalescing into a sphere at shoulder height. Before he could poke it, the contents splashed against the glass.

"It's not the same." Ember raised her chin. "And I found another outlet."

Dear gods. A Water Elemental. It was possible their line mixed with Lord Wulffrith's. Close pairings over the years stunted the branches on Faeblood family trees.

For her to possess not one, but two exceptional lines of magic…

Ember was wrong. She was remarkable.

The revelation stunned him. It was as if he tried to drink directly from Ashmere Falls. Too many secrets spilling over. All at once.

What did this mean for him? Ember, tucked away in the Militia territory, could practice her new powers in secret. It would be difficult for Erik to do the same. And what if his father found out? Perhaps he already knew magic could transform under duress.

And what of the others? With the Faeblood's general lack of magical education, did they know? Did they suspect?

Few practiced their casts, more concerned with parties and couture and social standings. Once parents confirmed their child inherited the expected powers, they returned to non-magical carnal pleasures. There was no formal schooling for offspring to hone their talents. No defined curriculum to guide young casters through the process.

The High Table neglected to develop the strength of the lines.

A division of labor in the peninsula made them all too wealthy to care. Too lazy to cultivate their powers. And his father, content with growing his influence, was likely unbothered that the others floundered with each generation.

"Do you understand the implications?" Ember clutched the sleeve of his tunic.

"If my father discovers your new abilities—"

"Forget about me. This could change the course of battle. The odds were near insurmountable before — sorcerers against human chattel — but if the Lords wielded secondary powers..."

She didn't need to finish the rest.

"You support Xavier's war?" A question masquerading as a statement.

"I support change. I hope it comes to pass without bloodshed."

"The dismantlement of every kingdom begins and ends with bloodshed. The suffering of the populace paves the path forward."

"Not if it rots from within," Ember said as if she didn't grasp the enormity of what she implied. "Not if it weakens from underneath."

He turned his back to her.

"Erik." Her faint touch seared his tunic. "It is time to take your place beside your father. Your destiny is to rule."

"I am not fit to rule. At least, not anything more substantial than what I place on my supper plate."

He never admitted, even to Maia, why he feared his father. Oh, he let everyone think he held no ambitions to sit on the High Table. It was easy to play the indifferent son, one raised in luxury, untroubled with the politics of running a kingdom.

But even before the bottom of his magic vanished, Erik

worried about its depth. He knew his powers ran deeper than his peers, even with their lack of practice.

His father was pure evil. His magic seemed limitless. But at what cost? What price did they pay the gods for such power?

"I cannot be trusted with such a position," he whispered. "There is a darkness inside me. A struggle between my sire's blood and our mother's. If I start down that road, claim my birthplace beside him, I fear I will lose the battle. I will lose what little good she passed on to me."

"Have you ever once used your powers to harm?"

"No. Never."

"Have you succumbed to the temptation to force others to do your bidding?"

"Of course not—"

"Have you thought about wielding magic to strike an innocent?"

"No. But that's beside the point—"

"That is the point. One you missed because you witnessed, as a child, that absolute power corrupts, and yet, your actions prove the opposite. Look around you. Think, Erik. Consider your loved ones. Think of your family."

He staggered.

"I have family." He repeated, quieter this time, "I have family."

"You've always had a family. Oh…" She smirked at his grimace, rightly guessing his thoughts. "Not the man who sired you. Blood is not the only binding element. Gavyn taught me that. And if you don't believe me, Maia will show you. She is your mate."

"Maia must return home," Erik said, ignoring the implications. Mate. Mate. *Mate*. "I will not risk her safety at the Castle."

"We lose the light," Gavyn warned.

Their time was up.

"Maia deserves a choice." Her eyes flicked to Gavyn. "The

greatest gift you can give anyone, human or Faeblood, is the chance to choose their path."

She traced the outline of her cuffs.

"It can be as simple as supporting their decision to fight." She stood and leaned into Gavyn. "Or as grand as striking the torch they will use to burn down a cruel monarchy."

"I would do it. I would light this place on fire for her." Erik scoffed. "That doesn't make me an idealist. It makes me a male in love."

"Aye. But here's what the greatest love stories leave out, the ones with the fair maiden whose kindness all but glows. The ones where the hero is smart and strong and never fears evil."

She turned to face Gavyn as if she spoke the words to him.

But Erik knew, without her searching his gaze, she reserved the next for him. For her. The perfectly imperfect characters in the world. Their mother was one. Her father another.

"History does not judge us by the flawlessness of our beginnings. True love — a mate — will teach us to come to the light. Until we take the steps ourselves, our stories begin when we follow theirs."

She cupped his cheek.

"We are not our parents. Good or absent or pure evil. Cast off the weight of their mistakes. Make your own, if you must. But it's worth the risk... taking a chance on love."

Maybe their mother knew that too. Despite the odds, she found a slice of happiness in her commander.

Erik wanted to be a better male. For her, his mother. For Dezee and the others who stood by him even when he never believed that they might return his affections. Now for a sister. And his Kitten.

Ember was right. Maia deserved a choice to become his wife.

They would drink Stella's potion, unbinding the oaths they pledged under duress. She may punch him for not confiding about the fake elixir, but who didn't like a little foreplay?

Maia would forgive him because that was her nature, always the better person. Then he would get down on one knee and ask her to marry him in front of the entire militia.

He smiled wryly. She would need a new dress (not pink) and an enormous bouquet. Lea could be their flower girl.

And after… when it was safe for him to return to the Militia territory to claim her, he would make her his wife. But first, he must convince her to stay there, protected by her family, until he cleansed Morvak of his father's rule.

Then, they could have a proper wedding night.

Maia stirred, her brows pinching together in sleep.

He rearranged the covers, tucking the heaviest under her chin like she preferred. It was the sincerest form of torture not to slide next to her.

They still needed to discuss the extraction plan. With her safety on his mind, Erik kissed Maia goodbye, lingering as long as he dared, then beckoned Gavyn and Ember to follow him to the clock tower.

CHAPTER THIRTY-EIGHT

Two hundred hands of rope dug into Mikel's shoulder. A month prior, he'd stolen it when his scouts delivered Xavier's message detailing his plans. It was the one thing that had gotten him through these last weeks — a definite exit date from this hellhole.

He needed to get Maia away from Erik. He was bound to break her heart. It was their nature.

She stirred under the heavy blankets, rubbing her eyes. Her color returned while she slept. Hopefully, she gained a bit of strength as well.

"It's time," he said in lieu of a greeting.

Mikel bent and inspected the linen binding her middle. Still white. Good. Her wound should hold.

"Tell me where you keep your leathers, your boots." He shrugged off the heavy rope.

"Over there." She sat up, swung her legs off the side of the bed, and pointed to the end. "In the trunk. Grab the dagger, too."

Mikel rummaged through the contents, finding her favorite olive pair. He grabbed the rest, closed the lid, and set the garments beside her.

"If you need help, I'll be on the balcony."

Mikel tested the wrought iron spindles. Once he deemed them sturdy enough to hold his weight, he looped one end of the rope around several, tying it in a miner's knot. He fished the other end through and lowered it hand-over-hand so it didn't splash.

Xavier planned to smuggle them out across the lake. He bit back a smirk.

Erik's father would have spies monitoring his every move, so the heir would act as a decoy. Oh how Mikel wished he could've seen the Erik's face when Gavyn explained his role.

Bree, the servant girl with a penchant for wandering, would escort Erik to the hidden passage in the clock tower. It led to the opposite side of the lake. From there, they would pretend a romantic tryst, drawing any tails deeper into the northern forests.

"I'm decent," Maia called out.

"Give me your foot." Mikel strode over to the bed, bent down, and finished lacing her boots.

"I'm not going." She nudged him with her other foot. "In a moment, I suspect several guests will parade through my rooms. I did not wish to greet them half-naked."

"Don't be ridiculous." His head jerked up. He dropped her boot and stood. "You can't stay. These people. This place. It will drain your soul."

"Sit." When he didn't immediately, she softened her tone. "Please sit. We have little time."

Mikel snatched the stool from her vanity and sat down in front of her.

"Thank you," she said. "For coming here. For watching my back. For Lea. I know I didn't make your task easy, but words cannot repay what I owe you for these past months."

"You owe me nothing." He rested his elbows across his thighs and leaned forward. "Others would've done the same."

"Perhaps," she hedged. "But the others don't share your history with the Castle."

"I was the obvious choice." He studied the pattern on the heavy covers. "It made sense."

"But the cost to someone else wouldn't have been so severe."

He cupped the back of his neck.

"I don't know your entire story, Mikel." She placed two fingers under his chin, tilting it up. "And it's not mine to explore. But my path is different. Before you leave, I have one last request."

She dropped her hand.

"Find someone who will listen. It helps. The talking. And forgive me for not recognizing something was amiss sooner."

"Nothing to forgive," he mumbled. "Nothing to tell. And that's two requests."

"Very well." She closed her eyes, exhaling. When they opened, she added, "At least tell me you convinced Lea to leave."

"What do you think I've been doing these last few hours while you lazed about in your plush bed?" He didn't need to touch the corner of his lips to confirm his smile was in place.

Knock. Knock.

"Should be her now."

Except it wasn't Lea in the corridor.

"You," Mikel spat through the narrowed opening. "What do you want?"

"A butler and a bodyguard… how resourceful you must be," Lady Stella purred. Her companion had the grace to look appalled at her tone. "I am here at Lord Siodina's behest. Step aside. I must speak with Lady Maia."

Mikel sighed for their benefit.

Lady Stella was persistent. No chance she would leave if he shut the door in her face. Whatever this was, he needed her in and out. Quick. Time faded.

"Very well. Make haste." He disappeared on the balcony, using his body to hide the rope.

"I understand you will leave tonight," Lady Stella said, her voice carrying outside.

He didn't hear Maia's reply.

"I am surprised you are awake. Not with…"

Mikel stuck his head into the room.

"Not with my injuries, you mean?" Maia stood, yawning.

"Not with the potion I gave Erik, you simpleton. It's meant for Faebloods. I assumed it would knock out a human."

"The pain draught? Sure, it made me sleepy."

"No… I meant." Lady Stella wrapped an arm around her companion. "Never mind. Erik tells me you plan to rejoin your band of merry militia fighters. You will take Talia."

"Whatever my husband told you, he is mistaken."

"We made a bargain." Lady Stella's palms glowed. Her face remained impassive. "I'm calling in his marker. As his wife, the debt belongs to you as well."

Lady Talia found the carpet interesting. To her feet she said, "Please. I can't stay."

This was how they ensnared you. Promises. Guilt. And when those weren't enough to entice you to act, Faebloods threatened with their magic. Lady Stella favored potions. But the glow emanating from her hands suggested another line of power.

Maia's mouth twisted into a frown. He knew the moment she decided to help.

"Head up. Look at me," Maia said to Lady Talia.

The Lady regarded Maia through her lashes.

"Have you poisoned anyone?"

"No."

"Stolen from anyone?"

"No."

"Killed anyone?"

"My Lady, I—"

"Do you belong to anyone in this Castle?"

"No. I'm an orphan. There is no claim—"

"Mikel travels to the Militia territory. I need your word that you are here of your own volition."

Maia pointed a finger at the Lady's chest.

"You understand they will escort you to my home? Xavier Northcott will command your future. You must sever all ties to the Castle. Should you resist... should you cause trouble... should you attempt to flee... I will hunt you down."

"I understand."

"You can never return to the Castle. Someone will assign you duties. You will earn your keep."

"I understand."

"Your correspondence will be monitored. Your every move will be questioned."

"I understand." She inclined her chin and repeated, "I understand."

"Very well." Maia flicked her wrist at Lady Stella. "Leave us. Unless you, too, want a job at the compound. The laundry is never-ending."

Lady Stella sneered.

"Right." Maia strode toward him. "See yourself out. The rest of us are busy."

"Your backside is indecent in those pants." Lady Stella threw the parting insult over her shoulder.

"Go to bed, Stella. Jealousy doesn't complement those bags under your eyes." To Mikel she said, "She tests my nerves."

"You're the one who wants to stay for tea parties."

She shot him a look.

Gong. The clock tower chimed eleven times.

A hand grasped the railing, followed by a foot. Ada climbed over the side. She stumbled onto the balcony, popped up, and dusted off her hands.

"Ahoy, Mates. Are you ready to walk me plank?"

Mikel's mouth gaped. What—

She wore billowing red pants tucked into tall black boots lined with gold buttons. A black and gold corset cinched a plain white tunic. She'd tied a red bandana around her forehead, the ends snapping in the breeze.

All she was missing was an eyepatch and a talking parrot.

"Ada, dear gods, what in all the realms are you wearing?" Maia pinched the bridge of her nose.

Lady Talia's eyes flicked between the three of them.

"What are you doing here?" He growled. "You should be at the compound. *You can't be here.*"

"Is that how you greet your captain? If I didn't know better, I would mistake you for a scalawag."

She winked.

"Captain Ada Sharkbait at your service, milady." Ada bowed low to Lady Talia. "Don't stare. It's rude. You won't find the bite, it's hidden under me—"

Enough. Mikel grabbed her elbow and steered her back to the railing. He peered over. A boat bobbed in the waves, anchored next to the rope.

"I sailed a long way in me ship to rescue you lot and claim any treasure in your possession as me own."

"Ada, you can't be here." Maybe if he said it again, he would wake. This was all some horrible nightmare.

"You three appeared marooned." Ada tapped her foot. The gesture was so familiar that he almost missed a step. "My crew saw the white flag."

"Ada," Maia hissed. "Drop the act."

Ada pouted. He didn't know whether to strangle her or kiss those insolent lips.

"Bunch o' ninnies. Where's your humor?"

"A-d-a." Maia enunciated the three letters with the patience of an tutor instructing their younger charge. "Where is Gavyn? Xavier?"

"Gavyn waits with Ember on the other side of the lake." Ada huffed at a lock of hair escaping the bandana. "You know he won't leave her. Xavier stayed with Jade after I convinced him we wouldn't all fit in the boat."

"Xavier allowed you to come alone?" Mikel asked, the question sour on his tongue.

"You and Maia offer plenty protection."

"Ada?" Exasperation replaced Maia's patient tone.

"You keep saying my name as if I forgot it. I told Xavier my idea. He and Gavyn debated its merits, but they were taking too long." She switched back in character, altering her voice. "I set sail without me crew's blessing."

There would be no kissing. Only strangling.

This was too much. Even for her. He opened his mouth to let her have it, but the chamber door creaked.

Mikel and Maia drew their daggers at the same time.

Ada shoved Lady Talia behind her, unsheathing her own blade.

"Maia," Leatrix shrieked and sprinted across the room. She flung herself in Maia's arms.

"The Lords and Ladies dine in the great hall." Dezee closed the door, following at a more dignified pace. "I can't stay long. King Siodina suspects something. Earlier, he visited the kitchens. When he couldn't locate Lea in the infirmary, he searched the barracks."

Mikel had hidden Lea in the pantry, rearranging the space so a heavy butcher block concealed the trap door to the root cellar.

"I informed him of her demise." Dezee smiled. "I told him we already buried the body."

"Did he believe you?" Mikel asked.

After Erik healed the lass, they explained their plan to Lea. She could leave tonight with them or take her chances with the Lords. She had taken one look at his mangled wrists and decided.

"I cannot be sure, but it was the best I could do."

"Thank you," Maia said, hugging Dezee. She crouched down to Lea's eye level. "I wish I could be the one to show you my home."

"You're not coming?" the lass asked, her voice quiet.

"No. My place is here, with my husband. Ada will take good care of you."

"Arr. She stays with me. I need a first mate."

"My home is yours." Maia rolled her eyes, the gesture wrenching a half giggle, half sob from Lea. "My rooms are yours... when you are ready."

"You'll visit?"

"Of course. How else could I ensure you are growing strong and hitting all your targets?"

The lass wrapped her arms around Maia.

"Careful. You risk choking me with your strength."

Another sob-laugh.

"You listen to Miss Ada." Dezee rested her hands on Lea's shoulders. "I don't want to hear tales of you not minding your manners."

"Be a help, not a hinderance," Lea recited.

"Take care of yourself." Dezee wrapped her arms around Mikel. "It brings me great joy to know you found a family of your own."

He inclined his head, swallowing past the lump in his throat. Mikel returned the hug, whispering his gratitude for her friendship so long ago. He pulled back and pasted on another roguish grin.

Dezee gave Lea one last goodbye, smiled at Maia, and left.

"Who's first?" Ada rubbed her hands together, breaking the thick tension.

"I'll go with Lady Talia." He glanced in the Faeblood's direction. She tried her best to blend into the wallpaper. "We don't have time for you to change."

She blushed. It wasn't as if she could climb down the rope in pants, anyway. Plus they couldn't leave her gown behind as evidence.

He held out his arm, gesturing for her to hold on.

She stepped into his embrace, clinging tightly. Something jabbed him in the side. Perhaps a trinket of some sort. Foolish, but one look at her wide eyes told him not to protest. Let her bring her baubles.

"Lea, you follow. Ada next." To Maia, he said, "Toss the rope after us."

Mikel hoisted himself and Lady Talia over the balcony. He grunted, not from the effort. She weighed nothing. But the blasted object poked him again.

"Hold on."

She tightened her grip and counted. Her voice wavered for the first ten, cracking on number fifteen.

"That's it." He doubted she was aware she spoke out loud. "Watch my hands. By twenty, we will reach the boat."

His feet struck starboard at twenty-two. He tightened his hold and widened his stance, trying to dampen the sway. This close to the foundation the waves were choppy, relentless.

"Take care where you step," he said, trying and failing to soften his voice.

Lady Talia let go and stumbled on the uneven planks. She righted and scrambled to the center, clinging to the splintered mast.

Lea rappelled next, her freshly-healed wounds not slowing her down.

Ada slung a leg over the balcony's railing, sent Maia a jaunty salute, and jumped. She slid down the rope. Fast, too fast.

Mikel's heart lodged in his throat.

A second before she would've crashed, Ada snaked the rope around her ankle, tightened her grip, and landed on the boat with enough force to drag them away from the wall.

"Pull the anchor." She popped up, dusting her hands on those obnoxious trousers.

Lea and Lady Talia hauled the heavy anchor over the side as the rope landed with a thud, its end tangling in the mast.

Ada handed him an oar and untied another for herself.

"Teamwork, aye?" She flicked her chin at Mikel.

Together they rowed to the shore. He rested every third stroke so Ada could straighten her side. Lea gripped the wall while Lady Talia sat silently on a crate near the bow.

He didn't dare speak. He didn't dare breathe until they reached the banks.

Xavier and Gavyn trudged into the water. Together, they hauled the small vessel the rest of the way to land.

Mikel hopped out and carried Lady Talia, depositing her in the tree line next to Ember and Jade. Lea followed behind him, unconcerned with her wet stockings. Ada right beside her.

"Mikel?" Xavier asked, nodding to their unexpected guest.

"Lady Talia Owenspaete." Mikel gnashed his teeth. "A gift, from Erik."

"Just Talia, please." She pulled a small journal from her skirts.

So that was what poked him.

"From Lady Stella." Lady Talia handed it to Xavier. "She said this shall serve as payment for my safety."

"You are welcome in my territory for as long as you wish," Xavier grabbed the journal. "Payment or no."

"Where's Maia?" Jade asked, her gaze bouncing between them.

No one spoke. What was there to say? History repeated itself. He couldn't convince Dezee to leave all those years ago. Now, Maia chose to stay.

Xavier kept silent as he tucked the journal in his waistband and walked away.

Mikel tied and retied his boot laces.

That damn book fractured the last of his calm. He couldn't

vomit his supper. Nor could he swallow past months of anxiety for Maia's safety. Years of anger from childhood.

Emotions flooded him. Too many at once.

They melded into something unrecognizable, a beast thrashing the against the bars of his self-control. Maybe if Maia had journeyed with them... Or if Ada had stayed on the banks protected by her family instead of flouncing around pretending to play pirates...

But they didn't, and he couldn't contain it any longer.

Ada grabbed his arm. "Mikel, what—"

He spun around, catching her before he knocked her into the lake. The moment stilled. He bent Ada backwards. Her mouth, for once, fell silent.

He did the one thing he swore never to do. Not because he didn't want her. Dream about her. *Obsess about her.* No. He held himself back because of who her brother was. Because of their age difference.

Mikel smashed his lips to Ada's.

And he kissed her until the beast quieted, retreating into his cave.

much more [illegible]

[illegible]

CHAPTER THIRTY-NINE

Erik led Bree deeper into the northern woods.

A trio of Red Guards followed, carefully keeping their distance. He gritted his teeth and scuffed the forest floor with his boot, baiting the trail. A little more. Just a little farther.

"Why Lord Siodina... where ever do you lead me?" Bree asked, her voice loud and saccharine. Too dark to see her lashes, he imagined them dramatically fluttering.

She giggled.

Erik glanced behind him, curbing his response.

Right. Lovers. This was to be a tryst. Mikel's idea. Curse Xavier for agreeing.

"A little longer, my sweet." He halted, drawing her in his embrace. In her ear he whispered, "Let's give them more time?"

Erik bent to brush a kiss on her mouth but turned his cheek the moment before his dry lips skimmed hers.

"My Lord." She wiggled against him. "Let's have some fun."

He pulled back, alarmed at the glint in her eyes.

"Up ahead, there is a cave." She cupped the side of his ears, keeping him close. "We can head there hide from our friends. What do you say? I haven't spooked a Red Guard in ages."

Erik had no memories of Bree at the Castle before his time in the militia. Nothing.

There were hundreds of servants, but he would've recalled one so outspoken, one unafraid of the Red Guard. Who the hell was she?

He brushed a lock of hair behind Bree's ear and grabbed her hand, lacing their fingers. Perhaps this was the distraction he needed. Red Guard taunting was a favorite pastime of his.

He knew the cave. It was another half mile along the ridge, hidden behind a bend. It would take them farther away from the Castle. From Maia.

A breath tore from his chest.

He hadn't said goodbye. And he was a bastard for it.

Maia slept in his bed while he'd met Xavier for last-minute instructions. After, he meant to return to their chambers, but his feet took him to the kitchens then to the pantry. And once he ensured Lea remained safe in her hiding spot, he found Lady Stella and her minion, Lady Talia.

They'd waited for him in his greenhouse, Stella guessing tonight was the night Xavier would collect his family. They exchanged heated whispers as Stella handed over two parting gifts.

Erik had eyed the pouch of gold. And he kept his mouth shut when Lady Talia slipped the small, navy journal in her voluminous skirts. Then he kicked them both out of his sanctuary, asking for five minutes alone.

He'd lasted three before storming out.

He couldn't find the words to tell Maia about the elixir or Stella's involvement. He never assembled the correct combination of phrases for an apology. Erik considered praying to the gods for guidance, dismissing it as quickly as the solution entered his mind.

They'd already answered one plea today. Best not push his luck.

Erik feared Maia would never forgive his betrayal. He worried the elixir wouldn't work. But neither was what kept him from his chambers.

No, the truth was rather simple. Painful, but simple. Erik couldn't bring himself to say goodbye.

Instead of escorting Lady Talia to his chambers, he'd fled like a coward. Bree had been kind enough not to argue when he'd shown up in her rooms, demanding they leave sooner than planned. She'd taken one look at his scowl, perhaps detecting the slight mania in his voice, and led them to the lake and forest beyond.

A branch snapped under foot. Bree's palm warmed against his. Too distraught from his own cowardice, Erik didn't notice.

"This way." She tore a piece of her apron and hung it at eye level.

Bree slipped between a break in the understory brush and followed a path so narrow its only chance of discovery was if another traveler revealed its location.

The goons, so elated to find the clue, wouldn't question how the fabric got there.

He followed her into the cave's entrance, the cool air prickling the hair on his nape.

"Once we return to the Castle, stay in the kitchens for a few weeks. Don't attend the families in their chambers. Stick to Dezee. When she isn't around, find something to occupy yourself in the pantry."

There would be repercussions for his interference in the Grimoire Games. For both his sponsorship and for tending the wounded.

Then there was Lady Talia. It was foolish to hope she stayed beneath his father's notice. Now, Mikel's scheming brought Bree in the mix.

"Stay hidden," he clarified.

Bree gave him a funny look but inclined her head.

Shouts echoed in the cave.

"Play time." A mischievous smirk crested her lips. She shimmied through a narrow crack, gesturing for him to follow.

They tiptoed around the curved wall and looped back to the entrance.

"I swear I saw them duck in here," the first Red Guard said.

"Sure. And where did they go, eh? Lord Siodina is naught but a healer, a stodgy gardener. Don't suppose he cloaked them with an invisibility vine."

Two guards snickered.

"I know what I saw."

"Let's go. We should divide and meet back at the front gate."

Bree cupped her mouth and howled.

If Erik hadn't been standing next to her, he would've sworn the cry came from an animal.

"What's that?" the first guard asked, stumbling back. "Did you hear that?"

"Aye, you fool. You led us straight to a den of timber wolves."

Bree howled again. Deeper this time.

Erik peered around the opening, holding in a snort at the guards' fumbling.

They formed a small circle, their backs to each other, moving in small, unsure steps.

Another growl curled over his shoulders. Deeper, it bounced off the stone walls, rumbling longer than her last.

"W–w–wolf."

The three Red Guards pushed and shoved, dashing from the cave.

"That was a delight." Bree clasped her hands together. "I haven't had that much fun in ages."

"Who *are* you?"

"A lowly servant, milord." She curtsied, the gesture neither out of respect nor decorum.

When she didn't elaborate, Erik leaned against the cool wall and slid down. He sat, his legs splaying out in front.

She cocked her head and joined him.

They stayed there, side by side, for who knew how long. Bree seemed to know he didn't want conversation. And Erik, overwhelmed by the events of the night, let the question of her identity rest.

The clock tower bells pealed. Midnight.

"Let's return you to the kitchens." He pulled her to stand and muttered, "Thank you for tonight."

She didn't dignify his feeble attempt at gratitude with a response, leaving him in the cave.

Erik caught up with her on the main path.

"Dezee mentioned you are trustworthy." The trail widened. He hurried to walk beside her. "If you run into trouble in the Castle, find me."

Tomorrow, Erik needed to figure out a way to sneak off to the Militia territory to confess his sins to Maia, but he could start acting the Lord now.

"If you need anything at all—"

A pair of boots fell from the tree. Erik unsheathed his dagger as a man unfolded to his full height.

"Fancy finding you here," Commander Lukas said to Bree.

How long was he on the trail? Did he follow them this entire time?

Erik nudged Bree behind him, angling his body to block her from sight.

"'Tis alright, milord." She stepped around Erik, a hand on her hip. "It's Lukas, coming to drag me home."

Erik looked between them.

Years ago, he and Commander Lukas had come to an understanding.

Erik didn't recognize Lukas's rise to power after their mentor's death. And Lukas didn't acknowledge Erik's heritage.

Any time they spotted each other in the corridors, they changed direction instead of brushing past one another as ghosts.

Bitter rivals in training, Lukas had never gotten over Erik's infiltration into the former commander's good graces.

And Erik, a hotheaded teenager battling his own demons, had never sought to cultivate a friendship with the bitter human who stumbled into the Castle, looking for a handout.

Commander Lachlan must've seen some good in Lukas because he bucked tradition and invited him to stay at the barracks. He started training the next day.

Lukas balled his fists at his side, his gaze never leaving Bree's.

Ah, so the commander wasn't here for him. Erik bit back a smirk.

"Come along, Lukas." Bree rolled her eyes and started up the trail. "I must've gotten lost again in the woods. Lord Siodina was kind enough to show me the way back. Though, I suppose, you could take it from here."

"Your father dines with the Lords in the great hall," Lukas threw over his shoulder. "I suggest you return before he notices your absence."

"Perhaps I will." Erik grinned. "Or perhaps I'll stay out a little longer and allow you to answer uncomfortable questions as to my whereabouts."

Kindness, it seemed, would take some practice. Maia would understand.

Maybe after a year or ten, he could be civil to Lukas. With that cheerful thought, he saluted and set off for his mother's grotto. After, he could return to his greenhouse and bury himself in the never-ending work.

The night was young. He rubbed his chest. This burn wouldn't allow sleep, anyway. Better to spend his energy doing something useful rather than staring at his empty bed.

MAIA WOKE TO THE SUN STREAMING THROUGH THE BALCONY windows.

The blankets next to her were unruffled. Huh.

The sleeping draught imprisoned her in a dream-filled slumber, so she wasn't surprised when she didn't wake upon Erik's return last night. But he didn't normally straighten the covers.

Her stomach itched. She unraveled the linen binding her torso and trailed her fingers over the shiny pink scar. The wound was long, spanning from her lower ribs down past her hipbone. It was a miracle her guts didn't coat the arena stage.

She gingerly poked and prodded and stretched the skin, everything she could think of besides scratching it. Perhaps Erik had a cream. All things considered, she was lucky to live with the minor discomfort.

Maia rose and snagged one of his tunics from the trunk.

The balcony beckoned. She opened the doors and inhaled the salty breeze coming off the lake.

A mixture of brine and the unmistakable odor of fish, she'd never given its scent much thought. Peculiar, since land surrounded the body of water on all sides.

A falcon landed on the railing next to her hand, its striking reddish-brown feathers gleaming in the morning sun. It regarded Maia with wise eyes and held out a yellow, scale-covered leg.

She untied the missive, careful not to brush against the beast's sharp claws.

The messenger took flight. A signal that her reply was unnecessary.

My Dearest Maia,

It was wonderful to see your grand home, even if we never made it past the courtyard. But what were you thinking? A Lady doesn't compete in the Games. You almost died! And that poor servant girl. Perhaps her defeat will prevent you from partaking in other foolish endeavors.

Xavier is furious about your loss. You know he tolerates nothing less than perfection. You are to be stripped of your title. Your militia rank. Any prior assignments are null. But I think I can persuade him to allow your return to the territory for the occasional visit.

The compound will host another wedding this winter. Gavyn proposed to his mate. Perhaps time will cool Xavier's ire, and he will allow your attendance. If he proves stubborn, I will remind him of your status in the Castle. No one refuses a Lord and his wife.

Mikel returned to the compound with us. He assures me you are happy and settled. How could you be otherwise, given the luxury in which you live? The handsome Lord you ensnared. Write when time allows. No need to make haste, my dear friend. I look forward to your next.

Yours in Friendship,
Jade

P.S. I discovered a new author. Happenstance, really. The book appeared when I least expected it, full of gory battle and tarnished knights and evil dragons! I don't know who to thank for the lovely gift, but my heart wishes it to be Rowan.

Maia reread the letter.

Any prior assignments are null...

The book appeared...

Could it be? Did one of them smuggle out the book Xavier sought? Perhaps Mikel discovered its whereabouts? But why wouldn't he mention it?

Jade reads romance tales, her appetite almost as large as Ada's. Another clue. If that was too subtle, the use of Rowan's name was akin to swinging a battle axe to kill a fly.

Write when the time allows.

That line, she understood. Xavier trusted her instincts, no longer requiring constant correspondence.

And Gavyn proposing to Ember... she chuckled. He'd lasted longer than she'd expected.

Things back home would return to normal. Well... as normal as they could be with Xavier plotting against the Castle. Now, she needed to set her affairs in order here, at her new home.

And she knew just where to start.

CHAPTER FORTY

Maia climbed the steps to Erik's greenhouse.

She'd expected to find him covered in soil, tending his favorite specimens.

But he wasn't at his potting bench. Nor in the Gillyflower patch. She wound between flower beds, too hurried to appreciate the splendor of riotous color. Not here, either.

Movement on the deck caught her attention. It was difficult to determine the source through the condensation on the glass. She went to investigate.

The heavy connecting door closed behind her, its noise echoing down the ravine.

A pity.

Erik had been moving through sword forms. Barefoot, without a shirt. The lacing of his trousers loose.

Sweat glistened on the hard lines of his chest, and beads rolled down to the pallet of blankets at his feet.

His eyes widened.

She registered two things at once.

One, he slept here last night instead of coming back to their chambers. And two, if he moved toward her, she would forget all the words they needed to share and spend the next hour licking every groove and contour of his body.

"Put on a shirt." Bollocks. That came out harsher than intended.

He straightened, tossed the blade to the side, and started toward her.

"I mean it Erik." She raised her hand. "Stay there. Put on a shirt. I can't think when you… when you look like that."

He seemed to appreciate her dilemma because he reached down and tugged on his tunic. With the simple act, his entire expression changed from focused to unreadable.

"What are you doing here?" He ran a hand over his hair.

"I stayed."

"You stayed—" His voice croaked. "You stayed."

Under different circumstances, Maia would chuckle at catching her husband off guard. But she needed him alert, not fumbling for words as if a left hook caught his chin.

"I stayed." She wasn't much better.

He crossed over to her, his strides devouring the distance. Erik cupped the back of her elbows and rested his forehead on hers. Heat emanated from his body, enveloping her like a cape.

She braced herself for his censure. He would protest her decision and order her back to the compound, especially now that Xavier had the book.

There was no reason for her to remain. And if his father suspected her involvement, even if she never so much as set eyes to it…

Time beat around them. Blood pulsed in her ears, marking its passage.

And still… she remained silent.

He inhaled deeply, as if trying to capture their scent, his body memorizing the blend. And slowly, with deliberate care, he leaned back and cupped her cheeks, then admitted the last thing she expected.

"The elixir was a fake."

The statement fell between them.

"I lied. The serum I gave you before our wedding vows was nothing more than a mixture of apple cider and Crimson Gillyflowers."

She swallowed. The individual words made sense but strung together... she would need him to repeat it.

"Maia, do you understand what I am saying?"

One at a time, she touched the tips of her fingers to her thumb. Tiny pin pricks sparked under her nail. Not a dream.

"The marriage oath still binds us," Erik said. The clarification unnecessary.

"Why?" Why what? Why didn't he tell her? Why lie in the first place?

"At the compound, when Xavier revealed his plans, you looked... lost. It was as if he hurled you off Ashmere Falls, then commanded you not to make a splash at the bottom. I couldn't stand that look. Your anger — your sharp claws, sharper dagger — would've been easier."

His thumb caressed her cheek.

"I spent months watching you in the training barn, telling myself I couldn't have you, comforted because whoever earned your love would also need to be strong enough to brave your headstrong will."

He loosed a breath.

"We never spoke about our dreams, but I knew you gave up one of yours to wed someone you didn't love. What else could put that look on your beautiful face?" He laughed, the sound harsh and bitter. "You would walk to the ends of the realm if Xavier asked. It was the only reason that made sense."

"So you lied."

"Aye. I promised a falsehood. But I found a solution."

Erik reached into his trouser pocket, producing a small vial of liquid.

"I made a bargain with Lady Stella. Find a spell to nullify the oath. In exchange, I was to speak with her father about her betrothal."

"Only she requested passage for Lady Talia? Her lover?"

"I never asked. But her request, while risky, wasn't unreasonable. As for the potion, I planned on confessing last night. You deserved to return home free of me. Only I couldn't face saying goodbye, not with your anger between us. After I completed my part of the plan with Bree, I went to mother's pool. Then I came up here, unable to sleep in our bed with your scent lingering on the covers."

He faced the vista.

"I planned to meet with my father, offer my services for tracking your whereabouts. Oh, nothing would give him greater pleasure than for me to be made the fool by a human wife, but he could twist the story and use it as propaganda in the territories to paint our family as the victim of Xavier's schemes. He would need to be certain of your location, anyway."

Erik offered her the vial. She shook her head.

"It sounds ridiculous this morning, but I wasn't of sound mind last eve."

The wrong thing for the right reasons. She should be furious with him for lying. A part of her was disappointed with herself too. She should've known, especially since her print keyed open the magical storage room.

She resisted the urge to smack her forehead. And to top it off, she'd help him brew the potion. The irony. She could strangle him for that alone.

Maia recalled their time together. The many chances to tell her. She sighed. No wonder he fought off her advances.

"No more lies." She tipped up her chin. Her foolish husband thought himself alone for so long. That nonsense ended now. "There can be no more lies between us."

"No more lies," he agreed easily. "But you deserve a proper

courtship, a proper wedding ceremony. You decided to stay, but I want to do it right this time."

She covered his hand with both of hers as he tried to remove the stopper.

His eyes shot up.

"You owe me a favor."

Their kiss. His mouth parted as if he only just remembered their bet.

"Is this elixir suitable for another purpose?"

"No. My magic tailored the spell to our plight. I took no chances. At midnight tonight, we must speak our marriage vows in reverse."

"Can you repurpose the ingredients? Distill the contents for future use?" It would be a pity to waste them, given their uncertain future. A potion that unbound oaths from the stars… it might come in handy.

"No," he said simply. "I cannot."

"Then chuck it off the mountain." If she had her bow and arrows, Maia could use it for target practice. A symbolic start to their marriage.

"I won't." He gripped the vial, letting his hand fall to his side. "I promised myself to set this right."

She knew that look. It was the one Xavier and Gavyn and every other hotheaded male in the militia wore when they decided something. Stubborn. Immovable. And only one thing would change his mind.

"You owe me a favor."

"Maia—"

"A bet's a bet. I have your marker."

She stepped inside his guard. Their chests touched.

"Perhaps it's my turn for a promise. I promise I bind myself to you, Erik Siodina, of my own volition. To have and to hold. In sickness and health. In war and at peace. In this life and beyond the Veil."

He clenched his jaw. She held her ground.

"There's no way back."

"I know—"

"I cannot brew another."

"I understand."

"I mean it, Kitten."

She almost purred at the nickname.

"I used the last of the Helispore."

"I was there."

"So be it." He chucked the vial, his whole body given to the throw.

They watched it fall until it became a speck. Then out of sight, disappearing beneath the canopy of trees.

She leaned back against him and steadied herself.

Their breaths evened out. Perhaps they could stay here a little longer and snuggle under the blankets in his inviting pallet.

A quiet way to start their union, a peaceful moment before their new adventures began.

He wrapped his arms around her. The weight of his chin rested on the top of her head. And before she suggested they lie down, he nipped her ear and growled, "Turn around."

~

SHE STAYED.

Maia spun in Erik's arms. He kept his hands on her, afraid she would disappear at any moment.

He didn't deserve her. Typical Maia, he meant to confess and give her a choice. He should've known she would balk at his plans.

Perhaps he could've worked harder to plead his rationale. He promised Ember as much. But he was selfish, offering little protest. Besides, he knew that look.

Maia listened but decided the opposite.

He wasn't entirely sure she'd forgiven him. Still, he owed her an apology.

"I'm sorry for lying. For all of it. I had my reasons, but they seem feeble now."

"I know. And I forgive you." She craned her neck to the side.

"That easy?" He chuckled and kissed down the column of her throat. "Maybe you can think of a way for me to make it up to you. I am at your service, my Lady."

"It's that easy." She grabbed his ears, guiding his nibbles. "Though I suspect you will not forgive yourself for some time."

Erik scooped her up in his arms.

"As for this morning…" she said. "I could pin you to the armory wall. Tickle your feet until my heart's satisfied. Or you could spend the day groveling, serving my every whim."

He smirked and deposited her on the pallet. While he wasn't one to relinquish control, he might enjoy being her private servant. Erik settled between her legs. His hard body nestled into her soft curves.

"No more daggers to the head," she said, her tone serious. "And while I might enjoy ordering you around, I do not require your submission."

Aye. She would always be the better one. Easy to forgive. Always doing what was right, no matter how difficult the task.

While he enjoyed their banter, now was not the time for play. Not their first joining.

"You have all of me. Marriage oaths or not. You had me from the moment I set eyes on you in the training barn. I don't need a promise to the gods, nor fancy earrings, nor my mark on your neck."

He propped himself on one elbow, brushing an imaginary tendril of hair off her forehead.

"This…" He trailed the finger down the bridge of her nose.

"This is what I need. You. Any way I can have you. Beside me. Under me. Next to me."

He removed his mother's chain.

"Would you do me the honor of wearing her pendant? It was a gift from her grandmother upon her marriage, a relic passed down for new brides. It's not fancy, nor valuable, but it's yours."

The charm warmed between his fingers.

"She would have loved you, my mother. Ember's mother."

"I'd be honored to wear it." Maia looped the chain over her head, twisting the pendant to the back of her neck.

"You have two options," Erik said. "We are both exhausted. I can draw a bath, and you can relax in our chambers while I finish my workout and tidy up the greenhouse. We are not expected anywhere soon. The Court will sleep past midday after last night's celebration."

A feather-light touch brushed over his waistband and tugged on the leather bindings of his pants.

"And if I want to stay right here?"

"Then I will make you my wife in every way."

She dipped her hand inside and cupped his hard cock.

"I gave you a chance to flee." He pressed his hips into her palm. "You didn't take it. Now you're mine."

"Am I trapped?" she asked in a way that suggested she would enjoy those sorts of games.

"You'd like that? Me tying you up. Would you prefer leather cuffs or something more dangerous?"

He ran the tip of his nose down the column of her neck.

"Wicked Kitten, is that what you thought when I pinned you to the armory wall?"

"Perhaps." She arched against him. "Perhaps I imagined you up there at the mercy of my clever tongue. How long would you last before you begged?"

"A bet for another day." If she didn't stop voicing ideas, this would be over before it began. He wanted their first time to last. "Lie back."

Maia pushed against his palm on her chest, straining against his control.

Erik added more pressure, guiding her shoulders flush with the pallet. His other hand slipped to the button on her leathers. It popped open. He peeled them down her thighs along with her utilitarian undergarments.

She kicked them off.

He sat up, pulled his tunic over his head, and waited, giving her one last chance to stop.

"Please," she said. "I need you."

"As you command." He cradled her head and closed his mouth over hers.

Maia's clever fingers explored his bare chest as if memorizing every dip and crevice and scar. She mapped his skin, branding it.

He dipped a finger inside her. Then another. Her heat coated his hand like stolen honey. He brought his fingers to his lips.

"Delicious." He bunched her tunic and kissed his way down her soft curves, too impatient to explore her hardening nipples.

The wound healed nicely. He frowned. He'd been too close to losing her.

"Erik," she said, bringing him back. "You can fuss another time."

She massaged the pointed tips of his ears.

Ache gathered at the base of his spine. Erik nuzzled her folds, slowly at first, savoring her scent. He swiped his tongue along her seam, laving at the center.

Maia arched into his touch and rubbed herself against his jaw. Whether in invitation or need, it didn't matter.

Erik growled and cupped her backside, thrusting his tongue where her body demanded.

"More." Her legs shook as her thighs clamped his head.

Fingers replaced his mouth, pumping inside her and rubbing against her inner walls. He found a rhythm that had her writhing under him.

When her legs thrashed — when a soft keening tore from her — he brushed the pad of his thumb over that sensitive nub peeking out from under its hood. Once. Twice. Then in methodical circles until she cried out his name.

Her core spasmed. It took the last vestiges of his restraint to let her ride out her release on his hand and not free himself and thrust inside.

Maia's legs slid off his shoulders. Her eyes, so often full of heat and ire and resolve, glazed over. They softened as she regarded him through heavy lids.

He let her float down but couldn't help but draw her in for a lazy kiss.

The wait was torture. Erik held her prisoner with his lips until she took over, her tongue ravishing his mouth.

"Your turn," she said.

His pants came off first. Then her tunic.

She gripped his hard shaft.

He wanted to plunge inside her, but her nimble fingers pumped him, mimicking his earlier rhythm.

"Enough." The word clogged his throat. "Soon, I'll mark your skin with my seed. But not today."

He entered slowly. Inch by inch. Liquid heat coating him. Erik gritted his teeth, studying her.

She took a shuddering breath. Her eyes were stormy and dark.

"Let me hear you scream," he said.

"What makes you think—"

He gripped her thighs, pulled back, then thrust inside.

Dear gods. He tilted her hips, adjusting the angle so she could take his entire length. He had no patience for teasing. His motions were hard. Consuming. Every slide sent a jolt of pleasure radiating down the base of his spine.

Her body seared him.

And his magic… warmth gathered in his palms as if it demanded an outlet, too. He ran his hands over her chest. Her nipples. Her neck, feeding power into his touch.

She clamped around him and gasped.

He tweaked one nipple, then the other, soothing the sting with his tongue. He kept pumping, the heat and pressure building inside him.

"Erik," she cried out, spasming around him. Not exactly a scream, but he grinned all the same.

She shook through her climax.

His magic demanded that he follow. Not yet.

He kissed her neck until she stopped shaking.

Maia lay limp under him.

His. He didn't deserve her. But she'd stayed. Maybe if he said it a hundred times, he would believe.

"You are the most beautiful thing in the realm." He propped himself on an elbow and brushed his fingers down the side of her arm.

They lay like that, him still hard inside her. Maia looking at him as if he could conquer Morvak. His magic tugged and nagged, the calm dissipating, giving way to a sharp need.

He flipped them over so she straddled his hips.

Maia grinned. The corner of one lip tugged higher than the other. His Kitten.

She scraped her nails over his chest and rode him.

It was his turn to yell.

His skin heated and burned as if she had lit him on fire. He didn't know where to touch, skimming his hands all over her. The saccharine taste of a cast coated his tongue as he exploded. Erik arched into her, letting her milk every drop from his shaft.

A primal shout wrenched from his chest.

He didn't cry out her name. Didn't remember his own.

She reached for his hands, locking theirs together above his head as she nipped along his jaw until his breathing slowed. When her neck came close, too near to resist, his teeth latched onto its base.

A soft cry escaped, but she held still, allowing him to soothe the pain with his tongue.

"Mine," he whispered into her hair.

"Yours," she said simply.

One day, he'd allow himself to believe it.

They snuggled, her on top of him. Sweat-soaked and sated. Feeling returned to his hands.

He caressed her back, massaging her muscles. When goose bumps erupted on her skin, he tugged a cover over them both. He fought to stay awake, wanting to savor this moment. The calm before a spring hurricane.

She yawned.

"I love you." He said simply, kissing her hair. "I vow to be the husband you deserve. The male you see in me."

"I love you, Erik Siodina. For the male you are today. The male you've always been. And the male you fight to become. If you don't trust yourself, then trust my instincts. I'd never marry a fool."

He chuckled. "No, you wouldn't."

Her breathing evened out. She dozed on his chest.

They would have to agree to disagree.

Erik was a fool. But a fool could always find other foolish sheep to lead. And he would don the shepherd's mask if it meant gathering an army. Because overthrowing his father was the first battle. And the war... the war was not the fight to rule Morvak. No... it was the fight to clear the rot his father left behind.

Erik wasn't good.

But his wife was.

And the Court... the realm... the very foundation of Morvak, with its long history of oppression and antiquated customs, demanded she change.

He would never allow it to transpire. Maia was perfect, as she was, so he would lead an army, defeat his father.

And change the realm for her.

CHAPTER FORTY-ONE

They spent the next three days wrapped around each other.

When restlessness hit, Erik led Maia from their chambers to his greenhouse. Or his mother's grotto. Often to the woods for his new favorite pastime — strip archery. Somehow, he always ended up naked while Maia remained in her leathers.

Not that he was complaining.

On the fourth day, a messenger shoved a royal purple envelope under their door, interrupting their belated honeymoon.

"Do I want to know the contents?" Maia lazed under the blankets.

He slid a finger under the wax seal and removed the folded parchment. It was a summons for this eve, containing an official announcement for his father's coronation.

According to Dezee, a pair of elaborate thrones arrived this morning. Commissioned from the Artisan territory, dozens of crafters spent the better part of a fortnight carving the monstrosities.

Why two, though? The realm wasn't in danger of inheriting a queen.

At the bottom, he recognized his sire's slanted penmanship.

Bring your whore. It is time you take your rightful place by my side.

Not a queen. A prince. He waited for a heavy lump to form in his gut. None came. He rested on the side of the bed.

"Charming, your father." Maia curled around him, rubbing small circles on his lower back. "Do you think he will ever learn my name?"

"Be glad. The moment he uses it — the second he assumes you are more than a mere plaything — you are on a one-way horse back home.

They'd argued fiercely about it. The selfish part of him was glad she stayed. But if father took an interest in her…

He handed Maia the letter.

"Ah, looks as if your father will claim you as his heir. Prince Erik has a nice ring to it." She nudged him with her shoulder. "It must rain Crimson Gillyflowers and dwarf dust because you may get me on my knees after all. You should know that my needlework is rubbish, but I will begin a tapestry in your honor at once."

He tackled her to the bed. The letter forgotten.

"As much as I'd like to punish your pert mouth, come." He kissed the corner. "We have plenty to do before we depart for the great hall."

He bopped the tip of her nose and pulled her to the vanity.

"Not another set of jewels." She trailed a hand over her earrings.

Erik had refitted them after the Games.

"Between your mother's necklace and these, I have everything I need."

He bent down, unlatching the false bottom on the middle drawer. His fingers fumbled around until they grazed the cool glass.

"It's time we answer for our transgressions." He handed her a small vial filled with emerald-green liquid.

"Do you jest? You want me to consume another elixir?"

"This one is real." He grinned. "An antidote to truth serum. Dezee is convinced my father suspects our involvement in Lea's *death*. He will probably question us in front of the Court."

"This should last until tomorrow morning." Erik uncorked the vial, drank half, and handed the rest to her.

She pinched her nose and swallowed her portion.

"My entire body is itchy, tingly."

"And your ears are red. It's working."

Only Erik didn't experience the same.

Lately, his magic had been off. Different. He kept waiting for secondary powers to manifest as Ember suggested, but nothing changed except its intrusion when he found release with Maia.

He'd tried explaining it to her, but Maia informed him she'd experienced the same, suggesting mating with a loved one was more intense. So he let it drop.

"What's wrong?" she asked.

"What's wrong?" he repeated, forcing a smile. "Many things. Most important of all, I cannot spend the night locked in our chambers with you. But I have a gift that will improve my mood."

He led her to the wardrobe.

"I commissioned new evening wear." Erik opened the armoire's double doors and removed the outfit hanging in the back. "If you like it, Jille can sew more in different colors."

He held out the pistachio green bundle.

Maia grabbed the pants first.

With thick ankle cuffs, a thicker waistband, the satin material would hug her curves but still allow her freedom to take down an unruly Lord. Intricate beadwork decorated the outer seams, the scroll adding a touch of luxury.

She held them against her legs, the length perfect.

"They are divine. I would bend to fashion and wear the uncomfortable gowns, but this... this is..."

"Try them on."

She stepped into the pants. His tunic, the one she'd claimed as hers, hung past her waist.

He grabbed the hem and pulled it over her head.

"Eyes up," she said.

His gaze flicked to her lips. Erik smirked. "Now the top."

Three-quarter length sleeves dove into a dramatic *V* on the front. A contrast to the boat necklines of most bodices. Made from the same satin, the fabric would cling to her chest.

She pushed her arms in and fished her head through the wide opening. The hem stopped below her belly button and left a sliver of her olive skin on display.

It was that tiny patch his hand found a moment later, stroking and teasing and reassuring him she was indeed there.

"Wear fighting leathers for all I care, but there may be times you wish for something more formal." He traced the beading. "It makes a statement, generating enough distraction for you to draw a blade."

"You left no place for a dagger." Maia twirled. "I suppose it's time I learned how to throw a star."

"Do you like it?" he asked, unable to disguise the gruffness of his tone.

"It's perfect. Functional. Scandalous. And best of all, a thoughtful gift." She kissed his chin. "I'll speak to Jille and commission one in black."

Her scent shifted. Instead of the spicy cloves from his borrowed soap, it took on a sweet smell. Not vanilla. He couldn't quite place it.

~

WITH THE ADDITION OF THE TWO NEW THRONES AND THREE dozen banners, the great hall became an obnoxious display of patriotism. His father, the King, had spared no expense.

Erik forced a smile.

Two wooden chairs commanded the center of the raised dais. The scrollwork on the legs alone must've taken artisans weeks to chisel. Plush royal purple cushions adorned their seats, golden tassels hanging from their corners.

The one was taller and almost double the width of its neighbor. With his father's slim frame, he would resemble a child playing pretend.

Erik stared at the other. If he hadn't shunned power before, the sheer gaudiness of the chair would put him off. He crooked his elbow.

Maia tilted her chin and looped her hand through it.

Most of the Court awaited them. Scattered throughout the room, all heads turned in their direction. A path dividing the floor opened.

At two bells before supper, servants wound between the Lords and Ladies, carrying trays leaden with Fae wine and mead.

Perfect. Drinks on empty stomachs. This should be interesting.

Three strides into the crowd, his magic acted up.

He recognized the scent of hundreds of sage-infused candles. The various perfumes and colognes the nobility favored forced him to swallow back bile. Whispers swirled around them, chased by an oily aroma — a mixture of unwashed bodies and carrion.

He was going to be sick.

"Deep breaths," Maia said. "You look ravishing tonight."

There it was again. That sweet smell from their chamber.

"Say something else." He stopped. "Say something true."

"I let you win the last time we had target practice." She bit her lip.

He parsed the notes. Sun-ripened strawberries and Crimson Gillyflowers and...

He sniffed the column of her throat.

Honeyed toffee.

The taste of a cast.

Dear gods, he was a Sniffer.

He could smell lies. And he was impervious to truth serum, to compulsion. A talent so rare he'd read a single line about it as a lad, promptly dismissing the author's words.

No wonder he felt nothing when they drank the antidote earlier.

And that foul stench filling the hall, well... the Lords and Ladies never spoke an honest word to one another.

Maia's eyes widened. She probably thought him daft, smelling her in front of the Court.

"Later," he whispered in her ear. He smiled, giving her that lopsided grin he reserved just for them.

Heat gathered in his palms.

I am a sniffer. An image of a dripping faucet flowed into his mind. He grabbed the handle, turning it tight. *I control this power.*

Ah, he could breathe again.

"When my father enters, I must leave you. Find Lady Stella. Do you trust me?"

"Aye, with every fiber of my being." She cupped the side of his cheek. "That look in your eye says you are about to doing something reckless."

"I strive to keep your life interesting." He pushed into her hand and nipped her palm.

Lady Stella slipped in the back, winding her way to her minions.

"Stella is here." He nodded in her direction and grabbed Maia's hips.

"Good luck." She searched his face, went on tiptoes, and kissed him.

Maia strode down the center aisle. He recognized the moment she spotted Stella in the crowd. Her gait changed, but she recovered quickly.

The new outfit was Lady Stella's idea.

He'd visited her, inquiring about Lady Talia's departure, warning her not to send correspondence. Erik mentioned commissioning a gown, something Maia would feel more comfortable wearing to the events they couldn't skip.

Stella — with her knowledge of fashion and fabrics — suggested the daring design. The best part, she'd commissioned a set for herself. A bold red with beads of gold sewn on the hem.

"By the next full moon, every Lady will wear this look. You must compensate Jille for her time."

"Why?" he'd asked simply.

"I can't allow Maia to have all the fun. Plus, I can pull it off better".

He wouldn't admit it, but judging by the Court's reaction, he owed Stella, especially since she didn't object when he told her the rest of his plans.

Dozens of Blackbirds flew into the chamber.

"Your king enters," said the Master of Ceremonies.

The Lords took a knee. The Ladies suspended in a half curtesy. All heads lowered.

Boots echoed on the wooden floor. A hand rested on Erik's head.

"Rise, my son," his father commanded. "We have matters to discuss before my official coronation."

Erik followed, focusing on the newest addition — a crown of obsidian encircling his head.

His father climbed the steps in front of the larger throne, gathered his robes from behind, and sat.

A servant scurried over and presented a scepter and a vial.

"You may rise," his father said to the Court. "I hold in my hand an Elixir of Truth."

One could hear a mouse squeak in the hall.

The serum was a perfect symbolism for how his father intended to rule. If he drugged his heir during his coronation, what would he do when someone who wasn't blood acted against him?

Erik needed to take the offensive.

"I, Erik Siodina, son of our noble King Emsworth Siodina, so willingly ingest the serum. Let it be known that I intend to serve this monarchy with a clear conscience."

No sour taste filled his mouth. Perfect. It would be difficult to cover his reaction if his new magic also alerted when he, himself, told falsehoods.

He inclined his head and took the vial. Erik spun to face the crowd, raising it aloft, then drank it in one swallow. Water. He wanted to laugh.

Instead, he scrunched his face for the Court's benefit and went to a knee.

"I shall answer your questions." It was a balance, the showmanship. He must remain assertive but not enough to irritate his father. This was his special day, after all.

"Did you willingly pledge your support of your wife's entrance into the Grimoire Games?"

"Aye." Erik paused for effect. "My human wife has had difficulty adjusting to Court. I assumed training for the Games would keep her busy. We spoke the marriage oaths, but I admit I took them in error. I was hasty, but she is an enchanting creature."

A few of the braver Lords chuckled.

"Very well. You are not the first Faeblood to be led astray by your rutting."

A sweet scent teased his nostrils. Truth. Erik bowed his

head. It took every ounce of control not to sigh. His father didn't suspect Maia's true purpose in coming to the Castle.

He was so relieved he almost missed the next.

"... I will accept no children from this union. You will breed Lady Stella who shall henceforth be known as the Princess Consort."

The Court gasped as one.

His father continued on without care. "... any Faeblood offspring shall carry the name *of Siodina*. I will acknowledge them as rightful heirs. You may keep your whore."

Gods, Stella would love this.

"Might I make a request?" Erik asked. Maia meant it when she gave him her trust. This was one of those times he would test it.

"Granted." His father waved his hand.

"Allow Lady Stella to move into our adjoining chambers. The rooms are vacant."

They could keep a closer eye on her activities. She could be a powerful ally. Or a cunning adversary.

"Excellent choice. See that the servants move her at once.

"As you are a most magnanimous ruler, might I trouble you with one more request?" He had to be careful. But if he'd learned anything from his fearless wife, some things were worth the risks, so he added, "It would benefit the Castle."

"Indeed." He sneered at Erik, likely debating how far to allow this exchange in front of the nobles. "Quite the diplomatic heir."

"Allow my wife to earn her place by tutoring the servants in the Castle. She is... more comfortable among her kind. And the small amount of education, reading and writing, may assist the Lords and Ladies with their correspondence."

"Hmm." His father drummed his fingers on the throne's arms. "I'll allow it. But only for two hours during the day, at most. They still have duties to attend. And she will have responsibilities in the Red Guard academy."

"My King." Erik dipped his head.

"It's a pity, though, that the child... what was her name?" His father snapped his fingers at the Master of Ceremonies. "The servant girl who competed with your wife?"

"Leatrix," the Master of Ceremonies supplied.

"Ah, yes. L-e-a-trix." His father drew out her name as if trying it for the first time. "What ever became of the child?"

His father suspected...

"Dead," he said quickly and without a hint of emotion in his tone.

Hopefully, Erik's answer would prevent him from sending scouts to search the territories for the lass.

"Died in her dormitory. There is speculation Wystan committed the atrocity," he added on a whim.

"Shame." His father flicked his wrist. "And what of the male who accompanied your wife?"

"Mikel returned to the militia."

"Very well. Am I not a generous ruler?" His lips curled. He clapped his hands. "Let us begin."

The coronation lasted an hour. Erik spent most of it down on one knee.

His father had brought in a holy man from gods knew where. They never kept one long at the Castle, religion being an afterthought amongst the nobility. Worship was unnecessary when they themselves possessed god-like powers.

The pontiff sprinkled blessed water on the crown and spelled the thrones for prosperity. He anointed the scepter for long life.

His father's perpetual sneer faltered at the last.

"Long live King Siodina," the crows squawked in unison. "All hail the King and Prince Erik."

The Court joined the next several iterations.

They didn't present Erik with a crown, nor a sword. At least he didn't need to swear fealty. Though it would be another boon if his magic nullified any oaths he took under duress.

"You may rise," his father said.

The Court stood.

Erik spied Maia in the crowd, her arm linked through Stella's. The soft smirk on her face was for him. Oh, he would pay for his surprise.

Heads swiveled in their directions as they made their way to the front, parting the whispers as they strolled nearer.

If glares could slice a man, Lady Stella's would make him a eunuch. She seemed to remember her place because she bowed low.

Erik patted his lap and Maia didn't hesitate. She settled on his thighs, draping her legs off the side. A careless display but expected.

As much as he enjoyed the feel of her, he despised this role. He reminded himself it didn't cheapen or tannish what they shared.

"Lady Stella will poison you in her sleep," Maia whispered in his ear. "You must have a death wish."

"Perhaps," he hedged, the wolfish grin more for her than the crowd watching eagerly. "I wouldn't want things to dull after the excitement of the Games."

He stroked a thumb along her inner thigh.

"It appears as if you have a chamber to move," he said to Stella. "I'll send servants along to pack. They will bring a meal to your rooms."

He dismissed her with a wave of his hand.

Maia pinched his side.

"Behave." She nipped his ear. But before she could chastise him further, Commander Lukas strode to the dais, his steps hurried.

"My King." He bowed low. "The two Red Guard you sent to

monitor the southern tunnels are missing. The area shows signs of a struggle."

"Lazy humans," his father said, ignoring the last. "They are probably in the barracks. Find them. And when you do, make it clear to the others that no one abandons their posts."

"We searched the barracks. When we didn't locate them, I sent men to comb the Castle and stables," Lukas said to his feet. If he bowed any lower, his nose would scrape the floor.

"You pulled men off their stations."

"Father," Erik said. "You've had a long day. Allow me to handle this. Enjoy your feast."

Erik gestured to the servants setting the table. To the appetizers circulated in the throng.

His father regarded him down the tip of his nose. His lips curled as if he smelled something foul.

"Perhaps you are right. You, girl." He flicked his wrist at Maia. "Run along and assist Lady Stella."

She uncurled from his lap and sauntered through the hall, taking her time to snag a few appetizers off roving trays and speaking with those who approached.

His father sneered at Maia's back. He turned to Erik and said, "Perhaps you need additional responsibilities beyond siring the next in our line. Commander Lukas?"

"My King?"

"From this moment forward, you will report to my son. His years of wallowing in the training pit seem of use. Find the missing guards. Punish them. Report to Prince Erik when it is done. Dismissed."

Commander Lukas inclined his head and left.

"See that news of the coronation spreads throughout the territories. Do not disturb me further."

His father stood, swept his robes behind him, then slipped out the back of the hall.

Two Red Guards followed.

He was up to something… something beyond seizing power and eliminating the High Table.

His father spent more and more time in his laboratory. And less and less time flaunting his status in the great hall. He didn't eat. Never drank from anything other than the decanter he hid beneath his robes. Though, after poisoning Lord Bierling, he was likely just taking care.

Erik exhaled, stifling the urge to slump on his throne.

His new cloak of power chafed. He no longer feared it… nor feared what he must become. Still, it felt heavy, stifling.

Ember was wrong — his destiny wasn't to rule. But he would abuse his new rank to take down his father. And when he finished, Erik wouldn't balk at transferring his authority to someone more worthy.

A weight lifted off his chest.

Maia blew him a kiss from the entrance doors and slipped into the corridor. As if she'd known he needed one last reminder of them. What was at stake.

He loved her, not for the delectable Kitten she was, but for who he was when he was with her.

Erik wasn't sure someone like him deserved a wife like Maia, but he would spend the rest of his days trying to become the answer to that riddle.

History told of two sides of every conflict. A line divided the good. And the evil. The winners and those who faded into obscurity.

Storytellers never wrote about those who dwelled somewhere in the middle. Those who sullied their hands maintaining that distinction.

No one claimed Erik belonged on the right side of Morvak's tale. He didn't fit in with kind, pure souls. But his wife wanted him to try. His mother and sister would too.

Erik stood, surveying the Court.

While many things needed upheaval in the Castle, he would

start with the territories — improving supply lines, reestablishing trade with the Northern Isles, and creating a welfare plan for Morvak's most vulnerable.

His father handed him a gift with the Red Guard.

The entire ranks needed thinning. As with the servants, good men existed amongst the rot. It would take time to subvert their loyalties to the kingdom, away from his father's whip. Plus, it gave him an excuse to visit the academy, observe his wife's *training.*

Erik couldn't save the Mikels of the realm.

Though when the moment came, he would end the Rite of Ortus. His prior indifference was appalling. It took his wife and a six-year-old child to wake him up. His skin heated, not from magic.

No one claimed Erik belonged on the right side of history.

But he would protect those who were. He would no longer remain idle while they fought.

With Maia, he knew who he was. Erik Siodina was a husband first. A mother's son and older brother second. He was a friend and a fighter and a Faeblood heir.

He was the male who would hold the line and raze his father's world to ashes. Then he would help them rebuild.

For her.

And maybe one day, for himself.

EPILOGUE

Ada

"Are you really a pirate?" Leatrix, Maia's friend and all-around wicked partner in the Grimoire Games asked.

"Hmm," Ada said, tapping a finger to her lip. "You spent three days in my company. What do you think?"

At the time, the costume seemed fun.

She'd bartered with a traveling merchant, fixing his book-keeping in exchange for goods or wares. He had little, mainly odds and ends. After the tithe, his business had barely earned enough coin to pay for his meals. So she'd selected the loud corset and even louder pants — items he'd lugged around unable to sell — for giggles.

"I want you to be one." A child-like confession. Simple, but laced with something more.

Lea was young enough to still believe in sirens and witches and Nightwalkers. Understandably, she wanted to cling to an imaginary world.

"I am when the time calls." Ada opened the door to her rooms in the training barn, ushering the lass in first. Maybe the world needed more pirates. Out of the side of her mouth she said, "But me crew is out to sea, and I shall toil amongst the land dwellers until they return."

Leatrix giggled.

Ollie, her tabby kitten, blinked from his favorite spot on her bed.

"How'd you get your name? Not your real one..." The lass plopped down next to Ada's fur baby, burying her face in his orange coat. "Your pirate name?"

Ada rubbed her chin, dramatically considering her answer.

More giggles.

"Captain Sharkbait?" She leaned in close. "These dirt-lovin' scalawags think it's a jest. But the ocean knows I prefer its monsters for company."

The girl's eyes widened.

Dear gods, Ada had spent too much time around stuffy militia soldiers. This was the most fun she had in ages. A perfect distraction.

"Perhaps we should figure out your pirate name. You won't strike fear into the hearts of the Northern Isle's Commodore answering to *Lea.*"

Ada stuck out her tongue, pretending she tasted something foul.

"I'm not so good at making up fun names." Lea hung her head. "My friend Jasper tells the best stories. He has the best imagination..."

Ada wasn't sure what happened. One minute the lass laughed along with her, the next she looked like someone stole her treasured bow and quiver.

"I'll never see Jasper again, will I?"

Ahh. The events of the past few days caught up to her.

Long ago, Ada fled her childhood home. But she was older than Lea. And had Xavier and Jade and Gavyn. Still, she remembered when she realized they would never see it again.

Ada sat down and rubbed small circles on Lea's lower back.

"I cannot promise you'll return to the Castle. But you are safe here. We will find you new friends. Maybe Xavier, my brother," she added the familial title for Lea's benefit, "will allow you to write, perhaps even visit, when it is safe."

"You think I will find new friends?"

Goodness, to be young again. To want such simple things. Relationships were more honest. More straight forward. Innocent.

"Aye. Dinna I ask you to crew for me? Perhaps I was not clear." Ada swiped a silent tear from Lea's cheek. "I only allow friends on me ship."

"Thank you." The girl hugged Ollie tighter. "I know you don't have a ship."

Bollocks. And here she assumed she'd hoodwinked the lass.

"Shh." Ada pressed a finger to her lips. "Don't let the others know. But I do have a secret hiding spot. And a kitten. Cats are more fun than talking parrots, don't you think?"

"Can I stay with you again tonight? I know Maia offered her chambers but—"

"You shouldn't be alone in a new place." Ada untied the strip of leather binding her braid. Her boots came off next. She wiggled her toes. "Stay as long as you like."

"Cook said I could help in the kitchens. I never minded the dishes at the Castle. Better than standing still in the shadows."

Lea snatched the ends of Ada's hair, unwinding the plait. The girl always kept her hands busy. Whether from restless energy or to cover her nervousness, Ada wasn't sure. But she was the same.

"... then I am to practice in the training barn. Mister Gavyn..."

Ada tidied the piles of clothes and parchments strewn on her quilt, arranging and rearranging them, so that when finished, it looked the same as before.

Nope. She was never one to sit still. Her mind didn't settle, either.

It drove her family crazy. And when a particular riddle took hold, especially one she couldn't solve, Ada barely slept. If it wasn't for Mikel, most days she wouldn't eat.

She rubbed behind Ollie's ear.

Lea wasn't the only one who struggled today. Maia's absence hit her too. There was something about knowing her friend would never return.

For so long, it had been just the two of them at the compound.

Ember was a recent addition, but her clinic kept her occupied. When she wasn't tending the bruised and battered trainees, she spent her time wrapped around Gavyn.

Jade lived in the village, rising before the roosters to feed the neighbors. Exhaustion, or Xavier's bossiness, kept her away from the training barn most days.

And Zoie, their resident brewmaster, lived in a small cottage on the outskirts of the territory. An introvert at heart, only the weekly fight night pulled her out of her sanctuary.

And the one person who she could always count on for company was ignoring her.

Ada had reasoned it was because of Lea's presence. But when he avoided her loft... when he never came to scold her for wandering the nearby field alone...

She sighed. Mikel was just... busy.

Few knew of his role as scout leader, unable to look beyond that irreverent mask he plastered on his handsome face. With tensions rising across Morvak, it made sense that Xavier sent him out more and more.

She never managed to tail him beyond the compound, but she always knew when he returned, if only because he sought her out.

Ada didn't imagine it — their kiss.

The longer she went without seeing him, the more she had to remind herself it was real. It wasn't her daydreams running amok.

She sighed.

Something had shifted at the compound. It was subtle, she couldn't describe the feeling. And for the first time, she was an outsider watching everyone else go about their days.

Sure, her brother never shared his plans. But Ada, whose mind wandered even when occupied with her books, whose ears detected every nuanced conversation around her, hadn't heard a word. Not a peep.

"... and then Rowan promised he'd take me and the other village kids to Ashmere Falls," Lea said, a hopeful expression on her face.

The lass still spoke? Ada swallowed another sigh. Then there were other days when her mind struggled to latch onto a single word.

She needed rest.

"You'll love it," Ada said, picking up the last threads of the conversation. "I have an idea. Do you want to sneak some supper? Take a basket to the new watch tower? I'm friendly with the guards on rotation. We can eat our meal while scouring the horizon for enemy ships."

Lea's eyes lit up. They darted around the room as if checking for spies.

"Arrrr," the lass drawled, unsure at first then louder.

"You'll make a fine first mate. We can—"

Xavier coughed from the threshold. Her brother gripped the doorknob, his gaze shooting to Lea.

She knew that look. Somehow, she was to blame. This time, Ada had no clue what she did. She must feign an apology, if only to hurry him along so she could cheer up the lass.

"I have business with the Port Master." Ada stood, yanking

Lea up beside her. "Secure the rations. We climb the mast in half a bell's time."

Lea clicked her heels together and saluted, throwing a roguish grin over her shoulder before she disappeared down the hall.

"Don't get attached." Xavier shut the door behind him. "The girl can't stay here."

"But Maia—"

He raised his hand, cutting her off.

"For now. When this is over, when I don't feel the weight of the Castle monitoring my breathing, we will bring her back. It's too risky. Her performance at the Games, while fierce, was too memorable."

"And what of Lady Talia?" she asked, uncaring if he spoke the truth. "I suppose you'll keep her instead."

Her brother didn't deserve her ire, but he was a safe target. "I'm sorry, Xav. It's only—"

Xavier waved her off.

He must be under more strain than she'd realized to dismiss her apology outright. It wasn't too long ago he would've gloated then forced her to grovel, claiming he failed her as a stand-in parent.

"I have something for you." He handed her a small navy journal, the spine peeling at its edges. It was the one Lady Talia smuggled out of the Castle. "It's the book I asked—"

"You asked Maia to find." Ada grabbed it, opening the front cover. "She might've mentioned..."

Rows of strange marks started on the bottom half of the first page. They continued the entire book, running right to left and breaking every so often in random spots. The symbols were complex. More elaborate than any language she'd ever seen.

"What is it?"

She ran her finger across a row, the words faded but still visible. In the margins near the spine, someone had used darker ink. No, fresher. Notes, perhaps? She thumbed through a few more pages. Closer to the end, someone had underlined a few sections.

"I don't know," Xavier admitted. "For years, Siodina carried that very journal on his person at all times. Right before Erik joined the militia, it disappeared. My contact at the Castle confirmed it."

His contact. Not Lukas. Not brother.

It made sense. Xavier would not risk Maia's presence at Court on a mere rumor.

"Lady Talia claims Lady Stella found it in an older section of the library. It would be dumb luck if the gods willed it to us without Siodina realizing its absence."

"I don't understand. Why gamble on a book?" She shrugged.

Books were magical. Ada had spent half her life with her nose in one. Mathematical texts. Tomes on scholarly explanations of the formation of realms. The patterns of the moon and planetary alignment.

Romance tales when her brain needed to process the latter.

"It's a feeling in my gut."

A rare admission. But every one of their adoptive family members would follow her brother to otherwise certain death based on his instincts alone.

"Too many unusual movements in the territories happened when it vanished. Too many for me to ignore." Xavier strode to her sole window and studied the stream out back.

"And you need me to read it." Decipher more like. The lure of the pages was hard to resist.

"It should keep you busy," he said, his tone shy of dismissive.

It didn't bother her though.

Xavier had always shown pride in her achievements. First in school. Then later, when her affinity for figures earned them all a tidy profit. Even when boredom loomed and her escapades threatened to tinge his temples gray before he reached forty summers…

"I do not recognize this language." They were letters and phrases, not equations. More certain the longer she looked. "Without a cipher or some inclination of its origins, the translation may be beyond my capabilities."

"Lady Talia thinks it hails from the ancient City of Atlantia. She spent a fair amount of time in the library trailing after Lady Stella."

"A scholar?"

"An infatuation. She claims no interest in history, nor other subjects." The corner of his lips tipped upward. "When one spends hours amongst texts, they are bound to pick up something."

"Didn't work for you," she said, smirking. "All those years in the schoolhouse and you graduated with knowledge of your letters and an ability to trace Jade's profile in your sleep."

"Leave it."

Prickly, so prickly, her brother. A part of her continued to push him in this. Not because she wanted Jade as a sister-in-law. But because his long-suffering refusal hurt her friend.

"Everyone has their talents," he said, ignoring her taunt. "You know the territories better than most. If a cipher or text existed, where might the realm hide it?"

True. Ada, with an amount of privilege foreign to many scraping a survival in the peninsula, had traveled extensively.

She enjoyed new things — experiencing new villages, establishing connections with their residents.

Every community had a story to tell. Trinkets to purchase. Books to acquire for her collection in the loft. With most of the human population forgoing formal education in favor of working the family trade, written works were few. And lucky for her, usually inexpensive.

In every village, she found a kindred soul who enjoyed

reading as much as she did. It was why Jade reinforced the seams of her travel satchel. She filled it with volumes to trade, often purchasing additional ones.

But there was one place she hadn't explored fully. Likely the largest collection outside the Castle's library.

"The Huntsmen's territory. If any text exists, it would be there."

"Are you sure of this?" Xavier asked, his tone hesitant. "There is no better place to start?"

"Aye. I am friendly with the curator." She grinned. Well... if one considered endless questions and good-natured pestering... friendly.

Xavier seemed to consider. His silence rubbed her patience raw.

Their village was a day's ride. She could be there and back before their next fight night.

"What's wrong?" Her lips flattened. "What are you not telling me?"

Knock. Knock. Knock.

"Come in," Xavier said, his gaze never leaving hers.

Mikel and Rowan entered. The latter leaned against the door, a dimple forming in his cheek.

"Close it." Xavier cupped his mouth and ran his hand down the column of his throat. To Ada he said, "I will ask again. You are certain there is no other place?"

Rowan straightened.

Mikel crossed his arms. The wordless greeting, after so many days of silence, was too much.

Ada stood, not quite toe-to-toe with her brother, but she wouldn't hear this sitting.

"This isn't a game," was all Mikel said.

Of all the—

Heat climbed up her spine.

He likely didn't even know what they discussed. But he

knew her… her tells… her propensity to push for the sake of a reaction, and assumed she was up to no good. Still, he thought to chastise her without evidence of a folly.

"Whoa. Whoa. Whoa." Rowan stepped between them. *Rowan,* who never spent more than two sentences on a serious topic unless it led to his evening entertainment, diffused her next remark. "As much as I enjoy your sparring, this room is too small."

Heavy hands rested on her shoulders. She unclenched her fists.

Please, Xavier's eyes said. *This concerns all of us.*

They'd always had a bond.

It benefited Ada when he stepped in between her and their parents, taking charge of the room. Usually after another one of her antics. When they tired of having a whirlwind of a child. It was always Xavier who defused the situation.

She blinked twice. *I'll listen, but don't expect me to stay quiet for long.*

"Mikel, what news do your scouts bring from the Huntsmen's territory?" Xavier asked.

"The same." Mikel wouldn't look at her. "Empty cabins. Tracks heading west following game. No signs of families."

"Very well." Xavier's hands dropped to his sides. "Gather supplies and a dozen of your best. You leave at sunrise tomorrow. Ada and Lea will accompany you. Find them. All of them."

The hunters. There was no menace in his tone. If an entire territory went missing…

"No," Mikel snarled at the same time Rowan asked, "Why Ada? What's going on?"

"Where is this collection you seek?" Xavier opened her chamber door.

"Housed in a smaller cabin nestled in the woods. There is a hidden trail on the western side of the village. It takes you past old ruins then to the homestead."

Ada willed her grip to relax, not bothering to check if she bent the journal. So careless.

"The cabin flanks the crumbling stone pillars."

"Perhaps I may be of help. A hidden cabin. An abandoned structure. Sounds like a perfect way to spend All Hallows Eve." Rowan crossed to her. "What do you say, fire nymph? Are you up for an adventure while Mikel and his band of misfits do their thing?"

She didn't need to look to know a scowl marred Mikel's face. And Rowan, the compound's resident rake with a reputation as maligned as hers, extended an olive branch. She would be a fool to ignore it.

"I suppose we could seek ghosts while we scoured for a text I need."

She forced her hip to the side, a cocky stance she'd observed some of the more experienced women in the village use when the interest of their affections neared.

She probably looked ridiculous.

This entire exchange was ridiculous, considering All Hallows Eve was another month away. But she had a bit of meanness in her, borne from a sliver of hurt caused by Mikel's callous attitude.

"Lea travels with the group," Xavier said. "See to it that Cook sends her with a set of paring knives."

Right. Because the wee lass could fend off an attack with her deadly aim. Because this was not some light-hearted jaunt.

"Tomorrow," Rowan said and pecked her temple. He disappeared down the corridor.

Xavier followed.

Mikel strode toward the door.

"Did it mean anything to you?" The kiss.

"It was a mistake." His arm shot out and braced the frame. He refused to look at her. "It won't happen again."

Her gaze followed his retreat. His broad shoulders curled

around the corner. His stubbornly wide shoulders holding up a stubbornly thick neck and stubborner head. Was stubborner even a word?

Ooh. He made her daft.

If Mikel thought he could ignore her, he had something else coming.

She knew his feelings for her ran deeper than a familial bond. But she couldn't figure out why he refused to act. Ada had made it plain she returned his affections.

If his adoptive brothers knew his reasons for staying away, they wouldn't tell her. Bonds between males, and all that.

Perhaps she could use this trip to her advantage and finally force some answers from him.

She couldn't keep going on like she was. Her heart breaking a little with every rebuff. Besides, Gavyn and Ember and now Maia and Erik, figured out their relationships when forced to share a bed. Maybe the gods would favor them, too.

Mikel was a riddle.

And if there was one thing Ada excelled at — beyond annoying her brother and rescuing kittens and keeping the soldiers on high alert with her pranks — it was solving riddles.

Join Ada and Mikel as she leads him on a merry adventure and uses her considerable charms to once and for all get him to admit they belong together in *The Mask of a Savage.*

Want more Erik and Maia?
Join my newsletter at mklorber.com to receive a special bonus epilogue.

THE FAEBLOOD SERIES
The Curse of a Faeblood: Gavyn and Ember
The Sins of an Heir: Erik and Maia
The Mask of a Savage: Mikel and Ada

ACKNOWLEDGMENTS

They call it the sophomore slump.

After completion of a full-length novel, it's common for authors to struggle to write another. Why?

There are lots of theories. One, the bloom is off the rose on this whole writing gig. We don't possess the luxury of innocence we carried during out debut.

Other times, it's because our creative well runs dry. Most of us pour our heart and soul into the first book. Throw everything in there that we ever wanted.

Hot, grumpy hero. Check. Magic to solve life's mundane problems. Check. Kickboxing and beautiful, sweaty people grappling with each other. Check. Check. Somehow, I ended up with a weird ode to mixed martial arts set in a magical medieval world. With kissing.

Then, instead of continuing that setting, past Melissa yanked you (the reader) out and threw everyone into high society. Past Melissa is a scalawag, as Ada would say.

But as I sat down to draft, I found the layers of conflict between the magical nobility and the human underdogs enjoyable. And as someone who cut her teeth on historical romance, the setting came easily.

Maia wasn't the issue, either.

I will undoubtedly weave a thread of myself into every heroine, and our fish-out-of-water protagonist was no exception. My story is not unique: I was uncomfortable in my skin in high school. College was marginally better. Perhaps aided by liquid courage. It wasn't until my late twenties, early thirties that I not only accepted who I was but also embraced what brought me joy. Maia was an absolute delight. A new adult character who acknowledged her differences and her struggles to fit in, staying true to herself... Check.

No, dear reader. Erik was my hang-up.

In my first three drafts, he kept being *nice* to Maia. With words. And gifts. Even his actions were nice. After all, my girl was going through some things, and I wanted a ride-or-die next to her.

But that's not who he needed to be. Once I got the hang of his transformation arc, Erik came to life. Because of him, I will forever have a special place in my heart for morally gray heros who worship their loves. Even in the most misguided ways.

Then there was the length.

This beast of a book is long. And thick. Maybe not as girthy as Gavyn's thighs, but it took all the note cards and the spreadsheets and the string plots to keep it on track. As a result, it came in right under the pre-order wire. And I owe a tremendous amount of gratitude to everyone who carried me to the other side of the finish line.

Foremost, a heartfelt thanks goes to my editor, Casey, for not pulling her punches when I needed some sense knocked into me. You are the best corner person/coach/teammate a girl could ask for.

Shout out to Jen Prokop and Jess Snyder for their fabulous critiques of Erik and Maia's love story and political shenanigans. To the entire HEA club (and its kind overlord) for their endless support and pocket friendship. To Marie, for her razzle-dazzle copyedits and proofing.

To my incredible family, none of this would be possible without Chris and our human babies. Thank you for feeding me and pulling me out of the social media pit and believing in my dreams.

And to you (dear reader), who trusts me enough to take a chance on my words. There are too many outstanding books in the world and not enough time. I am eternally grateful you spent some of yours with my characters.

Finally, my sincerest gratitude goes to my younger self. I will unabashedly draw on all of our mistakes and heartbreak and hard lessons along this journey. If I could send a letter to you with all the wisdom of age, I'm not sure I would. Everything we've ever done — all the struggles and uncertainty, the late nights eating our feelings, the escapes into a fictional worlds as we figured our shit out — it's brought us to this place.

Plus, you're too damn stubborn to listen anyway.

-Melissa

ww.ingramcontent.com/pod-product-compliance
ghtning Source LLC
ambersburg PA
HW011025190726
290CB00011B/2706